THE BETELGEUSE ORACLE

The Betelgeuse Chronicles,
Book One

A Novel

Joseph Macchiusi

Cover design: Sara Slater

Acknowledgements

I am very grateful to all the people who offered their valuable time to read this story: Peg Frye, Lou Macchiusi, Kate Watsa, Mag Stewart, Libby Dalle Rive, Iolanda Perciballi, Nina and John Dawson, Chris Martinello, Malcolm Campbell, Vali Stone, Jeff Smith, Elaine Stirling, Heather Goodman, Jose Napoleon Alaras III, Jim Stewart, Mark Conway, and Rachel Ironstone. Your advice, suggestions and support have been incredible.

Thanks to Richard Brooks, MD, for advice on medical matters. Sara Slater did an incredible job of designing the book cover. Cheers to Rose Tassone for editing my rubbish Italian.

Special thanks to Jen Hale for believing.

Ancient Egyptian transliterations and translations are from the excellent *How To Read Egyptian Hieroglyphs* by Mark Collier and Bill Manley. All additions and alterations are mine, in order to make translations easier to read. Information on alchemy was gleaned from *The Lure and Romance of Alchemy* by C. J. S. Thompson.

This book is dedicated with love to Karen and Malcolm, without whom I would hardly be a human being, let alone a writer. You are my world.

Surely some revelation is at hand;
Surely the Second Coming is at hand.
The Second Coming! Hardly are those words out
When a vast image out of *Spiritus Mundi*
Troubles my sight: somewhere in the sands of the
desert
A shape with lion body and the head of a man,
A gaze blank and pitiless as the sun,
Is moving its slow thighs, while all about it
Reel shadows of the indignant desert birds
The darkness drops again; but now I know
That twenty centuries of stony sleep
Were vexed to nightmare by a rocking cradle,
And what rough beast, its hour come round at last,
Slouches towards Bethlehem to be born?

     -- W. B. Yeats, *The Second Coming*

Prologue:
The Winery

Ten years after the world turned over, Sheilagh crouched in the baking female slave pen. Pressed her bony back against the hot steel of the shipping container and whispered to the girl on her left, her lips almost touching the girl's ear. Important to be very quiet, but more important still to tell the tale. Sheilagh's voice only a hint of sound, a breath of meaning. So long had she spoken this way, forming sounds without using her voice box, that her throat burned dry, a faint squeaking clouded by straw dust.

Across the pen, an emaciated woman with barbed wire tattooing around the hose of her right biceps, squatting over the stinking crapbucket, diarrhea spouting hollowly. From further in the cloudy murk, a moaning cough. The sounds of exhaustion, of power wrung from the bodies of forced laborers.

Enough at least to hide Sheilagh's words. Caught speaking, she risked twenty lashes on the wheel. Twenty strikes of the cane against skin unprotected by fat, skin drum-tight over hard bone. Enough to kill. A few days of teeth-clenched agony while infection or shock greedily slurped her life away.

"The Circle," Sheilagh panted. "The Circle was our net."

Greedier they were for tales than for food, these slaves. Thirstier for hope than for water. Needing to know of something outside the endless rows of grapevines, of hallowed existence free from the lash. Far away from this vineyard, far across desolate landscapes, in the quiet of the world after it had turned over, the Circle had been salvation. Not for many. Only twelve. Twelve of them around the fire, the huge moaning arctic wind whipping muscular and black through miles of creaking barren trees. The Circle had kept them alive.

"Tales do magic," said Sheilagh, and in these words was the measure of how much she had turned over as the world had done. Before, magic was to be scoffed at, denied. Now she knew very different. Knew it with an urgent certainty more real than anything she had known before the lights went out.

Before.

Sheilagh put the back of her shaved head against the steel wall, mouth opened to gulp fetid, dusty air. Surely it had been more than ten years gone. Sure, it seemed an age since the time before.

"Tell me more," whispered the girl on her left. No more than a teenager, yet drawn haggard. Used. She would have been little more than a child when the world turned over. Her memories of the time before would be faint. Impressions of light, speed.

Sheilagh wondered if such a creature could know the depth of change.

"Please," the creature pleaded.

Sheilagh brought her mouth very close again to the ear that smelled of sweaty cheese. "Tales do magic," she repeated. "Tales told in the Circle saved us. Held us together. They had power."

"You remade the *power*!" gasped the creature, loudly enough for Sheilagh to wince, hold a finger over her lips.

The fervency of the word 'power,' so sad in its naiveté that Sheilagh needed a few moments to collect her thoughts.

"I have heard told such like," the girl pleaded. "That you created great things, wonderful things – from the time before!"

"No," said Sheilagh with unintended harshness. She had heard many of these stories passed around the slave pens since she'd arrived here. Secret societies with electricity. With wonder weapons even, only waiting for the right moment to come and set all the captives free. Poor souls so desperate they believed even the most fantastic tripe.

"But you told of magic," the girl whimpered.

"Not of that sort." Sheilagh wanted to hug her, such was the crushed hope on the teen's gaunt face. "Nothing can remake the power of the time before. It is gone. But tales do hold great power, in the telling, in the sharing. There were twelve of us who formed the Circle. Twelve only, thrust together when the world turned over. As..."

She'd been about to say 'As castaways from a sinking ship,' but how much resonance could this phrase carry for this girl?

"As twelve who escape the slave pens," she said instead, and the girl's eyes rounded in deep wonder. Yes, that had done it. Sheilagh supposed this youngster had never heard of anything quite so fantastic as twelve fugitives evading capture.

"You came back. You came back to make us free."

"Child," said Sheilagh, reaching out to clasp her bony knee. "We were betrayed by one of our own, who delivered us into the hands of your master." At this, Sheilagh needed to breathe, to resist tears. It had been her love, the one she'd thought of as her mate, who had betrayed them all. Tears wouldn't do anybody any good now. All she could do was tell the tale. Weave the magic.

"Some of us are dead," Sheilagh continued. "Some... some, I don't even know what's happened to them. We are scattered, the

Circle is destroyed. But know this: there are others, there are many other groups beyond the vineyard fence. They are free and await you. You mustn't abandon hope. You must plan, and work towards escape."

Suddenly the steel behind her head clanged *BANG!BANG!BANG!* and she jumped, they all jumped, whooping in fright. One final *BANG!* of ringing steel as a guard outside pounded it with his truncheon.

"Shut up in there!" he shouted. "So help me, by Lichboegh's teeth, I'll stick this in your fucking snatch!"

Sheilagh quaked. The straw between her legs was damp where the pee had squirted from her in a terrified stream.

Across the container, the severe woman with the barbed wire tattoo shook her head furiously. She'd finished on the bucket, then slunk back to her place. There were other sharp looks of panicky disapproval. They heard the guard's boots crunch away and all of them, twenty skinny squalid women, fell back into the stifled silence of captivity.

Sheilagh blew out hard, expelling the fear, the hapless rage. *Fek yis*, she spat in her mind. *Fek yis all witchyer guns and yer fekin brutality.*

Going on six months now, she'd been in the pens with the rest of these cattle. Harsh assessment, but *Jaysus* the state of these women! Some of them had memories of freedom, sure they must. To look at them now, you'd think they'd been bred for slaves. Programmed, like. Happy enough to lie back and just take it up the arse, as Graham might have said.

Even here, squatting in the urine-damp straw with the heat prickly in her skin like the bites of a hundred deer flies, even here Graham made her smile.

The one with the stupid tattoo kept glaring at her. She'd noticed Sheilagh smiling, must've taken it for malice, that she was happy to have gotten them in trouble.

Sheilagh grinned all the merrier, giving her the finger all the while. Screw her. She was the worst of the lot! One of Lichboegh's stooges. Sheilagh made sure not to look away from that stony glare.

Six months now. Sheilagh would find a way out. Or die trying. That was it as far as alternatives in this shithole. And that tattooed slag with the deep furrows in her cheeks and the sinewy neck could die trying right along with her.

Don't test me, you bitch. You don't know. You don't know what I've done.

Finally, Sheilagh's adversary blinked and shifted her bitter eyes to a weaker target.

Sheilagh closed her eyes. Tried to shut out the heat-tempered hacking and moaning echoed by the unforgiving steel.

Nothing else mattered now, nothing but James. His face in the volatile fire light of the Circle, his high cheekbones clutching at hollows above his jawline. His tale had held the most magic of all. She still did not understand how James had become the locus of their Group. The kernel.

His slack-jawed fugue states, his turning eyes staring into nothing. Almost boiling in their jittery searching. The Stone. A chant slithering through the nighttime wood, slippery as a pack of ferrets. The Stone The Stone... *The Stonethestonethestone...*

Dead creepy, when he was like that.

He'd hypnotized them. James had cast a spell, flung the irresistible longing he felt for the Stone onto them, an invisible bridle around all their heads. They'd had to follow him, just as surely as if they'd been drugged to it.

Follow him, or whatever force – whatever *thing* – was inside him.

Or had they just acquiesced, like all these cows?

Whatever was to happen now, James was still the kernel. No certainty of it. That precious gem had vanished along with the electricity. But a sense. A mystery. Something else she would have haughtily dismissed in the time before. She could even hear herself chattering away at a grad student: *Well either ye know it or ye don't, goodness sake! Don't be plying me wityer 'feelings' or yer 'intuition'. Scientists need facts!*

The last ten years had taught her cruelly the need to pay damned close attention to her intuition.

James might even be dead now, and that was the truth. If he was dead, there wasn't much hope. None at all.

But she *felt* it. He was *alive*. Somewhere, and *Jaysus* she had absolutely no idea where. It was like she could hear his breathing, very faint, a hint of air.

Dozy, the deep sliding respiration of REM sleep.

Chapter 1
James Muir

Sheilagh had heard James breathing in his sleep. Somehow Sheilagh's sense of his dreaming breath stretched back into her past, already ten years gone in its grave. Back to James, comfortable in his own bed.

The day the world ended, James Muir stirred out of a light dream-plagued doze at about five in the afternoon. Another scorcher. Even the basement apartment was no longer a cool shield against the humid halitosis of the city.

The narrow window near the ceiling was shut up with cardboard and duct tape, a barricade against the light. But from a breach in the upper right corner, a thin ray of hot afternoon glared into the room. The heat scenting his sweat, scratching its way in for a lick.

James smelled something as well. Gamy, like an animal stall. Dirty straw, tinged with piss. Great, the apartment probably had mold now. Yeah, that'd be a good next step. Nothing like the knee-slapping good times of a mold infestation! In a basement apartment, no less!

James kicked off the sheet, rolling his eyes at the shouts and squeals that had woken him.

"Sara give me the book. Sara!"

"Jenny, sweetie, Daddy's sleeping. Please be quiet."

Good stage whisper, Stace. You'd be able to hear that from the back of the auditorium.

"Sara took my boo-oook!" For months now, Jenny had been talking in that irritating baby-voice, jealous of all the attention her little sister demanded.

"No. My book! Mine!"

"Gimme my book Sara! Saaa-ra!"

"OK," Stacy snapped. "Both of you into the living room. Now, before you wake up your father."

The voices of his family faded to a low drone. Then something went thump, and Sara caterwauled in the morally indignant outrage that only three-year olds could muster. That two-noted wail: "*AAAAaaahhh...Ah-ah-ah-ah... AAAAAaaaahhhh... Ah-ah-ah...*"

James sighed and rolled over. Every sound drumming into his

5

ears: the kids, a pot ringing in the kitchen, the whirring A/C, thumping footfalls in the apartment upstairs. Every goddamn afternoon, the neighbors came home and tossed their bags down.

He had the dry mouth and foggy numbness of boggy daytime sleep. Wading through shallow slumber, occasionally plunging headlong into freakish carnivals of vivid dreams. Then back to a brittle, restless slumber so easily shattered by even the smallest noise.

He twisted onto his right shoulder, looking across Stacy's side of the bed to a bent Ikea wardrobe, on which he and Stacy had stenciled the Camus quote they both loved:

Do not walk in front of me, I may not follow;
Do not walk behind me, I may not lead.
Just walk beside me and be my friend.

A long time since they'd painted that. Jeez, that would have been a couple of years before they'd had Jenny even.

Gradually, his breath deepened. He dreamed about Maggie, that time she'd started the hallowed tradition of drunken stripping.

"Wake up Maggie I think I got something to say to yoouuu!"

You could bet your ass you'd be hearing that old chestnut being belted out in aggressive inebriated choruses nearly every weekend at Maggie's place. One night, in the middle of a particularly drunken party, Maggie pulled out the album and slapped it down on the turntable, the needle making that horrible warping sound across the vinyl. She told Auntie Lenora to hold the needle until she was ready.

Then there she was, clinging to the stairs, revealing her pendulous swaying breasts, like drooping yeasty dough.

Every man in the room roared with hungry approval. Much beer was spilled in sloshing toasts and from the corners of grinning mouths.

"It's late September and I really should be back at school!" You would have thought it was an intimate and interactive Rod Stewart concert, such was the enthusiasm of the collected degenerates.

She's gonna fall, James thought in the refracted way of dreams. They weren't really Maggie's stairs, of course not. It wasn't even the right house. His brain presented him with an oddly out of tune dreamhouse. But the characters were real, ladies and gentlemen. Real as rain. And he knew she would fall.

At first she did real well, actually managing to shake her hips. James was no more than eight, but even he could tell it was a good move. She boogied down the stairs, lapping up the attention, grinning like a pig in shit. Not just proud – *drunk* proud.

6

Then her left foot came down on the second last step and it was like her leg was suddenly made of paper, it just folded under her. Maggie came crashing down and thank God she'd only been on the second step, cause she would have gone ass over tea kettle if she'd fallen near the top.

Uncle Randy and Uncle Glen helped her up, everybody doing that strange, stiff-legged dance of the macho rural white handyman. Maggie twittered, tucking her hands under her chin and fluttering her eyes like Betty Boop. James could see her left wrist going all purple. He said she should go to the hospital, but Maggie got all sullen and told him if he was going to be such a poop he could go off to bed this instant!

That same night Donnie cut up Jamie's doggy with the garden shears. First the paws, just to make it scream, he said. But Jamie was old enough to know that stuffed doggies don't scream, even when you snip off their legs with garden shears.

Donnie snickering as he slowly, slowly squeezed the shears. Metal blades grinding through fabric and stuffing. The muscles twitching in Donnie's bulging forearms, making the big heart tattoo on the right wrist look like it was beating. When Jamie burst into tears, Maggie finally stepped in and told Donnie to lay off, for Christ sake, you're upsetting him!

By then, Donnie had snipped off two legs and Doggy's head.

"Faaaack," he'd spat at Jamie, disgusted at his tears. Throwing the shears into the pile of shoes by the front door, grabbing his beer.

But it wasn't the harm done to Doggy that hurt Jamie's feelings; it was that somebody could be so cruel to just a little kid. The aquifer-deep sorrow of dreams.

James went wider and wider in the dream circle, drifting through various trance-memories made sinister by the acute paranoia of that state between wakeful and gone.

That enormous dock spider he'd seen at Mare's cottage last summer. He'd been clinging to the tip of the dock like a sailor after the ship had gone down, desperately embracing bobbing flotsam.

Finally, he convinced himself to venture further out into the water, kicking off the dock a bit, enjoying Stacy's teasing cheers and Jenny chanting "Da-dee! Da-dee! Da-dee!"

Then his feet felt the cold depth of the lake, the merciless space beneath him. Panic jerked his limbs. He groped for the dock. As long as he could get his hand on the dock he'd be fine, but then there it was! The hugest spider he'd ever seen outside a zoo. Its legs twin fans of grey fingers, translucent but furry. So large it seemed outrageous: a spider that size had no business living in North America.

His frantic hand splashed water on the dock and it reared back. So quick, he knew it would sink its fangs into his finger before he had a chance to yank it back, before his brain even had time to send the signal. James had never been the type to get freaked out by spiders, he actually thought they were kind of beautiful in their own way, but this spider! The mammalian furriness of its plump body, that moment of sudden defiance rather than fear. Standing up to him!

With nothing to hang onto, his head plunged into the brown cold water thrumming with its own alien language.

Panicking, James just managed to get his nose up to the air. Sputtering, coughing, he reached around to the narrow side of the dock, ninety degrees from the spider. He clung on, sighting the creature along the flatness of the lumber. The butt end of the dock was a two-by-six board, and damn it if those hairy grey legs didn't stretch the entire width!

The spider sparkled. He realized with creeping horror that he was looking into its eyes. The damn thing was so enormous, sunlight glaring on the water reflected in all eight of its eyes. Light keener than slivers of glass. A fecund, vicious hunger. Watching him.

He could even see its mouthparts moving – zap! it nabbed a tiny fly, chewed it up with relish.

Can I get some mustard with that?

"Ha ha ha ha ha! Haaaww-haw-haw-haw!"

Again James was ripped awake.

"Jenny!" Stacy hissed. "What did I tell you?"

The bedside alarm clock went off.

"Jenny bad! Bad Jenny!" Sara's chance now to get her digs in. James swore and slapped the alarm clock quiet.

*

Demands, forcing ever closer, eating up space. Gobbling freedom.

Just as he did every morning – because he still thought of this portion of his day as "morning" despite the fact that it was after five in the afternoon – he took a moment to be thankful. For his beautiful wife, his wonderful daughters. He asked for strength and safety tonight. He forced himself to remember why he needed to be grateful.

The bedroom door opened and Stacy came in. "It's time," she announced, raising her eyebrows.

James couldn't help but see cruel glee in those wise eyebrows.

He had to get up, whether he wanted to or not. As she came into the room and nestled against him, he chalked up his annoyance to chronic exhaustion.

"Sleep ok?" she asked.

"Same as always." He breathed her in, the smell of chamomile shampoo and freshly sliced cucumbers. She was making a salad for dinfast. The meal that was a freakish blend of dinner and breakfast.

"Did you get any work done last night?" Her breath tickled the hair on his chest.

By 'work' she meant writing. Editing was probably the more appropriate term. The damn manuscript was *written*, but needed a massive overhaul.

This was their only chance to discuss anything. When he got home from his shift around seven in the morning, Stacy would be waiting like a sprinter in the blocks with Sara scrubbed and in her daycare duds. Quick pecks instead of kisses. Her turn to rush away to work.

"When was the last time we had sex?" he asked.

"Don't change the subject."

At first their ridiculous schedule had reduced them from spouses to roommates with benefits. Now even the benefits had been axed.

"Got a fair bit of work done, actually," he lied. Stacy had her cheek on his ribs, looking down at his feet, so she couldn't see his wince. Lying still irritated his conscience, but he found with lazy satisfaction that the more he told the lie, the less he cared. He kissed the top of Stacy's head, tracing her shoulder with the tips of his fingers, hoping that this dabbling affection might be enough to offset his dishonesty.

"So you might have enough for me to, you know, actually read at some point?"

"Mmmm..."

James's job when he got home from work in the morning was to get Jenny up, make her breakfast and supervise her increasingly bellicose attempts to get his attention. Then it was a rush to get her ready and out the door to school, a few blocks away.

At least then he could trudge back home, collapse into bed from nine in the morning all the way through till five. Their sitter Mrs. Benjamin picked up Jenny from school, and Stacy picked up Sara from daycare.

"Jenny's so excited about summer vacation this year," said Stacy.

"Yeah?"

"Only another week to go, boyo!"

Ah, the mockery of that phrase – *vacation*. For James, summer was as much a vacation as Jack, Ralph, and Piggy's little jaunt to the deserted island. Since Jenny was home every day anyway, they pulled Sara out of daycare. A golden opportunity to save the fees, which James's job barely covered. So she'd be home every day as well, and wouldn't it be fan-damn-tastic to be the umpire for Jenny and Sara's Olympian shouting matches!

Laughing all the way! Ha-ha-ha-ha-ha!

"So how many words?" Stacy asked.

"Hmmm?"

"How much did you get done last night?"

"Oh," he said, blinking himself alert. "Uh, I dunno..." His mind wasn't exactly a blank. More like a chalkboard that hadn't been washed for years: a gray, unfocused mess.

"C'mon, c'mon!" She smacked his belly. It seemed to him the kind of corrective you'd give a dog who didn't come when it was called. "More than a thousand?"

"Are you for real?"

"What?"

"A thousand words?"

"Well that's why I'm asking, Mr. Man!"

"Oh, Stace, I don't know. A few hundred?"

Not exactly a lie, after all. He had done some work on the manuscript last night. Fighting through that infuriating sixteenth chapter. The lynch pin of the whole damn book, and he just couldn't get it right. At least seven rewrites, maybe eight on that chapter alone.

He hadn't added anything close to a few hundred words. But he said it anyway, just to keep her happy.

The entire premise of her question was faulty. Stacy couldn't seem to understand that when he went to *work* there was actually real *work* to do, funnily enough. That left him hardly any time or space to do any meaningful writing, editing, any damn thing.

"You were dreaming," she stated.

For a breathless second, he thought she was calling him out. As in, "You're dreaming, fella, if you think I believe you did that much work." But no, he realized she was speaking of real dreams. "Yeah," he said, "some weird ones."

"You were yelling."

"Yeah?"

"Do you remember what it was?"

James shifted under her. "One was about... about slaves? Slaves I think."

"Is that supposed to be some kind of commentary on your life?"

James chuckled. An apt one, at that. "No, no, really. A bunch of female slaves."

"Oh, I see. Slave chicks..."

"There was one slave who was Irish," he persisted. "Her and a bunch of women in some kind of huge metal box. That's all I remember. About that one, anyway."

"Well..." Stacy pushed herself up on one elbow, giving his chin a nibble. "It's time to stop fantasizing. Get up and fight the good fight, soldier."

"Yeah."

"Cheer up! Tonight's another chance to consummate your bromance with Dr. Rivers!"

"Sure."

"Just two more days and we're up at Mare's cottage again. Two days, that's bearable, isn't it?"

"Ok." He put some spunk into it so he wouldn't seem sulky. At that moment two more shifts seemed ridiculously punitive. "Two more days in the Gulag."

"The Gulag," she mocked. "That the kind of hyperbole that's gonna win you the Booker?" She bounded to her feet with smooth, graceful athleticism. It was the thing about her he'd fallen in love with first. She stretched, fingertips brushing the low ceiling. "Maggie called."

"She wants money," said James flatly.

"She talked to the girls, sent her love."

"Right."

"You're so mean," she laughed. "Your own mother, your own flesh and blood."

James sat up, arching his aching back. "I'll call her before I go, alright?"

"You should. Jamie."

"Aw, don't, just don't."

"Ok *Jamie*, get your ass up and out. Dinner'll be ready in fifteen."

She left and he climbed back in to his uniform: the blue shirt with embroidered shoulder patches: Gunnarson Security Services. Trousers with a red stripe down the outside seam. Blue and boxy enough to single him out for abuse from students and faculty alike.

The proximity of Maggie's call and his dream jarred him a little. It wasn't a coincidence. This morning's dreams were *bright*. That was the term he'd used since he'd been a boy. Dreams in Day-Glo colors, with very crisp edges and a deeply woven sense of veracity. It's like being there, folks! Step up and take a ride, come one, come all!

Once or twice a month, a bright dream whispered cryptic omens. This morning – this afternoon – was a classic example. He'd dream a bright dream of her and Maggie would call.

For James, it was just the nature of things. There wasn't much to reflect over, any more than if he'd just discovered a new mole on his arm. Or another gray hair in his whiskers.

Staring at his own silvery stubble in the bathroom vanity mirror, turning his head back and forth, James was aghast at the age creeping into his features. He plucked at the loose pouch of skin under his left eye. When his fingers let go, the skin remained drooped! *Ick*, a slowly receding chunk of gray dough. Very much like a miniature version of his mother's breast.

He smirked. What a comparison! With an unpleasant twang, he realized that even at the beginning of her long stair-strip-teasing career, with an eight year-old son, Maggie had been a good deal younger than he was now, father of two daughters aged five and three.

"These hours are writing age on my face," he said, still peering in the mirror. "Like..." C'mon now. Rev up the old simile machine! Like an ancient, indecipherable language etched into soft stone.

Not bad, he thought, lathering shaving cream. *Cosi-cosi*, as his friend Massimo would say. He wasn't overly taken with *indecipherable*, that mouthful of a modifier. But it would do in a pinch.

Faaaack.

Donnie's slur still sharp in his ears, even after twenty damn years. A sump from which corrosive self-criticism so often echoed. Fuck you, he thought sourly. The razor shushed through his stubble.

If he had any idea how to find Donnie today, James would write him a note of somewhat sardonic thanks. Whenever he had doubts about his own dubious manhood, all he needed was a glance in the mirror at that bent aquiline nose: another heirloom courtesy of Donnie-boy! That, and the v-shaped scar on the middle knuckle of his right hand. Ah well, at least the nose lent his lean face the Gallic, enigmatic look that so slew the ladies. What a laugh! Good times, Donnie. Good times.

As he came out of the bathroom, Jenny and Sara barreled down the hall from the living room, screaming "Daaaa-deeee!"

James crouched down, sweeping them both off the floor. Warm pain creaked down his spine, Jenny getting too big and heavy for this, but he did it anyway. It was important. Knees and elbows and ecstatic faces pummeling him, he clutched their wiggling

12

bodies, swinging them back and forth.

"Did Daddy have a good sleep?" Jenny asked, as if cradling one of her dolls.

"Sleepy sleepy sleepy!" said Sara, drooling down her chin.

"What does a guy have to do to get some peace and quiet around here!" James laughed.

"Smooooooth!" Jenny crooned, caressing his cheek.

"Daddy! Daddy, look! My tattoo! It's so booootiful—" Sara did indeed have a new butterfly tat on her plump forearm, the kind applied with a wet washcloth. It would stay there for days, until it was no more than a gray blur. Even then, Sara would insist they not wash that part of her arm. "My booootiful budderfly!"

"Hey Daddy," Jenny insisted, "I'm a bird. Peck-peck-peck. I'm a bird daddy! I'm pecking you!"

The twin streams of consciousness babbled as perfectly as water over smooth pebbles. As monotonously, as endlessly.

Adding to the noise, Stacy had put on Jenny and Sara's favorite CD, a collection of children's ditties by a local musician named Sammy Peterson. Relentlessly upbeat, the cover of the CD featured Mr. Peterson dressed in a bright blue tee-shirt with neon green polka dots, peeking out around a door. The grin on that merry face was enough to send chills down the spine of any sensible parent.

I love ice cream, ice cream's yum-my!
I love ice cream when it's sun-ny!
Melty, creamy in myyyy tummmmy!

The girls sang along. Bobbing to the beat, James carried them into the nook where the supper table was laid out, plopping them into their seats. Jenny in her 'big girl chair', Sarah in the highchair with her back to the living room, which was a disaster of far-flung toys, board books, dolls. He went through to the kitchenette to pinch Stacy's bum.

"Thanks for putting on Sammy Pedophile." He couldn't resist using this nickname.

Stacy smacked his arm. "Stop," she said, handing him Jenny and Sara's juice cups.

Stacy had laid on all the fixings for a cold supper: deli meats, cheese, mustard, and the crusty Italian buns he enjoyed. Humus and pita torn into wedges. Pickles.

James plucked a fat one out of the brine and took a bite, relishing the huge salty crunch between his molars.

Can I get some mustard with that?

Very funny, Mr. Spider, but I've got my eye on you!

Stacy put down a huge bowl of salad, sprinkled with roasted

walnuts. The toaster oven was the only heat she would think of adding to the apartment on such a humid day.

Already, James felt his uniform shirt sticking to his back.

James and Stacy set about making the girls their sandwiches with the quick efficiency that can only come through years of dedicated practice.

"No I don't want mustard!" Jenny cried.

"Well what do you say then?" James asked.

"No mustard please! But I wanna pickle!"

"Sara, do you want cheese?" Even as the question left his lips, James closed his eyes, rebuking himself. Why, why was he so stupid?

"Cheesy-cheesy cheeeeseeeee!" Sara began chanting, and then both of the girls, at the tops of their little lungs, were in on the mad game. "Cheesy-cheesy cheeeeseeeee! Cheesy-cheesy cheeeeseeeee!"

Stace gave James a murderous look. "Sorry," he mouthed, shrugging his shoulders in abject regret. Amazing how such wee bodies could produce such earsplitting volume.

"Okay, okay!" James had to shout. "Girls! That's enough, thank-you!" But he had to repeat "Thank you" several more times before the volume dropped to the point where they could continue a normal conversation.

"But I don't want cheese!" Sara whined as James gave her the sandwich.

He hung his head. Putting the sandwich on his own plate, he started another for her.

When things had finally calmed down to a dull roar, James went to the fridge for a beer, returning to Stacy's frankly accusing glance.

"It's just a beer!" he insisted.

"Right before work?"

He laughed, and regretted the edge of bitterness in it. "It's not like I'll be driving."

"Okay. *Jamie.*"

"Nice," he nodded to acknowledge the pregnant jibe. And then, to change the subject, a neat segue to their daily dinner ritual. "Jenny, can you tell me what you're thankful for today?"

"Ummm..." she said through a huge mouthful of half-chewed ham sandwich.

"Daddy shouldn't be asking while you've got your mouth so full," said Stacy.

"Can I do anything right?" he snapped.

"Someone woke up grumpy!" Stacy snickered. "Is Daddy a

14

grouchasaurus rex today?"

Sara giggled, legs bouncing happily beneath the plastic tray of her high chair. "Yeah! Daddy's a grouchee-saw-wus!"

"I'm thankful..." Jenny began with solemn formality. "I'm thankful for the whole world!"

"Yeah!" Sara squealed. "Me too! The whole world!'

"Hey no fair! Mommee! Sara copied."

"She's allowed to be thankful for whatever she wants," said James, intervening in exactly the way Stacy found irritating. He felt a pang of childish satisfaction, took a gulp of beer. The icy cold felt magic in his throat.

"Sara," said Stacy, pointedly ignoring James. "Is there something else you can think of that makes you thankful?"

"You and Daddy!" she replied immediately, her face sunny with a wide milk-toothed smile. So much like her mother with her round little face and her straight corn silk hair.

"I wanna be thankful for something else too!" said Jenny.

"Alright," said Stacy. "What else?"

"Hmmm..." Jenny knitted her brow and frowned off to one side. In this expression James saw clear echoes of Maggie's pouting self-pity. As when the beer money ran out, for example. "Me thankful for the flowers!"

There it was again, that nasal baby talk that made James's hair stand on end. "Can we talk like a big girl?" he asked, winking at her.

"What you thankful for, Daa-deee?"

"I'm thankful for you, and Sara and Mommy."

Stacy sat up straight in her chair, and James braced himself for whatever was coming. "I'm thankful that Daddy might finally have his story done for me to read. Sometime soon." She stuck out her tongue at him, and both girls giggled with delight.

James took a bite of his sandwich. For a while, they all settled in to their eating. Even the girls calmed down enough to jam some food into their faces.

From the cache of toys Jenny kept stashed under the table, she produced the singing puppy. Lord help me, James thought. A birthday gift from Stacy's folks, the kind of torture implement so enjoyed by grandparents. Jenny pressed the red button on its front paw and it started to contort with a stiff, mechanical whine. The jaw flapped up and down, as a tinny version of 'I Can't Stop Loving You' emanated from its stuffing guts.

All the while, the brown plastic eyes that were supposed to look baleful and sweet stared with the empty cruelty of a deep-sea hunter.

"Jenny, please put that away, or it'll get covered in food." James was conscious of keeping his tone light. That dog really creeped him out.

Jenny sulked and removed the thing just as it went into a wolfish howl that ended the routine. Truth be told, it was already filthy, the fur greasy and stringy. If James had his way, it would be buried in the Goodwill pile.

Thinking of Goodwill reminded him about Chapter sixteen. A key scene took place in a Goodwill emporium. Stacy was being catty about the damn manuscript, but fair enough. It had been four years now since he'd finished the first draft. The thick wad of paper that sat in an inert lump under his laptop on the chair behind Jenny, the one pushed back to make room for Sara's highchair. The millstone, he'd come to think of that manuscript in his own mind.

No, he suddenly realized. Not four years at all! Jesus, you moron, Jenny just turned *five* last month! Five years! Somehow, the extra year hit him low in the gut. Half a decade now, and the goddamn thing was no closer to finished than it had been the day he cut Jenny's umbilical cord, severing her from Stacy.

"Look, Daddy. I'm a bird." Jenny began tapping her finger on James's forearm again. "Peck-peck-peck, Daddy. Peck-peck-peck!"

"That's pretty funny, Jenny. Can you finish your baby carrots please?"

The first draft he'd pounded out in those six months of heady arrogance after Stace had announced she was pregnant. They'd seen themselves as *artistes*, groovy cosmopolites, above the pedantic fray of children, of normal lives led by normal people. Stacy had been on the pill, a proud cobalt-haired urban warrior. They'd joked in bed at night about James's swimmers, how not even the pill could stop a Muir from procreating. Sure, they'd never planned on children, but so what? They could do it. How hard could it possibly be?

From under the table, that damned uncanny dog started baying again. He realized Jenny had slipped underneath.

"Jenny, can you sit back down please?"

The wobbly voice drawled in an exaggerated yokel accent: "*I cayn't stawp luuvin yew...Ah made up ma maaand...*"

It clashed with the jangling banjo-plagued romp through the fecund twisted mind of Sammy Pedophile.

"Jenny!" Stacy snapped. "What did your father ask you to do?"

Jenny appeared over the edge of the table, a mawkish expression on her face.

Deep underground, James had always doubted he'd make a

16

decent father. Too much negative emotional radiation oozing from the veins of awful memories laid down by nearly eighteen years under Maggie's roof. Until he'd met Stacy, he'd dismissed it all as 'bullshit'. But Stacy – bless her – had convinced him that he'd gone through blatant abuse.

Donnie. That bony face, shiny drunk, twisting in contempt. The way he spat *Faaaaaaack*, as if James was nothing. Lower than the shit on the soles of his work boots.

James shivered.

He looked at Stacy, who was making a silly face at Sara. She'd long since let the cobalt blue grow out. Her hair looked way better blond. He wouldn't have agreed with that assessment when she'd dyed it, but now – her face was getting rounder, as he'd known it would. The ash blond hair framed it in long straight petals, emphasizing her grace.

"You're beautiful," he said, grasping her hand on the table. Irritated by the wan close-lipped smile she gave back.

By the time of Jenny's accidental conception, Stacy had already established her career as a freelancer, with several published articles in her portfolio. Her pride and joy had been a piece on the environmental impact of chemical fertilizers. It had been picked up by Lifestyle@Home, the type of glossy mag found on wire racks in grocery stores. The tag to her story on the cover – the cover! – had been "ARE YOUR LAWN CHEMICALS KILLING YOU?"

Unlike the few short stories James had published in obscure journals, it helped pay the bills. And before Jenny was born, that had been enough. A life of stylish shabbiness. Writing, attending demonstrations, workshops and ad-hoc committees.

Charting the growth of Stacy's belly, they assured each other their lives wouldn't change. No way. They both knew what they wanted, both had plans etched too deep to be abandoned for a mere *child*.

"Mooommmeee..." Jenny droned, keeping her gleeful eyes on James. "I fullllll..."

"Can you talk like a big girl please?" he asked, forcing a smile.

"Alright, fine," said Stacy. "Go and wash your hands."

"I told her she needed to finish those carrots." Right away, James regretted the heat in his words.

"Fine."

"No, I'm sorry, go on Jenny and wash your hands."

Sulking, Jenny went down the hall to the bathroom.

"I'm just tired," he said, trying to catch Stacy's eye. But she frowned down at her plate, jaw working the sandwich.

A mere child. Right. That attitude had been smashed by reality.

Then, just after Jenny turned two – more great news!

"Quite the swimmers, Muir," Stacy had muttered, staring at the pee-soaked dipstick with the blue cross or red checkmark or whatever the fuck it had been that signed the death warrant for their pretensions.

James remembered cracking, "How can that be possible, Stace? Dontcha need to have sex to do that?"

Stacy had buried herself under the blankets and angrily turned her back on him.

Now, he looked at Sara, and realized she was just playing with her food. He took the initiative, getting up to wipe her face.

"Ugh," James made a stinky-poo face at Sara. "You sure do smell!"

"I pell?"

"You do, you pell."

Jenny ran back from the bathroom and plunged her hands into the bowl of humus.

"Oh, Jenny!" Stacy cried. "What do you think you're doing?"

"Acting out," James stated, giving Jenny a no-nonsense look. It was well practiced. He set Sara on the floor, reaching for a napkin. "Why would you do that, honey?"

"Tension." Jenny splayed her humus-caked fingers, barely suppressing a huge shit-eating grin.

"Attention, sure. Well you've got my attention. Please don't do that anymore, ok?"

"Kay."

"Now you need to go and wash your hands – yet again!" That's it, he thought. Turn it into a lesson. *Lessonize* the situation, y'all. "You see how that's kind of silly?"

"No," she said sadly, as if she pitied his utter stupidity.

Stacy snickered into her hand.

"Mommy thinks you're very funny," said James.

"I am funny."

"Go and wash those hands please."

"J," Stacy said, "if you're gonna call Maggie, you should do it pronto."

He glanced at his watch, and shit she was right, it was almost quarter to six. "Yeah, alright, I'll call her after I change Sara."

"No, I'll do it." She got up. Without actually touching him, she scooped Sara off the floor. "Call your ma."

James rubbed his face, trying to massage some life into the muscles hanging on his skull. He felt unwell.

"Jenny, what did I ask you to do?" he snapped, glaring at the ceiling.

"Waaaawsh handzzzz..."

"Jenny! *Please* stop the baby talk. You just sound like a little girl pretending to be a baby, and not really succeeding at it."

She rolled her eyes and flounced off, spreading her arms dramatically.

James was already so irritated that he didn't notice the cup in her left hand until it knocked against the wall, spilling mango juice all over his laptop, down the edges of the manuscript.

"Jennifer, Jesus Christ!" he shouted, smacking his thighs.

Instantly Jenny was in tears, no less so than if he'd hauled off and smacked her. And of course she made a beeline directly to Stacy. Maybe Marx had it right after all. Every act is political.

In the lightning clarity of his anger, James could see the accident was his own fault. For leaving the damn laptop so close to the table. For not paying enough attention to his daughter in the first place, tempting her to act out. These realizations just made him even more angry.

He seized Sara's Minnie Mouse sippy cup and hurled it into the kitchen. It struck the wall next to the fridge with a whack that satisfied his teeming brain. Until the top came off and the dregs of Sara's juice bled out all over the damn floor.

Almost crying with drained frustration, he got down on his knees with the dishcloth to wipe up the mess.

Within half an hour he'd be saying goodbye to his family for the last time. He would never see them again.

*

Of course the laptop was fine. He'd blown his stack over nothing. The juice completely missed all the vitals, and thank God for that.

James had it open at the table, the phone squeezed between his ear and shoulder as his call rang through to Maggie.

"Jamie!" Maggie crooned. She'd snatched the phone up even before the first ring had died.

"Maggie," he responded, beaten.

Despite her chronic shortage of money, Maggie would never give up luxuries like call display. That way she could avoid her creditors. She was in so much money trouble that her phone service wasn't even in her own name. The bills she ignored were addressed to Shirley Meisner, one of the identities she cycled through her endless series of pogey and disability scams.

"How's my love?"

James snorted. "Dunno. How's he doing?"

"Oh very funny, Jamie, you're a real hoot and a half, love."

Half love. Yep, James thought, that's about what it amounted to. There was an email from Allistair Rivers. James opened it.

hey man —

good news: MAJOR breakthrough on the project!!!!!

come to the lab and see!

game for drunken debauchery friday in celebration???

that fuckin novel finished yet ;)

rainbo

"Still all tied up in knots when I call you Jamie, eh sweetie?"

"Nobody but you, Maggie. You're still the only one who still calls me that."

"Well how else would you know it's me talking to ya?" He heard the satisfied grunt of Maggie inhaling nicotine.

James clicked the respond button and started typing.

Stricken by ennui, rainbo. Drunken debauchery to take place Friday pm in cottage country. Debauchery to include: generous abuse of alcohol (hence "drunken"), sordid naked acrobatics and neo-feminist discourse on the hegemony of the male gaze in western literatures. You simply cannot compete. Try not to be heartbroken.

J.

Rainbo. James got a kick out of that. Allistair's hypersensitive irony apparatus had been stimulated by a story he'd heard about a Russian mistranslation of the movie Rambo.

"It's been ages, Jamie. Ages and ages." The smoke deepened her whining tone. "Keepin' busy, are ya?"

"About all I'm doing," he muttered, hitting send, getting up to pack a lunch.

"Eh? What's that?"

"Yeah, yeah, I'm keeping busy." He folded some ham into a bun.

"You sound flustered. Tell Maggie what's the matter."

Well, Maggie. I've got a head crowded with a riotous mob. No torches, pitchforks or scythes though. No, this mob's armed with money worries, the nightshift, chores, the endless tumult of kids. The mob is on the hunt for my creativity, see. And my creativity – my will to write – is so terrified it's cowering in the deepest cellar of my imagination. And now I've gotta spend my last few precious moments before I go to work talking to you. "I'm fine, Maggie, I'm fine."

"*Nothing could be finer to be in Caroliner in the mor-orrrr-ning!*" she sang, and then he heard Auntie Lenora's croaking laugh in the background, joining in on the next line. "*No one could be sweeter than my sweetie when I meet her in the mor-orrrr-niiing!*"

Even when all of Maggie's other drinking buddies had finally buggered off, Lenora clung fast. Like a greedy chigger that doesn't know it's full. 'Auntie' was a meaningless abstraction. Lenora and Maggie were sisters in a deeper way than genes could provide. Their love affair with booze would never be torn asunder.

"How's the enabler?" he asked, filling his water bottle at the sink.

"Oh stop, Jamie." Maggie made the raspy chuckle that more than anything else had come to define her in his mind. Then, in a hoarse call that made James wince and hold the phone away from his ear: "Jamie says hi, Len!" Lenora's fluted laugh, as distant as he wished some of his memories could be. "Lenora says hi ba-ack!" Maggie sang.

"*I love you! You love me! We're all one big fam-i-ily!*" James sang into the phone along with Sammy Pedophile, his tone cruelly etched in the acid bath of his resignation. His uniform shoes did a shuffling dance across the kitchen linoleum into the living room to hit the power button on the stereo, finally killing that god-awful shit coming out of the speakers.

On his way back to the kitchen he stepped on one of Jenny's dolls, cracking the head in two. God-*damn*-it!

"I spoke to your lovely wife earlier," Maggie said. "You're a lucky man, Jamie, and just you remember that. That Stacy is just so lovely."

James stopped at the table to shut down the laptop. There was a response from Allistair. As always, he need the last word:

YAWN been there done that — nobody can fellate your ego like that wife of yers — sure you'll have a BALL.

MAKE SURE YOU SEE ME IN THE LAB TONITE!

"Jamie," Maggie said with exaggerated gravity. "You've got to get that family of yours out of that awful apartment."

He rolled his eyes at the same advice she'd given him a hundred times. He put the laptop into his knapsack.

"A cellar, Jamie," she lilted. He pictured her in that rickety yellow reading chair, crossing her vein-marbled legs. "A cellar is no place to raise your children."

"First of all, it's not a cellar, it's a basement."

"Well, whatever you want to call it—"

"I call it a fucking basement because that's what it is—"

"No sunshine for the girls, no fresh air—"

"Stop it. Just stop." He kept his tone level. He felt no need to explain himself yet again. It was a huge apartment for the rent they paid, and the vacancy rate was very low. Besides, they were in a good area, right in the middle of Corktown with lots of other young families, parks. Just a short walk to Jenny's school. "Let me worry about my family, Maggie."

"Well, they're my family too!" she croaked.

"You're even more loaded than I thought!"

"Well, Jamie, it is after five, honey!"

"What do you want, Maggie? Hard up for dough, then?"

"Aw, Jamie, can't – can't a mother just call and say hello to her son? Eh?"

Let me know, James thought sourly. Let me know when you're a mother, and we'll talk about it. "Everything's fine at this end, Maggie," he stated.

"You knew I was gonna call, didn't you Jamie? Had one of your dreams? Did ya get a peek over the horizon, love?"

This was her phrase for what James thought of as bright dreams. Maggie claimed to have similar experiences. She treated them with a careless tripping-down-the-yellow brick road type of jocularity that always struck James as akin to farting in the middle of a church service.

"I dreamt of the time Donnie cut up my stuffed dog." He went to the fridge and pulled out another bottle of beer. Pressed the frosty glass against his forehead.

Maggie sniffed, raking through her ash heap of memories. "Donnie never did that." Flatly dismissing the possibility.

"He did," James insisted. "With the garden shears." He twisted off the beer cap.

"Bullshit," she droned, sounding tired of him now. "Even if he did, it's no wonder after what you did to him."

James sighed. Right. Bent nose, scarred knuckle and all. "No, no, Maggie. Try to keep up. He did it when I was a kid!" He downed the beer in one go, chugging until foam dribbled from the corners of his mouth. The whole bottle in one groaning chug-aroo!

"Jamie, Jesus H. Christ, then it was *years* ago. You need to let go."

"Well, if Donnie never did it, then I suppose there's nothing to let go of. Is there?"

"Smartass. How's the book coming along?"

"Fine, Maggie. Look, I've got to get going, I'm going to be late for work."

"Ah," she scoffed. "They can wait."

"No, Maggie, they can't wait. I need this job." Carefully, so that Stace wouldn't hear the door, he opened the hall closet and slipped the empty beer bottle into the case. So Stace wouldn't find it. Right, he told himself, belching in Maggie's ear. He didn't want Stace to worry.

"Every job needs you more than you need it, Jamie. Take it from somebody who knows."

"Right!" he snickered. "When's the last time you had steady work?"

"Jamie, stop it. I'm still on the disability. My wrist is killing me. You do remember my wrist?"

James tried to suppress a giggle.

"Oh, you find it funny, do you?"

He heard Lenora pipe up: "Tell him he's your son, Maggie, he's your fuckin' son and he owes us!"

"Maggie, I gotta go. I'll call you next week."

"No, Jamie, no you won't." Her voice cracked.

"Alright, I won't," he said, the words distorted by his giggling.

"You're a real asshole sometimes, Jamie."

"Right back atcha, Maggie-Mae!"

"Could you at least send the old girl a few bucks? Eh?" Another suck at the ciggie.

"Oh yeah," he said. "Tell you what, I'll cut a check against the gold Visa. Would that suit you? Nah, nah, I got it, I'll whip out the platinum MasterCard, ok Maggie? How bout I just fire that off to you?"

The last thing he would ever hear of Maggie in life was a choked sob as the phone crashed down. The line went dead.

*

That conversation was in fact the last time he'd ever use a phone.

Half an hour later, he was struggling to stay awake on a streetcar without air conditioning, staring at a paperback copy of Cormac McCarthy's *The Crossing*. To write, he needed input. But he gaped at the text without reading.

After the conversation with Maggie, Stacy had come into the kitchen. Looking gravely disappointed as the silently threw condiments back into the fridge. Not wanting to leave his family in a state of turmoil, he'd have to make the first move.

"Jenny's pretty upset, huh?" had been his faltering gesture.

"Pretty upset," Stacy turned on him. "James, she's wrecked.

She's never heard her father yell at her like that."

"Shit."

"What's going on with you?"

The two of them, arrayed against each other across the narrow kitchen. "I'm tired, bone tired, and it – it just..."

"Just what?"

"It was just too much. That's it. I don't know what else to say."

"Here I am trying to pick you up." Keeping her voice low and tight so the girls wouldn't hear them going at it. "I'm trying to boost your spirit, and you're looking at me like I'm being a catty bitch."

"I wasn't."

"You were!"

"No, I mean I wasn't thinking that. C'mon, now."

"No, James, you were," she insisted.

Now the streetcar ground to a halt. Passengers shuffled on and off. As much as his eyes wouldn't focus on the on the page, his ears couldn't stop hearing the words spoken around him. A woman behind, prattling on and on about her boss, how she should just tell him to stuff his damn job, stuff it you-know-where.

A Chinese man across the aisle, giving his wife shit. James couldn't understand Mandarin or Cantonese, but the emotion came through loud and clear. You're a disappointment to me, he jabbered in her downcast face. You shame me.

Everyone, determined only to have what they did not have right now.

Most of them were on their way home from work, destitute of happiness. Oh, he saw people smiling, some laughing. But he saw little real joy. The only gladness most people felt was the negative kind: glad *not* to be at work, *not* to be that panhandler.

Unable to stand the prickly sweat on his shoulders, he stripped off his uniform shirt and stuffed it into his knapsack. Now a bare-chested heathen, earning distrusting glances.

"You know, I realized earlier," he'd told Stacy after a few moments of tense silence, "I'm older now than Maggie was when I was Jenny's age. A lot older."

"So what?"

"Here's so what: even Maggie had a roof over my head by that point. Despite everything, even she provided that. And what do I provide?"

"James, what are you talking about? We have a roof over our heads—"

"No, no – she owned her place, Stace. What was she, twenty-two, twenty-three, and she already owned her own house. Can you understand how hard that is for me to realize?"

Stacy smirked, shaking her head. "You're insane!"

"I'm insane."

"You are. You're fucking bonkers, James. Of course she was young! She got knocked up when she was seventeen! Besides that, the only reason she owned anything was because she extorted it from somebody. And you're a terrible poet."

He'd blinked at her, uncomprehending.

"Place, Stace... just doesn't work for me."

That had been enough to make him smile. A real smile. They hugged, James pressing his cheek against hers, holding her tight.

"So," she summarized, "you're asking me to pity you because you're making an honest living, providing as best you can for your children?"

"Is that what I'm asking for?"

"That's what it seems, boyo."

"Easy for you to say, you who's working as a writer— "

"Oh, please—"

"A professional writer, Stacy."

"Gawd, James!" She wrenched her head out of his grasp, glaring at him. *The Corktown News*? Stilted bits on why people don't pick up dog turds in the park, little cameos for the Corktown Merchants Association? Is that your definition of a successful writing career?"

"I didn't use those words. I said you are a professional writer, and you are, by definition: somebody who makes a living as a writer."

"What happened to the man I married?" She raked her nails through his work shirt, down his shoulder blades. "The man I married didn't wallow in self pity, and I don't feel like spending the rest of my life with a self-pitying fool."

"You won't."

"Good. Yuck! Your back's all sweaty!"

He transferred from the streetcar to the subway, flowing in a river of bodies down into the windy tunnels smelling of hot oil.

Just before leaving, he'd drawn Jenny into his arms. "I wish I hadn't yelled," he whispered.

"I wish I didn't spill the juice on your com-pewter."

"It was just an accident, sweetie. Daddy shouldn't have yelled like that."

"Just a accident," she'd repeated, as if to ward off the possibility of him changing his mind. The fragile hope in her voice broke his heart. "Is it broken?"

"No, sweetheart," he said, jarred by the proximity of her

question and his thought. "It's just fine. Okay?"

"Kay."

Difficult for him to leave after that. The sense he was a fleeing coward. Still clinging by the very tips of his fingers and toes to the slippery cliff face of the early parental learning curve.

He rode to the end of the subway line and climbed the stairs to the York University campus. The westering sun loomed through a sulfurous sky, an eldritch omen shrinking him to an infinitesimal point. An ant creeping among the vast blocks of sweltering concrete.

James called it the Gulag because Stalin would have felt right at home among the brutalist slabs of its buildings. Crossing the pavement towards the hulking cement coffin of the administrative building, he felt a tickle of fear. A current was already in the air, a stir of something so vast it could not be seen. Not yet. As with so many other things in this time before the world turned over, James was blind to it. But somehow, below consciousness, he felt it. In the slipstream of wind behind his body, a creeping.

Again, the venomous constellation of that huge spider's eyes filled his thoughts. Glittering in the silken water light under the edge of the dock. Watching. Waiting.

Chapter 2
The Campus

The security office was an airless cube buried deep in the cryptic bowels of the administrative building. His shift started at seven. Shrugging on his uniform shirt, he strode in with ten minutes to spare.

The scene was the same one he'd witnessed for years. The scarred, battered lockers, the faded, wrinkled Bruce Lee posters. The smell of stale coffee scalding on the hotplate. Framed photos of Lars Gunnarson in his prime as a sixth-degree black belt, sparring, smashing boards with his bare hands.

There was Lars himself, leaning back in his desk chair, plucking his acoustic guitar. Rangy legs stretched up on the desk, his pointed cowboy boots indicating the dusty ceiling tiles. He was finger-picking along with Dust in the Wind, tinny on the antique desktop radio, spooky and distant. Off-key, Lars crooned the final lyric, *"Everything is dust in the wind."*

As if to contradict this notion, Massimo posed in the opposite corner, stripped to a flimsy undershirt, pumping huge dumbbells. Panting through gritted teeth, the olive skin of his broad face and bulky arms satiny with sweat.

"Hey Jimmy," said Lars in his Zen way. James often thought that the Earth could collide with another damn planet, and Lars would make it his sworn mission not – repeat *not* – to get even a little ruffled.

"How's it going, Lars?" James went to his locker and put on the heavy utility belt with the loop to hang the big MagLite they all carried. He clipped the microphone on his shoulder. The coiled wire like a telephone cord hung across his chest, connected to the radio on his belt.

"Jimmy!" Massimo grunted as he finished his last biceps curl.

"How's it going, Mass?"

"How's it look like it's goin'?"

"You're looking good, Mass, looking good."

Massimo flexed his engorged muscles for James's benefit. "Fuckin' right I'm lookin' good," he growled.

Artur stomped in. Lean, wearing mirrored aviator sunglasses and a flat-top crew cut, he looked like an instructor at a Top Gun fan club boot camp.

"Hey Massimo! Ya balding Dago!"

"Artur," Lars warned.

"Screw you," Massimo grunted, looking at himself this way and that in the mirror on his locker door.

"Massimo, decorum please," Lars ordered.

"Jimmy!" Artur roared. "You dudes ready to kick some ass!"

"Fuckin' A," Massimo rumbled, still fussing with the little hair that remained clinging to his shining scalp.

"Give it up, you mendacious Italian!" Artur snickered. "Check him out, Jimmy! Barely got enough pubes on that head to cover his woman's snatch!" He paused just long enough to let that barb sink in. "But wait, that's right! Massimo doesn't have a woman!"

"Artur," Lars groaned, but even he was struggling not to smile.

Massimo's narrow eyes swiveled back and forth, searching desperately for a comeback. "You're an asshole," was all he could manage.

James had just finished gearing up when Lars barked "*Shugo!*"

James, Artur and Massimo lined up shoulder to shoulder behind Lars, facing the small shrine on the wall between Lars's desk and the lockers. Only a squat wooden table displaying a Japanese bell and a reproduction samurai helmet. For Lars it held a mystical significance. Just as in a karate dojo, he began all the shifts with *mokuso*, a period of meditation.

"*Tsuke!*"

All of them stood to attention.

"*Seiza!*"

Following Lars, they kneeled on the carpet, sitting on their shins. Lars reached forward and rapped the bell with a small mallet. The resonating bronze filled the room. The idea was to follow the sound as it faded to silence, leaving behind all the worries and cares of their private lives.

When James had first started working here, all this ceremony had been hard to take seriously. Now it was an important part of his day. Another rare opportunity for quiet focus.

The bell faded to a tiny pealing sphere, very far away. Eyes closed, James could hear breath whistling in Artur's nose, the humming ventilation system. He tried to empty his mind, but it remained harried. His knees hurt. He thought of the manuscript, that damned millstone. He thought of Jenny whispering "Just a accident" in his ear. "Just a accident."

Okay, sweetie, just a accident. Okay.

The phone on Lars's desk rang and he twitched. It rang and rang, a pale electronic murmur. Lars had instructed them to acknowledge, to accept such interruptions instead of spending energy shutting them out. James couldn't suppress the urgency he'd felt since getting on the streetcar downtown. Something was amiss.

It was Stacy calling. Something was wrong with one of the girls.

Stop, he told himself. Just stop. He deepened his breathing. Tried to find some calm.

Stacy's last words as he'd gone through the door: "Get some work done on that book. I don't wanna hear any horseshit tomorrow morning! Real work!"

"*Mokuso yame*," Lars murmured. Stop meditating. "Artur, the Gunnarson Security Services *kun*, please."

"GSS *kun*!" Artur barked. "Seek perfection of character!"

"Seek perfection of character!" they all chanted together. Artur went through the rest of the code, throwing out the exhortations like a drill sergeant, the rest of them responding in repetition.

"Be faithful!"

"Endeavour!"

"Respect others!"

"Refrain from violent behavior!"

"*Shomen ni lei*!" Artur barked. Bow to the front, to honor the shrine.

They all bowed to the shrine, touching their foreheads to the backs of their hands like Muslims at prayer. Lars turned around to face them, his face a studied mask.

"*Sensei ni lei*!" Artur shouted, and they all bowed to Lars.

Lars cleared his throat. "Thank-you Artur. Please try to remember the *kun* tonight. Especially the bit about respect."

"Yessir."

Lars gave him a skeptical look. "We're not expecting any trouble this evening, gentlemen. I have word from the physical sciences building: apparently those folks in the basement have something important going on, so they will be around tonight. James, be mindful: that's on your circuit. *Hai*?"

"*Hai*," he acknowledged.

"Let's hope they're not getting ready to blow up the world or something," Lars winked.

Artur guffawed as if it was the funniest joke he'd ever heard.

"Serve and protect," Lars said. "It's that simple. Keep up the circuits, stay in radio contact. Let's stay safe out there."

They let Lars get to his feet before rising. James winced at his snapping knees, feeling old and stiff.

*

James had always wondered how the three of them must appear as they marched together across the rotunda of the Vari lecture hall building towards the big bus roundabout where they started their circuits. Strutting toughs, cop wannabes. Fascist assholes. Maybe all of the above.

"Have a good, safe night," said Massimo as they pushed through the glass doors outside.

"Ah, kiss my ass!" Off Artur strode, sixteen-hole Docs thumping across the concrete. MagLite swinging in one fist. Against regs, he wore his uniform pants tucked into his boots, to make them look like jodhpurs.

"God help anybody getting in his way tonight," said James. Artur's circuit was the southern part of the campus, the graduate student apartments, and the track and field center. Most nights, they saw nothing of him. Which suited James just fine.

It was a gorgeous evening. They stood in the shadow of the building, the breeze combing James's hair. Warm, but it had lost the torrid anger of the earlier afternoon.

"Gonna be a nice one," said Massimo, sucking air through his big nostrils.

"Be safe, you big ape."

"You too, buddy."

They punched their knuckles together in macho solidarity.

"You okay?" Massimo's forehead creased with concern.

"Yeah, okay."

"Girls good?" James nodded. "That wife of yours still begging for some Italian sausage?" James grinned, but Massimo still wasn't satisfied. "You seem bummed."

"Something... something's weird," James stuttered. He kept looking back over his shoulder.

Expecting to see those eight eyes. Shining slivers of glass. *Watching. Waiting.*

"Whaddaya mean?"

James shrugged, putting on a game face. "Probably just tired, man."

"You think you're tired now, just give it a few hours!"

"You got that right."

They parted company.

James cut through the Student Centre, which was really just a tawdry little mall of fast food outlets. His circuit started on the other side, at Stedman Common, a tree-shaded cobblestone court. Probably designed to evoke Harvard or Oxford. Students lounged around waiting for the eight o'clock summer evening classes to start. Jeez, all of them were on cellphones. Gazing into little glowing screens, thumbs skittering on keys. Plugged in to their own solipsistic digital universes. Something eerie in the uniformity of it, the vacant faces.

What was it that Margaret Thatcher had said? 'There is no society, just a collection of individuals.' Something like that. Brought to mind Gold Hat: 'Batches? We don't need no stinking batches!' In his head, James modified the line, but kept the contemptuous voice: *Civilization? I don't see no stinking civilization!*

Ah, quit your whining, he admonished himself. You're just jealous because you can't afford a cell phone of your own!

Soon after Jen was born, he and Stacy realized the stupidity of flirting with the poverty line like Olympian gymnasts on the parallel bars. One night they ran out of diapers, and there'd been literally no cash to buy more. A grand total of one dollar and sixty-five cents in their savings account.

James remembered holding poor little Jenny. Babbling, drooling. Completely unaware that the next poop or pee to exit her body would be caught by nothing more than a paper towel.

Stace had gone to her folks, humiliated to ask for a couple of hundred to tide them over.

That's when they both started looking for steady work that paid more than the odd freelancing check. One afternoon, returning from the latest in a long string of dreary job interviews, James ran into Massimo. They'd been acquaintances since university, but hadn't seen each other for a while. Mass mentioned he was working as a security guard, which struck James as very funny – squat, stocky mass in uniform!

When Mass mentioned in passing that Lars was looking for new recruits, James's humor withered like a leaky balloon.

Within a week, James had been certified in first aid and CPR. And he'd started the Lars Gunnarson short course in basic self-defense. Now here he was, a straight-up pro.

As if.

Tonight he needed the peace and relative solitude of the campus. York University sprawled across the suburban northwest of the city, in an area of vast industrial parks and wholesale outlets. Very quiet at night, especially in the summer term. Classes were light, the student dorms sparsely inhabited. James was looking forward to the cool, placid dark, doing his circuit under the midsummer stars. Good for the soul. Or so he hoped.

The shoulder mike crackled, Lars's voice coming in staticky. "Radio checks. Muir?"

James reached up and flicked the button. "Loud and clear, Lars."

"Roger. Faccini?"

James heard the subtle irritation in Massimo's response. Mass saw this routine as just another Lars cop fetish. Maybe he was right. But James liked the radio unit. It was a connection. He knew that under the right circumstances it might even be a lifeline.

He headed for the Physical Sciences building. That email from Allistair had said something about a breakthrough.

James did a routine walk-through of the offices upstairs, then rode the old clunking elevator belowground. Officially, he only needed to check that the door to the lab was locked and secure. "Malvern Lichboegh Neutrino Observatory," the stencil on the door read. "Authorized admittance only."

But for months now, he'd been using the swipe card to go through the security door, down the long ill-lit hallway to the steel stairs plunging even further into the earth. Ten flights, shoes ringing on metal, deeper and deeper.

The massive underground structure had originally been built as a bomb shelter. At the bottom of the skeletal stairwell was another dim hallway that ended in a huge lead-lined steel door, now hanging open. Inside, the antechamber of the shelter had been turned into an office that looked like a submarine's command room. Low blue light cast by large monitors displaying charts and graphs and figures. Pipes and tubes snaking in every direction. The air was stifling hot.

"Something crazy going on!" Allistair Rivers shouted as James went in. "Something crazy!"

Allistair Rivers, PhD in astrophysics. Bent over a monitor, one slender hand pressed to the crown of his tall head. As if to stop the escape of troubling ideas.

James stood back near the door, out of the way.

"Holy shit!" Allistair's colleague was a muscular Asian guy named Chen, wearing nothing but a swimsuit. He threw his fists into the air as if his team had snagged gold in the freestyle event. "This is incredible!"

"Where are we?" Allistair asked, his Scottish accent barbed, nervous. "Give me the numbers Chen!"

Chen's eyes darted to the screen. "You're not gonna believe this—"

"Talk to me, talk to me!"

"Edging up towards a hundred billion!"

"Jesus Christ!" Allistair sounded ready to faint. He swiped a hand across his face. Finally, he noticed James. "Jimbo! For fuck sake, you think you could do something about the bloody air con?"

James smiled. "Not my department."

"Bollocks!" Allistair laughed, beckoning James to come forward. "You've gotta see this, Jimbo. This is once in a lifetime, my friend!" Allistair was the kind of person who demanded attention. Tall, pearish, his long face hanging on a deeply slouched neck, mockingly grave. He had a tall hedge of electrified dark blonde hair.

Chen slurped a can of Coke, eyeing James across the cluttered desk. "Who's this?"

"Dr. Hieronymous Chen, meet James Muir – a good bloke with a good Scottish name."

"Don't worry," James said, "I'm no spy." He and Chen had met a few times before, but it was always the same with academics engrossed in a project. No memory for anything else.

"He's a damn civilian, Chen, but don't let that fool you. This one's actually got something of a brain."

"What's all the excitement about?" James asked.

Allistair cackled, putting on his best mad scientist routine. "Eh Chen, what're we so excited about?"

Chen glanced down at the screen. "We're up above one twenty."

"One twenty!" Allistair enthused. "One twenty, Jimbo! Can you believe it?"

"One hundred and twenty what?" James asked impatiently.

"One hundred and twenty billion neutrinos!" Allistair shouted. "This is it, Jimbo! When I sent you that email, what was that? Two hours ago? Even then I didn't see how big it is! This is fucking it, my friend!"

Now Allistair was yelling, and James felt a nibble of unease. Because he could see that Allistair wasn't just excited. He was scared too.

"Fuck me, is it hot down here!" Allistair turned back to the monitors. Sweat stained the back of his shirt.

"You're not really my type," said James, trying to defuse the tension.

"What's that?" Allistair rounded on him so quickly that James actually took a step back. "Oh! Sure, yeah, very funny Jimbo."

"One forty!" Chen called out, sounding winded.

"Shit!" Allistair's gripped his own face with both hands. "It's accelerating!"

Over the years, Allistair had filled James in on the basics of his project. He'd received tens of millions in funding from a magnate named Malvern Lichboegh (pronounced 'Lickbow'), a billionaire who'd mushroomed his fortune by providing military contractors for Iraq and Afghanistan. Lichboegh's money funded Allistair's dream of building a state-of-the-art neutrino detector. It crouched behind a sealed steel door looming massively on the far side of the room, like the entrance to a bank vault. Allistair had shown James a photo of the apparatus, a transparent polyethylene sphere more than fifteen feet wide, filled with heavy water, suspended a few feet off the floor. This was surrounded by a geodesic steel scaffold. The scaffold was hung with what looked like large flattened light bulbs. Allistair had called them 'photodectectors'.

"One fifty!" Chen croaked.

The whole apparatus had to be sealed behind tons of lead and steel because to work properly, the detector needed to operate in an ultra-clean environment. Allistair had told him once that even if someone had smoked a cigarette the previous day, they'd still be exhaling enough junk to pollute the environment and spoil the project.

"Okay, so you remember what neutrinos are, Jimbo?" Allistair cocked a gimlet eye at him.

"Ghost particles," he responded dutifully. "They're extremely small, created inside stars. They fly out of the sun in very large numbers."

"See, Chen? I told you: a civilian with brains, eh?"

"Who knew?" Chen cracked, clearly irritated by the distraction.

"What else?" Allistair prompted James.

"Uh, neutrinos don't have an electrical charge."

"Which means?"

"Which means that they pass right through the Earth without hitting it. That's why they're called 'ghost particles.'"

"From a neutrino's standpoint, we don't exist at all, it's like the damn planet isn't even there. Right?" Allistair's eyes glinted in the low light. "That's the magic of these things. We know we're in a torrent of neutrinos, they're flowing through us all the time, a hundred trillion every second! But we can't see 'em, can't feel 'em."

"You're tracking them because they can tell you a lot about how the sun works," James parroted, feeling ridiculously pleased with himself. "Even about the origins of the universe."

"For the past twenty-four hours we've seen an exponential increase in the number of neutrinos detected by our device. Right now we're sitting at – where're we sitting, Chen?"

Chen's eyes flicked down to the screen. "Nearing two hundred."

Allistair looked utterly flabbergasted. "That's two hundred *billion* neutrinos that we've detected, just in the past twenty-four hours."

"But you've always said that there are trillions of these things passing through every second—" James began.

"Yeah, yeah, but just remember, we only actually detect a tiny fraction of what's really there. The way I've designed this detector, there's an array of electromagnets and they act like a lens. Works just the same way as a magnifying glass focusing a ray of sunlight into a spot hot enough to burn paper. You ever do that when you were a kid?"

James nodded.

"Alright, you can visualize it then. The magnets focus the neutrino flow into that big sphere of heavy water. So because the stream is focused, concentrated, we detect more."

"And," Chen spoke up, "we don't need to build our detector a mile underground. So we can work here instead of deep in a nickel mine, like the Sudbury Neutrino Observatory."

"Right. Which brings me to my next point. You should be astonished by that number I just told you, James. Two hundred *billion* of the buggers—"

"Two twenty," Chen snapped.

"Two hundred and twenty billion neutrinos have collided with that heavy water in there." Allistair pointed a shaking finger at the huge steel door.

"And every time it collides you can see a flash of light," said James.

"No, no, buddy," Chen scoffed. "Can't *see* it. Way too faint. The photo detectors, they magnify the light so that our computer can track them."

"Picture the wake of a boat," said Allistair. "This is similar, only in 3-D. Instead of a triangle spreading behind the boat, you've got a cone that spreads out behind the neutrino. A wee shockwave. And the cone glows a faint bluish color, just for a millisecond, mind. Ever seen a picture of the glowing bits in a nuclear reactor?"

James nodded again.

"Same stuff – it's called Cherenkov radiation, okay? Only in this case, as my esteemed colleague pointed out, you can't see these streaks because they're way too tiny..." Allistair's voice drifted off, his eyes widened. He snatched a pencil off the desk and started scratching on a piece of paper.

"What is it?" James asked.

"Nothing, nothing," said Allistair in a distant voice. The pencil scribbled, filling the paper with the hieroglyphs of advanced astrophysics. Then he dropped the pencil, and now he didn't look scared. He looked terrified. "I want you to think about this Jimbo," he croaked. "The Sudbury Neutrino Observatory operated for about 20 months—"

"Nineteen," Chen corrected.

Allistair rolled his eyes. "In just over a year and a half they reckon about ten billion trillion neutrinos passed through their detector. Ye get that, Jimbo? That's a ten with twenty one fucking zeros after it, yeah? Some perspective for you, on just how large a number that is: how long would it take you to count that high? Counting at the rate of one number per second?"

Chen snickered.

"Can't do it!" Allistair chortled hysterically. "If you started counting at the birth of the universe, okay, and you counted – one number every second – never stopping that whole time until this very moment – sorry, pal! You're only halfway there! You'd need more time than has existed in the entire history of the universe! You've got that many neutrinos going through, and how many did SNO actually snag?"

"About two thousand," Chen said.

"Two thousand out of ten billion trillion!"

"But hold on," James interrupted. "You've got that magnetic lens focusing them, so you're just seeing more."

"We've been in operation now almost as long as SNO was, and until yesterday afternoon, we'd managed to snag 20,000 of the little buggers."

"So, ten times more," said James.

"Very good!" Chen mocked.

"Think about it, civilian," said Allistair. "Twenty thousand in eighteen months. Now, we've seen *twelve million times* that number just in the past day!" Allistair's long face, emphatic with sweat.

"So there are more neutrinos coming out of the sun," said James, weirded out by Allistair's mania.

"A whole shitload more, my friend!" Allistair slapped the desk. "And not from the sun!"

"Where from then?"

Allistair leaped to his feet, and dragged James by the arm to the wall. His finger spiked a laminated star chart, and James squinted to read the name of the star.

"Betel..." he stammered, pronouncing it like it rhymed with petal. "Betel... gay... use?"

Allistair snickered, the shrill sound of air whistling through a punctured tire. "It's pronounced 'beetle juice', Jimbo. A red supergiant star in the Orion constellation."

"Like that movie, Beetlejuice— "

"No, no, no!" Allistair shouted. "Not like the fucking movie, Jimbo!" He was ranting now. Allistair trooped back to the desk. "All bloody day we've been watching this. More and more and more caught in my wee trap!"

"It shouldn't be happening!" Chen exclaimed.

"I mean, think about it – the sun is right next door to us, and Betelgeuse is four hundred and twenty-five light years away. And still, its neutrinos are overwhelming us!"

"And the number's rising all the time. Three sixty now!"

"Holy Jesus!" Allistair's fists drummed the desktop.

James felt worms crawling at the base of his spine. "What's the big deal? I mean, there's millions of times more of them, and you still need all this equipment to even tell the difference."

Chen's laugh combined panic and scorn. "I'll tell you why, Mr. Security Guard! Betelgeuse is about to go supernova!"

"Shut up Chen!"

James saw Allistair's shaking lips, droplets of sweat glistening on stubble. With a thunderclap of alarm, James realized Allistair was on the verge of tears.

"But it's four hundred light years away!" James said, dry-mouthed.

"Ah, Chen's just talking out of his arse!" Allistair's laughing voice creaked rustily. He pressed the heels of both hands into his eye sockets and breathed deeply, clearly struggling to calm himself. "But you know what, Chen? You scoffed, but it turns out Mr. Security Guard was right about the Cherenkov." He gestured at the hieroglyphs he'd scratched a few minutes ago.

Allistair slunk to a security keypad and started punching the buttons.

"Rivers!" Chen raged, jumping up. "What the hell are you doing?"

"It doesn't even matter anymore," Allistair gulped, and now there were tears running down his cheeks.

The seal around the big bank vault door hissed, and a motor whirred as the door swung open.

"Ah, shit!" Chen screamed.

A blue glow drained from the gaping room beyond. James saw the apparatus, the geodesic frame just a black geometric frame against the glowing bulb of water.

Chen made a frantic gulping noise.

Allistair went through into the apparatus room, splaying his hand against the glowing sphere. James realized what he was seeing and his legs turned to gelatin. The water itself was aglow.

A sick silvery gleam that was like, oh no, my God, it was just like one of the spider's eyes, blown up to gargantuan size, filled with its own seething intelligence.

"What the hell's going on!" James yelled.

"I can feel the heat!" Allistair brayed.

James swore he could see the bones of Allistair's hand, picked out sharply, as if by an x-ray.

"You can actually see it getting brighter!" Chen's voice, strangled by awe.

Allistair spun to gaze back at James, a cracked stare betraying the collapse of all he thought he knew. "Pay attention, James. Nobody's ever seen – *ever* – what you're seeing right now." He sounded like he was speaking a eulogy.

Then he was laughing again. A high, breathless twitter.

The laughter electrified James. The way seeing a demon's face in a haunted house mirror stabs you with fear. I need to get out of here, he thought. I need to go now.

He turned towards the door, almost driving headlong into Chen. Chen in miserable rapture, standing agape in the sharp light.

*

When he got back to the surface, James needed a few minutes to catch his breath. The cooling breeze felt cleansing after the suffocation in that pit, but even the clear evening sky seemed to be alight with the sickly silvery glow. Water enfolding its own light.

No, he decided abruptly. There was no way. Allistair and Chen had played a trick on him, the pricks. It had all been a cruel hoax. Jesus, he'd been so scared down there he'd almost peed himself. He rubbed his mouth, took a few deep breaths. He could not get the image of a great spidery eye out of his mind. Somehow he felt it was still watching him. An all-seeing organ directed by a terrible, cruel intelligence.

"No," he said to himself, hitching up the utility belt. "Stop it."

Walking east to finish his first circuit, he followed his own shadow, starved and desiccated by the sinking sun. He looked at his watch and shit, he'd better get a move on because he was damn late.

Entering the Stong College offices with his magnetic swipe card, he stalked the cubicles. The place was deserted, all the lights extinguished. The sun seeking him through the Venetian blinds, throwing glowing steel rulers across the beige carpeting.

In the odd half-light, James stopped for a few seconds, listening intently. He'd heard something. A soft sibilance. A breath, or a muffled snicker.

But there was nothing. Hearing his eyelids blink, the wet fricative sound of his lips peeling away from his teeth as he smiled at his own paranoia.

Then a phone rang on the desk behind him and he jumped, blowing out a shocked breath. Just a soft warble, but it made his skin crawl, bleating like a little plastic sheep. James found himself longing for the cold, solid ring of an old-fashioned phone. A real bell.

He sensed something creeping in the shadows. From around the edge of the very next cubicle, little gnomish hands would crawl, like—

Like the legs of a giant spider!

He shuddered and moved quickly, completing his round through the offices, and back out into the restive air.

Next on his itinerary was the aerospace building, then the science library. Everything still and quiet. Expectant.

Lord, it seemed like even the quiet he sought would torment him tonight. He had the sense of things scurrying away just as he rounded corners, barely eluding him. Alien things.

"You're being stupid," he told himself, but had to clear the dryness from his throat.

By the time James finished his second security round, the evening had deepened to indigo. The clear western sky a vast sheet of red hot glass slowly cooling.

Finally, it was break time. James sat on the edge of a big concrete planter behind the biology building. At last a chance to chip away at the damn millstone. Classes were ending now, students hurrying along the lighted footpath. On their way to the parking lots or buses, carrying books and bags, chattering on obligatory cellphones. Or walking silently, plugged in to iPods or whatever. Closed inside their own perfectly manicured worlds.

He opened his laptop, pressing the power button to enter the world born in his own mind. Well, he thought. At least I'm not using it to prattle on and on about nothing.

"You're such a snot!" he scolded himself, sipping the coffee he'd bought on the way over. Damn that hit the spot. Bull's-eye.

The scrawny maple tree struggling in the concrete planter fluttered in the strong westerly breeze. Storm's a-coming, he thought, and true enough, there were distant thunderhead spires way off to the southwest, brooding purple. The only clouds in the sky.

He unwrapped his ham sandwich and took a big bite. Despite the razor's edge of tension pressuring him all afternoon, he found himself hungry. This was his favorite time. The unmeasured border between night and day, indefinable. The domed sky as deep as a fathomless ocean. From now until the end of the shift, he could expect to see almost nobody, and that was good. As old Stalin himself had said, people are the problem. No people, no problem.

"Can't agree with your methodology, Joey," he said, clicking on the icon entitled *Opus*. "But I can certainly see where you're coming from." He drew in a deep breath, blew it out slowly. "I think you'd like it here, I really do."

Opus. He didn't even have a firm title yet. He'd toyed with *Lilac's Dream*, but that seemed flat, bordering on stupid.

Okay, alright, stop with the negativity.

From across the campus, roared the opening chords of Anarchy in the UK.

Rrrrrright now! Hahahahahaha!

Sounded like it was coming from the Stong College residence. James smiled. Chances were he'd be over there within the hour, asking them to turn it down.

More distantly came the monotonous bass boom of the Underground, the club in the Student Centre.

The laptop screen presented him with the opening line of the dreaded chapter sixteen. The cursor blinking, daring him to continue.

"Lilac rose from a fitful sleep," he'd written. "Today was the day. She knew it. Knew it with a pregnant fullness in her bones. Today was the day she'd finally get away from Roger."

This – this is what counted as the 'fair bit of work' he'd told Stacy about. Probably the fifth or sixth incarnation of that opening line. A Rubik's cube of prose: no matter how he rearranged the words, it never seemed to come out the way he wanted.

Before Jenny was born, back when he'd still thought of himself as a *writer*, it had seemed like a grand idea to create a great piece of literature from a woman's standpoint. A woman in the middle of an abusive wreck of a marriage. A way of stabbing back at the parochialism of Maggie's world. A world of hangers-on, handsome-handy types that she told James to call 'uncles'. This would be a work of fiction to scramble the pallid brains of those types, who only ever read instruction manuals.

I wanna destroy possibly cause I wanna beeeee an-ar-cheeeee!

Trouble was, this Lilac bitch had gotten so far into the workings of his own brain that he could no longer describe her, feel her thoughts. It was like turning to look at himself without a mirror. He just kept turning, and turning.

Well, give those handsome-handy types some credit: at least they knew how to get shit done. When they weren't loaded, of course.

Okay, okay. He reread the first line of chapter sixteen aloud. "'Lilac rose from a fitful sleep. Today was the day. She knew it. Knew it with a pregnant fullness in her bones. Today was the day she'd finally get away from Roger.'"

His fingertips rested lightly on the concave surfaces of the home row keys.

James's childhood was filled with dozens of uncles. Drifters, migratory day-laborers, handymen who could do almost any job – except straighten out their messed up lives. Flocking to Wilberforce, Ontario. Population 815. Chasing the cottager business in the summer months, when the population swelled to four times that number.

Getting wasted get what you want! I is so pissed I is arressssst!

Ain't that the truth, Mr. Rotten. Ain't it just. What would Lilac think of Uncle Randy? Not much. Lilac was a bit of a stiffened old prude. Ruined by Roger's abuse, poor thing. Worse, grown stale by her extended incarceration in James's mind.

Randy had been one of James's favorites, a thin swarthy man with a huge Adam's apple. There were a lot of, well, *impeded* things about Randy. James would never know for sure, relying as he did on hazy childhood recollections, but he was almost certain Randy had been developmentally delayed. But damned handy.

Like so many others, Randy bartered with Maggie. A warm – if unclean – bed in return for fixing the eaves troughs or replanking the deck or whatever. James remembered his knobby jean-clad knees sticking out from under the kitchen sink, surrounded by curlicues of cigarette smoke and the choking fumes of his plumber's torch. Repairing the pipe that froze and burst after Maggie forgot to pay the electricity bill.

"Okay, Jamie, gimme the pipe wrench," he'd call in his simple, aw-shucks way.

"Oh, Randy! Stop that nonsense and have a goddamn drink!" Maggie, draped cross-legged at the kitchen table, dribbling CC and Coke down the front of her Algonquin Park sweatshirt.

Maggie. James took another bite of his sandwich and smiled, shaking his head. "I'll say one thing for ya, you certainly gave me a unique perspective on life."

He'd just swallowed his mouthful of sandwich when It happened. If he'd still had his mouth full, he probably would have choked to death like so many others.

A violent seizure rammed through his body, racking his spine, his thighs snapping up to his chest, catapulting the laptop away.

He heard the shoulder mike screech in deafening feedback:

41

wee-weeeee-WEEEEEEEEEeeeeeeeeee! as he was thrown backwards into the planter. His body arched and thrashed like a trout drowning in air, flinging him to the ground, a jerking spastic corpse.

Then all was darkness.

Chapter 3

The Thrall of Betelgeuse

James. Enclosed in complete stifling blackness for a very, very long time. Nothing but words in the infinite dark.

Heru screaming a mighty war cry. Mekhenty-er-irty. He Who Has No Eyes, bewailing his blindness. Heru, the Distant One. Mighty but sightless. Kemwer, the Great Black One. The hunting falcon!

Then James gasped, sucking air greedily. Down on the pavement, on his side. Every part of him ached. Hard to catch his breath.

Unsure where he was. Then little sips of reality crept back into his mind.

Somewhere far away he heard somebody screaming. The cry of a hunting bird.

The pounding beat of the Underground at an incredible speed now, almost no interval between the booms.

A clammy wetness in his crotch.

Screaming, screaming.

"Alright," his voice creaked. "Okay, take it easy..."

Hold on, hold on. He listened intently to the fast thumping. That wasn't club music he was hearing, it was his own heartbeat. The speed frightened him. It didn't seem possible for a heart to beat so fast and remain alive.

He gasped, putting his hand to his chest, willing himself to breathe.

The screaming continued. A woman. She was calling.

He sat up with a grimace, feeling the clamminess in his groin. Lord, he thought, I've peed myself!

He reached down the front of his pants, fingers wiggling into his underwear, into the sopping pubic hair, and the urine was still warm. He'd only been out for a few seconds, then.

But it wasn't urine. Slippery fluid, mucous. He smelled his fingers. Semen! What in God's name?

Okay, he thought. You've had a seizure. There was a nasty lump on the back of his head, where it had smacked against the pavement. That would need looking at. His shaking hand reached for the radio mike on his shoulder, thumbing the send button.

"Lars," he croaked. "Muir here. Lars, I've got an emergency."

But there was nothing. Not a sound, except the plastic click of the button against the housing of the mike.

He tried again, pressing the send button until the edges of the thumbnail bit into his skin. "Lars, come in."

Nothing.

Shit. Quite a time for the radio to die.

Damn it, some woman was still wailing. "Help! Somebody help me!"

James looked blearily across to the footpath. There she was, a woman in a pantsuit, her face hidden in shadow. Kneeling beside a prone figure.

"Please! I need help!" Edging on panic, her voice ragged.

James struggled to his feet, stumbled down again, ripping a hole in the right knee of his pants. It took enormous effort to get up, drag himself twenty yards to where the woman knelt.

The prone figure was another woman in the midst of a grand mal seizure. Even in his foggy state, James's first aid training kicked in. "It's going to be okay," he rasped. "It's going to be okay."

He rolled the spasming woman onto her side, fought to fold her legs up into the emergency position.

"Omigod, omigod!" the woman in the pantsuit wailed. "What's happening?"

A professor, no doubt. With a PhD in uselessness.

"She's having a seizure," James answered, laying his hand on the stricken woman's forehead.

"I know that!" she screamed at him. "Don't you think I know that already! Something happened! Just a few seconds ago! I had one too!"

Her meaning slowly crept up on him. Jeez, James thought. So did I. What are the chances?

"Holy Jesus!" The words shuddered out of the woman as if she'd just been doused with cold water. "Holy Jesus Christ, look! Look!"

Still hazy, James followed her shaking pointing hand, looking straight down the footpath towards the admin building. All the way along the asphalt path there were people down, just shadows, people getting to their knees, people crying and groaning. He blinked, trying to clear his eyes. Something seemed to be dimming his vision.

Then he realized with dawning disquiet that all the lights along the footpath were out. It took his frazzled brain another few seconds to see that there were no lights on in the huge admin building either.

It hulked, a black monolith against the deepening sky.

Shit, he was kneeling right under a light standard! He should be helping this woman in a pool of light twenty feet across. Instead, there was nothing but the dusk, ink dim.

He looked around, left, then right. Behind him. Not one light to be seen. Not anywhere.

The spasming woman erupted with a scary burbling sound, her body still jerking, twisting, pumping. The seizure shouldn't be lasting this long, James thought. She should be coming out of it by now.

Automatically, his hand went up to the shoulder mike again, thumb pressing the send button. Automatically, his head twisted down to the left, speaking into the dead hunk of plastic. Shit, no, don't do this to me! Terrified, he pressed again and again, but there was nothing.

Now the spasming woman was making an obscene sound, as if trying to speak. "*Oowa!*" she burbled. "*Oowa! Oowa oowa!*" Something dark spilled from her mouth.

James realized it was blood. Lots of blood. "She's choking on her tongue!" he yelled.

The spasms came on more rapidly, more like shivering now, her limbs rubbing manically against the asphalt, faster, faster.

"Do something!" the other woman shrieked, pounding his shoulder with her fists.

Yes. Definitely a professor.

"What do you want me to do!" James bellowed at her. He was panicky now, heart still racing. She was dying, and there was nothing they could do but watch.

The stricken woman made a sickening gulping noise. Blood poured from her mouth, her nose, and she was utterly still. He pressed his fingers into the softness under her jaw, feeling for a pulse, digging for it.

Stillness.

James slumped back on his seat, eyes wide. She had just died, right in front of him.

"Omigod!" the professor chattered. "Omigod, omigod, omigod!" Holding her rigidly splayed fingers inches away from her face, as if they smelled of the woman's death and she couldn't help but sniff them. Her eyes popping, shining in the murk like wet marbles.

James got to his feet again, and his knees felt jellified. The ground tilted and yawed under him. Nausea dug at his guts and he was disgustedly aware of the congealing mess in his underwear. Every step a sloppy, sticky chill.

Up the footpath about fifteen yards, another woman lay face down, arms and legs tucked neatly in line with her body. As if she'd been dragged by the hair. Even before he rolled her over onto her back, James knew she too was dead. Her nose smashed flat by the fall, her face opaque with blood.

He turned away, just enough time to avoid puking all over her. Masticated bits of ham sandwich poured out of him all over the grass at the edge of the path. Stinking of cheese and coffee.

"Gotta get outta here!" the professor in the pantsuit cried, sidling backwards down the path. She turned and started running so fast that her feet slipped out of her high heels.

I need to get back to the security office, James thought dully, wiping his mouth on his sleeve. Need to get instructions. Lars will know what to do.

"Security!" somebody shouted. "Security!"

James looked up. A face came at him, just an oval smudge in the gloom. Bisected by a dark gaping mouth.

"Ya gotta help me, dude!" He was a young kid, probably a freshman, in a dark satiny tracksuit. Cradling one arm against his chest. "Fuck, ya gotta help me!"

He pulled his arm away from his chest, and James saw a wide gash spreading open all the way from wrist to elbow. James realized the tracksuit was actually some pale color. The top of the tracksuit only *seemed* dark and satiny because it was soaked in the kid's blood.

Blood gushed from the wound in a black stream.

James ripped out a pair of latex gloves from the cargo pocket of his pants. Hard to put them on, his hands were shaking so badly. He got the kid to sit on the grass, tearing open the two packs of gauze bandages he carried – standard light first aid kit. He pressed them on the wound, binding them with the sling. Then, when he saw the blood soaking through those, he stripped off his own shirt, detaching the mike, binding the shirt around the wounded arm as tightly as he could. Right away the blood spread through the blue fabric. Menacing black. A blossoming storm system as seen from orbit.

"Shit!" the kid hissed.

"Keep pressure on it," James told him, guiding the kid's other hand over the bloody patch. "Don't let it up, just hold your hand there."

"I'm gonna die, I'm bleedin' to death ain't I, I'm bleedin' bad!"

Okay, James thought. Talk to him. Take his mind off it. "I'm James. What's your name?"

"I fell!" the kid croaked, still gaping down at the black stain. Blood squeezed through the fingers of the pressing hand now, crawling along the lines of his knuckles.

"What's your name?" James asked again, tying another knot in his shirt. This bleeding keeps up, he thought, this kid really is gonna bleed to death.

"Somethin' happened, dude! What the fuck was that?"

"I don't know."

"Fuck! Sounded like a bell, a fuckin huge bell ringin' – BONNNGG! y'know? Next thing I know, I'm on the ground, fell on my bottle, man! Fuck, it hurts, dude, it stings!"

"Your bottle." Now James smelled the booze. Probably on his way to party at the Underground. Enjoying a cheap starter on the way. "At least the alcohol will disinfect the wound." No infection, at least. If you live.

"Well what're ya waiting for, dude! Use your radio, get me a fuckin' ambulance!"

"Radio's not working."

"What! What'd'ya mean the fuckin' radio's not fuckin' working! Call me a fuckin' ambulance now, motherfucker!"

"Take it easy. Keep up the pressure!" He pressed the kid's hand back down on the impromptu bandage and the kid shrieked with pain. Might still be glass in there. Impossible to tell without some goddamn light. "D'you have a cell?"

"Take it easy? Fuck you, ya fuckin' pig! Get on the fuckin' radio! I need an ambulance right fuckin' now!" The kid reached for the radio mike, now dangling limply on its cord. James slapped his hand away.

"Listen to me," James said directly, fighting to keep control. "The radio's not working. You wanna live? Keep your fucking hand on that bandage, press down hard. Do you have a cellphone on you or not?"

"Yeah, okay, okay," the kid cried, reaching for his pocket.

Again James replaced the hand on the bandage, fishing the device out of the kid's track pants. He pressed the power button, but the little screen remained dark. "It's not working!"

"Service got cancelled, fuck!"

Lord, what a mess! Campus security carried such a light first aid kit because the protocol was supposed to be that easy: get on the radio, summon EMT. So they were only outfitted with a pair of rubber gloves, a few packs of gauze, a fabric sling, and some Band-Aids. Injuries happened all the time.

Not like this one. James had never seen human skin gape open like that. But minor cuts, bruises. At least once a month during the fall and winter terms, when the campus teemed with thousands of students. Drunken kids doing stupid shit. Click the send button on the mike, and like magic ten minutes later the EMT guys would be on site. Fifteen minutes after that, the injured kid would be on an ER gurney. Problem solved.

They took the damn radios for granted, but they were the weak link in the chain. Without them, the whole system just stopped. Now he'd need ten minutes just to get back to the office. The way the blood was coming out through the kid's fingers, James knew the time difference could be lethal.

He stood up, looking for the woman in the pantsuit. But she was gone – that's right, he reminded himself, he'd seen her take off. Get it together, Muir, come on! He waved at a woman coming down the path. "Hey! Hey, I need to use your cell, it's an emergency and my radio's— "

His words choked off when he saw the woman's face. Frozen with a wide-eyed rapturous grin as vacant as a blank screen. A lobotomized Cheshire Cat.

The grinning woman paused. Turned slowly to face him. The chilling expression never shifted. Not even a twitch in the crescent of bright teeth.

James felt such a needle of unease that he actually heard himself make a little whoop.

"Ya gotta help me!" the injured kid screamed.

The woman never even looked down at him. Slowly, slowly she pivoted and just kept walking west. A stiff-legged grinning automaton.

The next woman he stopped reared back as if he'd spat her in her face. At least she seemed lucid.

"Sorry to disturb you," he began, "but I need to—"

"Go fuck yourself!" she screeched at the top of her lungs, snarling at him. Frantically, she started running. "Fuck you asshole!" she screamed over her shoulder as she sprinted away. "Go fuck yourself up the ass!" So manic, she ran headlong into the grinning woman, knocking them both to the pavement.

Hoping against hope, James tried the mike one more time. But the result was the same. That hollow, mute click of plastic on plastic.

"Can I help?"

The voice startled James. He turned and found himself staring at a calm woman with a blonde bob. He approached her as if she was a loaded rat trap. "Can – can I use your cell?"

"Stupid thing's dead!" she exclaimed, brandishing it at him. "Isn't this *ridiculous*?"

He saw with some relief that she was scared. Not insane. Just scared. He took the phone, jabbing the buttons. The screen remained black. Not a burr. Not even a hint of a chirp.

"What the fuck's going on!" the injured kid wailed.

Indeed, James thought. A chill crawled under his skin. What the fuck *is* going on? Fighting hard against panic. "My radio's out," he explained to the woman. "I have to go back to the security office to call 911. I need you to stay with this gentleman. Can you do that for me?"

"Absolutely," she said, nodding. "I'm a bio major." As if that explained everything.

"I gotta come with you!" the kid keened.

"No, you have to stay here."

"No, please— "

"You can't move. Stay here and I'll be back— "

"Don't leave me here, dawg!" the kid whined. "Ya can't! I'm gonna die! Don't leave me, I'm sorry I called you a pig, dawg, I didn't mean nothin', I'm just scared, I don't wanna die!"

Jesus. "You're not going to die, man. But you need to relax. The more upset you get, the more you're gonna bleed."

"He's right," said the bio major resolutely. "Your blood pressure will rise and— "

"Please! Pleeeease!" The pleading dissolved into sobs.

"Stay here and don't move," James ordered. "I'll be back before you know it."

"Did you hear that?" the bio major asked suddenly. She froze, tilting her head.

Shit, James thought. She *is* insane!

"There! There it was again!"

"What?"

"Listen, listen!"

James was about to tell her he needed to get the fuck going – and then he did hear something. A low resounding thump. It reminded him of the dull bumps in the ceiling at home. The people in the upstairs apartment dropping their shit.

There it was again. Distant thunder, he thought, remembering the storm clouds he'd seen earlier. Then he heard another. No, it definitely wasn't thunder. Too flat. That, and he'd felt the vibration through the ground.

"Something's exploding!" said the bio major.

"Big fuckin' explosions!" the injured kid rasped, eyes wide.

Yeah, thought James, but far away.

Then a whole bunch of people were shouting. He heard a voice raw with fear, scream "Oh no, oh my God!" and piercing brightness ripped through the dark twilight behind them, their shadows slipping across the ground like frightened animals as a mighty fireball ploughed into the sky. A huge roar erupted, powerful enough to resonate in his chest. Now the ground gave an angry dog rumble.

"Holy fuck!" the injured kid shrieked.

From behind the biology building a column of black smoke twisted into the sky like a huge charred muscle. Sharp evil flames leaping over the top of the building. People all around stood in naked disbelief, pointing, holding their heads in their hands. Silhouettes swimming in the firelight.

"There! Look!" somebody shouted.

"Oh my God!"

Some of them pointing skyward. Putting his head back, James saw a huge air liner, far up in the clear blue evening. So high it still caught the dying sun's light, glinting as it slowly rotated.

"Naw, naw!" somebody screamed. "Please, naw!"

"*It's dropping!*" somebody else declared.

"No," said James. Unable to accept what it meant. An airliner couldn't just *fall*. Yet he saw the wings slowly cart wheeling. Like a broken gear, he would say later. An eroded clockwork gear with only a few broken cogs, winding down. "It *is* falling!" he choked, feeling as if the ground opened up under his feet. Unable to believe the words leaving his mouth.

"My lord almighty!" the bio major whispered, clapping her hands over her nose and mouth.

None of them could take their eyes away from the plane. One of the really big ones, a 747, maybe even a 777. Tumbling slowly, achingly towards the earth.

James thought of the final image in the film Koyanisquatsi.

"Huh?" the injured kid scoffed. "Koyana what?"

James started at this. He must have said it aloud.

"Fuck!" said the injured kid, awestruck. "It's like 9/11, dawg! Another attack! Them fucks is dropping planes on our city! Those assholes, those fucking assholes!"

Steadily the plane grew until they could discern its markings, a bright green and red tail fin, dark windows arrayed neatly along the fuselage. It seemed to be accelerating as it got closer to the ground. James imagined horror-stricken faces pressed against those windows. Already, they were pallid ghosts. Then the airliner slipped into the earth's shadow, an ember fading to a cinder. A bullet now, whipping down. Disappearing behind a line of trees.

Moments later, they heard the thump of its demise. Now it did sound like thunder, rumbling from somewhere to the north-west.

"Fuck this," the injured kid spat. "I'm fuckin' outta here!" Shakily he got to his feet, cradling his arm.

"No, wait!" James yelled, but the kid was off in a spidery canter, fading into the gloom.

The bio major kept her face buried in her hands, retching sobs.

All around, muttering shadows, heads shaking, aghast. All of them searching the sky with terrified apprehension for more falling planes. They saw none, but heard several more explosions – one from the distant west, somewhere near the airport. Another to the south, close enough that they heard the shockwave belt off the surrounding buildings.

Then a macabre stillness as the evening faded to night. A smothering stillness James recognized from his boyhood in the bush near Wilberforce, far from the city. Uninterrupted by sirens or the blaring horns of fire trucks.

Jesus H. Christ! James pressed the heels of his palms desperately into his temples. Power out. Communications down. Planes falling out of the damn sky. And not a siren! No response at all! Nothing but the groaning wind.

*

James enjoyed working nights because the nighttime painted the world in different shades. As if presenting him with a backstage version of what most people experienced day to day. Sleepy yet hyper alert. Presided over by stars.

Before tonight, he'd never realized how lit it had been. Even though he'd spent the first seventeen years of his life in a place where moonless or cloudy nights were dark enough to steal your vision, his urban sojourn since then inured his eyes to the pinkish, jaundiced twilight of electric illumination. Even the shape of light had been comforting, the regular geometry of circular pools beneath outdoor light standards, the squares and rectangles of lit windows.

Now he stood aghast, staring at the impenetrably black smoke boiling over the campus. A final gray pallor of dying sun still clung to the western horizon, but already there were more stars in the sky than on the clearest, darkest city night. Far more. The Big Dipper afloat in a vast field of beady twinkling eyes. A thin crescent moon brooded just above the eastern horizon, a brittle bone sickle. Already the Milky Way stretched in a steamy arc north to south. He hadn't seen it in years. The brilliance of the sky scared him badly, in a way he couldn't define.

Yeah, he thought. Yeah, you can define it: a hundred slavering spiders. Staring right at you.

He looked around. The bio major had disappeared. People drifted in murmuring schools towards the crash site behind the bio building, as if drawn by some magnetic force. Like migrating lobsters.

Desolately, James wandered back to the tree planter. His laptop sat on the pavement on one end. He picked it up. One of the hinges had snapped off, leaving the screen askew. Feeling close to tears, he pressed the power button. Nothing. Of course nothing. He tried to close it, but because of the broken hinge the screen wasn't square with the keyboard and it wouldn't latch. He wondered doubtfully if he'd ever meet Lilac Spencer again. He imagined her, an unfinished emblem. Forever trapped with that bastard Roger.

He tucked the dangling mike in his pocket so it wouldn't drag on the ground, took the laptop with him. Joining the thin crowd, wandering as if asleep.

"It's a magnetic bomb, eh?"

He turned, confronted by a strange toothy grin. A guy shuffling along with his hands in the pockets of army surplus shorts. An unwashed marriage of Kurt Cobain's hair on a bespectacled mask of John Denver's cornbread charm.

The grin widened. "Magnetic bomb, man. Sends out an electromagnetic pulse, disables every electrical device for miles."

"Yeah," said James uncertainly.

"Look, I'm in electrical engineering, so I know what I'm talking about."

"Okay."

"Don't 'okay' me, asshole—"

"Easy, man, easy."

Cobain Denver's toothy smile never faltered. "Just don't 'okay' me, okay? I hate that. Isn't this amazing though?"

"Amazing?" James was aghast.

"You're a pretty miserable jerk, eh?"

"Aren't you a bit freaked out?"

"Why should we be freaked out, man?"

James shook his head and moved away from Cobain Denver.

The crowd moved quietly in small hushed groups, as if entering a cathedral. Very badly, James wished he heard the wail and scream of emergency vehicles or the chatter of police radios. Shit, this was an enormous disaster. Planes down all over the damn city, thousands dead. Emergency services should be stretched beyond the limit.

In the parking lot north of the lab building, he saw lots of stalled cars. Hoods and doors open, drivers waving their arms at each other. He saw a man smash the driver's side window of a

Buick, helping a woman crawl awkwardly through the empty frame, a beetle emerging from a dead stump.

Before they got to the crash site he smelled it: choking fumes of jet fuel and noxious smoke, a hot metallic stench that made James lightheaded. The airliner had come down on the sports field west of the lab building. A crater large enough to bury a decent-sized house was engulfed in hyperactive flames forty feet high. The force of the explosion had sprayed burning fuel everywhere. Nobody could get closer than ten yards before being repelled by the heat and stench. Even at twenty yards, it was like standing in front of an open oven.

It seemed the crashing plane had opened a portal. That fire had erupted from unknowable deep. Crawling, avid to engulf the entire campus. Then the city.

A landscape crowded with scraps of torn metal and melted plastic, tufts of insulation. Subtle details that would have been invisible without the red glaring firelight. James imagined the instant of impact, a huge machine obliterated, reduced to widely scattered rubbish in a millisecond. The view from the cabin as it had plummeted. Had there been panic? A mute rigor of terror?

Pieces everywhere... hands... feet...

One of the engines, the size of a panel van, black and smoking, lay in a crumpled heap against a charred tree. The branches denuded, bereft of leaves, a premature, permanent winter. Torn rags flapping.

Somebody pointed into the treetop, gaping. A shredded seat caught in the branches twenty feet above, a limbless torso trapped in the seatbelt. Obscenely, the first thing to strike James was one of uncle Randy's jokes.

What do you call a man with no arms and no legs hanging in a tree?

Dunno, Randy, what d'you call him?

Lief!

James shook his head, appalled at himself.

He squatted, seeing a naked plastic doll. A doll without a head. One of the legs twisted awkwardly up. For some reason, more than anything else, this headless doll stuck in his mind. For several minutes he simply squatted and stared.

Over to the left, James saw Cobain Denver pick up an arm, lips wrinkled in disgust. Torn, meaty strings dangled.

"Hey!" James shouted at him, getting back to his feet. "Put it down!"

The Cobain Denver freak dropped it without even looking in James's direction, daintily wiggling his fingers. James felt a crushing desire to run across and strike him full in the face as hard as he could, a bolt of rage so powerful his entire body shivered. The offender disappeared through a veil of smoke, still browsing.

After some time, most of the onlookers started drifting away. Their silence was most striking, a sad, hunching resignation in their slow gaits as they realized – as had James – that there was nothing to be done.

Then James noticed somebody waving at him. Lars! Gratified relief flooded into him. He couldn't remember the last time he'd felt such a desperate need for a familiar face. He walked quickly over to him, plowing unapologetically into several people. Massimo and Artur were there too.

"Good to see you in one piece," said Lars, smacking his bare shoulder hard enough to sting. "What happened to your shirt?"

James told him everything in a rushed stream of consciousness that would have made little Jenny proud. By the time he'd finished, tears were burbling in his voice.

Lars kept his steady hand on James's shoulder. "You did your duty," he said, his sharp chin wrinkling with emotion. "No shame in that, Jimmy. There's people down all over campus." Even with the frenetic firelight on his face, Lars acted as if he was giving a pep talk after losing a karate tournament.

"I just can't understand what's going on," said Massimo through the hand he held over his mouth and nose. His dark eyes searching, really scared. "I saw a guy— " Massimo's voice cracked. "I saw a guy, like, running into a wall. With his head down, like a bull for God's sake! Just kept on running into the wall over and over. Until his head was... ugh..." He shook his head rapidly, as if to deter a wasp.

Artur stood stock-still, head back, basking in the light. He was still wearing his mirrored aviator shades. The lenses creeping with the bright twitching fire. "It's wicked," he breathed in a post-coital whisper. He looked like a statue of a man with fly's eyes.

Looking at him, James felt a wriggle of something deeper than fear in his groin. He thought of the woman with that crazed smile on her face. The way she'd turned so slowly at him, the expression never changing.

"When people get scared they do strange things," Lars offered simply. The interval between Massimo's tale and Lars's explanation belied the Zen tone. Lars was scraping deep.

"I'm one of them," said James. But that woman with the grin, she wasn't afraid. She was insane. Utterly brain fried.

"Gentlemen, I want to thank you for your good work, but I need to remind you: we still have a job to do." Lars looked at each

54

of them in turn. "Especially under these circumstances. People need our help."

"Fuck yeah!" Artur snarled.

For a second, they all stared at Artur. Into the depths of those shades. His mouth somewhere between a smile and a furious grimace, his tongue working wetly at his grinning lower lip.

"I don't know what's going on," Lars continued, keeping a concerned eye on him. "Any more than you guys. I do know this: we are the only chance some of these people have for comfort, for order tonight. Serve and protect."

"Serve and protect!" Artur shouted.

"Serve and protect," James and Massimo muttered together. They exchanged a rueful glance.

"Now, we're gonna stick together for the rest of the shift. The radios are obviously deep-sixed, so there's no other way for us to stay in contact."

Despite his misuse of the term 'deep-sixed', James felt a ridiculously deep appreciation for Lars's genius. He didn't want to spend the rest of the night alone. Not this night.

A gust of wind billowed noxious smoke at them, and they coughed miserably.

"Let's get away from here," Massimo suggested, already backing off.

"What the fuck's going on over there?" Artur barked, pointing towards the physical sciences building.

They all turned to look, the squat brick structure bathed in the swimming red of the flames. James saw a group of men in black, standing around the front of the building. Waves of smoke were pouring from the door. Flameless black being sucked away by the night. Allistair, he thought. Something had gone wrong down there. Badly wrong. He was dead. Roasted alive down in that tomb.

"Good eye, Artur, good eye." Lars set his jaw and they followed him towards the physical sciences building.

The building was about a hundred and fifty yards away. As they closed in, James saw the figures in black were wearing the kind of outfits worn by SWAT teams. They'd taken up a defensive position around the entrance. One of them had a handgun unholstered. Finally! he thought. Someone to take charge!

"Cops," Artur sneered.

"No," said Lars. "Those guys are wearing berets."

"Then who the fuck are they?" Massimo asked.

"Let's find out. Don't do anything until I give the word. Artur, you hear me?"

"Yessir."

"They got guns, they mean business – we need to find out exactly what business they have here."

They closed in on the physical science building. The paramilitaries were men with angular, sinewy faces, intent and watchful. A squad of ten. The murder James saw in their glowering eyes flooded his chest with urgency. His blood seemed hot in his veins. Serve and protect my ass, he thought. I'm not being paid enough for this kind of trouble.

The squad stood in cordon around a pair of figures, one of whom was very fat, clad in a bright red cassock. A grinning white face, bloated but with sharp features. Like something out of the apocalyptic paintings of Bosch. Gleefully malevolent, he seemed to be sniffing the air, his pointed upper lip twitching as he strode through the security straight at James.

"Hermes!" shouted the one he'd just been talking to. "Where on earth are you going?"

"Hey!" said Artur. "That's Malvern Lichboegh!"

For a moment, James was distracted from the red cassock barreling at him. Not every day did one lay eyes on one of the world's richest men. Lichboegh was wearing an ornate generalissimo's uniform, complete with jackboots and jodhpurs, red sash and gold epaulettes. He looked like a member of a fascist marching band.

"Captain!" Lichboegh snapped his fingers at his guards and trotted after Hermes, the one in the red robes.

"*Ho!*" said the Captain. "Get out, get out, flanks, flanks!"

The gunmen spread in a widening chevron, overtaking Hermes, weapons pointed right at James, Massimo, Lars and Artur.

"Shit!" Massimo grunted. "This ain't good! This ain't good at all!"

Artur bounced. "Yeah, motherfucker!" he growled. "Yeah! Yeah! Yeah, motherfucker!"

"Okay, okay, okay," Lars stammered, the fear in his voice scarier for James than the guns. "Easy, now, easy. Hey!" he called. "Campus security, fellas! We're unarmed! Easy, now, we're unarmed."

"Shut up!" The Captain snarled, thrusting his pistol at Lars. "Stay where you are!" He had an Italian accent. A vituperative voice, made for shouting into megaphones.

Shit! This is it, thought James bleakly. We're about to die. Here and now.

The fear finally clarified his boggled mind. I need to get home, he thought. Now.

"Hands up! Hands where we can see them!" The Captain's

stout Roman nose flared, dark eyes obstinate.

Meekly showing their hands, James and the others froze next to a row of pine trees. In the firing line. James couldn't take his wide eyes off the guns. Until the one in the red cassock shoved through the gunmen and stood before him.

Up close, James smelled an oily, goatish odor. Completely bald, coated in sweaty beads. He reached at James, stubby sausage fingers tipped with long, sharp nails. A grinning ogre with a huge swollen nose, pitted like a lemon rind. Wispy dark whiskers sprouted sparsely over his shining face. His yellow tongue rooted among rotten teeth.

"You!" He giggled. Most terrifying of all were his eyes, just slits in folds of fattened flesh. Whitely opaque, completely without irises or pupils. And yet this Hermes seemed able to peer right at James with a merry intensity that made him quake.

"Hermes!" Lichboegh came up. "What is the meaning of this?" He was a balding man, iron-gray hair combed straight back over his round scalp. He had a wide middle-aged face, well groomed and pampered.

"The meaning of all! The meaning of all!" Hermes chanted, gently clapping his pudgy hands. The milky orbs of his eyes frozen on James. "I see now why we came here tonight!"

"*Signor* Lichboegh," James heard the Captain warn. "We must leave. Now, sir."

"A moment, Captain Alvarro! Hermes—"

Hermes held up a hand that cut off Lichboegh's words like a hatchet. The evil grin widened around the creeping, yellow tongue. The firelight of the downed plane lapped his shiny face. "I wonder," he lilted to James. "I wonder if even *you* know."

"Know – know what?" James stammered. He felt very cold now, holding his own arms across his bare, vulnerable chest.

"Hee hee!" Hermes giggled, and James shivered violently. "You! *You* will be the one to find it! One day soon – very soon!" Abruptly Hermes's hand darted forward, briefly gripping James's head, the gesture of a demented faith healer. The heel of the palm smacked James's forehead hard enough to snap his head back.

"Hey!" Lars shouted, coming forward. "Don't you touch him!"

Captain Alvarro jumped ahead, putting the muzzle right against Lars's chest, but Lars pushed it aside, confronting Hermes and Lichboegh.

All of them started shouting at each other, but James only heard the weird unworldly mumbling of Hermes's speech. The jolly dissonance. He and Hermes remained at the center of the scrum, face to face. Hermes a big man, taller than James.

Then he heard a funny sound. Like wind in a badly sealed window. A faint green glow appeared in front of Hermes's chest. James looked down. Hermes held his pudgy hands a foot apart. Between them, an amorphous smoky light curled and churned. Within a few seconds the glowing smoke had resolved into a small glowing ball, green as a wine bottle. As James watched, thunderstruck, the hovering, hissing ball expanded and contracted. As if breathing, but slowly growing. Now the size of a squash ball. Now a tennis ball. Then a grapefruit. Clear and glassy. When it was about the size of a volleyball, James could see his own reflection on its fluid surface. Eyes wide with fright.

Hermes giggled, merry and malevolent. Abruptly his hands snapped into fists and the glowing green bubble disappeared with a soft pop. James gaped into the blind white face. "Just you wait, my lovely! Wait and see what I can do when you have done your wee task!" Spoken in sing-song cadence, just loudly enough for James to hear through the din of arguing voices. "Bring it to me!"

"Gentlemen, gentlemen!" Lichboegh held up his hands like a conductor readying his orchestra. The babble died down. "We mean no harm," he said genially. But he was clearly upset by Hermes's behavior. His heavy-lidded eyes kept swiveling towards the man in the red cassock, then flicking to James.

"Then drop your fuckin' guns!" Artur bellowed.

"Artur!" Lars shouted, rounding on him. "Shut up and stop being so stupid!"

"Clearly we have zealous employees, we two," said Lichboegh to Lars, brimming with casual authority. He motioned to the guards, who lowered their weapons. He peered at the embroidered badge on Lars's shirt. "Mr. Gunnarson, I presume? I apologize about the weapons. I agree they are... off-putting, shall we say? But you must understand the circumstances." He indicated the burning football field behind them. "I am the patron of the neutrino observatory in the basement of this building. I am only here to ensure the protection of my facility."

Lichboegh's manner was very gracious, truly disarming. His smile solicitous, but even. His guards had yet to holster their weapons. That option was clearly still on the table. Lichboegh focused on James. "It seems my colleague finds some interest in you, Mr...?"

James's pasty mouth opened, then closed again with a snap.

Lichboegh's smile widened. "Hermes can have this affect on people," he said to Lars with a meaningful wink.

"No kidding," said Massimo.

Hermes giggled again, a sound that liquefied James's

intestines. "Misssster Muir, I presume!" He waved a finger in Lichboegh's face, as if to tell him what a naughty boy he was being. "No, no, no! That is for later."

"What's for later?" Massimo asked. "What's this freak talkin' about?"

Now Lichboegh regarded James with the keen fascination some people might reserve for a religious relic. "Well! I am very sorry for all the fuss, Mr. Gunnarson. We'll be off. I bid you—"

Something whizzed past Lichboegh's head. A dagger thudded into one of the pine trunks behind them.

"Down down down!" the Captain screamed, jumping on Lichboegh, shoving him to the ground. All of the gunmen swung their weapons towards whoever had just thrown the dagger.

Another dagger flew from the shadows, striking a guard's throat. The guard went down squawking, gargling blood.

A third blade bounced off the Captain's Kevlar vest, clattering to the ground.

"Throw down your guns and fight like men!" A very tall figure leaped from the shadows into the firelight. James got a quick impression of a fierce bearded face, long dark hair. He dashed forward with a chilling scream. Brandishing a sword.

A sword!

It was all over in seconds. Gunfire cracked the air. Somehow the swordsman avoided the bullets, darting forward to impale the closest guard.

Lars kicked the feet out from under the gunman closest to him. As the gunman fell, Lars applied a precise upward hold on his arm, pinning him to the ground. Artur clubbed another guard's skull with his MagLite.

Everybody was screaming.

The swordsman leaped back and forth, sword flashing, gunmen falling all around. "Ha!" he kept yelling, teeth bared. "Ha! Ha!"

"Yeah!" Artur shrieked, swinging his metal club. "Yeah! *Yeah motherfucker!*"

Massimo wrestled with another gunman.

James got a quick impression of Lichboegh squatting, hands raised to protect his head.

"Put him down!" the Captain shouted. "Put him down!"

Through it all the one called Hermes stood implacable, cataract eyes fused on James.

All at once the clamor died.

"Tribe's gone!" one of the guards shouted.

"Where did he go? Where!"

The pavement was littered with bleeding bodies. Only the Captain and another guard were left standing, both with their weapons leveled at Lars, Artur and Massimo.

Lichboegh jumped to his feet, thrusting a shaking finger straight at Lars. "Shoot them all!"

The Captain smiled, relishing the moment. He fired several quick shots, stitching holes up the center of Lars's chest.

"*No!*" Massimo screamed.

Lars pitched over backwards, squirmed and was still. The guard he'd pinned got shakily to his feet. "Fucker broke my shoulder!" he squealed.

The Captain leveled his gun at James. "*Arrivaderci!*" he snarled, and James turned his head away with a grimacing squint. As if from driving rain.

"No no no!" Hermes cried. He spread his arms, stepping in front of the Captain.

Lichboegh rounded on Hermes. James saw the black fury in those dark eyes. Lichboegh's voice remained calm, but the murderous hatred beamed through like a torch. "You insolent—"

"He must live!" Hermes stated.

"Come, come!" the Captain panted. He hooked a hand under Lichboegh's arm and hauled him away. Another guard did the same to Hermes, the final guard following, pointing his gun at them with his unbroken left arm.

The last James saw of them was Hermes's bloated face peeking out around the corner of the physical sciences building, wiggling his fingers at him. "Toodle-dooo!"

Massimo fell to his knees beside Lars's corpse, his face battered by miserable grief. There was blood all over the concrete, splattered in great black octopuses, draining down the slope to the grass. James heard it pattering into a storm sewer. Seven of the guards were dead.

Artur snatched a weapon off one of them, caressing it like a long-lost heirloom. "Sweeeet," he crooned.

James felt he was no longer there; that the campus, the bodies, Massimo and Artur, were all manufactured. That he himself was unreal, a mere figment.

The falling plane, burned into his mind. Replaying over and over. Gleaming sunlight crawling along the edges of the wings, slipping unctuously over the fuselage.

Creeping terror nibbled at his extremities. Mesmerizing firelight. He wasn't having a nightmare. No, he was caught in the nightmare of another. The nightmare of a madman.

His last flutter of awareness was a single thought: I have to get home. Back to Stacy and the girls.

*

He was aware of cold. Damp, bone aching cold and brilliant light. He was aware, piercingly aware—

Heru, son of Isis. Horos, so-called by the barbarian Greeks. Har-nedj-itef, avenger of Osiris, the One Who Cast Down Seth. One eye the golden boat of Ra, one eye the ghost face of the moon!

New morning sunshine pierced his eyes. He lay in wet grass, splendorous with glinting dew. Buried deep in his head a migraine jackhammered. Mauling him with pain every time he moved. Every time the voice roared in his head—

One eye the golden boat of Ra!

Jesus! The last thing he remembered was the bloodbath at the physical science building. Just thinking of it afflicted him with waves of nausea. A pulsing thread from his churning gut to his splitting head.

Hold on, hold on. There were other memories. Jotted against a sea of jilted, blurred dreams. All of it jumbled together in his foggy mind, a hand-held documentary with no cohesion.

The students had built a heaping pyre on the quad last night, lit with a flaming branch from the plane crash. Wriggling flames catapulting swirling clouds of sparks, dying as they ascended like immolated fireflies. Bony shadows heaving dorm furniture into the huge bonfire, feeding the light. Besieged by all-encompassing night, they'd fought with the fierce determination of an army under siege—

Heru son of Osiris, he who bears the crown of white!

"Oh, shut the fuck up!" James's voice dusty dry, the pathetic rasp of laryngitis.

He drew his knees to his chest and sat hugging his calves for some time, fighting to clear his head. He couldn't get away from the image of Horus—

—so-called by the barbarian Greeks! —

— a brilliant Egyptian figure blasted onto his mind's eye like the afterimage of a flashbulb. The falcon-headed god.

He shivered, his pants soaked through, his hair damp. He was in a grove of scotch pines along the rear wall of the graduate student apartments. Through the trees across the quad he saw the heaped, smoldering corpse of the fire. Puddles painted sky blue along the curbs. That's right, that's right. It wasn't dew sparkling on the grass. It had rained last night. Clouds rolling silently in, blotting out the stars. Crowds of kids, panic-stricken as the rain lashed down, dousing their fire, leaving them groping in unforgiving pitch blackness. Nothing but unrelenting torrents of rain hissing like invisible snakes in the impenetrable dark. Terrifying.

Now the sun was just creeping above the horizon into a perfectly clear sky. Robins warbled in the still trees. Not another sound.

He glanced at the blank face of his watch, then remembered. Okay, he thought, get it together. Judging by the sun it's about five in the morning.

Where was his damn laptop? He looked around, but it wasn't there. Shit, the manuscript!

Then he saw the figure standing at the edge of the trees, no more than thirty feet away. A big kid in a red football jersey. No, not big – huge. An ox. Seeing the look on the ox's face froze James's blood. An expression of eye-rolling, slack-jawed hatred.

"You and me," he muttered lowly. "You. And. Me." And then something else, another language: *"Ir quin'k ar ib'k meh'k,"* he growled. *"Quin'k im herdew'k zin'k hemat ma'k per'k!"*

James gaped at the ox. Somehow, he knew this was ancient Egyptian. Somehow, he could understand. *If you are brave and control your heart, you shall embrace your children, you shall kiss your wife, you shall see your home!*

What the holy fuck!

The glowering ox came towards him. James got to his feet. Mouth ashen. Heart heaving. This kid was gone on some drug, and he was raging. Bottom teeth bared like the razors in a shark's grin. James reached for the MagLite at his belt, but it was gone. So much for a weapon.

The red jersey was grimed, the Ox's jeans caked with filth at the knees. Hair hanging in his face, bedraggled. He rocked slowly back and forth, fists at his sides. Cords taut in his wrists.

Worse, the ox had a coterie of snickering, vulpine toadies. They crept around James. "Come on, Johnny!" one of them whined. James couldn't tell if it was meant to encourage or reproach the Ox. The thug reeled woodenly towards James. Moving just like that damn woman last night with the vapid ecstatic grin.

James held his ground. "Back off," he croaked, holding up a hand. He felt his testicles squirm up into his abdomen.

"Hate assholes. In uniforms." The Ox's scary eyes were rolled up, as if he was on the edge of passing out.

James knew he wasn't that lucky. He feinted left, just as Lars had taught him, out of range of that big right fist. "Back off!"

The Ox turned on his heels, following James, staying face-on. "Gonna rip. You. A NEW ONE!" The huge right fist rose. James saw a damned Blackberry jutting from the bottom like a Paleolithic hand tool.

Plasticolithic, James thought and actually started laughing, the panic juicing his emotions like a stroke. Nowhere for him to go. The Ox's little helpers walled James in.

The fist-mounted Blackberry came down hard, James dodging left again. It missed his head, but clubbed his shoulder with enough force to stagger him. Fucking thing was hard enough to do some serious damage.

James spread his feet, bent his knees, grabbed his right fist in his left hand, and swung his right elbow at the Ox's jaw. Just as Lars had taught him he screamed. What the Japanese called a *kiai* – a sudden release of focused energy at the point of impact. The Ox's head turned with the blow, but that was it. The Blackberry slashed down. James felt the whip of air, it passed that close to his ear.

Shit! He'd hit this monster with everything he had, and the Ox hadn't even felt it.

All around him he heard the cruel snickering of the Ox's coterie. Slithering weasels eager for blood.

James kicked the Ox right in the balls, giving everything, but now his *kiai* contained a thin note of desperation. The blow hard enough to hurt James's ankle and that should have been enough to put anybody down. But the Ox just took a small step backward. Not even a flicker of pain in those evil rolling eyes.

The Blackberry caught him hard on the cheekbone, starring his vision. Oh lord, James thought, I'm going to pass out, and when I pass out he's going to—

Suddenly a gunshot split the air.

It was Massimo. Massimo with a damn handgun for God's sake. Combat-stanced, leveling the gun at the Ox. "Stand back, asshole!"

For a few seconds the Ox froze, upper lip wrinkling in a snarl. But even someone in his state of so-called mind saw the stupidity of going up against an armed opponent. He backed off, his crowd of grinning acolytes scurrying away.

"Get the fuck outta here!" Massimo growled.

The Ox shuffled off with the unsteady stiffness of a punch-drunk boxer. Peering over his massive shoulder back at James. Muttering.

"Thank Christ for you, Mass!" Gulping air, James realized he'd been holding his breath.

"Yeah, yeah." Massimo seemed distracted and off-put. He stuck the gun down the front of his pants like a seventies TV vigilante.

"That guy is fucking insane!" James's voice quavered.

"Lotta that goin' round." Mass wiped his forehead with the back of his hand, eyes darting back and forth.

"Mass, did you see my goddamn laptop, man?"

Mass's shoulders slumped. "Your fuckin' *laptop*!" He laughed, but it was a desperate sound. The sound of a man fighting for life in a raging river. "That's all you gotta say to me right now?"

"You okay man?"

"Okay. Yeah, I'm doin' great, Jimmy! Just fuckin' great, and thanks a lot for fuckin' asking. Where the fuck have you been?"

"I, uh – I don't really know..." Feeling ridiculous, James shuffled his feet.

"You don't really know. What's that shit all over you?"

James gaped down at himself, seeing his arms, his entire torso covered in jagged brown lines. His shaking fingers pawed at his face, coming away smeared with more of the same. It looked like henna. Hieroglyphs scrawled all over him. "Jesus..."

"You look like a goddamn fag!"

"Hey! And what if I was, a fag! Eh, Mass? What would you do then?"

"Aw, c'mon, don't give me that holy than thou garbage, man!" He waved his thick hands in the air. "This ain't no tutorial discussion."

"Fuck you, Mass! Don't *give me* your homophobic garbage! And it's holi*er* than thou, by the way." James felt a dribble of sweat on his right cheek, but when he wiped it away, there was blood on his fingers. His right cheekbone felt bruised and sore. Shit, that goddamn Blackberry had done just the trick! Now his whole skull thrashed with furious pain.

Massimo crossed his arms, shot a truculent glare at James. Now James saw with a flush of pity that Massimo was at his wit's end. Frayed and torn. His wide mouth nervously working, as if chewing sunflower seeds. Struggling not to break into tears.

"Look," said James calmly. He put a tentative hand on Massimo's shoulder. "I don't know what the hell's going on, okay? Last I remember – last I remember is Lars going down..."

"Don't remind me," Massimo choked.

For a few moments they just stood. The attachment of James's hand allowing a current of emotion to flow between them. Massimo wiped his eyes and sniffed angrily. "You just wandered off."

"I did?"

"Yeah, you fuckin' did!" Massimo shook his head. "Sorry. Sorry, Jimmy." He took a deep breath, blew it out. "This fuckin' situation... It's... it's doing my mind. Y'know?"

"Yeah, I know."

"You don't remember nothing?"

James only shook his head.

"Okay, so for a coupla minutes you stood, kinda staring down at Lars's body. I was – I was pretty broken up. I asked you something, like are you okay, something like that, but you just kept this blank look on your face. You didn't answer me. So I'm thinkin', okay, alright. Figured even *you* could be at a loss for words, moment like that."

"Thanks, Mass."

"Well, ya know..." For a second they shared wan smiles. "Then, next thing I know, I looked up and you were gone. We were supposed to stick together, Jimmy, that's what Lars said."

"I know, I know. I... I just can't remember anything – except the fire on the quad."

"Fuck, how could you forget? Then that rainstorm, holy shit! Never considered myself scared of the dark, but fuck! Creepy, being outside in that kinda black."

"What about Artur?"

"Fuckin' Artur, he's off on his own... crusade, some shit."

Suddenly another memory leaped into James's mind. Artur in the raging light of the heaped pyre, bare-chested. Standing on a table. Artur with the head of a giant fly. Standing with his feet wide, both arms out, slanting up from his shoulders. A double Nazi salute. The tumescent bulbs of compound eyes glittering in the frenetic firelight. James shook himself, but the image would not clear. "Do I really remember him taking a gun?"

"Damn right he did. It's enough to scare the shit out of a sewer pipe. Even in all this, that kinda help I don't need. I tried finding you all night, man. Spotted you coupla times, but then you just disappeared into the crowd again. You were... I dunno, like yelling about something."

"Was I?" The furry, insect mouthparts of Artur's fly head, vigorously squirming.

"Yelling in some weird language, sounded like Hebrew... Arabic, some shit, I dunno."

"But I don't speak Hebrew or Arabic."

"Yeah, well, no kidding. What else you remember?"

"Next thing I know, I'm waking up here with that fucking Ox on me. Crazy son of a bitch!" James rubbed his temples with his fingertips, gritting his teeth.

"Like I said, lotta that goin' round. Whatever happened last night, it fucked a lotta people up. Bad." Massimo bit his lip, gave James a strange look. Skeptical, but a little scared too. "I was worried, Jimmy. Thought you were one of them, buddy. You okay? You don't look so good."

Who says I'm not one of them? James thought. *Who says I'm not just as crazy as the Ox? Wandering around all bloody night in a blackout? Speaking in tongues! What a party! Call in the faith healer!*

But that only reminded him of the fat weirdo in the red cassock. Hermes. The pudgy hand darting out, smacking his forehead. The glowing green sphere, hovering between his fingers.

As if to confirm the anxious squirm in his belly, James looked at his blank watch again. "Do you have any idea what's going on?"

"Damned if I know, Jimmy." His eyes scanned the campus. "Everything's still down."

Right. Including planes, James thought. Thin smoke still curled up from behind the bio building, almost half a mile away. Sewage-hued in the morning sun.

"Cars. Lights. TV's, phones. Even the landlines. Nothin's working." Massimo raised his eyebrows, searching for an answer – any answer – from James. But James felt blank. Seeing the gnawing fear in his colleague's twitching jaw muscles, he experienced dull despondency, a throbbing desire to simply leave this place. Get home. Stacy needed him.

Suddenly Massimo snickered. "Man, you look like some freak on a Pride Parade float. We gotta get you cleaned up."

"Scuse me," said a voice behind them. "I can't seem to find my way..."

Massimo whipped out the gun, pointing it at a stooped figure coated in soot, with the lower half of his face swathed in bloody bandages.

"Mass, Mass, put it down, Jesus!" James put his hand on Massimo's wrist.

"Whaddaya want?" Mass snapped, jostling away from James.

The man with the bandages raised his hands. "Easy, pal, easy." It was a dirty t-shirt knotted around his face. It needed changing. The blood edged with that yellowish color that said infection. "What a travesty!" he remarked. "One armed to the teeth, the other painted to the fuckin' gills!"

The voice sounded so familiar to James.

"We're doin' the best we can, okay?" Massimo's voice quavered.

"Jimbo, can't you tell him to lay down?"

"Allistair!" James cried, running forward. "God, are you alright?"

"Do I look alright?"

James introduced him to Massimo, then compelled his friend to put the damn gun away. "I thought you were dead. What the hell happened?"

"Thought I was dead too, mate. That bloody tank of heavy water blew. When the pulse hit, it exploded like a bloody bomb."

"Pulse?" Massimo asked.

"Piece of it nearly took off my left cheek." He sounded like he was talking through a mouthful of cotton balls.

"What about Chen?" James asked.

Allistair shook his head. "Chen's dead," he sobbed. "Ah, shite, you gotta hold it together, son. Stiff upper lip and all that!"

James patted him on the back. "That's awful, man."

"Eh, well, he died doing what he loved, anyway. Few people can say that, I suppose."

"You said there was a pulse," Massimo insisted. "Will you tell me what the shit you're talking about?"

Allistair's eyes came alert, tears twinkling above the sopping bandage. "I'll do better than tell you, my buff friend. I'll *show* you!"

His excitement abruptly buried his grief. The sudden change wasn't natural. James felt a prickle of fear.

Allistair started leading them towards the oblong bulk of the administration building.

"Whoa, whoa," said Massimo, looking very nervous. "I don't wanna go in there again. No way. Tried getting down to the security office last night, it's blacker than shit down there."

"C'mon, c'mon," Allistair motioned to them impatiently. "We're not going to the basement, we're going to the roof!"

James and Mass exchanged glances. "I've gotta get in there anyway," said James. "I need to call home, make sure Stace and the girls are okay."

Allistair snickered.

Massimo looked at him as if he had just sprouted antlers. "Weren't you paying attention? I already told you, phones ain't workin', guy! They're done! Lights are done, radio's done, it's all fuckin done man!"

"Alright, okay, take it easy," said James, not feeling very easy himself.

"Will you two hurry your arses!" Allistair, hopping eagerly.

As they went on, the anxious feeling in James's belly crept up to his lungs. As if the effort of walking was making him pant like a sprinter. Things were bad. Very bad.

He didn't like the way Massimo was acting. Massimo was not the type of man who showed tension. He was the kind of man who buried it, kept it deeply hidden. Now his burial pit must be full to overflowing. He kept touching that damn gun in his belt, tracing the line of the butt.

My God, Massimo was packing a *gun*! That fact alone was enough to tilt the perspective on things. Distort them like a funhouse mirror.

There were bodies everywhere. Strewn on the grass, laid out along the footpath. Allistair didn't seem to notice them, but James saw Mass cross himself every time they passed one. James watched the pallid, still faces. Gaping mouths. The way the breeze animated their hair, a mockery of death.

"Gotta take care of them," James heard Massimo mutter. "This heat... gonna get bad quick."

Massimo was right. The damp chill was being driven away by the sun. Getting warm enough that James was no longer uncomfortable shirtless. Jesus, they must have passed fifteen, twenty corpses on this path alone. Extrapolate that over the campus, mix in a sweaty humid day like yesterday – it didn't bear thinking about.

There were only a few other people out and about. Stunned, it seemed. Nearly robotic. They passed a couple spooned together on the grass. His arms around her as she wept into in her hands.

They ran into a cop who said he was cutting across the campus, trying to hoof it back to headquarters on foot. Massimo asked him what he'd heard, James focusing on him as if he was a prophet.

"Sweet F.A." His face drawn and hollow, as if he doubted his own sanity. He kept looking at the gun on Massimo's belt, then quizzically to James's painted body. Massimo tried to explain about the weapon, but the cop waved him off. "You're security here, you're gonna need it, buddy. And you didn't hear me say that, by the way. I abandoned my cruiser about twenty miles west of here. Been walkin' all night. Same everywhere. Nothin's working. I seen thousands of people, walking the streets and roads, headin' wherever they need to get to." He shook his head, peering off into the distance. "And when I say nothin's working, I'm talking, like, people's *heads*, too, okay? Time was, craziness was at a premium, right? You can forget that now. You know how to use that?"

Massimo nodded grimly.

"Just you be sure, use it right, you understand me? Time's gonna come, all this shit'll be cleared away, you'll have to answer for it. Good luck, now." He shook all their hands, hitched up his utility belt and marched off.

They watched him go, James trying to swallow the bitter taste in his mouth. Authority, shit. What good was it?

Massimo gave a bitter laugh. "*Thousands*, Jimmy! That's what he said, right? Like, thousands of people on foot! So you know what that means – it means this isn't just about the campus, man! This is all over!"

"Ach, Jesus Christ!" Allistair spat through his bandages. "Of course it's all over, pal! C'mon, c'mon, and I'll show you!"

Allistair's manner was starting to feel absurd, like that waiter near the end of Monty Python's *The Meaning of Life*. The one who kept gesturing at the camera, saying "Just a little further now, just a little further!"

When they entered the admin building, it didn't take long for James to see why Massimo had balked at coming back. Even on the ground floor, they hadn't gone more than a hundred feet down a hallway before the light faded to a grey murk that made it difficult to see anything except shadows.

Allistair took them to a windowless stairwell that would have been pitch black if not for the candles lit on each landing. Even with the faint, wavering light the climb to the roof was spooky, full of their scraping feet and pounding breath.

When they came out on the gravelly rooftop, the sudden brightness stung their eyes. The roof was dotted with people, most of them standing at the southern parapet, the narrow end of the rectangular rooftop. All of them oddly quiet, awkwardly unmoving, like mourners at a wake.

There was Artur, lounging in a folding aluminum lawn chair, strumming a guitar. Helmeted by his blond flattop, eyes hidden behind those damned mirrored sunglasses.

Fly eyes in the firelight.

A knot of ten or twelve people sat in the pea gravel around the lawn chair, some holding the metal tubing as if hoping for a healing miracle.

His gun sat on his lap, half-hidden by the guitar body.

James and Massimo followed Allistair, crunching through the gravel to the southern end.

"Take a look, take a look!" Allistair enthused, casting his arm southwards.

From the York campus the terrain slipped down, away to the south, spreading the vast cityscape out before them in a limitless grey concrete and asphalt heap.

Dimly, as if from a great distance, James heard Massimo's hoarse whisper. "Holy fuckin' shit."

Despite last night's downpour, broad areas of the city still burned, sending up curtains of black smoke miles wide. Slanted eastwards by the prevailing winds, the smoke merged into a sooty pall high in the atmosphere.

James felt his breath stolen through his numb, gaping mouth. His eyes turning back and forth, his field of vision not big enough to take it all in. Far to the southwest, something still raged with fire, flames tossing so high they were level with the tops of surrounding apartment blocks.

"What happened, fuck sakes?" Massimo gasped.

"The planes coming down," James snapped. "They set the city alight and the fire crews can't get to them because the trucks aren't running!"

It was the silence that stifled anything but fear and stinging apprehension. A wind-murmuring quiet so complete it seemed unholy. The undead muffling of the world.

All except for Artur's twangy strumming. The steady creak of the lawn chair as his body gently rocked with the beat of "Hangman." Artur's hiccupping singing, *Friends've got some silver*," he sang. "*Gotta little gold... what did ya bring me, my dear friends, keep me from the gallows pole?*"

"Quite something, isn't it?" Allistair's awestruck tone was such a jarring mismatch with James's dread that he shivered.

Distantly he heard three echoing firecracker pops. Then a single sharp crack that splintered away. James had spent enough November deer seasons in the north bush to recognize the sound of a high powered rifle. He supposed the first three shots had been from a handgun. He thought of the cop.

Allistair was staring at a light suspended just over the eastern horizon. The landing lights of a plane! James smiled with a pang of cringing gratitude so sweet it could only come from bone-deep fear. Some planes had survived! At least one! He smacked Massimo's shoulder and pointed it out. He put his hands together and turned his face to the sun. Not everything was gone. Thank you, he thought. Thank-you!

The light hung in the sky below and just to the left of the sun. A bright silvery spark, fanning out cold beams.

"Betelgeuse," Allistair croaked. A warble of supplicant joy, of madness.

"It's a plane," said James, now uncertain. "It's the landing lights of a plane..."

Allistair turned and looked at him as if he was crazy.

"It is!" squealed a woman to James's left, hopping up and down, pointing. "It is! A plane, a plane!"

More and more of them started doing it, hugging each other, crying.

"I knew they'd take care of it," somebody exalted. "I just knew it!"

Artur's sneer hissed, a stridulating rattlesnake uncovered beneath a paving stone.

"You're all daft!" Allistair spat through his bandages. "Fuckin' dafties, the lot of you!"

Betelgeuse. The star emitting all those damned neutrinos. Now James recalled what Chen had said the night before. His manic smile traced in the dim blue light of the monitors.

I'll tell you! I'll give you that for fucking free! It's gonna go supernova!

James stared hard at the light in the sky, willing it to move. It must move. It *must* because it was a plane coming in from somewhere east of here. Some kind of relief flight. Landing lights on, flying towards the airport... but it wasn't moving.

"Allistair," he said, breathless. "Tell us what the hell's going on. Just give it up."

"It's Betelgeuse!" Allistair shouted, as if he'd just seen a celebrity.

"The fuck you talkin' about?" said Massimo. "That shitty eighties movie?"

"No, no, not the movie," Allistair shouted.

"Johnny Depp," Massimo continued.

"Nah, nah," Artur scoffed at him. "Michael Keaton, ya stupid wop!"

"It's got nothin' to do with any fuckin' movie, alright?" Allistair shouted. And then to James: "D'you know what a supernova is?" He sounded like a professor having to revisit something he'd already reviewed a hundred times.

"An exploding star, right?"

"Yeah..." He waved his arms emphatically at the bright sparkle in the east.

"You're tryin' to tell me that's a star?" Massimo scoffed. "But it's daylight!"

"Yeah," said a guy behind them. "And it's way too big to be a star. Too bright."

Allistair shook his head miserably. "For Christ sake, think, just think for a second, yeah? Betelgeuse went supernova about ten hours ago – well, no that's not correct, actually. Actually, it happened about four hundred and twenty five years ago, it's just that the light took that long to get here."

"Then how come we didn't see it last night?" somebody piped up. "When the blackout hit?"

"Because," said Allistair pedantically, "Betelgeuse crosses the sky in daytime during the summer. When the pulse hit last night, it had already set, well below the horizon. And it just rose a couple of hours ago. It's always been there, every day, every summer. You just couldn't see it until now."

"No need for the attitude," Massimo growled.

"Just try to pay attention, beefcake. This star, Betelgeuse, is fuckin massive, like a thousand times bigger than the sun." Allistair giggled. "So think about this for a second: if you imagine the sun as being the size of a basketball, at that scale the Earth would be about the size of a peppercorn. Now, take that basketball and hold it in your hands. At the same scale Betelgeuse would be as big around as a domed stadium, like the Roger's Center. Even before it exploded, Betelgeuse shone sixty thousand times brighter than the sun. Can you even imagine that? Something that size explodes, it's gonna make a fuckin' bright light!"

"So you're trying to tell us that this... this super thing caused all this shit?" Massimo stood with his hands on his hips, challenging Allistair.

Allistair's gleaming, bloodshot eyes rolled towards the burning cityscape. "It would seem so." He admitted, as if not wanting to give his damn precious star a bad name.

"How?" James demanded. "How can that be possible?"

Allistair shrugged, and to James it seemed maddeningly dismissive. "Dunno. You were there, in the lab last night."

"Neutrinos did this, Allistair?"

"How the fuck should I know!"

"What the fuck are you guys talking about?" Massimo raged.

"That's all you can say?" James yelled in Allistair's damaged face. "That's it?"

"Hey, fuck, it's not as if I've done it! Fuck sakes, it's like blaming a weatherman when a tornado destroys your house! A massive blast of neutrinos, some kinda electromagnetic pulse, I'm fucked if I know, Jimbo. When a star goes off like that, you're talkin' massive blasts of x-rays, alpha, beta and gamma radiation way off the fuckin' charts. We're in completely unknown territory here, my man."

Territory rhyming with tree, house rhyming with moose. Allistair's Scottish pronunciation only made James's seething resentment burrow deeper. The pretension! "My God, you're an asshole!" he screamed.

"You're fulla shit," Massimo stated. "I don't believe a word comin' outta your mouth."

James, alarmed to see Massimo's hand resting on the butt of the gun.

"Christ, what's not to believe?" Allistair laughed bitterly. "You can see it with your own bloody eyes!"

"You knew!" James thrust a finger at him. "Chen tried to warn me – you knew this was gonna happen as well as he did and you shut him down!"

Allistair snorted. "I didn't know any of *this* would happen! Who could've seen that? Besides, what would you have done, Jimbo? Run away?"

"Should string you the fuck up!" Massimo snarled.

"What is this, the fourteenth fuckin century?"

James couldn't tell if Allistair was outraged or scared out of his mind.

"Fuckin' A!" Artur was grinning now. That slack mouth, the same sagging smile they'd seen on some of the corpses below. He picked absently at the strings, plucking the odd high vibrato as he projected his honking voice. "Beware the witching hour, people... beware the witching hour."

Only now, James saw that it was Lars's guitar.

"Fantastic," Allistair laughed, shaking his head.

Artur's retinue around the chair swayed with the music, a few hooting, whistling. Artur's fingers found a rhythm on the strings and he started strumming, and then in a high, rough wail: "*Beware the witching hour!*"

A lanky guy with bushy red hair hooted through a shit-eating grin. James had run into him a few times over the past few months. A hatchet-faced physiology student who'd been researching the effects of sleep deprivation on reflexes, something like that. Steve, Simon, he couldn't remember which. James remembered him saying that he kept himself awake for days at a time.

Steve/Simon gazed up at Artur just like the others, rapt, nodding solemnly, some of them clapping time as Artur picked up the pace, hitting the strings hard. "*BEWARE THE WITCHING HOUR!*" he shrieked.

Artur pulling them in place, iron filings around a magnet. Those awful glasses, fused to Artur's face, seeing nothing and everything at once.

It was in the smooth distortion of those lenses that James saw a couple climb up onto the parapet, hand in hand. He turned around just in time to see them jump off.

"Noooo!" somebody screamed.

A second later, the loud wet smack of their bodies striking the pavement seven stories below.

A girl on the other side of the roof in hysterics, screaming "No, no no, no, no!"

People with wide unhinged eyes. People sobbing, making ugly retching sounds.

Allistair, turning his face away from everybody. James realized he was actually laughing.

"Hey, relax," Artur drawled, still strumming. "Just means less for us to kill later."

The physiology guy hacked out a laugh. His bulging eyes screwed tightly into dark sockets, bucked yellow teeth leering. Drinking Artur in. They all were, in that cluster around the chair.

"The fuck're you talking about, Artur?" Massimo asked.

"The putsch, you putz! They're making a grab for the reins, for everything, man!" Artur was assured, calm, but stony now, the slackness in his face frozen into a chilling smirk.

"Who?" Allistair demanded. "What the hell are you rabbiting on about?"

"The cops! The man!" Artur hissed at Allistair's naiveté.

"I need to get home," James heard himself say, no longer feeling quite awake. Not quite *there*. "Take care of Stace, the girls."

He started towards the door behind Artur, but then the guitar was quiet. It was quiet because Artur's picking hand was holding the gun, pointing it straight at James's chest. James's feet squelched to silence in the pea gravel. Nothing now but the crawling, moaning wind.

"Nobody's goin' no damn where," Artur grinned. The sun and the eerie new daystar – Betelgeuse – dual flaming pupils in each of his freakish bulbous eyes.

Massimo shouldered James aside, yanking out his own gun. "What the fuck're you doing?"

"Jimmy, man, I'm doing you a favor, buddy," said Artur. "You really think you're gonna get back downtown anytime soon? You gonna enjoy your thirty mile hike?"

James felt the breath knocked out of him. Until that moment he'd been assuming an hour aboard city transit would get him home. An hour or so and he'd be putting his key in the apartment door. But how could that be? Jesus Christ, how could that be with everything shut down? They'd even seen the buses in the roundabout below. Huge dead caterpillars. Thirty miles, yeah, at least that. Maybe more. If he was lucky – lucky! – he'd see his family by dusk tonight after a 12-hours of straight walking.

"Artur, you have to let me get out of here."

"Do I?" He snickered. "Do I, my peeps?"

"Fuck no!" they all chanted as one, a few laughing, pointing at James's abject horror.

"We're in new times," said Artur, cold as the breath of winter.

74

"We're here! We're queer! We're not going away!"

"You're mad as a hatter!" Allistair squealed.

"He's saner than you!" Simon/Steve the physiology student shrieked. Spit sprayed from between his bucked teeth.

No, James thought. None of us are sane at all. You fell asleep. Your experiment failed. *You're* the one having the nightmare that's trapped us all.

"Artur's right." A girl with long auburn hair, standing on the southern parapet, pointed down at the bus roundabout. A note of snotty I-told-you-so in her voice. "The cops are already here, to take us all away."

A sudden rattle of machinegun fire. James and Massimo ran to the parapet.

Chapter 4

Quentin Tribe

James tried not to see the three bodies on the sidewalk below. Smashed into jagged bloody pools. Across the grass oval in the middle of the roundabout, dozens of men in black paramilitary jumpsuits were setting up a stockade of modular wire fencing, the kind that comes in sections, made for use around building sites.

"It's the guys that killed Lars!" Massimo called out. "Lichboegh's guys!"

The half of Allistair's face visible over the bandages drained pale, the color of raw bone. "Lich-Lichboegh!" he stammered. "He's here?"

James watched students being hauled into the stockade, hands bound behind their backs with plastic zip cords. There were men with guns everywhere. About a dozen on horseback, riding from the south, hemming the students in. Others with huge black Alsatians lunging at terrified kids.

Allistair crouched behind the parapet, blowing out a despairing breath. His eyes swung back and forth. He thinks Lichboegh's men are after him, James thought.

There was a struggle near the entrance to the student center. Several guards were wrestling a kid to the ground. It was the Ox in the red football jersey. Fighting ferociously, the Ox knocked his assailants back. Again they attacked him, putting the boots to him, driving him down to the concrete. He struggled ferociously. A guard calmly stepped up behind him and pumped three bullets into the back of his head. The shots echoed across the quad. It was the Captain. Stocky, with big forearms. Alvarro.

Artur's retinue clapped and whooped heartily.

Now it was Artur's turn to hop onto the parapet. James was horrified to find himself wishing he would jump off like the others.

"My people!" he hollered. "We are on the cusp of greatness!" A murmur of compliant joy shuddered through the small crowd. James noticed metal glinting on Artur's pecs. Safety pins, stuck through his nipples. Each one lined with speared flies.

More gunfire, the snap and ricochet of bullets.

"It's the guy with the sword!" Massimo yelled.

James peered over the edge, seeing the tall figure, with long black hair. His sword caught the sunlight as he dashed into the student center, closely followed by a trotting squad of gunmen, led by Alvarro. Like hounds after a hare.

"We gotta get down there," said Massimo, eyeing Artur.

"Are you out of your mind?" James demanded.

"That asshole killed Lars." Massimo ejected the gun's magazine, checked the loads, and slammed it back in.

"Fuckin' cops," Artur growled, still grinning. "Swingin' their dicks."

"They aren't cops, you idiot! You're gonna go up against guys with automatic weapons—" James was cut off by Massimo.

"They killed Lars," he said quietly, jaw muscles twitching. And then to Artur: "You gonna let us off this goddamn roof, or what?"

Artur's big square teeth glistened. "Fuckin' A." He turned to address his retinue, putting his arms out, an imprint of James's memory. The double Nazi salute, the handgun in his right fist. Those fly-encrusted safety pins. For a second, just a second, Artur had the head of a giant fly again. Only a flash. Furry dexterous mouthparts twitching. "My peeps! We are going after them! I may not return. Do not mourn me, but celebrate the dawn of the New Age!" The acolytes all cheered.

That cop earlier: craziness used to be at a premium. Got that right.

Artur hopped down from the parapet. Then he pressed the muzzle of his gun against James's forehead. Grinning. "And you're comin' too, asshole."

*

James's frantic heart slammed his sore head in the silent murk of the student center. Fast food counters shuttered tight. A girl toting a pile of clothes wormed out through a hole that had been wrenched in the gate of a boutique. Artur pointed his gun at her and she fled through the north exit. They crept another twenty yards, feet gritting against the tiles.

Those gunmen, they'll hear us, James thought. They'll come back and then – and then—

They peeked around the corner of an ATM kiosk, seeing the Captain and several other gunmen fifty yards ahead, slipping through the glass door of the library.

"Now!" Artur panted, avid for blood. "Let's kill those fuckers!" Bouncing on his haunches.

"Shut the fuck up!" Massimo snapped. "We fire on them now, we're dead. Up there, in the shelving, we gotta fighting chance."

"You're crazy!" said James. "Those guys are pros, with automatic weapons, with—"

The metal snout of Artur's gun rested coldly against his temple. That bright, slavering grin.

"Don't you got any balls?" Massimo accused him.

They crept past the library's long check-out desk, then up the frozen escalator, careful their feet didn't clang. The second floor atrium yawned three storeys above them. Dim papery light through the foggy glass ceiling.

Two sets of poured concrete staircases opened to the atrium, one on either side. They saw the gunmen creeping up the eastern steps, their quarry leading them all the way to the fifth floor.

Insane, James thought as they crept up behind. A last stand. Sword versus firearms. And we'll be in the middle of it.

This isn't happening. This *can't be* happening!

When they got to the fifth floor, they looked both ways down the length of the library. Enameled metal stacks stretched into darkness in both directions. They saw nobody. Not a sound except their own hushed, dry gasps.

"Artur you go left," Massimo whispered. "Don't try to be shit-hot. Get in tight—"

"Yeah, yeah, yeah." Artur crawled left, disappearing into the stacks.

"He's just as likely to shoot you as anybody," James pleaded with Massimo. "Come on, for fuck sake!"

Massimo's hard eyes glittered in the gloom. "You're such a pussy."

James's mouth was very dry. Knowing now that he would never see Stacy, Jenny, Sara again. Never again.

James and Massimo went right, along the aisle, then down one of the stacks. James saw they were in the section housing books on the history of arms and armor. How fitting. At the other end, the space opened out. Wooden study carrels squatted under slanting safety glass, looking out over the roof of the student center.

There, sitting on the carpet with his back to one of the carrels, long legs drawn up, sat the swordsman. A book nestled in his lap. He seemed deep in study, as if there was nothing else to concern him. James heard the dry slip of a page as he turned it. He was powerfully built. The only sign of tension on his lean, hard face was the flare of his long nose. That and the sword lying on the carpet. Ready to hand.

The heavy silence pulsed.

"Tribe!" called a biting voice. James jumped, jamming his fist into his mouth as if suppressing a cough. It was the Italian Captain, just a few rows down. "Tribe, give it up. We've got you."

The swordsman leaned his head back against the carrels, eyes rolling to the ceiling. "Come and get me, then," he growled. A sonorous, gravelly voice that came from deep within the throat behind his long, bushy goatee.

"Tribe. Don't be stupid."

James looked behind him, and shit! Massimo was gone! Hyperventilating, James turned back to find the deep blue eyes of the swordsman boring into him. The swordsman raised a long finger to his lips. And winked.

"Come out and face me, Alvarro," he said, still glaring at James. "Put down that cowardly machine. Pick up a blade and fight like a man."

A callous, stony chuckle. "You hear that, boys? Eh? Mr. Tribe over here bids me to a contest of men – in a library!"

"Only a deeply retarded intellect would find such a notion amusing," Tribe growled. And then, loudly calling: "You men who call Nicolo Alvarro your Captain! Surely you know what a coward he is. Over a decade now he has refused to face me."

"I could snap my fingers and have you sawn in half. Right now. But Lichboegh wants you alive."

"I know it."

"Will you overlook this gift? Stand up, leave your weapon on the floor. You talk to me of being a man, Tribe. Why don't you be a man? Face Lichboegh."

"On his terms?" Tribe snorted. "I think not!"

James saw Tribe's eyes flick right. Right and back to James, right and back to James again. Eyebrows arched with some meaning. Rightwards, and back again. James shook his head, gesturing. Hearing the pasty click of his tongue as he mouthed *I don't understand what you mean—*

Suddenly the quiet exploded with gunfire. Down the stacks, far to the left. *BAM! BAM! BAM!BAM!BAM!*

A blizzard of confetti blew out towards the study carrels. Books eviscerated by bullets.

Artur ran screaming down the aisle between the stacks and the carrels. *"THE NATIONAL REVOLUTION HAS BEGUN!"* he shrieked.

Then the earsplitting shred of automatic fire: *BRRRRRRATTT!*

Artur catapulted backwards. Tackled by bullets, legs bicycling.

The swordsman – Tribe – leaped to his feet as gunmen poured out like great black beetles.

"Hup!" he shouted, lunging, driving the sword deep through a gunman's chest. The tip of the blade sprouted from his back. Still the gunman struggled to raise his machine pistol. Tribe's left hand exactly mirrored this final defiant spasm, jamming a dagger into his forearm.

The gunman made a gorping sound, his weapon clattering down. He grabbed at the blade in his chest. Vomiting green bile as he fell. Tribe tore out both blades and several of the gunman's fingers fell off. Steel zipping from bone and flesh, a thick sucking. A fine bloody spray against the study carrels.

Tribe's grim face, his flared nostrils. The way he'd stepped up to the gunman, as if to embrace him. Obscene, reptilian, incredibly graceful all at once.

BAM! BAM!BAM!

Men shouting. Screaming confusion, barely heard through the gigantic din.

Tribe hurdled the study carrels, ducking and weaving as bullets split the wood.

Another gunman came out of the row to James's right. Lowered his weapon on Tribe's back. So intent on his target, he didn't see James crouching at his feet. Now James understood the meaning of Tribe's gesturing eyeballs.

A pulse flashed down James's spine. He seized the heavy tome Tribe had just flung aside. A weighty plank of paper bound solid between hard leather covers.

James's *kiai* was a raging "*Heee!*" as he jumped up, the book's spine knocking the gun upwards. It fired, shredding ceiling tiles.

One flash of the gunman's face. Wide-eyed, twisted in shock. James smashed the book down on the gunman's wrist. Again the gun fired, bullets tearing into the carrels. James snapped the book spine back up, jamming it hard into the gunman's throat. The force of the impact numbed James's fingers.

The gunman sprawled backwards into the stacks, pulling a rockslide of books down on top of himself. James watched in glutinous horror. The gunman's ballooning blue lips, bisected by a hideously gaping mouth. His legs kicked, hands pawing frantically to his throat through the spilled books. Even through the overwhelming noise of combat, James heard repulsive sucking. The sound of a blocked drain.

I crushed his windpipe, James thought. I got him right where Lars taught me to aim, right at the trachea. *I killed this man.*

Emerging from the gunman's last grimace, a swollen tongue erect as a black mushroom.

A hand gripped his arm, pulling him away. Tribe. "Get a move on!"

They dashed down the aisle past the carrels, past Artur's bloody body – the insane grin frozen. James dimly aware that the gunfire had died down. Just the odd shot now, flinchingly loud.

Massimo ran behind them, arms furiously pumping. "Go, go, go!"

Then there were three gunmen in front of them, and they dodged left, back into the stacks, their faces full of dusty confetti as books were torn apart by gunfire. Bullets twanged off metal shelves. Both Tribe and Massimo were shouting, but James couldn't hear what they were saying.

Suddenly a gunman was in front of them. Filling the space between the shelves. Gun raised at them – Tribe's arm flicked out. A knife buried itself right in the gunman's mouth. He keeled over, a blood fountain between his teeth.

"Holy shit!" Massimo yelled.

As they passed the corpse, Tribe stooped to yank out his weapon, just as another gunman fired at them from the next row.

They jogged right, then left, then back right again. Deeper and deeper into the maze of shelves.

"No, no – wait, wait, wait!" James cried. The three of them hunkered down, panting, wide-eyed. Tribe using a book to wipe the blood from his knife. Massimo putting a new magazine into his pistol. "We've gotta head back towards the stairs, or they'll trap us!"

"Nah, nah," Massimo spat. "They'll be waiting for us by the fuckin' stairs! Where's that third guy? Where is he?"

"Just shut up and listen!" James spat. "We'll head through the stacks, around the atrium – towards the stairs on the west side!"

"I'm tellin' you, we head that way, we're dead!"

"Will you just make a decision!" Tribe hissed.

"Who's spent more time up here," James asked. "Me or you?"

Massimo gave a reluctant shrug.

James became aware of a crackling sound. The stinging smell of smoke.

"God's teeth, they're setting the library alight!" Tribe yelled.

"Tryin' to flush us out!" Massimo barked.

They got moving. Before long, the air was thick with smoke. Invading their lungs, making them choke and cough. Already dim away from the windows, the air browned out until it was hard to see anything.

Finally they found the stairs on the western side. Across the atrium, they saw a rearguard of three gunmen watching the top landing of the far staircase.

They dashed down, staying low, behind the concrete balustrade. But they were spotted. A deafening rattle of gunfire. Bullets smacking the concrete.

As they dashed across the atrium floor towards the escalator, Alvarro's hubristic scream echoed behind them: "I AM NICOLO ALVARRO, CAPTAIN OF THE SICARI! I WILL NOT REST UNTIL YOU ARE DEAD!"

*

By the time James, Massimo and Tribe made it back into the brilliant sunshine, black smoke was roiling from the top floor of the library, a rope pulling into the limitless blue sky.

They hid behind a concrete pillar at the foot of the admin building. Staring aghast at hundreds of students penned within the wire stockade in the middle of the bus roundabout.

More students being hauled in, hands bound.

A guard marched back and forth, a pistol in one hand and an old-fashioned megaphone in the other. He shouted into the metal cone, the tinny amplified voice a hollow mechanism. Berating the prisoners, cowing them.

"What the fuck is all this?" Massimo still gripped the pistol. James told him to take his finger off the damned trigger.

"I suggest we make tracks," said Tribe grimly. He sheathed his sword.

"But all those people—" said Massimo.

"You're planning a rescue operation?" Tribe snorted. "Very gallant."

Massimo's nostrils flared. "It's our jobs, man!"

Not my job, James thought. My job is to get back home.

"If you think your *jobs* amount to a peck of shit just now, you're fools! If you think you can actually make a difference for those people, you're *damned* fools. How long do you think we can linger here before they spot us?"

"What do we do?" James sounded whiny, desperate.

"I'd suggest leaving," Tribe snapped. "You two know this campus far better than I. How can we evade the Sicari?"

"They gotta have the campus surrounded by now!" said Massimo.

"No, no. They don't have anything like the manpower to be that ambitious."

"Who are these people?" James asked. "What in God's name is happening here?"

"No time for that now! Damn it, can you not listen!"

James and Massimo looked at each other.

"South?" James asked, thinking only of his family.

"Let's just get the fuck outta here, man."

Yes, south. Away from this senseless brutality. Yet at the same time, the idea of moving in that direction filled James's head with even greater, hammering pain.

They had to cross a broad open patch between the admin building and the Arts Center. For those few excruciating seconds, exposed to view, every footfall seemed nailed to the asphalt. The world had taken on a muted, brief quality. Dreamlike. James's stubborn migraine, the odor of burning books on his painted skin. They heard gunfire, but far distant, somewhere off campus. Everything seemed distant now, even his own shaking hands.

When they were on the south side of the Arts Center, they were hidden from the impromptu stockade on the bus roundabout. The sense of oppressive chase eased, but they remained watchful for black uniforms. Sticking to the line of pines along the south side of the Arts building, going single file towards the graduate student apartments.

Above, climbing into the far blue dome of the sky, the sun and its new companion, the bright silver arc light of Betelgeuse.

Protect them, James whispered. In case anybody was listening. Protect my family from harm.

They were almost at Keele Street, the eastern edge of the campus, in line with a small bush lot of trees just opposite the student apartments, when they heard a commotion behind them. A large throng of students with placards, marching from the apartment block towards the center of campus. Chanting and shouting, banging pots and pans, waving crudely lettered signs like strike pickets.

"*WE MARCH FOR PEACE! FUCK THE POLICE! WE MARCH FOR PEACE! FUCK THE POLICE!*"

Down with Police Brutality! declared one of the signs. Another: *WE DEMAND FREEDOM!*

"What on earth do they think they're doing?" said Tribe, shaking his head.

"Least they're doin' *something*," said Massimo.

"And what good will come of it, pray tell?"

A line of men appeared atop the admin building. Men in black. James saw them readying their weapons. "Look out!" he shouted, but the marching pickets were too boisterous. Flighty panic swirled in James's chest. Sure he was about to puke. The world shrinking away from him to a faint echo, dimly seen as from across eons. Still, James could pick out every tiny detail. One of the signs reading *Mine eyes hath seen the coming of Artur!* A black handprint on it. And yes! he could even see the smudged lifeline across the palm!

Northeast! Northeast you must go!

"What?" James asked. "What did you say?"

"I didn't say nothing." Massimo giving James a narrow, distrusting look.

Gunfire from the roof of the admin building, an echoing metallic clatter across the campus.

Northeast! I command you! Northeast!

Students screeching, falling. Their placards fluttering down. The throng scattered like a bottle of roaches dumped on a table. More gunmen appeared over a rise, giving chase with batons, hauling them down, furiously beating.

"Into the trees!" Tribe commanded, shoving James from behind. "Into the trees!"

Feeling himself shoved into the bush lot, pressed down into the moist fungal earth. Through the leafy screen, seeing fleeing students wrestled, struck down.

Then the leaves seemed to fold inward, swallowing him. Deep, deep, into unknowable black.

Chapter 5
The Pharmacy

James choked, rearing back as if a bucket of cold water had been flung into his face. Stumbling, falling hard on his side. He was on a wide suburban road, big box outlets on both sides.

"Whoa!" he heard someone shout. "Easy, buddy, easy."

Floating behind the road and the big box outlets – as if everything in front of him was reflected on glass – the swollen, asphyxiating face of the gunman with the crushed windpipe, eyes wide. Breath boiling, sucked through a water pipe. "*Heru, the Distant One, he who is called Kemwer, the Great Black One, bids you northeast! You must go northeast!*"

"Hey! Back the fuck off!" Massimo bawled, waving a gun at Allistair.

And a very tall, fierce man with a long goatee.

Reverberating gunfire, somewhere behind them. Close.

"We must get off the road," said the tall, fierce one. He was dressed in ratty sneakers, black track pants and a strange-looking loose black blouse. A widow's peak cleaved his high forehead, the long black hair swept back and hanging down to his shoulders. James noticed the long scabbard on his belt. Tribe. That's right, his name was Tribe.

"Must we?" Massimo indignant, the gun hopping frenetically from Tribe to Allistair, back to Tribe again.

"You don't need the fuckin' gun, pal." Allistair's improvised bandages were hanging off his face. Beneath, just a peek of his gashed, swollen cheek. "Let's get him to his feet, get the fuck out of here— "

"Hey!" Massimo barked. "Keep away!" And then, more quietly, in James's ear. "That you in there, buddy? Talk to me, man. Say something."

James opened his mouth to ask Massimo where the hell they were. His dry throat produced nothing but rough ribbitting. I sound like a bullfrog, he thought. It struck him as very funny, but still there was the horrible blare of that bubbling voice. The man he'd murdered, screaming—

"*Har-nedj-itef, avenger of Osiris, the One Who Cast Down Seth! Commands you to go northeast!*"

He lay back against gritty pavement. Warm and rough. The

petrified scales of a giant reptile.

"For Christ sake, let us help him!" Allistair pleaded.

"We need to get him off the street," Tribe insisted. "It's getting on to evening."

"Fuck you both!" Massimo grunted. "I'm in charge."

"Are you?" Tribe sounded amused.

"Fuckin' Beretta says so."

"Sir, I grow weary of your bullying. It is my sworn mission to protect the life of this man." James realized with a dull pang that Tribe was talking about him. "If you do not let me fulfill my mission—"

"Then what?" said Massimo. "Gonna pull out your big gay sword?"

Tribe smiled coldly. "This is why I object to firearms," he growled. "They turn men into gaping monkeys."

"Monkeys!" Massimo jumped to his feet. "You better shut the fuck up, man."

"Had I?" Tribe laughed.

"Simmer down, both of you," Allistair pleaded.

Massimo stalked forward until the gun was just a couple of inches from Tribe's nose and then an extraordinary thing happened. James only saw a flicker of Tribe's arm swinging up. Suddenly Massimo's gun hand was twisted away, so violently Massimo sucked painful air. The gun clattered to the pavement. With one hand, Tribe gripped Massimo in a wristlock; his other hand held a dagger against Massimo's Adam's apple.

"Anything else you'd like to add to the discussion?" Tribe's glib tone mocked him. "Before I insert my blade into your spinal column?"

"Fuck you!" Massimo hissed. But he was helpless. Completely at Tribe's mercy. "You were gonna do it, you would've done it by now."

Tribe raised an eyebrow. "True," he admitted, but he seemed impressed by Massimo's machismo. "Remember just one thing: I don't take orders from anybody."

He shoved Massimo backwards. Tribe was a good foot taller than Massimo, and the push sent him over on his ass. Very calmly, Tribe sheathed his weapon. Bent at the waist to pick up the gun. He held it out to Massimo, holding the barrel between two fingers. Like something dirty.

"If you point this infernal thing at me one more time, I'll take it from you again, along with your head."

Glaring black rage, Massimo got to his feet and snatched the gun.

"Tribe's right. We need to get off the street," Allistair twittered. He looked frightened.

"What do you say?" Tribe asked Massimo, who was still rubbing the spot under his chin where Tribe had pressed his dagger.

"You two assholes just go ahead and do whatever you want," he said, squinting into the sun. He offered James his hand. "C'mon, buddy. Let's get you up, on your feet." Carefully enunciating every syllable, the way some people talked to the mentally impaired.

As Massimo hauled him up, James saw a blue reflectorized road sign. Markham. Population 250,000. As far as he could see in both directions, streams of exhausted people shuffling along the attenuated road. Long lines of dead cars gleaming in the sun. Sitting right where they'd been when It happened. All these people, left stranded. It was like looking back in time to something epic. The exodus from Egypt.

His head hurt badly. His mouth, a foul gritty wound. At some point, they'd put a dirty tee-shirt on him. DON'T BLAME ME, it announced. I VOTED FOR OBAMA.

Behind them, the sun blasted its orange heat. Near evening, that's what Tribe had said. James turned to look, seeing again the hard glint of Betelgeuse suspended just above the horizon. The western horizon.

Only now it dawned on him what that blue road sign said. Markham! Hot fear squeezed his throat. Jesus H. Christ, what the fuck were they doing all the way out here?

Northeast! He commands that you go northeast!

He shook himself, tearing his arm out of Massimo's grip.

"Whoa, buddy!"

"Fuck whoa!" James rasped, voice as raw as his burning throat. "I need to – I need to— " He felt dizzy, extremely foggy. Even with a rough idea of west and east, he found it hard to concentrate, find the direction he needed to go. Stace and the girls! He needed to get back to them. So if west was behind him, then south would be—

Northeast!

"No!" James insisted. "I won't go north fucking east!"

"At least he's gone back to the Queen's own English!" James heard the mistrust in Allistair's merriment.

"Gotta get down into the city, back home..."

Finally it was Tribe who focused James. Stepping forward, grabbing him by the shoulders and cuffing him across the face.

"You're an asshole, you know that?" Massimo cried.

It wasn't a hard blow, just a stinging slap. Enough to make James draw a breath, come to. He stood bent at the waist, hands on his knees.

"I'm sorry, but you needed it," said Tribe.

"What the fuck are we doing out in fucking Markham?" James croaked.

"We followed *you* here!" Allistair screamed, bobbing up and down.

"Christ, it'll be days before I can get back to Stacy and the girls – they'll be frantic."

A few seconds of awkward silence. James straightening up, seeing all three of them exchanging knowing glances.

Another volley of gunfire made all of them jump. A way off to their left, they saw people scatter across a huge parking lot. Chased by a fat naked man with a shotgun. The gun barked as he fired again and again, dropping people on the pavement like tenpins.

"Holy shit!" Massimo choked.

"We need to get out of here!" Allistair screeched, still bobbing like a boxer.

"Come on," said Tribe.

They made for a big box Shopper's Drug Mart on the south side of the road. As they got closer they saw that the front windows had been smashed, shelves inside tipped over. The gaping space within was dark, the tangy odor of makeup and medicine. Tribe and Massimo went in first, to make sure they were alone. Then Allistair and James joined them, climbing carefully over toppled metal shelves. In the dim recess at the back of the store, they hunkered down behind the prescription counter, out of sight.

James was dismayed at the deep shame he felt, as if he was cheating on Stace. Walking even a few hundred yards south was enough to prompt accusation from the gurgling nightmarish voice: *Northeast! Northeast!*

He had to concentrate, focus on preventing himself from getting up and running east down the road. It was that hard.

"I'll tell ya one thing, Jimbo, you're a fuckin fast walker, pal. That forced march could've put a horse down." Allistair hissed as Tribe removed the dirty bandage. In the orange failing sunlight, the wound looked bad. Yawning, weepy.

"Markham," James wondered again. "Lord, that's got to be fifty clicks from the campus!"

"You were raving, speaking in tongues, pal! Your mate here even tried pointing his gun at your head – even that wasn't enough to stop you. Christ!" Allistair hissed as Tribe poured peroxide on the wound.

James turned to Massimo.

"I tried holding you down," he said, big shoulders rolling.

"You bit me!" He showed the crescent of bright pink teeth marks across the back of his hand.

"He kidnapped us!" Allistair pointed at Massimo.

"Will you sit still!" Tribe barked.

"Fuck you!" Massimo keened.

James held his head in his hands. All of them had gone mad. Yes, stir-fried frigging crazy!

Massimo hunkered down beside James. "Out near the student apartments, when we saw those kids with the signs and shit, I saw you were…you had this blank stare, and you looked…I don't know, you looked…crazy."

James did have a dim memory. Of feeling swallowed. Of soil and roots, a damp claustrophobic grave.

"Artur was right," said Massimo, as if hardly able to believe the words coming out of his mouth. "I thought he was whacked, but he saw it all coming!"

"Your crazy friend with the safety pins through his tits?" Allistair snickered. "Bollocks! Those fuckers weren't cops. They were looking for me! That dago fucker with the hair like one of the Bay City Rollers…" He touched his new bandage with ginger fingers. Tribe had managed to cover the wound without hiding his blood-soiled mouth.

"Nicolo Alvarro," said Tribe, as if tasting something very bitter. "Captain of the Sicari. Dr. Rivers, I suggest we start you on a round of antibiotics." Tribe started rooting through the mess left by looters.

"Yeah," said Massimo skeptically. "And how did you get away from them, then? Huh? If they were looking so hard?"

"You stupid bugger, I'd got half my face hidden behind a bandage!" Allistair's bitter laugh was underwritten by chilling mania.

"Yeah, okay." Massimo spat. "Alls I know is, you worked for that Lichboegh prick, just as much as that Alvarro."

"This is how it was, Jimbo—"

James was about to tell him he didn't give a damn how it was, but he realized it was as futile as trying to stop a moving train with a car. Energy surging around them, through them, conductive in the air.

"I'd gone back to my flat at the graduate students building. Thought maybe I could change the bandage, right? Then I heard the shooting and I knew I had to get out of there fast. So I'm legging it down the road and next thing I know I've got this fuckin' gorilla jumping out of the bushes with a gun on me!" He turned back to Massimo. "So, entertain us! How're you any better than those goons on campus, eh?"

"Hey, I got right on my side, buddy."

"*Right!*" Allistair cackled. "Oh, Jesus that's precious, pal! *Right!* You're a right wanker, I know that!"

"If you're not allergic to penicillin, take two of those now," said Tribe, tossing a big plastic bottle into Allistair's lap. The pills inside rattled like a maraca.

But Allistair ignored the medication. He got up, started rooting through collapsed display racks.

"It's all just as well," said Tribe, taking a seat on the floor. "Following James got us far from the campus, far from Alvarro's men."

Allistair came back with his arms spilling packs of new batteries, a box of aluminum foil and a bunch of other junk. "Okay!" He was wild-eyed. "Okay, okay, okay."

"What the fuck are you doing?" Massimo asked.

"I am about to prove that basic science hasn't failed," he boomed.

"Will you keep it down!" Tribe hissed.

Allistair's shaking hands tore open a pack of batteries, inserting them into a new flashlight. He flicked the switch. Nothing happened. "Right!" he panted. "Make yourself useful, simian!" Allistair tossed a pair of scissors and a ream of paper into Massimo's lap. "Cut me, say, two dozen paper discs – but make sure they're no bigger than quarters!"

Massimo shook his head. "What the fuck?"

"Just do it! You, mister blademan, I can't remember your name, you can do the same with the foil. But remember, you both – no bigger than quarters, right?"

They looked dumbfounded.

"Look, you want electric light? Do as your told!"

Tribe and Massimo got down to cutting.

Allistair scrounged for a small metal bowl. He poured in some white vinegar, slopping a good deal on the floor. "Okay," he kept whispering. "Okay, okay, okay." The intense mantric quality of his voice made James want to back as far away from him as he could.

Allistair caught James's quizzical look and cackled. "North fuckin' America!" he raved. "Every goddamn outlet has just what you need, when you need it, eh?" He dumped a handful of salt into the vinegar, stirring with his finger. The acrid scent of the vinegar was the smell of his psyche burning white-hot. Burning out. "You think I'm a fuckin' daftie, Jimbo! I can see it square on your pasty face! But you see, it's just simple science. What's salt?"

James could only blink.

"Come on, come on!"

"Sodium, right?" said Massimo.

"Five outta ten!" Allistair screeched.

"I'll tell you if you will please keep your voice down!" said Tribe. "Sodium chloride."

"Full fuckin' marks to the man with the phallic symbol! What I'm doing here is dissolving sodium chloride in an acidic solution. We're going to test our preconceptions in the *acid bath* of experience! How's that one, eh?" A frenetic birdsong of giggles burst from him. "The acid separates the sodium – which is a positive ion – from the chlorine, which is a negative ion. You got them paper discs done yet!"

"Hold on, hold on." Massimo concentrating on the circular cutting with the intensity of a ten-year old.

"I see what you're up to," said Tribe, still working on the aluminum. "The ions should create a mild electric current."

"Not just a gay blade after all, then!"

"Will you stop?"

Allistair ran to the plundered cash register at the front of the store and brought back two fistfuls of quarters. He soaked the paper discs in the vinegar solution, and started making a stack: a foil disc, a paper disc, and a coin. The stack continued, foil-paper-coin, foil-paper-coin. Allistair's hands shaking so badly he could hardly get it right.

When he'd stacked maybe twenty-five coins this way, he spread his hands like a cheap street corner busker. "Volta's original battery pile, you fuckin' twats!" he proclaimed. Then he suddenly clubbed the flashlight against the corner of the prescription counter, smashing the lens open. "Light bulb!" he cried. Then he rolled out two pieces of foil into thin wires. "Aye, okay, fucker, okay!" He touched one wire to the bottom of the stack, the other to the top, then both to the little light bulb.

Nothing happened.

James felt the room sag. The floor actually drooped like a trampoline mat. All of them had invested far too much in that tiny bulb. All of them, balefully staring at it in the failing light.

Hold on, James was about to cry, hold on, it's working, I see a glow – I see—

Then he saw it was only the last of the twilight gleaming on the bulb's surface. He felt sick.

Allistair scrubbed his scalp with his vinegar-soaked palms, teasing his hair into a tangled mess. "Should work!" he choked. "Fuckin' thing should fuckin' work. Basic physics," he giggled, bulging eyes fixed on the stack of coins and paper and foil. "Right?

Bloody basic. You can almost understand how an electromagnetic pulse could ruin batteries, fry electric motors, generators and all that, but shit, this is basic fuckin' *physics*! Positive ions to the cathode, negative ions to the anode, y'get electrons flowing, y'have fucking *electricity*!"

The frustration jolted from his body, scattering the battery pile across the tiles. His head slammed back against the wall. "Fuck!" he kept mumbling. "Fuck, fuck, fuck!"

"Easy," said Tribe.

"But that's just it! It's supposed to be easy! I mean, this whole process, electrolytes letting ions move about, Jesus Christ, it's how our nerves work! So fuck, how's it possible for all of us to be *alive*!"

For a long time they just sat, slumped on the floor of a Shopper's Drug Mart as the sun slipped away from them, the very end of the first day of a new world. One in which it was possible for their hearts to beat, their brains to think, all in the absence of electricity. James felt as if the inner surface of his body, his skull, had been scraped down with a scaling knife.

When the air had blued to gunmetal, Massimo was the first to stir. "I really need something to eat, I'm fuckin' starved." Vague in the gloom, he got up again and hopped over the counter. For a few minutes they listened to him rooting through the wrecked shelving and toppled merchandise. He came back with two big bottles of water, bags of chips, and boxes of granola bars.

All four of them ate and drank. Ravenous, James wolfed down half a box of the bars and a whole bottle of water himself. The last thing he'd eaten was half his ham sandwich the previous evening. Lord, it seemed a lot longer ago than that.

Soon it was getting dark enough that they couldn't see much. Allistair scrounged up a bottle of rubbing alcohol. He poured some into the bowl, carefully setting it alight with his lighter. "Thought this might come in handy," he said triumphantly. The fumes burned with a sluggish, blue flame. Just enough for them to see each other's tired faces.

The light seemed to give Allistair's heady emotions a jolt. For the next while, his mouth was an engine with no exhaust but words. "None of this should be possible," he was babbling, "none of it, but hey – when I was a kid they used to go on about how 'according to the laws of physics, bumblebees shouldn't be able to fly,' right? Wings're too narrow, right? Shouldn't be enough lift, okay? And I was always all, 'For Christ sake – they obviously *can* fly, can't they – there's all the evidence you need that the much-vaunted 'laws of physics' aren't what they're cracked up to be. But here we are:

shouldn't be possible, but it is..." On he want, on and on.

James wished Tribe's bandage had muffled Allistair's mouth after all.

A throaty, hungry howl echoed from outside. They all froze. Even Allistair shut his gob. The sound of running feet slapping across the parking lot, a voice screaming "*No, no, noooooo!*" Then silence again, punctuated only by the intermittent gunfire that had was already starting to seem commonplace.

James got up, feeling wobbly. Tribe and Massimo both jumped up like the place was one fire.

"Relax," he croaked. "Just need something for this throat."

"Lemme get it," said Massimo.

"Just sit down. I'm fine." But he felt about as far from fine as he ever had in his life.

He took Allistair's lighter and went out into the store. Dark now, the sun gone. The floor slippery with something slick. Liquid soap, the sharp aroma stinging his nose. Those helpful signs still dangled from the ceiling, waving in the unsteady light: Feminine needs. Colds/Flu. Pain Relief. But it took him some time to find what he needed. Aspirin. Cold medication. The whole time, hearing the other three speak in hushed voices.

"It's probable!" he heard Allistair's whispering frenzy. "The pulse that knocked the electricity out clearly had an effect on some people – makes sense, after all, like I say, the brain does work on electrical impulses."

"Made some of them fuckin' whacked, is what you're sayin'," said Massimo.

"I'm no expert," Tribe murmured. "But it seems to me he's suffering from a type of epilepsy. Going in and out of trances."

"Temporal lobe hallucinations?" Allistair squealed. "One way or another, he's fuckin' bonkers and I can't do another haul tomorrow. Wasn't for beefcake here putting his gun on me, I'd be dead, I'm tellin' you."

"So what're you sayin'?" Massimo asked.

"You gotta let us go."

"Speak for yourself," Tribe interrupted. "I have an obligation to fulfill."

"Aw, bollocks!"

"That man saved my life." Tribe's voice was heavy with emotion. "I'm honor-bound to return the favor."

"You'll be following a man with a spunk stain on the front of his trousers – on some kind of fuckin' dream quest! Prattling on in that gibberish he was shouting all fuckin' day! You really up for that kind of business?"

James smiled grimly. Why don't you take a glance in the mirror, Allistair? James had spent enough time with alcoholics and drug addicts in his life to recognize manic behavior.

As if sleepwalking, James made his way to the front of the store. Behind the check-out counter there was a phone on the wall. He lifted the receiver, but of course there was no dial tone. He punched the buttons, dialing his home number, hoping against hope. He put his forehead against the wall, still grasping the receiver, hearing nothing but the hollow squelch of the plastic cupped against his ear. Stacy, he thought. Stacy. Stay safe. I'm coming.

Then he went to the cold cabinet for another few bottles of water. Not at all cold anymore, but it would do. He took a few Gatorade bottles too. He felt as if his body had been saturated with dust.

He joined the others back behind the prescriptions counter, gulping down a couple of Aspirins and a Sinutab with a whole bottle of Gatorade.

"But you see how a star, even one so far away – I mean, I mean it's actually close in celestial terms, okay? Right in our backyard, you might say – but you see how it can affect the way we live, the way we act? I mean, every atom in your body was manufactured in a star. It's all about Betelgeuse, right, I mean it's undeniable— "

Finally, James had had enough. Enough to sink a container ship. "Allistair," he honked. His throat felt raw, aching. "Can't you please just shut the fuck up, for two goddamned minutes?"

Massimo smirked, nodding enthusiastically.

"Please, let us try to maintain some decorum," said Tribe.

"All – all…" James took a deep breath, then lowered his tone a few notches. "All I want to do is pick up a phone. And call my family. I need to hear their voices. Right now. Right fucking now."

"Chin up," said Tribe.

If it hadn't been for that damned sword, James would have booted him for saying that.

"Can you help me talk to my family, Allistair?"

"Nobody could help you with that," said Allistair. Pityingly, talking down to the defective.

"Then. Please. Just a few minutes of quiet. Is that too much to ask for?"

"We should sleep," said Tribe, perhaps trying to find a compromise.

"We need to keep watch," Massimo snapped, getting to his feet yet again. "I'll go first."

Allistair blew out the alcohol lamp. They lay on the floor of the Shopper's Drug Mart. Dropped into fitful, frightened sleep.

*

Despite his exhaustion, James fought against sleep. Terrified he would wake to find himself in some strange place, even further from home.

Northeast! Heru commands you!

He woke suddenly in the dark of night. Hearing a tapping noise. *Tap-tap, tap-tap, tap-tap, tap-tap.*

"Jenny," he moaned, still half-asleep. "Jenny, stop with the noise. Daddy's trying

to—"

Only then was he fully awake. Shivering, aching from hours on the unyielding floor. Very dark. What in God's name was that noise? *Tap-tap, tap-tap, tap-tap.* Joined now by a dissonant fluting. To his sleepy mind, it seemed a malevolent code. *Tap-tap, tap-tap, tap-tap.* Only when he felt a cold stir did he realize it was something in the store being wrestled by the black wind.

Outside, but very close, another jarring howl caromed through the night. Almost a laugh, a human voice brutalized by slavering madness.

James shivered violently. Deep inside, a firm tug. A force. Somewhere, far to the northeast, something pulling him. Compelling him towards it.

Don't get up, he begged himself. Resist. Forcing himself to remain on the floor took the same strength of will it had taken to move in the library against men with guns. More, even.

What was happening to him?

Unseen, blind in the blackness, James held his shaking hands together and prayed.

Chapter 6

Homeward

They were on the road again at dawn. Wary, on edge. But it was very quiet. Except for the distant cawing of crows. There were dozens of bodies strewn along the road. It occurred to James that the crows were celebrating. A carrion bonanza!

James's thighs and calves were sluggish with the deep-rooted ache of miles. Thought I felt old when I got out of bed yesterday, he thought. No, wait. That was *the day before* yesterday. He didn't know until now what old felt like. They headed south, back towards the city.

The wrong way, the wrong way!

An insistent force, as painful as his legs. A hidden tendon hooked into his ribs, connecting him to whatever thing beckoned far, far to the northeast. Pulling, stretching until it felt his lungs would be torn from his chest.

No, he kept thinking. No. I must see my family. I must see my family. The tuneless chant skipping like a scratched CD. Before long, his chapped lips were murmuring the words, over and over and over.

Massimo had filled a tote bag with more of the granola bars, chocolate bars, and bags of chips. He and Tribe ate as they walked. The thought of eating seemed as appealing to James as shoving one of those insipid bars up his ass. Allistair didn't eat anything, chain-smoking from the pocketfuls of cigarette packs he'd taken from the pharmacy.

"Fancy that," he said to nobody in particular, breathing smoke. "Haven't had a cigarette in years and years!"

It occurred to James that Allistair hadn't eaten last night, either. Too busy spewing shit. After Allistair's whining about being force-marched, James was tempted to ask him why he didn't just go ahead and fuck right off instead of joining them this morning.

The day was lightly overcast and humid, the sun dawning torrid red. A tropical sun, casting the glow of sweaty fever dreams. James kept looking to his left. Waiting to see Betelgeuse crawl over the eastern horizon. When it finally appeared, a hole punched through the high cloud into a nuclear furnace, Allistair clapped his hands and actually did a few skips along the sidewalk.

"You think it's bright now, Jimbo!" he sang in time with his skipping feet, "just wait until December! By then it'll be rising at night, see, and it'll be bright enough to cast a shadow!"

Nobody commented. The rhythmic chock and scrape of their feet a numbing cadence. They moved through a suburban housing development. Just a few years old, by the look of it. Dead quiet. Not a bird, not a chirrup of an insect.

"Look guys," said Massimo after a while. "I know I was being an asshole yesterday, okay? I was thinking about how the pulse or whatever coulda had some kinda...effect...I dunno. When it hit, I passed out for a while, but I'm not trying to make any excuses." He spoke haltingly, as if the words coming out of his mouth failed to meet the standard he'd rehearsed while he'd been on watch last night. "Anyway...uh, I apologize. Okay?"

"Apology accepted!" Tribe shouted, vigorously shaking his hand. "I admire a man who admits a fault. Shows character."

"Yeah, well..." Massimo held out his hand to Allistair too, but he refused to shake. "I don't blame you, buddy. It was wrong, what I did. I guess I was *freaking*, and then I saw you on campus, running away, and I thought..." He chuckled, shaking his head. "Jesus, I don't know what the fuck I was thinking."

"Look," Allistair snapped. "This isn't Oprah, alright? I'll just say 'apology accepted' and let's move on, shall we? Can I just ask a key question: Now what?"

"Well, you know, Jimmy's talk last night about his family, hit me pretty hard. Then I had a dream about my Ma, my Dad. I gotta get back home to them, see if they're okay. I can't frigging believe I wasn't, like, *running* to get back down there last night. So I was thinking. I'll stay with you guys until we're uptown, then I'll split, head west."

"That's all well and good for you lot," said Allistair, snide and self-pitying. "I don't see myself trotting off to Glasgow to have a head-to-head with my kith and kin."

"Hard to see how that's our fault," James remarked.

"Didn't say it was your fault, did I?"

"Seemed to be tossing the blame around pretty good last night."

"Now, now," said Tribe. "Where's this going to get us?"

"Why'd you set up your experiment or whatever over here, anyway?" Massimo asked. "Why didn't you just stay over there?"

"Because the prick who funded the project insisted I come to this godforsaken wasteland."

"Right, that Lichboegh asshole," Massimo mumbled, mouth full of sour cream and onion chips. "You worked for the guy. Tribe, you were tryin' to kill him. Fill us in, for fuck sake."

Massimo and James had been walking ahead of the other two on the sidewalk, looking back over their shoulders to carry on the conversation. Only now, it occurred to James that they didn't need to confine themselves to the sidewalk anymore. No danger now of being hit by a car. Pavlov's dogs, he thought, pulling Massimo onto the asphalt.

"Lichboegh first contacted me a few years back," Allistair began, "when I was doing postdoc research, developing my ideas for the neutrino observatory. Never with a hope in hell that I'd ever have enough dough to get it off the ground." Allistair's quick Alesse sneakers faltered, a scraping break in the rhythm. "Lichboegh knew this was going to happen."

"What do you mean, 'he knew'?" Tribe asked.

"What the fuck d'you think I mean, pal? He knew the lights were gonna go out. Or at least, that something was coming."

"How can that be?"

"It's that Hermes, ugh…" Allistair couldn't even say his name without shuddering. "He's the one that warned him."

James remembered the macabre, gleeful grin on Hermes's pudding white face, popping around the corner of the physical sciences building: *Toodle-do!* The quick wiggle of fat fingers. Those hideous white eyes. James's turn to shiver, feeling sicker than ever.

"About him I know next to nothing," said Tribe. "Except that he is a nut."

"Oh aye, he's about the biggest of the lot, my friend, and I'll tell you that for nothing."

"What's with the red robes" Massimo asked.

"Ach, he's got a whole gang of them, all dressed the same way. Hermes calls them his 'Collegians.' Can't understand why Lichboegh hangs around with that creep. Lichboegh's far from stupid, I'll say that for the fucker. He's a member of Mensa, and all!"

"Mensa, *please*," said James in his sandpaper voice. "My mother's in Mensa, and she's never done much of anything."

"So you think Hermes predicted the lights going out?" Tribe asked.

"All I'm sayin' is, Lichboegh *knew* something was coming," said Allistair. "This was five years ago, when he first approached me. I was doing post-doc work at Oxford, and he'd read some of the stuff I'd published. He told me he knew something was gonna happen. He told me my research might be able to prevent it. He said he didn't know exactly what form it would take, or when it'd be, but that when this event happened, it would be catastrophic."

"Yeah, well, no kidding, he got that part right," said Massimo.

"So I asked him, right, 'How the fuck can you know all this?' He just out and told me, Hermes predicted it. He said Hermes had told him that whatever event it was, it would have something to do with neutrinos. I mean, Christ, how could I resist an offer like that? The deal was, whenever I came up with any unusual results, I was to contact him. Immediately. Lichboegh stressed that, over and fuckin' over. Immediately."

"Lichboegh was ready," Massimo grunted. "No doubt about it. He was prepared, the horses, that fencing. I bet my dick on it."

"Not much of a bet," said James, and Massimo punched his shoulder.

"It didn't occur that he might be using you?" Tribe asked.

"Naw," Allistair shrugged. "It didn't. All I wanted was money for my research."

"He lured you by letting you think you could help avert a disaster," said James.

"Perhaps."

"Perhaps, my ass, Allistair. Open your frigging eyes!"

"Ah, they're open, Jimbo, they're wide open! Lichboegh with his compound downtown, that private security squad he had set up. What is it they call themselves?"

"The Sicari," Tribe answered.

"What the fuck is that supposed to mean?" Massimo asked.

"It's a bastardization of the term 'Sicarii' which comes from a Greek word meaning 'dagger men.' Historically, they were members of a radical Hebrew sect who dedicated themselves to assassinating collaborators during the Roman occupation. But Nicolo Alvarro knows nothing of history. He was an amateur entomologist, and was especially interested in a family of spiders called the Sicariidae, apparently well-known for venom which rots the flesh. Particularly apt, considering Alvarro's toxic personality."

"I met that Alvarro twat when Lichboegh took me on a tour of his compound downtown," said Allistair. "They had enough firepower to take over a small country. Soon as I saw what he was up to, I knew – no way was I gonna give them the goods! Then, when Chen and I started detecting that massive neutrino stream – well, it was obvious that he only wanted me for a wee bit of advance warning, like. So I thought, fuck him! So I didn't call. Fucker, showing up on campus the very night of! What do you think of that!"

"I think, Dr. Rivers, that he no longer required your services!" Tribe chuckled coldly. "I'd been tracking Lichboegh's movements for months. His trip to the campus that night was absolutely a diversion from the routine. I can't tell you why they were there, but I can tell you that it was a sudden but well-organized excursion. Perhaps he had more advanced, detailed warning of what was coming than he let on."

"If that's the case, then why spend all the dough to set me up with the observatory?"

"An unanswerable question at the moment. Lichboegh's got more money than God," Tribe remarked. "What did he spend on your project? Tens of millions? For him, that would be of little consequence. Anyway, all this talk of predicting the future is probably bunk. I wouldn't give that Hermes any credit at all."

"So them being on campus was just a coincidence?" Massimo stated. "I don't think so."

"When I was a kid," said James, "there was a woman who lived around the corner, Mrs. Gritzner. She used to say that coincidences are God's way of letting us hear his voice."

"Easy enough if you believe in God," Allistair scoffed.

"You don't?" Tribe asked.

"You do?"

"I'd say I'm…hesitant, to think that all this is simply a random jumble."

"Einstein once said that God doesn't play dice. Meaning that the universe plays according to certain rules. That it's all ordered in some way. He was dead wrong, and he admitted it later on. Said that it was the biggest mistake of his career. What about you, Jimbo? Are you a true believer, then?" Allistair's tone was jarring.

"I believe in a creative force. Nothing like the damning, vengeful old asshole in the Old Testament. But something."

"Jesus, it's like being back in the Dark Ages, listening to the two of you!" Allistair shook his head.

"Tell me, Dr. Rivers," said Tribe. "Aren't we in a dark age? Hasn't God – *a* god, *the* gods, whatever one happens to believe – hasn't he/she/it cast the die?"

"What – and it came up AD 1200?" Allistair joked. "I don't think so, pal."

Thinking of the Dark Ages stirred something deep, deep in James's memory. A certainty. That glowing ball between Hermes's hands. Only the most recent manifestation of something very ancient. It was like remembering an event that had happened millennia before his own birth. "That Hermes dude, he sees himself as some kind of alchemist," said James. Suddenly, he'd been certain of this. Struck by the granitic truth of it.

"Quite the non sequitur," said Allistair. "Y'mean like alembics and secret codes and turning lead into gold?"

"Uh, yeah, that's what's usually meant by alchemy." James paused, wondering whether to go on. Against his own better judgment, he took a deep breath and told them about Hermes's glowing ball.

"No way," Massimo dismissed.

"A cheap illusion, James!" Tribe snapped.

"I'm only telling you what I saw."

"I'm telling *you*, you fell for a conjurer's trick," Tribe insisted.

"I was right there too, buddy," said Massimo. "I didn't see nothing."

"You were too busy thumping your chest."

Allistair snickered at that one. "You probably had some kind of hallucination, Jimbo. Makes sense, when you think about everything else that's happened, and all."

"The alchemists were very strong believers in the influence of heavenly bodies on their work," said Tribe.

"Tripe!" Allistair sneered. "When Lichboegh and Hermes came to see me at Oxford, Hermes went on and on about the heavens: the heavens this, the heavens that. What a load of crap!"

"I'm very surprised to hear you say that," said Tribe quietly. "Here we are, clearly under the direct influence of a distant star." His elegant hand indicated Betelgeuse.

"Ah, but that's different," Allistair responded. "That's physics, plain and simple."

"I don't think so," said James. "I think if you had to define anything as alchemy, this would be it."

Even Allistair seemed struck by this. For a long time, they walked in silence.

More and more people crowded the road. Refugees promenading down a midway at the carnival of the damned. The lost, the lame. They started seeing people emerging from their front doors. Angry and confused, watching them with feral suspicion.

"Hey!" a middle-aged man in an undershirt yelled at them from his front porch. "You know what the hell's going on?" Silence. "Can somebody please tell me what the hell's going on?" The strident helplessness echoing down the street.

They kept moving through miles and miles of suburbs. Endless strip malls and gas stations, blank, numb and empty. Almost every store they saw had been looted, vandalized. Around midmorning they heard the first gunfire of the day. Then, the first screaming. The mad wailing of the insane. James wincing as if he'd had an ice cube dropped into his underwear. Massimo took the gun out of his waistband. Tribe's hand fell onto the hilt of his sword, sharp eyes watchful. Pregnant expectation charged the air. Any minute, the gunfire they heard could pour deadly fast and accurate onto this road.

It bothered James that he couldn't check the time. He kept looking at his watch, kept telling himself to stop. He noticed Massimo doing the same thing. There was no way of knowing what kind of progress they were making. He saw the sun, he saw Betelgeuse crawling west. Hours? Minutes? Like a kind of blindness. Like they'd been waylaid and let loose in a strange wilderness. Still, the maddening tic continued, his right wrist rising, his eyes looking downwards, only to see the black watch face, only to remind himself of a habitual need that would not be fulfilled.

They came to an area that had been burned out. For a long time they walked through incinerated city blocks. Block after block, nothing but jagged charcoaled ruins, spuming smoke the color of dirty March snow. Whipped by the whistling wind into frantic snakes, slithering along the litter-choked pavement. Difficult to breathe. Filthy ash, caustic and dry, stinging the nose, coating the throat. They tore strips of fabric off cheap dresses they found flapping in a smashed shop window. James thinking, Lord now we're looters too. They wrapped their faces like bandits. Joining the trudging throngs of ash clotted refugees, masked and hidden.

*

The hike into the downtown core was a jilted rockslide of vivid images. The hulking tailfins of an airliner protruding from a wrecked apartment building. An office block with its top half smashed away, looking like a great broken tooth. The interiors of stores, of all buildings, like festering dark sores eating into blank, staring faces.

Looters, crowds of them, crawling out of shattered shop fronts. Lazy, leisured. Taking their sweetass time. A languid Asian man straining under a heap of clothes. Another guy, face as pink as a fresh burn scar, turning to leer at them, plasma screen TV under one arm and a Blu-ray player under another. All of them eerily calm. Sleepy as the blown ash.

"Good luck getting that shit to work now," Massimo remarked, nodding at the guy with the TV.

"You never know," Allistair piped up. "Get the scientists, the technicians and engineers to work, and all this could be temporary. Replace the coils and magnets in yer power generators, your electric motors, and you'd be tickety-boo!"

"What about your little battery experiment?" James's voice biting.

Allistair snickered. "Following Jimbo's cheery attitude, it could be even worse! The earth's magnetic field creates the Van Allen Belts, which protect us from the worst of the sun's radiation. So if the earth's magnetic field is blown – if I had a fuckin' compass I could tell you for sure – but if that's the case, then the Van Allen Belts have gone bye-bye! Could be by the time Betelgeuse is rising at night, Jimbo, we'll all be fried!"

"Great," Massimo moaned. "Just fuckin' great."

They saw a mob clustered around the base of a lamppost, chanting "Jump! Jump! JUMP!" Perched atop the light stanchion, a naked man, arms outstretched in exaltation, head back. A new idol for the new age.

Spears of shattered glass everywhere, jagged razor edges throwing back sunlight in hard silver veins. The squeaking crunch underfoot. Crystalline, purely cruel. One slip, one fall into those waiting fangs and they would slice to the bone.

An older woman dashed out of the crowd, grabbing Massimo by the shoulders, shaking him. "Do something!" she screamed in his face. "Why don't you people do something about this?"

You people. A profound realization struck James: Massimo was still in his GSS uniform. The man who'd called to them from his front porch, the looter with the pilfered gear who'd gaped back at Massimo with a 'come get me' grin, this woman – they all saw the uniform as an emblem.

"Leave him alone," James told the old woman. "He's not a cop."

"Not any more!" Her face contorted with disgust. She pushed off Massimo and disappeared back into the crowd.

Faces like hers would fill James's dreams, fuel his nightmares for the rest of his life. Faces stretched taut, the wrinkled half-smiles of miserable anguish. Hunched ghosts, creeping raggedly through the rolling smoke. The looted, the stranded, the grieving. A middle-aged woman in a burned housecoat, her light brown hair hanging in greasy wings. Her face a quaking tight-lipped grimace.

In many intersections, stacks of burning tires blackened the air. Abandoned barricades belching soot. Overturned cars and trucks, the first wave of dead behemoths in a mass extinction.

Popping, crackling gunfire chased the sounds of shattering glass, crumpling metal. People scattering, screaming frantically. They ran too, slipping on glass. A man in a tight t-shirt, gripping a handgun, jiggling into the street. The t-shirt too small for the bulging beer belly that peaked out beneath. Screaming, rabid-eyed. He gunned down a man who'd been walking right in front of them, blasted him with bullet after bullet, screaming "You ain't getting' nothin'! You bin bad! You ain't gettin' nothin'! You bin bad! Bad bad bad BAD!" He squeezed the trigger until the gun was empty, stumbling away sobbing like a child. The moniker on the t-shirt screeching in big red letters, flash-burned onto James's mind: YES! I GAVE AT THE OFFICE! The gunman did not even seem to notice his own bare feet, clumps of bloody-wet hamburger, shredded by the broken glass.

*

They reached uptown by about midday. "Well..." said Massimo, shuffling his feet as if unwilling to stop his progress south. "I guess I gotta be going."

Massimo offered his hand, but James hugged him, feeling close to tears. "You take care, you fucking gorilla." He didn't want to see Massimo go – right now, he was the only face both familiar and friendly.

"Hey – when all this shit clears up, come and see me. You been to my house before. Ma, she'll fry us some fatina." Massimo, trying to put on a brave face, but James could tell he had serious misgivings about setting off on his own. About the probability of anything clearing up any time soon.

After he'd shaken hands all around – even Allistair took his hand this time – Massimo headed west down Lawrence Avenue. They stood and watched until he was just a small figure, lost in a river of small figures, flowing past islands of glinting dead cars.

*

Their progress south was hindered by the growing maelstrom of mob violence. Rampaging crowds charged the streets. Armed with bats, knives, lumber. Chanting, baying like soccer hooligans. Time and again, they'd jog down a side street to avoid them, only to find themselves halted again by gunfire or heaps of smoldering rubble.

It also became clear that the violence was not simply the result of madness. That well-armed street gangs were taking the opportunity to war over disputed territory. Two or three times, James heard bullets part the air next to his face, the drone of enormous hornets.

The hellish maze of the smoking inner city turned them around until it became difficult to know the right direction. Street signs had been knocked down, familiar landmarks destroyed. James kept looking for the office towers of the downtown core, knowing at least that they lay to the west. But it was not always easy to see them through the blowing thunderheads of ash and smoke.

Finally, by late afternoon they were spent, their brains fried. Squatting with several others in an alleyway among bloated bags of garbage as a gun battle raged in the street. Over their heads, bricks pecked to red dust by smacking bullets.

"If we stay out here, one of us will be hit eventually," said Tribe, wide-eyed, breathing hard.

"We need shelter!" screeched a woman in a torn blue evening dress.

"I've gotta get home!" James yelled.

"Tribe's right," said Allistair. "This is crazy!"

"We're so close now – I can't spend another night without seeing them!"

Tribe snatched James's wrist and squeezed until it hurt. "Think man! Will you be any help to them with a bullet through your head?"

James struggled to breathe. As if it was something he needed to relearn after head trauma. Poor Jenny and Sara! They'd be frantic with this noise, terrified. Please, he pleaded in his mind. Please, just let them be alright.

Sensed dimly through his panic, a presence. An invisible companion he was only just beginning to sense.

Northeast! it whispered urgently. Yes, just a whisper now. Changing tack. Resigned to James's need to get back home. Then something else: information! James shook his head, unable at first to understand what he was being bidden to do.

They spied jagged silhouettes scrambling down the street, chasing each other through firecracker muzzle flashes.

Then James understood. "Hey Tribe," he said. "There's an outfitting place just around the corner!"

"Best idea I've heard in days!" said Tribe.

"Right," said Allistair. "Trouble is, getting there!"

"Lead us on!" Tribe gave James a nudge.

Growing dark, the air in the closed dim of the steep urban canyon thick with smoke, the fume of burning plastic. The gunfire had moved off north, fading to stuttering thuds, dim flashes in the twilight. Quickly, they crossed the street, dodging wrecked cars and chunks of looting debris. Eyes wide, wary.

They crept a few blocks eastward before more fighters spilled into the street, blocking their way. Exposed by the dying flames of a burning panel van, they hunkered down again between two cars in a parking lot.

James felt so alert, so alive. The terror galvanizing him. Every tiny detail traced intricately for his eyes in the gloom. A silvered hole in the metal skin of a Toyota. *Hey, my Lord, that's a* bullet *hole I'm looking at right now!* Chest bursting with the exhilaration of it.

Then a huge explosion. A heavy BOOM! that made James's ears pop. The whole street shook around them.

"What the hell was that?" Allistair wailed.

"Fuel truck?" said Tribe, shaken. "Maybe a gas leak."

Suddenly through the intersection up the street, a great mass of roiling dust burst into the open. A coiling worm rushing down the street for them.

"Run!" gasped the woman in the blue dress.

It overcame them, a blinding pyroclast. Smothering everything in a blanket of thick grey dust. James tripped, sprawling into it, fingers closing on powder, talc-fine. Around the corner they saw a building had collapsed, a mountain of concrete rubble spewed over the street.

Dusty myopia. The arid smell of it caked in their noses. Voices echoing in the gloom. Guttural. Growling.

Hacking in the dust, they followed James a few blocks south, to the Outward Bound store. Like everywhere else, stricken by the looting disease. But it didn't take them long to find candles.

James took the opportunity to wash up in the public washroom. When he turned on the tap, only a feeble coughing trickle leaked out. But there were gallons and gallons in the hot water tank. Still warm too. He filled a billycan from the spigot at the bottom of the tank. It felt so good to finally scrub the bizarre, jagged hieroglyphs off his skin. To smell of soap instead of ashes and sweat. In the candlelight, he examined the scabby bruise that the Ox's Blackberry had left on his cheekbone. Still very sore, but it didn't look infected.

He only wished he'd thought to pick up some razors at the pharmacy. His stubble was getting prickly. Toothpaste, too, that would have been wise. A toothbrush. Good hard soap instead of this perfumed treacle. Deodorant. But he had not thought of those things. Things that in his home had just jumped to hand. Entitlements. So customary, they'd become invisible.

If wishes were horses, beggars would ride. Yes, Maggie, and thanks so much for the insight. Wishes now mute, stolen from his mouth, his mind.

By candlelight, James found trousers and a long-sleeved shirt. Nerves still jagged, he felt giddy and silly. The click of hangers as he ripped off various pieces of clothing sounding ridiculously jubilant. This was home territory for him. His turf. His very own spree.

The woman in the blue dress eyed them, arms crossed. "But that's stealing!"

Tribe shook his head. "We've got a long way to go to get out of this hellhole – on foot. We need to be ready. If, as Dr. Rivers suggested, there is any hope in hell that the power comes back on and everything goes back to 'normal' – whatever that is – I give you my word of honor that I will reimburse this store for all items we take." He went back into the washroom to change. When James followed him, Tribe disappeared into one of the stalls. Oddly bashful, it seemed, about showing his bare body.

They bedded down in a storage room at the back of the store, away from the street. The woman in the gown had glared at them for the gear they took, but James noted she was more than happy to use a padded groundsheet. They were joined by a small withdrawn man with a sharp nose and a Beatle mop.

Metal shelves stacked with rolls of toilet paper, big wheels of refills for hand towel dispensers. Jugs of the liquid soap James had used to bathe. It was dark, the window above their heads admitting only a dribble of late evening. Allistair pulled out his impromptu lamp and lit it. The smell of rubbing alcohol seemed oddly comforting.

There were truncated introductions. The woman's name was Ann. The solemn guy mumbled that his was Bob. News was passed around, dealt out like comforting pills. Soma, James thought bitterly. Transitory, empty.

Ann had heard something about a bomb going off in the west end. Someone had told her there were soldiers with working vehicles moving out of the Downsview air force base. "It's being solved," she said. Definitively. As if the scenario had been written into eternal law. The Word made hopeful.

James didn't say anything, didn't want to shatter her hope, but the Downsview air base was just south of the York campus and he knew that it had been shut down over a decade ago.

"It's being solved," she said again with gritty determination, casting a jaundiced eye at the window. "Those bastards, the gangbangers – their time'll come. In a way, this is just what we needed."

"How do you mean?" Tribe asked.

Ann smiled edgily. "You don't need a PhD in social work to see what those people need. Now that they've had their – their little moment... the right people will see what needs to be done."

Allistair popped a couple of penicillin capsules in his mouth, tossed them back with a swallow of bottled juice. "Bullets all around, eh?" Then he pulled out a crumpled pack of cigarettes.

Ann nodded grimly, completely missing his sarcasm.

A dirty face appeared in the doorway behind them. Licked by the flickering blue light of Allistair's lamp. Weak-chinned, flaccid and sweaty.

"What do you want?" Tribe bellowed. James jumped.

"Oh please – oh please don't hurt me – puh-please…" A pudgy shape in Bermuda shorts, awkwardly full.

"That doesn't answer my question," said Tribe.

"I just need – please, puh-lease don't hurt me – can I just come in for the night, I won't even take up that much room…"

"Get inside before somebody sees you!" Allistair pleaded.

"Not advisable," Tribe grumbled.

"We can't very well say no, Tribe," said James. "We've got room."

"Do we?" said Ann.

The stranger shuffled in before any formal invitation. "Oh, thanks – thank you, so much, thank—"

"Just sit down and shut up," Allistair ordered.

"Allistair!" James's voice broke like an adolescent's. "I'm James," he warbled to the new guy.

"Walter," said the visitor, standing stiffly to one side. He was badly pigeon toed. He wore thick glasses.

"Sit down," said Allistair again, this time more politely.

The street actually grew quiet for a while. A windless evening. Thrashing silence, loud with petty noises. James heard the arthritic creak of the building, sounding so much like creeping footsteps. The icy clink of Tribe's sword as he unhooked the scabbard from his belt.

Quiet enough that when Walter spoke again, James shivered.

"Can I – can I buh-borrow one of them?" Walter asked, indicating their stash of granola bars with a shaking finger.

"No," Allistair snapped.

So James tossed him one. Walter offered profuse, stuttering thanks.

James took one too. Lost himself in the dry crunch between his molars. The way he could hear his own tongue squirming inside his head, a parasitic worm. Every digestive little smack. He felt like he was only now becoming aware of his own reality as a living being. Excreting, ingesting, a pulsing fluid sack. His mind incarcerated within the meat of another organism. When he put a potato chip in his mouth, his lips sounded like those of a nursing infant. Gentle puckering. He felt displaced, disconnected.

"I feel bizarre," he said faintly. "These – these episodes I've been having. Maybe it's PTSD…"

"Easy," said Tribe. "Easy now."

The accusatory look on Ann's face would have been comic under better circumstances. Looking at James as if he'd just turned into a huge insect.

"Jimbo," Allistair lectured, still high. "The PT in PTSD stands for 'post-traumatic,' yeah? Far as I can see, the trauma seems a wee bit current to be labeled post!"

"Am I losing my mind?"

Allistair snickered cruelly. The sound of February ice being chipped off a windshield. "I'll help you look for it if you want!"

*

James started, sucked in a sharp breath through his nose. He'd been dozing.

Allistair was back at it, insisting that there still might be a way of fixing things, getting everything back to normal. Ann, nodding enthusiastically, providing just the fuel Allistair needed.

Bob stood alone in a corner, one hand braced against the wall over his head, idly nudging a custodian's wheeled mop pail with the toe of his Birkenstock.

Then Walter spoke up. "Hey, you're Iranian, ain't you?" he asked in a very personable way, looking straight at Allistair.

Allistair blinked, perhaps not comprehending. "I'm Scottish, pal," he said in a tone that said everything there was to say about Walter's intelligence. James thought he even thickened his accent a little. The prig.

"Nah, nah," said Walter, grinning excitedly. "You're Iranian. I – I recognize the accent just fine, sure do." He wobbled back and forth on his generous butt like he was finding a comfortable spot on the rug for his favorite TV show.

Allistair and James looked at each other. James shrugged. He hoped as a signal for Allistair to just let it go.

"Yeah, alright, you daftie," said Allistair, waving Walter down.

"Teach me how to say something in Persian?" Walter pleaded.

Allistair was laughing now. "What word shall I teach you, then?"

"Nah, nah, not a word – a sentence!" Walter clapped quickly. "Oh, I know, I know – teach me to say 'I'm Walter, how'dyou do?'"

"Ish-ta-bish," began Allistair, laughing so hard he could barely get the syllables out. "Walter."

"Ish – ta – bish…" said Walter. "Walter."

"Tosh-to-tish?"

"Tosh – to – tish? Like that, like you're asking a question?"

"Right," Allistair choked out, "yeah."

"Ish-ta-bish, Walter, tosh-to-tish?" Walter sang it like do-re-me. He even managed to replicate the Scottish accent. "Far out, that's cool. Hey – what do you think of that Ahmedinejad fella?"

"Well, it just so happens I'm a member of his personal bodyguar – " Allistair never finished the final word.

Walter leaped at him, plunging a kitchen knife into Allistair's chest over and over. "This is what I think!" he screamed. Even much later, the sound of the knife would haunt James, make him wince just at the memory – he'd hear it again and again, the wet sickly *chok!* of the blade thumping through Allistair's ribs.

Allistair was bowled over, Walter on top of him, the knife pistoning. "*ISH-TA-BISH TOSH-TO-TISH!*" Walter screamed frantically, teeth bared. "*ISHTABISHTOSHTOTISH!*" His glasses flew off in the frenzy. Allistair's drumming fists against Walter's face. Blood flew, spattering thick.

Walter's foot kicked over Allistair's little alcohol lamp, splashing liquid fire across the floor.

Tribe stabbed his dagger straight into the back of Walter's neck. Walter fell, instantly dead. But twitching.

Bob was screaming, James was screaming. Ann scrambled to her feet and was gone.

Tribe pulled the corpse off Allistair.

Allistair's eyes were already flat, unfocused. A wet rattle pushed a plume of blood out of his mouth, painting his bandaged face. That was it. Allistair was dead.

Tribe tipped back on his haunches, sitting on Allistair's legs. Aghast. James remained frozen, gaping horrified at the corpse. Gouts of blood, thick glistening blackstrap splattered over everything. A fat coppery archipelago.

James couldn't breathe – he couldn't breathe—

He turned away quickly and puked in the corner.

Tribe frantically stamped at the flames, finally dumping a bottle of energy drink. It diluted the alcohol, and the room went dark.

James held Allistair's limp hand for a few seconds. Still warm. Tried to remember the Allistair he'd spent his breaks with. Who'd made him laugh out loud with his pithy droll commentaries on the state of the world. Or his monologues on the cultural significance of the Beatles song "Love to You." He wept.

"Let's go," said Tribe quietly after a while.

"We can't just leave him," said James.

"What do you suggest, a burial?"

Awkwardly, James folded the limp hands over Allistair's bloody chest. They vacated the supply room. Made sure the door was closed behind them. Chose a new spot at the rear of the store, shielded behind a canoe propped on its side. A night spent on ground sheets. Good ones, the kind that inflate automatically when the valve is unscrewed. After two nights on the ground or hard tiles, they seemed luxurious.

But James couldn't sleep. For hours he lay still, every speck of sound in the night warning his humming brain. Sensing Tribe and Bob were awake as well. Allistair, restless. Accusing. James had insisted on allowing Walter in. Pure truth. "I won't take the fall for that," he whispered into the mute dark. A feeble exorcism.

Already he'd seen enough to know. Enough death. Your time came, and that was it.

He made sure they were up, packed and gone long before the sun peaked down the street. The problem was finding the right gear in the wreckage. But it was all there for the taking. Numb, swollen with fatigue in the grey dawn, he and Tribe picked through all the gear they could think to grab. Packs, spare clothes and footwear, a camp stove. A two-man pup tent. They wouldn't need sleeping bags in the heat, but they took them for the journey. Mummy bags rated for arctic cold, neatly tucked away into light sacks no bigger than hand muffs. Best of all, they filled their packs with lots of foil-packed pre-cooked camp meals. Just snip, heat and serve!

Last, before they left, James went back to the supply room. One last good-bye for poor Allistair. The corpse was stiff and cold. The dozy expression waxed onto a face no longer Allistair's. The odor of shit. A vessel emptied, spent. James backed from the room, softly closing the door on his friend's tawdry tomb, shared with his murderer.

*

"Dr. Rivers was right," Tribe muttered soon after they'd left Outward Bound. He was staring at his newly pilfered compass. "It's useless!"

James looked at his own compass. He was walking as fast as he could, almost trotting, frantic to get home. The jerk of his legs made the compass needle rock lazily back and forth, indicating nothing. "Could just be the magnet inside the compass," he said. "It doesn't necessarily mean the earth's magnetic field is gone."

"It's gone," Bob confirmed sadly, shoulders hunched in

resignation under the straps of his pack. "We'll be roasted by solar radiation, just like that guy said!"

"Stop it, just stop it!" Tribe snapped. "Your insipid bleating will do more to doom us than anything else!"

Who cares, James thought, tossing away the obstinate compass. Just let me get home to my family. Everything else follows from that.

Outward Bound was no more than a half-hour walk from home. A couple of birthdays back, Stacy's folks had sent him a hundred-dollar gift certificate from that store. He remembered he and Stacy taking the girls in two strollers, enjoying the bracing Autumn air. A leisurely Sunday afternoon, golden, somehow warm and chilly at once. The city filled with clean, breezy light. Shopping for anything but groceries was a rare treat for them, so they'd spent an hour browsing, checking out all the cool gear the gift certificate brought into buying range, but he'd never be able to use most of it. When Jenny had gotten cranky and weepy with boredom, he'd settled on a mid-range Spring-Autumn anorak. It still hung in the bedroom closet, a pale cousin to the shit-hot foul weather hiking smock he'd rolled into his pack this morning. He couldn't wait to show it off to them.

He'd throw open the door and Stacy would fall gratefully, tearfully into his arms, the girls grasping his legs, chanting "Da-dee, da-dee, da-dee!" Then he'd introduce Tribe, and what a guest he'd make!

"Hey!" Bob squealed as they scrambled over a pile of rubble. "Wait up! What's the rush?"

Every step honed James's anticipation to a keener point. Prodding his back like Tribe's sword, urging him onward, faster, faster.

The debris-choked streets slowed them down, but there was very little gun fighting. Tribe attributed the lull to hunger.

"They've started to realize they need food more than they need to kill each other," he said.

Still early morning, they'd reached the Corktown neighborhood. The solid familiarity of shop windows and parks James saw every day thrilled his pounding blood. It seemed he hadn't been on these streets in months and months. He felt like an ecstatic tour guide, pointing out the corner store where they bought their paper towels, the park where Jenny liked the monkey bars best.

Then they turned onto Sackville Street. Turned north, past the beer store on the left, the big brick animal shelter on the right. The squalid stink of fetid ash. The fires had spread voraciously here, engorged on the tinder-dry lumber of century-old homes and buildings.

Stunning to see nothing for hundreds of yards north, west, and east. Nothing but black-heaped, smoking ruin. The noxious smoke brilliant in the rising sun. Incinerated desolation toying cruelly with James's memory. The destruction so complete he had trouble even locating his own street.

This city had been destroyed by fire before, in 1904. A time when electricity had still been an amusing novelty. Streets reverting now to early recollections of those flame-cracked bricks, those rubble-choked sidewalks.

Tripping like a drunkard, James unable to see the sidewalks or the pavement. The humped backs of cars in the wreckage like newly disinterred archaeological remains. Dumbfounded, finally seeing there was no house to host his grand homecoming.

James spied the blackened edge of the concrete foundation, the serpentine crack in the corner he saw when he returned from work every morning. His only certainty that this wreckage had been his home. The crack had been just left of the porch steps. The porch now a heap.

He fell to his knees. Felt the warm gravelly cinders through his new hiking pants. The remains of every house on the street, nothing but pits choked with charred debris. Bathtubs and smashed toilets peeking through, whiter than lost teeth.

His chest dissolved in heaving sobs. Crouched in the ashes on his knees, curled tight, feeling the gray powder leaking through his clenched fists. All he smelled was burned, cremated, pulverized. His tears sucked into the dryness, disappearing as tiny empty craters in the ash.

*

Tribe stepped up behind him, knelt down with a hand on his shoulder. "Don't assume the worst, James. Your family most likely escaped."

"So they're refugees – like the rest of the people we've seen? Is that supposed to make me feel any better?"

"Don't give up hope." It was Bob, standing behind Tribe "It's all you got."

James was on his feet, on Bob, shouting obscenities, throwing wild punches at his stupid glum face. Bob was a small weakling. Easy pickings. James felt ridiculous satisfaction dropping him into the swirling dust.

Tribe pulled him off. Faced him down, eyes wild with fury.

"Will you be a bully!" he roared. "If your family is dead, is this how you wish to commemorate them?"

"Fuck you!" James wailed, feeling his chin shake with smothering grief. "And fuck you too, asshole!" he shrieked at Bob. Bob still on his back, clutching his bleeding nose.

Tribe dumped him onto his back with a disgusted snort. He turned to help Bob to his feet.

James unslung his pack. "I've got to get in there."

"Don't," said Tribe. "It's damned dangerous, you'll kill yourself."

"I need to know." He trudged to the edge of the hole where he and his family used to live. The grave of all he'd known.

"Think, man!" Tribe insisted. "What will this accomplish?"

"I don't need your protection, Tribe, I never asked for it." James's voice shredded and raw, almost gone. "Take your honor and your obligation and go away – leave me alone!"

"Hey buddy!" Bob's voice still quavered from the shock of being beaten, shining tears jiggling in his eyes. "You think I don't know, but I know! I saw my dad, my sister get shot – right in front of my eyes! I got nothing! Nothing!"

"Then you'll understand." James sat on the foundation's lip, then lowered himself down into the fuming wreck.

*

Tribe was right. It was useless. Everything had been completely burned. The basement an impenetrable, black jumble of collapsed joists. Nothing recognizable. Difficult even to move a pace in any direction. James's nose, his entire head, clogged with the miasmatic stench of cinders and ash.

He crouched down with his back to the foundation. Back bent by useless, pitiless grief. In a mesmerized stupor. If he'd just taken the night off sick, he would have been here with them.

The other day – *just the other day* – Jenny and Sara had come into the bedroom, creeping quiet as little monks. While James had feigned sleep, they'd sat at the end of the bed and Jenny read her Franklin book to Sara. Whispered a running commentary on the pictures.

"Franklin is sick, so he needs to go to the hop-sital," she'd whispered. The softness of a turning page. "Franklin is scared to be at the hop-sital. Doctor Bear helps Franklin feel better."

"Bett-or," Sara chimed, fascinated.

He'd kept his face half-buried in the pillow. Wishing they'd go away. He should have sat up. Opened his arms to his daughters, snuggled them to himself and read them the story of Franklin going to the hospital to have his broken shell operated on by Dr. Bear. Should have, but had not. Stace had come in, maybe fifteen minutes later, given the girls royal shit for bothering Daddy's sleep. Poor Jenny and Sara!

As if from a great distance, he heard the squeak of his own ruined voice as he wept.

For hours he squatted in the pit, hardly moving. Only dimly aware of Tribe somewhere above, shoes crunching in the filth. Always there, hovering. It seemed a very short time before the afternoon waned. Tribe telling him they should move on, find shelter for the night. James refusing to answer.

Even now, he could hear the furtive tick of hot wood, the fire comatose but still alive, buried in its own feast.

Early evening drowned in muggy heat. Tribe got the camp stove going, tried to get him to eat. Finally James was compelled to climb up, take some. The slimy texture of vacuum-packed stew washed down by stale warm water. James sitting on the foundation now, feet dangling into what had been Jenny and Sara's bedroom.

"I need to go," Tribe said, "to find more water. Do you hear me?"

James nodded blankly.

"I'd rather not leave you alone, but I suppose you'll refuse to come."

James nodded again.

"Stay here. Don't move. Do you understand? I'll be back as soon as I can."

He heard Tribe's footsteps crunch away into silence. Then nothing but the ceaseless wind sniffing through the ruins all around. Bob had disappeared. Who could blame him?

James's clothes, his hair, his skin, all clotted with ash. The dry dead skin of the fires. He began to imagine himself dissolving into ash. The wind carried the smell of rotting meat. The city beginning to give up its dead.

Tribe was gone for a long time. James dimly remembered telling him to go away. So he had, and now he was utterly alone.

Even the Voice in his mind, so infuriating, so terrifying, had now abandoned him.

He had just decided that Tribe was not coming back, not ever, when he first laid eyes on the Dog Man. At first he thought he must be dreaming. Or hallucinating. A corpulent body in filthy jeans and work boots, and a sleeveless undershirt stained with blood and grime. Capped by an oversized grey felt doggy head, like something from a team mascot's costume. But the doggy face was odd – as if crafted by a demented child. Crooked red eyes, one a triangle, the other a crude oval, with white pinpricks for pupils. And a jagged oblong mouth, filled with teeth that would have been more at home in a hippopotamus. All square-tipped, like thick human molars, but again crooked, misshapen.

In one hairy fist the Dog Man carried a pump-action shotgun. Shuffling drunkenly through the wreckage, boots crunching broken glass, kicking aside a bent kitchen chair and chunks of scorched drywall. One of the plastic spade-shaped doggy ears bent halfway, bobbing with each oafish stride.

Watching the Dog Man from behind, James was seized by the first emotion he'd felt since that morning except numbed misery. An irrational, hot fear, the near-painful certainty that this creature – this *thing* – must be evaded at any cost.

As quietly as he could, grappling his pack, he eased his ass off the foundation, hopping down into the pit. Scarcely breathing, he searched for a hiding spot, hearing the Dog Man's assured boots coming closer, closer.

He crawled into a precarious teepee of blackened joists, finally having to roll over, edge in legs first. Desperate now, wincing as his foot clunked against metal debris. Yanking the pack in behind himself.

The distorted dog face appeared over the edge of the foundation. James froze. Face to face now. Nothing between them but the feeble cindered beams of the teepee.

Please lord don't let him see me.

His lips formed the prayer silently. Shivering with his pounding heart. The Dog Man stared down. Those wicked pinpricked pupils alert, white hot. James swore he saw the grimy felt snout twitching. Wiggling whiskers like plastic dry spaghetti. No sound but the asthmatic breath of fly wings, dozens of them clustering on the blood-stained undershirt.

James's eyes rolled with the Dog Man as it shuffled around the foundation. Hefting the big pump action, it fired. The blast smashed the wreckage. Charcoal sifted onto James's neck.

The Dog Man behind James now, where he couldn't see it. To James, his own breath a dead giveaway. Hiccuping with fear that stabbed his bladder. Sure he would piss himself.

The pump action cracked. A shell rattled down. Another blast. Rolling, echoing. Something sharp fell on James's left calf. A third shot, a fourth.

What the hell was it doing? Trying to flush him out?

As it came around to the front again, James pressed his chin into the ashes. *Please, please, please* his mortified mind begged.

He noticed the red heart tattoo on the Dog Man's broad right forearm. Frowned quizzically. That saying of Mrs. Gritzner's: synchronicity, the language of God. But what god had conjured this?

Then he saw something that froze his mind in a crushing singularity of terror. He bit his lip to stop himself from crying out.

Around the bottom edge of the dog head. Crudely sewn stitches. Thick, bloody. They might be leather thongs. Stretched tight between ragged holes in the dog head and the hideously stretched skin of the neck.

It can't be, he thought. It's impossible. *It can't be!*

And yet it was. Bloody holes teeming with flies.

Finally, finally the Dog Man's face disappeared, a macabre grey sun sinking behind the horizon of the foundation. James listened to the receding footsteps. Still, he dared not move. Body mingled with ash. Crumbling into the ticking, snickering dregs.

*

James had first met Donnie the morning after one of Maggie's colossal smash-up parties. Donnie, who was such a pig he didn't even earn the sobriquet of 'uncle.' James had spent the night sleeping over at a friend's place. Came home that morning to find the house in the usual state of chaotic disarray.

Some guy crashed out on the couch, another stranger on the floor beside the wood stove. Familiar banging, moaning, giggling from upstairs. Then as James ate his cereal at the kitchen table, peering through a forest of empty beer bottles, he got his first glimpse of Donnie. Here came the piston of the pornographic montage in Maggie's room. Creaking down the stairs. A squat, sweaty, hairless man with just the makings of a beer gut marring a powerful chest. Going to the fridge, wearing nothing but an enormous shining erection.

"Where's the fuckin mayo?" he grunted, not even bothering to look at James as he bent to peer into the fridge. Giving James a proctological viewpoint of Donnie's personality. But of course, at that point, James had yet to learn even his name. He'd never laid eyes on him until this minute.

"Old are you?" Donnie demanded.

"Ummm – seven."

"Ummm seven, huh?" Then after a pause long enough for a belch. "You gonna answer me, boy?"

"Seven, I said."

Bleary but cunning eyes appeared over the top of the fridge

door, face hungover-bloated. "Show some damn respect, you little asshole."

"Sorry."

"Not as sorry as you'll be, you keep being so rude. Now, where is the goddamned mayo?"

James, of course now on the verge of tears. "Should be in there – somewhere mister."

"Name's Donnie, chickenshit." The mayonnaise jar clanged against the shelf as he tore it loose, then slammed the fridge door.

To James's trepidation, Donnie ambled over to the table, fell into a chair beside him, and belched again. He waved the jar at James in a sly, knowing way. "That mom of yours…" he sighed, chuckling. "What she's thinking, keepin' a kid like you around this shithole."

"Yes sir."

"Don't you be disrespecting your mother!" Donnie bellowed, pounding the table. A beer bottle toppled to the floor.

James so scared he spat out a mouthful of half-chewed Captain Crunch. It ran down his chin onto his clean shirt.

Donnie laughed at him. "So much for your fancy churchey clothes!"

So Maggie had even told him that Mrs. Gritzner picked him up at nine every Sunday and took him to Mass. James felt betrayed, naked before this brute.

He flinched as Donnie's hand darted across the table and pinched his cheek so hard he yipped like a puppy. "Take my word for it, kid. You won't find the answers your lookin' for in a church."

From upstairs, Maggie's keening wail: "Donnn-nnnie! I miss you sweetie!"

Donnie chuckled, shook his head. "You go on, watch Scooby Doo or something, while I go fuck your mommy. K?" He scratched himself lazily, ropey wrist muscles twitching as he grabbed the mayonnaise jar. Undulating the red heart tattoo on his right forearm.

Then, abruptly, James was in bed with Stacy. Making love. He'd just slipped his penis inside her, just beginning to grind his pelvis against her. Stacy's hips thrusting up to meet him. His face buried in her sweet-smelling hair.

"Oh yeah, baby." She moaned, stroking his back. "Oh yeah give it to me, angel. Give it to me."

James unable to get the image of a red heart out of his head. Wondering why, where it came from.

"Oh yeah, fuck me, yeah…"

James stopped. This porn talk wasn't Stacy. This wasn't Stacy at all.

He reared back. Seeing her face swollen purple. The face of the man James had murdered in the library. Fungal tongue protruding. He tried to rip his penis out but it was stuck, gripped tight by the delicious hole. The gaping strangling face burping "*Go northeast! You must go northeast!*"

James shivered awake. Back in the ruins. Chilly, near dusk. Gunfire exploding nearby. Lots of it, a real melee.

"James!"

It was Tribe. He came back!

"James, damn it!"

"Down here," he rasped, shifting forward on his elbows, getting to his feet.

Tribe jogged to the edge of the pit. "By Christ I thought you'd gone! Come on, we need to move."

"Just a moment. I need it."

He saw a gleam in the flat, opaque grayness. A little glass bell, a relic from the tangle of Jenny's trinkets he was forever stepping on or tripping over. Somehow it had survived. Slightly flattened by the heat, it no longer rang true. The tiny clapper rattled, a precious cricketing that made him cry yet again. James's grimy thumb smoothed away the worst of the dirt encrusted on the glass.

Taking down the Christmas tree last January. Jenny had been delighted by the glass bell's tinkling delicacy. She and Sara dashing through the apartment with it, squealing laughter. Stacy telling her alright, alright, she could keep it, but not as a toy. She had to promise to leave it on top of her dresser where nobody would step on it. James had objected. Sooner or later, one of them'll leave it on the floor, he'd insisted. We'll end up in the ER waiting hours to have stitches put in one of our feet. Cease and desist, Stacy had said, blowing frustration at him.

And now here it was. He closed his fingers around it, closed his eyes. Please. Wherever they are. Just please let them be alright. Keep them safe. And please, please let me see them again.

"Are you coming or not?" Tribe snapped.

James slipped the bell into the breast pocket of his shirt. It would rest there just an inch over his heart. Rattling faintly as he walked. A small memorial cyst for his fingers to find when things were at their worst.

Tribe gave James his hand, helping him up and out.

"Thanks for coming back," James sobbed.

"Look at you! Like a mime in a black-face routine!"

It occurred to James that it might have been the soot all over his face that saved his ass. If the Dog Man was real.

"We need to move. The fighting west of here is damned intense – makes what we saw yesterday seem mild by comparison." Tribe picked up James's ash-caked pack, helped him put it on his back. He gathered his own equipment.

"They're alive," said James, trying to inject some hope into his voice.

"They are," Tribe agreed. "Somewhere. Believe it, and it will be so."

But the Dog Man remained stuck in his brain. The revolting stitches he'd seen binding the big fabric head onto the lumpy body. It must have been a nightmare. It couldn't have been real.

Could it?

Then those other dreams. Bright simulacra. Betelgeuse bright. He shook himself.

"I'm going northeast," he said. Just speaking the words was enough to make him feel intense relief. As if some hot pain had suddenly been palliated. Maybe the sore urgency would bring him back to his family. Maybe they were what was pulling him in that direction.

"Then I am as well." Tribe shrugged on his pack, and they started out.

"Why are you coming with me?" James asked after a while.

"I told you – I need to repay the debt I owe you."

"You've already done that."

Tribe huffed. "I believe that the Fates have brought us together. For what purpose I cannot discern at the moment. But I know it would be foolish to turn aside from the path lain before us."

"What does it all mean?"

Tribe laughed, but there was an edge to it. "It means, my dear James, that we must do everything in our power to survive. In the pursuit of survival, nothing is unjustified."

"Nothing? At all?"

"Believe me – nothing is more ignominious than dying."

James still felt uncomfortable with Tribe's assertion, but his head was as cluttered as the pit he'd just crawled from. He couldn't think of any riposte, so he let it slide.

He felt as if something had been ripped from his mind. Leaving an open wound. As they strode away, he couldn't help but feel intensely that he'd just forgotten to look properly. That if he turned and looked back over his shoulder just one more time, the house would still be there after all.

They headed north, then east along Dundas Street. Across the bridge over the Don River. James struggling to keep up with Tribe's pace, nearly a jog. Catching up behind them, an incoming storm surge of gunfire. Explosions. More and more refugees thronging the street, pouring onto Dundas from north and south. The bridge was packed, the dense crowd flowing around eyeots of stalled cars. James even saw people leaping right into the river from the western bank, swimming across in jerking strokes. Desperate fear on the air, vinegary and sweet.

A brilliant rose explosion leaped skyward, swelling the gloaming with light. People shrieking when the shockwave hit. A hot slap of air, a woman on the other side of the bridge clutching her wailing baby closer to her chest. Then a bullet sang past. Chopped into the back of a man just ahead of James and Tribe. The man went down. Now the crowd's shuffling trot surged into a panicked dash, a dense heaving throng like the start of the Boston marathon. The bridge wobbled under the bouncing weight. People sucked under, trampled by panicked feet.

"Stay close!" Tribe called to James.

More bullets pinged off the bridge's superstructure.

They went past a streetcar on its side. Then past the stained gothic castle of the Don Jail. The sounds coming from inside driving right into James's blood. Cries filled with more than desperation. It seemed to him that these were the shrieks of those fed to hunting cats.

James grappled Tribe's arm, pulling him through the impossible thicket of elbows and shoulders towards a derelict factory. A dark, hollow ghost, a decades-old premonition of what the entire city was starting to look like.

Shouts behind them, and no longer shouts of fear. Anger. Cruelty. The gunfire ear splitting. The way it gets only when it's very close.

They ran into a broad courtyard, surrounded on three sides by several stories of shattered windows and crumbling brickwork. The crowd hammering on a set of steel doors, surging forward as a single organism. Those against the doors were screaming, being crushed as the doors warped inward, then burst open. Scrambling into the dark factory space. Dank wood rot, the sting of ammonia. Years of accumulated piss. In the piddling light of dusk, vague forms shrank back into deeper shadows.

Shouts and screams echoed through the hulking space. The stamp of running feet.

Then, through a set of loading doors at the far end of the factory, muzzle flashes. The giant banging of guns.

James and Tribe skidded to a halt in a confused knotted crowd. Scrambling to turn around, but more and more were pouring through the doors they'd just entered. Cattle being run into the slaughter pens. Impossible to move against the crush.

More gunfire, ahead and behind. The throng whooped like a crammed stadium.

Armed men at both ends of the factory. Lightning and pounding thunder, impossibly loud. In the clarion moment of supreme terror, a bright revelation in James's mind: this is what it's like to be caught in a crossfire! Now you're gonna die!

Tribe had his sword out, snarling at people around them. Using his height and weight to plough through the huge, boiling scrum.

But it was too late. They were trapped.

Chapter 7

Graham McMann

This is what I have foreseen. Darkness
Three hours before the power died, Graham sat in the only halfway comfortable seat in the whole damn common room, the one with the red vinyl cushion and wooden arms. Staring through the window at the small houses squeezed tight from end to end along Knox Avenue.

The meeting was late.

Too late for a lot of things.

This is what I have foreseen. Darkness

Maybe an hour ago, maybe more, he'd pressed the ballpoint onto his notebook to write the next words: *so complete*. The pen still in his right fingers. In his left, the stub of the smoke he'd rolled. Long since gone out. Nicotine. The last, best addiction. Safe from the recrimination of the pristine cunts who ran this place.

The phrase *Darkness so complete* had seemed truer than scripture in his mind. Sure it had. But his hand had faltered. Suddenly it had seemed utterly inadequate to describe what he actually had foreseen. Truth be told, there was no way to bring such a vision to life, full as it was of death and pain and torment.

Some of the other inmates were creeping in to the common room to grab a coffee or a Coke. Stopping to read the notices stuck to the whiteboard with magnets. The shuffling distraction leading up to their evening group session. Inmates, right. Trapped in Counselor John's emotional gravity. In love with the arcs their orbits traced, going round and round and round that star.

But tonight, Counselor John was tardy.

Contemplation and awareness. The twin pillars of the Knoxwood detox program.

Aye, sure. But contemplation and awareness of *what*?

The look on that little girl's face two weeks ago. Staring up at Graham in revulsion. In utter contempt. In sorrow. The depth in those blue eyes, the *depth*. You could fall into them. Like Yucatan cenotes, they'd swallow you forever. How could there be such contempt in the face of such a wee girl?

You know how, you know exactly how Mr. McMann. What did you do to her? You leaned over her and—

For the first time in maybe an hour, Graham's muscles

twitched. His head turning away from the window. As if the glass televised the memory of what he'd done. Of what he could not revisit.

Awareness and contemplation. Kiss my fucking arse.

*

The room, dim enough that when somebody finally flicked on the lights Graham blinked at the sudden brightness.

Counselor John marched in, tucking in his weak chin with that expression of fanatical optimism. Officiously, he looked at his watch. Right in the center of the room, where all could witness his abject regret. "My word! We're almost forty-five minutes late. Guys, I sincerely apologize to each and every one of you. We had a crisis down the hall this evening. Couldn't be avoided." Absolutely the Sun King of this maudlin band.

Supposed to be friendly and helpful. Sorry, Johnny, but often enough you come across as the intrusive arsehole that you're struggling so hard not to be.

Graham flicked his fingers, launching the dead cold smoke onto the tiles.

Crisis down the hall. Do tell, Johnny-boy! Some sorry mucker in the throes of a DT nightmare? Nah, nah, they would have heard the screams.

Nah, probably an even sorrier mucker whose meat was marinated in sweet, sweet booze. Past the point of sickness into the zone of paralytic disgust. Graham knew that zone. Exactly thirteen days before, he'd woken up there. And he'd yet to tread all the way out.

They all dragged up chairs, sixteen alcoholics in the very earliest stages of recovery, forming the ring where Johnny became the radiant diamond, gripped in a setting of their needful attention. Graham was among the last to join up, shoving his chair back and shifting it around without even getting to his feet. The wood legs scraped with a dry whining protest.

"God," said John.

"God," all of them chimed in, Graham included. "Grant me the serenity to accept the things I cannot change, the courage to change the things I can, and the wisdom to know the difference."

"And the wisdom to know the difference," Johnny repeated. A reverent whisper, with all the aplomb and dignity the inmates projected onto him. "Tonight's topic is the first step, guys. 'We admit that we are powerless over alcohol and that our lives have become unmanageable.' Who wants to start?"

Fidgeting hands. The rubbery squeak of fingers against foam coffee beakers. Knees bouncing merry wee jigs, but their shoulders hunched, defeated. No eye contact. Ach, it was gonna be a long session tonight.

"Graham, why don't you start us out?"

Johnny's beady gaze gave Graham a giddy, sinking feeling. It wasn't that Graham minded speaking up in front of other people. In fact, he got a bit of a thrill out of it. Something about debasing himself in front of strangers, especially when the things he was relating were so raw, so open still.

"I suppose I was just sick and tired of being sick and tired."

A few groans. Just neophytes mostly, and already that phrase was becoming a sentimental rut.

"Put another way," Graham added, reminding himself that this was his third time through the detox mill. "I think I was sick and tired of slow-motion suicide."

That merited a few knowing nods.

"Good, good," said Johnny. "Would you care to elaborate on that?"

"Nah, to be honest. Nah." Graham dug out his works and started rolling another fag. Unsteady fingers spilling tobacco shreds across the notebook, still in his lap.

This is what I have foreseen. Darkness

Would you care to talk about the visions I've been having, Counselor John? That would do wonders for your sanguine wisdom! Jesus, I can't even bring myself to write them down, and they're from my own head! And another thing, by the way – this horrible stuff I've been seeing, I think it's gonna happen. Really and truly happen.

He licked the edge of the rolling paper, fingers expertly folding the wet end over. Then out with the lighter, just a bit of flourish lighting up, sucking the smoke in greedily.

Somebody else was droning now. A guy in his forties. Depressing tale of how he blew everything in his pursuit of oblivion. Lost his job. His marriage. Kids not speaking to him anymore.

Graham could have elaborated when Johnny had prompted him. The stories were legend, surfacing like wads of toilet roll floating on a swill of sewage. How him and Doxie used to go around the clock downing the voddy and OJ back at Doxie's place. Long haul sessions becoming common enough to be called a way of life.

"Breakfast of champions!" Doxie'd roar, gulping another huge glass. "I'm gonna bed."

Graham's cue to be off. Half an hour later he'd be home in bed. Struggling to read the glowing numbers on his bedside clock as they pitched and dodged in his drunk-sloppy eyes. The fact dawning on him that he needed to be up in just another *half an hour* to pick Doxie up for fuckin' work! Ah, them glory days, back before he'd lost his license on a DUI!

Then, he and Doxie'd be on the loading docks, still pissed, barely keeping their eyes open. Slurping one coffee after another. One of the great North American vices he'd adopted as soon as he'd stepped off the plane. So much better than tea to wedge your brain to an approximation of sobriety.

How about the time Doxie, in a stuporous hung over state, rolled over Benny Sweetwater's toes with the pallet truck. That was a rip-roarer too, Johnny, let me tell you! Sure, Benny would never walk properly again, having lost most of the toes on his right foot. But he wasn't wearing safety shoes, was he, in a clearly marked safety shoe zone! Sure, the union sided with Doxie over that poor fucker. And if Doxie hadn't been in a chemically-altered state of consciousness? Well…things best left unsaid, things best left unsaid.

A lot of things in that particular category, Johnny-Boy. The road to sobriety littered with erosions of the truth, lies you've been telling yourself for half your life. Jutting rocks just waiting to tear the oil pan right out from under you. It got to the point for Graham where he didn't know if the 'truth' he'd spilled in these sessions wasn't just some faint approximation of reality he'd carefully crafted to buttress a deeper need.

And some things just refused to improve with the telling and retelling. Like what he'd done to that little girl on the subway. The deepest of deep rock-bottom events in his young life. The latest one to give him the kicking he needed to get sober. Yet again.

Nah, nah, he thought, shaking his head. Nah, that story would never, ever be told. Not because the act of telling it would embarrass him, make him look like the arsehole he was. Because one thing that definitely could not be changed, and which Graham now had the serenity to accept, was that he most certainly was a perfect arsehole.

Nah, the problem with relating that little nugget was that it wouldn't do any good. He could tell it till he was blue in the face. He could tell it for a thousand years, engrave it on a holy stone and bring it down from the bloody mountain and it wouldn't change the fact of the violation he'd committed. Somewhere out there was the little girl living it still. And the girl's mother, who'd had to explain to her wee daughter how it was there were men like him in the world who did disgusting things to little wee girls on subways.

He tuned back into the conversation just in time to hear a dumpy guy named Marc going on about how his catholicity had been a light, how his God had seen him through such heartache and loss. *Catholicity*, that was the word he used. Y'see, Graham reminded himself. Perfect example of how sometimes the sharing of people's feelings really is pointless. And quite inane, truth be told.

"Something to add, Graham?" Counselor John presented him with the delighted smile he used to highlight his irritation.

Graham had begun to get on Johnny-Boy's nerves. Excellent, like! He smiled back. "Nope."

"Let me tell ya something, buddy," Shelby squawked. Tonight he sat three over to Graham's right around the ring. A small wiry man with a pink face glowing through a thin white beard. "You'll never get sober without a higher power, alright?"

Graham eased back in his chair. Beaming now. "I never said I don't believe in a higher power."

"Yeah, okay, that's not what the look on your face says," Marc grumbled. "What are you, one of them Orange Men, some shit?"

"Gentlemen..." Johnny-Boy getting agitated. Even his knee was starting to bounce.

Graham couldn't help but laugh at that comment. "Yeah," he snickered. "Alright. Sure."

At the moment, Graham's deepest dearest wish was that hairy Marc could have been there that night back home, the dregs of the session he and Doxie and Sparling had gone on to celebrate when he'd received the Duke of Eddie. Spray painting FTP on the ferro-concrete wall down Portrush Road in Ballymoney. What that would have done for Marc's fucking *catholicity*!

FTP, he thought, still glare-smiling at Marc. In his mind, vandalizing him. Fuck the Pope!

"Graham, it seems obvious you have something to add to the discussion. I do wish you'd be mature enough to just share." Johnny nodded his flushed face.

"I apologize for disrupting the discussion," said Graham, blowing smoke. And he meant it. Not so much the apology part, mind. More the fact that he'd inadvertently brought everything back around to himself again. You can accept the fact of your own arsehole nature without *sharing* it with strangers. "This shouldn't be about me – unless I want it to be. I'll say this, though – way I feel just now..." He leaned forward, putting his elbows on his knees, as if he were trying to shield the words he'd written on the notebook from prying eyes.

This is what I have foreseen. Darkness

"It's just…I really don't feel that I deserve to get over them things right now, the shite I've done. Won't change the fact that I done 'em. Won't change the fact of the hurt that people feel – *right now* – because I caused 'em to feel that way."

Surprised to have the room distorted by tears, Graham coughed, looked down at his shoes.

"You got a way with words, I'll tell you that," said Shelby emphatically.

Graham dug knuckles into his moist eye sockets. "Cheers," he said, and sat back.

Away with words would be more like it. Oh, they'd buggered right off, so they had. The very minute he'd started describing in detail the visions he'd been having the past three months.

He even remembered the exact date of vision number one: March 14. He'd been walking to the corner store for a carton of milk. Felled, as if by a high-powered bullet punching through his thorax. Flat out on the sidewalk, opening his forehead over his left eye. He still bore the hot pink scar.

Graham had been engulfed in a cold shroud of darkness. Darkness across the face of the world, smothering deep.

And then just as quickly it was gone again. Gasping like he'd been held under an icy lake to the point of desperation, blood stinging his eyes. Pedestrians quickly swinging wide of him, just in case he was crazy enough or stoned enough to reach for them. None of them even looking back.

The street, the traffic, a sound system blaring bass-heavy reggae. Graham's sudden vision had been just as real, just as vital and full as those realities. Been and gone, a flood of horrifying images, impressions.

Pitiless dark, a moonless nighttime, a wilderness of insanity waiting to pounce on him. On everything. That first vision left a residue of cold water around his heart. A tight pocket, squeezing. A certainty – *dead certainty* it was actually about to happen. A beast that had been *waiting* to attack, eagerly, greedily for a long, long time. And it couldn't wait any more.

Guess what, Johnny? Didn't end up buying any milk at the corner store. Almost seventy days of sobriety under the bridge by that point, but fuck that. Sure, Graham had walked on just that extra two blocks to the *liquor* store. For two twenty-sixers of voddy. And that had been the first day – the *first step*, you could almost call it, he thought with an inward snicker – in the epic binge that had finally ended thirteen days ago.

So epic in fact that even the infamous Doxie was quit with him after too long. Even *he* couldn't keep up with Graham's monumental gluttony for alcohol, his need to utterly swamp the terror inspired by that vision.

Normal folks, having had a sudden crippling vision of the end of the world might have gone off to the doctor. Gotten that forehead gash stitched up right and proper. Maybe checked to make sure they hadn't had a stroke.

Not Graham, not the glutton. Nah, the only doctor Graham McMann required at that moment was Doctor Alcohol. With more than a little help from his trusty assistants, Nurses Cannabis and Speed. AA's Big Book described alcohol as cunning and baffling. For Graham, it was fucking erudite.

More erudite than he'd managed to be.

This is what I have foreseen. Darkness

Not one word more than those seven at the top of the page.

"I know where you're coming from, Graham," said Johnny, all quiet, an almost religious quality to him. "Remember, I've been there too."

No you've not, Graham thought immediately. An alcoholic you may be, but you've not been where I am now. No way.

"Just try considering that it's less about the people you may have hurt, and more about learning to deal with those feelings without relying on alcohol." Probably, Johnny really was trying to show empathy, but Graham could tell he just didn't like Graham much, or put much stock in his odds of staying sober.

Fair play. Neither did Graham.

The conversation continued around the ring. The guy named Melvin, whose face was so mottled by freckles his skin looked as bright orange as his hair, he told them all his story of coming out of an alcoholic blackout with a gun in his hand and his dog bleeding to death on the sitting room rug. That was a good one. Bit of *bite* in that tale.

Jesus, Graham chided himself, what are you *like*? You really *are* an arsehole, and make no mistake!

Still and all, you couldn't live without at least a bit of humor. Especially in this dour setting. Graham had a personal rule: he took nothing seriously, but kept some things sacred.

Them visions, they'd held a kind of hallowed malevolence. A timelessness that had tricked him for certainty. It was coming! But then nothing had happened. Even in his drunken walking coma, that inescapable fact had been obvious. The visions weren't coming true after all.

"You guys have been really great tonight," said Johnny, breathing like he'd just had a particularly satisfying wank. "Thank you. All," he added, giving Graham a knowing look. "I'm *pumped* for tomorrow night – and I promise I'll be on time, okay?"

All of them got to their feet, all but Graham, who felt that his arse had fused with the vinyl leather seat. Thinking of how he'd violated that wee girl on the train. Seriously wondering if being sober could in any way blot out that particular stain on the soul of Graham McMann.

Then the lights went out with a loud clatter.

Something huge slammed into Graham's right side, knocking his wind out. It took Graham a few moments to realize he'd fallen out of the chair. That he'd hit the floor, not the other way round.

All of them were down on the floor. Marc clutching his head, groaning. Shelby whispering "Whoa, Jesus, whoa Jesus, what the hell?"

This is it! Graham thought, a triumphant surge through his belly, his groin. The visions *are* coming true! He recognized the occurrence like a half-forgotten odor. *Oh Jesus! Oh Jesus, oh jesusohjesus!*

It was dark, but Graham could see Johnny face down on the tiles. A black halo of blood spreading around his head.

"I think – I think he's dead!" Marc gulped, kneeling beside him.

Graham was ashamed of the thought bursting into his mind: *Good. Adios, ye irritating twat!* Ashamed, but not so much that he couldn't see the humor. He could always see the humor! He laughed. Getting to his feet, he felt drunk. *I've got them rubber legs!*

The clatter he'd heard were all of the magnets falling off the whiteboard and the fridge. Giggling like a brat, he picked up one of the magnets and held it to the fridge's metal skin. When he let go, the magnet fell. No longer a magnet at all!

Inexplicable, the excitement, the sheer joy ringing in his mind. Because way down below that, he'd never been more afraid in his life. Down deep, the cruelest terror swam those nighttime waters around his thrusting heart. A hungry eel. *Nothing's sacred anymore*, he thought. *Nothing at all!*

He pointed at Johnny-Boy's limp, prone body, and laughed. Laughed at Marc's expression of shocked sorrow. Hardly able to breathe, he laughed and laughed.

*

Shelby's white beard, aglow in the dusk time. His eyes pinpointed with eager light, sunk down deep into his massive grin. "Nuthin' for it," he kept saying, "nuthin' for it but getting' shitfaced!"

One of the last clear memories Graham had for what turned out to be the next three days. The nighttime he'd foreseen, but not as dark as he'd expected. Alive with fire, it was. The whole city awash in fierce golden light.

Streets turned into glowing aquariums, people dashing like ants on alert. Feeling the heat against his upturned face, basking he was. All the time knowing he should be terrified. He felt the terror, and make no mistake. Just the same as he had in the common room at Knoxwood. Laughing at poor Johnny's limp remains. Unable to respond to his own emotions, somehow.

Somehow, standing in the face of a flame-roaring building – the whole structure enveloped, and Graham could only raise his hands, jump up and down and cheer like he was in the Casement Park stadium back home and the home side had just scored against Londonderry.

The terror so wee, just a tiny mote – but still and all he knew it was gargantuan. The smallness just an illusion of how deep it was buried.

Turned out, Shelby was righter than rain. Within the hour after the lights went out, Graham was so shitfaced he could hardly stand. They'd just hiked a ways, down Knox, across to Woodbine where there was a beer store. They joined the crowd, took what they wanted. The cold effervescence of the ale and stout and lager fizzling down his throat!

"Don't it hit the spot though! Don't it just!" Shelby squawked, spitting beer down the front of his shirt.

Sure, beer was good for starters, but not enough to celebrate what had finally come upon the world! So up Woodbine they hiked, just a few miles north to the Danforth, to the liquor store waiting like a cool, black Mecca. Beer after beer bottle along the way, the dwindling case of twenty-four slung between them.

For what did it matter now? What did it matter what Graham had done to an anonymous little girl on the subway, who he'd never see again. Who'd probably not survive this anyway? Because very few would survive, that was obvious from the get-go.

There were screaming maniacs everywhere. Mindless violence that made some of the thuggery back home in Ballymoney seem like Sunday school pranks. Right away the looting began. The vandalism. He and Shelby marching north on Woodbine, and every beer bottle they drained smashed into the street, or against the dead, muted cars, or even through the dark windows of houses they passed.

For Graham, everything seemed outside, far away from

himself. So that even the bottle he chucked through the front window of a house seemed to have been thrown by somebody else. The angry feller shaking his fist at them, screaming at them down the street – he was angry at another person, not Graham.

No, you don't understand, Graham wanted to scream back. You don't understand at all, see, because it ain't me throwing these bottles. Looks like me, sounds like me, stands in my place and all, but it ain't because the mucker who threw that beer bottle through your parlor window is overcome with puerile hyperactive joy. Me, I'm as terrified and outraged as you are. Me, I'm scared to fuckin' death!

Then Shelby and Graham were jostling with the crowd inside the liquor store. Helping themselves to Jamaican 150-proof rum. A sweet, sweet burn to match the city. A case each, belting out "It's a Long Way to Tipperary" at the tops of their lungs.

All at once, Shelby was gone. The flames were gone, doused in vast clouds of smoke. The rising sun inflamed, tumescent through the smoke. Graham gaping at it through a dirt-fogged window. The taste of sickness in his furry mouth. He could feel the puffiness in his face and hands, the swell of a monumental drinking session. He heard firecrackers going off all around. He belched, bringing up a stringy splash of bloody vomit. *Oh shit, oh Jesus, that's not a good sign.*

His body encrusted with a sore, salty thirst that he felt could never be slaked, not in a thousand years. A bottle of Jamaican rum in each fist. The thought of putting more of that brownish piss into his stomach sent a shiver of revulsion across his shoulders. And still his filthy hands gripped the necks of those bottles, gripped them tighter than a seagull's arse in a power dive.

He felt his cracked, chapped lips scrape together, a smile that died in utero. Gone was the ticklish joy he'd first felt in the common room of the Knoxwood Detox center. Drained like the reservoir behind a burst dam, leaving behind only mummified remnants. Horrid things that had been swallowed by the reservoir long ago. Now spit back out.

Agonized trepidation came over him then, as two things occurred to him. First, that the sun at which he was so vacantly gaping was not in fact rising, but sinking. Lancing his squinting eyes. Second, that those firecrackers were actually gunfire. A shiteload of gunfire, and it was getting closer fast.

He was standing on the rotted mezzanine of what seemed to be an abandoned warehouse. Crumbling brick, oozing mortar long ago fossilized. Dusty bundles of rags up and down the length of the mezzanine turned out to be vagabonds twisting awake, snorting their fuzzy alarm at the approaching gunshots.

Through a hole in the floor ten feet across he saw tall doors on the ground floor bang open, disgorging a rushing, screaming crowd chased by a squad of soldiers with submachine guns. Soldiers, his gummy brain told him, because they were wearing black berets and jumpsuits. Bloodthirsty cunts, firing right into their backs. Deafening cascades of shooting, muzzle flashes like strobe lights in a hellish dance club. Screaming folks fell away, melting back like snowflakes blown against a hot stove.

Just go on standing there, you gormless fuck. Go on just watching them people be murdered!

The soldiers fanned out across the warehouse floor and the shooting abated as they knew they had the crowd trapped.

Then another set of doors on the other side flew open. Gates in a liftlock, admitting another torrent of runners, chased by another armed gang. These ones weren't in uniform, though. Irregulars, a ragged street militia blazing away with handguns.

Already there were dozens of dead. Dozens. Then the two gangs started firing on each other. The crowds between them collapsing to the floor with a terrified howl. Jesus, one of them had a sword!

Graham blinked, shook his sore head, but sure it was a tall bloke waving a sword, yanking another guy along behind, both of them bent double, struggling through the crowd to the side of the warehouse, away from the whipping bullets. The one being yanked along, fairly caked with soot he was, a lanky big-nosed guy shouting at the tops of his lungs. Through a brief gap in the gunfire, Graham heard his ragged voice. Shouting something about his tribe. A tribe of his men, a tribe, he kept screaming.

Something in the actions of those two men finally steeled Graham's poisoned nerves. Still gripping the two bottles of rum, he moved along the sagging mezzanine towards a rusty iron footwalk that stretched over the factory floor.

Chapter 8

The Fellowship is Born

Tribe gripped James's jacket, hauling him towards cover. Bullets punched through rusty steel drums. Whatever chemicals remained in them caught fire. More bullets thunking into bodies, splintering wooden beams. A woman shrieked as the crowd toppled her into the spreading flames.

"It's his men, Tribe!" James screamed above the din. "Tribe, it's Lichboegh's men! The Sicari!" He caught a glimpse of them through the bustling crowd, as people dived for the floor. The same black jumpsuits they'd seen at York. "How in the hell did they find us?"

Tribe pulled him in tight behind the remains of a ruined wooden kiosk against the warehouse wall.

James's lungs convulsed, his breath whooped through his gaping mouth. The tiny glass bell he'd disinterred from the ruin of his apartment felt atomically small in his shirt pocket, his fingers compulsively kneading its shape through the fabric.

The gunmen were almost abreast of their position now. There were only a few of them. James saw them kicking at prone figures on the floor, gripping them by the scruffs of the neck, rolling them over to see their faces. It seemed obvious they were searching for James and Tribe.

A tall thin figure strode into the warehouse. Wearing a long crimson robe. Instant memories of that bizarre Hermes character from the first night. His pudgy fingers wiggling. But no, this wasn't Hermes. This one had a head of thick black curls. What had Allistair called these characters? Collegians. This one stopped near the door, eyes closed, hands folded.

Only intermittent gunshots now. They seemed to have driven off the gang bangers who'd come through the other side. In a way, the quiet only increased the terror of exposure. Soon, they'd see James and Tribe. Only seconds now! Seconds, and then—

That's when James saw the figure standing on the rust-caked iron catwalk. Suspended maybe thirty feet above the warehouse floor. The gunmen so intent on searching the floor that none of them noticed. Then the guy on the catwalk dropped something. James saw a glint as it fell, and it struck one of the burning barrels with a loud clang.

Instantly a fireball exploded into the rafters. Several of the gunmen were aflame, screaming, and a few people in the crowd as well. Writhing, shrieking in agony. The crowd up and fleeing towards the far doors. Gunmen wrestling their burning comrades to the floor, rolling them over to dampen the flames. Too shocked to get off more than a few shots.

"Come on!" Tribe shouted.

They leaped to their feet. Back into the mad rush. There was another explosion, another one of the barrels going up. Then they were back out into the cool evening, dispersing with the crowds into the dim streets.

*

They followed the rushing pack, running several blocks. To James it seemed absurdly like the running of the bulls.

Finally, they ended up squirreled into the employee lounge behind a ransacked electronics store. The evening gloom followed them through the smashed front window, past malformed ghosts meddling with leftover merchandise. Fingering buttons. Gripping remotes. One guy with his hand pressed to a dead TV screen, caressing the blank surface, his mouth hanging open. All of them, mute as stone age tribespeople awed by unknown idols.

A tall kid with long kinky hair was bent over one of the shattered glass counters, fiddling with a cell phone. James saw he was replacing the phone's battery, his hands tearing at plastic packaging, ripping out the mirrored nickel units, fervently trying one after another. At his feet, a gleaming circle of cadmium batteries.

"Something must still be working," James heard him mutter. "Some goddamn thing!"

In the back they found a cabal of maybe twenty people. The lounge was really no more than a closet. The people crowded around the stark light of a Coleman hurricane lamp. The light slippery, ephemeral over the faces of those drawn in close for a small taste of its warmth. A few were perched on desk chairs. Others on pale wooden Ikea furniture twenty years past its prime. Tribe and James were among the last to arrive, so they had to join the majority hunched on the floor.

A few chattered about what had happened in the warehouse. Wide eyes striped with leering light, apostolic in the jittery telling of the tale for those who hadn't been there.

Most simply sat and stared. Bent coat hanger poses of miserable defeat. Dirty, scared faces.

Propped in the corner, tended by a sharp-featured woman with a greying page-boy haircut, a dark-skinned man with a bullet wound to the shoulder rocked and groaned with pain. Just watching the man's grimacing seat-dance was enough to make James squirm.

James felt ragged. Hearing phantom screams from the derelict factory still. In his mind a chorus of pleading cries, screeching of the dead he'd tended to back at York, the dead Sicari man in the library.

In the squeal of a desk chair's wheels he heard that Walter dude—

ISH-TA-BISH TOSH-TO-TISH! – ISHTABISHTOSHTOTISH!

Thunking the knife into Allistair's chest. The sewing machine jerk of his arm thunking the knife into Allistair's chest. The spray of Allistair's blood.

James cringed, but the wraiths could not be shunned. Christ, Allistair had been getting on his every nerve. For an instant, not even a second, when Walter had attacked Allistair, James had felt a delicious cramp of satisfaction. As if – as if he had willed it.

No, he thought. Not me. But *something*. Something in him had wanted it to happen and made it so. A chess master arranging the gaming board. Then – bam! It had been over. So fast, Allistair's lungs spewing blood for air.

James felt that presence again right now, an imminent stranger, unseen, unbidden. Within him, beside him – he couldn't decide. The Voice. Heru, the distant one. Called Horos by the barbarian Greeks. The falcon-headed god. Yes, that one.

And now Heru reminded him of the charred remnant James had once called his own home. The burned junk that his family's lives had become. And it wasn't the screams from the factory he heard now, it was Jenny and Sara screaming. Terrified little voices screaming and crying. *Daddeee! Daa-ddeee!* As if they were dashing past in the street right this very instant, and his leg muscles gave an involuntary twitch, a spinal jolt to chase after them.

Northeast! Heru whispered in his ear. Gone now was the stringent note of command he'd heard before. Now, just quiet satisfaction. *I told you*, that tone said. *I told you not to head south!*

Too much – too much to take, damn it! How much more could he be expected to deal with, for the love of God?

Tribe heated some camp stew in the billy can on the stove. James was hungry, ravenously so, but his hands were shaking so badly he couldn't even get the spoon to his lips without slopping it down the front of his shirt. Resentful frustration burst from him in a bout of sobbing.

"I'll have that, if you're not gonna eat it."

A pale, thin woman with dark curly hair reached a slender hand for the bowl. James's first inclination was to crouch over the food like an abused mongrel. A nasty, resentful greed that made him feel less than human. Her hand, so steady and bold. Delicate and strong at the same time.

"You'll not share what you've got?" She gestured again for the bowl, impatient, irritable. "Well why don't you just bin it then, and be done with it, instead of teasing us, waving it in our bloody noses all bloody night!"

"Sorry," he croaked, handing it over. Several pairs of eyes watched the bowl intently as it passed before them. James even saw a thread of drool hanging from an older guy's lips. He felt pity and shame. He undid his pack and got out a few more of his rations to prepare.

"Thanks," said the thin woman with the dark curls, and it sounded like *tanks*. "Thanks a lot."

"What did I say about survival?" Tribe muttered.

"Whatever it takes," James repeated. "Guess I'm not quite the Machiavellian you are."

Tribe reared back as if slapped. "I dare say you'll be more amenable to my way of thinking when you're starving!"

"Fuck sakes, Tribe!" James's couldn't stop his voice from trembling. "I'd rather not starve my conscience, if you don't mind!"

A low snicker on the other side of the room. "Nice one!"

"You two're awfully well prepared, with your gear," said the woman with the dark curls, chewing. She spooned some of the stew into the mouth of a chubby East Indian woman on her left who was so deadened she seemed catatonic. The directness, the plain practical grace of this gesture charged James with something that felt like fear.

"Who was it that said chance favors the prepared mind," said Tribe, glaring at James as he emptied the camp stew into the billycan.

Soon the camp stove had heated enough food for anybody who wanted to eat. They found some plates and cutlery in a cupboard underneath a useless microwave. The aroma of the camp food, though somewhat flat and dogfoody, seemed good and warm. Context was everything.

"I'm Sheilagh," said the woman with the curly hair.

The keen yet displaced sense of familiarity made James feel better. He couldn't explain how or why, but it didn't matter. He introduced himself, and there were more introductions around the lamp.

A guy with a stringy mane of metalhead hair and a long soul

patch named Mulligan. James wasn't clear if this was his first name or last. He had black sweatbands on each wrist and was wearing a faded Motorhead tee-shirt.

The one who'd drooled at the food, a heavy-set retired-aged man in a green golf jacket, told them his name was Ross.

James offered some of his Aspirin to the guy with the bullet hole in his shoulder. His name was Sam, and it was his wife Astrid taking care of him. She thanked James profusely, but as it turned out later, it might have been the Aspirin that contributed to his death.

"This here's Rohini," said Sheilagh, indicating the Indian woman on her left. Again she maneuvered a spoon of stew through the curtain of tangled hair to her loose mouth. Rohini's arms were crossed tightly over her chest. As if trying to hold in some vital organ. "She's not much for talkin' at the moment. Are you, Rohini?"

Rohini's lax lower lip clutched upwards in what could have been a muted reply.

Near the door, a delicate-looking Asian teen said his name was Mike. He'd been the one out front caressing the TV screen. During the introductions, he produced a wide chopping knife. James's eyes locked onto the gleaming blade. A single-tined tuning fork broadcasting intense humming terror into the center of his chest.

Everything had a subtle edge. Like he wasn't just seeing things with his eyes, but with his entire body. Behind or just to the side of everything – Mike's honed steel, Rohini's drooping face, a weeping woman cradling a little boy, Ross's mouth, slightly sunken – a dizzying simultaneity of vision. Of feeling. The whole room had a heartbeat, panic-quick. James was peeking around corners, behind hidden curves. He heard his own breath. Wind in a cave.

Many pairs of distrustful eyes swiveling back and forth. It was as if the sharing of names had become anathema to some of them. A taboo of strangers, like the sharing of saliva or the caress of private body parts.

"Does anybody know what time it is?" asked a waiflike woman in the corner near the door. James saw a few of them glance at their wrists, but there was no reply. Just a deflated murmur. Nobody had an old-fashioned mechanical watch.

That Mike kid kept flicking the pad of his thumb across the razor edge of his knife. Looking fascinated by the keen *sin-sin-sin-sin* of his fingerprint against sharpness that might slice through it. *Sin-sin-sin-sin*. The nervous sound filled James with a kind of drowning sensation. His teeth pressed together until his jaw ached.

"Son," said Tribe. Very quietly. The intense calm before a

deluge. "Why don't you put it away."

"Sure, there's no one's gonna hurt you here, Michael," Sheilagh instructed.

"I said it's Mike." An awful serration in his voice. But he put the knife away, glancing self-consciously around the group.

James noticed Tribe's hand relax from the handle of his dagger. The same one he'd plunged into the back of Walter's skull. James released a breath that felt hotter than steam. His heart was pounding.

For a long while, nobody said anything. The guy with the kinky hair who James had seen madly replacing cellphone batteries was one of the ones who hadn't said anything about himself. He kept fishing for the damn phone in his dirty cargo pants, flipping it open. The rubbery click as he thumbed the buttons, a rhythmic irritant. He peered intently at the little screen, jaw muscles bulging in frustration. He'd drop the phone into his pocket, only to reach for it again just a few minutes later. As if hearing it ring.

For James, watching him was the equivalent of waiting for Sara or Jenny to stop doing something after he'd asked them three times to cease and desist. His hands itched to smack the damn phone away.

"Dude, it ain't gonna work," the touchy guy named Mulligan growled after the tenth or twelfth time. "Just give it up!"

The cell phone man gave him a hateful look. "You never know, do you?"

"Actually, I do know," Mulligan responded with a self-satisfied pull on his cigarette. "Seems obvious to me. Everything that runs on electricity is pretty much fucked!"

There was more chatter about what had happened in the warehouse. Lots of questions about the gunmen in the black berets.

James and Tribe shared a knowing glance.

"What?" said the Mike kid. "They don't like guys with swords?"

An uncomfortable murmur of laughter greeted this.

"Not me, especially," said Tribe.

"All I know is, that crazy dude on the catwalk saved our fuckin' asses," said Mulligan. He had a cranky, sardonic voice. He flicked his lighter, touched the flame to another cigarette. In the light of the flame, James caught a glimpse of a nose that looked like it had been flattened in the boxing ring.

"It was like magic!" The cell phone guy sounded drugged. "Fire magic!"

"Nah, nah," said a groaning voice. The same one that had responded to James's outburst at Tribe by saying "Nice one" a few minutes before. A shadow within someone else's shadow. "Just Jamaican rum. Which I suppose can be magic enough, under the proper circumstances, and all." He had an unplaceable accent similar to Allistair's, but his voice was deeper. Resigned, James thought. That was it. Ground down.

"How can you possibly know that?" Mulligan asked, bitingly skeptical.

"Because I was the crazy fucker that tossed 'em," he answered, leaning forward into the light.

A heavy quiet. A lot of them like James, no doubt: still dealing with the tortured burning screams.

He had a heavily-built face. Lean, but big-boned. An angry red scar angled across the left side of his forehead. He was fiddling with something in his lap. Rolling a cigarette, James saw, but having a lot of trouble, his hands shaking even worse than James's. But those shakes weren't just rooted in shot nerves. No sir, James was pretty sure he was looking at the aftereffects of that magical rum.

"Yo, all's I can say," said Mike in a tremulous voice, "is that you saved our asses, like that dude just said. I had no idea booze could could burn like that."

"Thank-you," said Ross in a tremulous voice. He reached out, a chunky sports ring gleaming in the dull light. "Thank you so much for what you did, uh, Mr.?"

"McMann," he said quietly. "Graham McMann." They shook hands.

"Well you burned my friend too, asshole," said a girl on the other side of the lamp. She was about Mike's age, with spiky cherry popsicle hair. "Burned her right up!" She beamed more strenuous joy than a kid at her own birthday party. "So you won't be getting any thanks from me."

The guy named Graham gave up fighting with the rolling papers and loose tobacco. His face dropped to his chest. "I'm, uh...Jesus, I'm sorry bout your friend." With his strange accent, that last word came out as *fray-end*. Then he made a sound like somebody had just stuck a needle into his back. James realized he was crying.

"Would you rather you'd both been shot?" said Tribe sharply.

"Yeah," said Mulligan dismissively. His eyes flicked only briefly in the girl's direction. "Sorry, but it's collateral damage, right? I mean, I'm sure you're upset about your friend, but fuck...we're all upset!"

"Nice!" said the girl with the cherry popsicle hair. "Real nice!" She rolled her eyes, staring at the ceiling as big tears streamed down her cheeks, inked mascara black.

One of them had brought out a bottle of scotch, and they passed it around. James took a healthy pull. Then another to chase it down. The amber potion ringing in the glass as they each tipped the bottle to their mouths in turn. That Graham guy took the bottle hesitantly, like he was afraid of it. Staring at it with a look of dull horror that slipped into resignation. As his face tilted back to receive the mouth of the bottle, the unkind lamplight revealed unmistakable alcoholic puffiness. So much like the hangover of mourning.

He passed the scotch to Sheilagh, who swigged then gasped, her hand pressed to her mouth. Around the bottle went, then around again. The last of it splashing down Tribe's gullet. He smacked his lips and blew out alcoholic vapor.

"Not bourbon," he said, "but it will do."

"I can see where you're coming from, miss," said Ross. He was sitting next to the girl with the cherry popsicle hair, and he put a hand on her shoulder. "I'd be upset too if my friend was hurt."

"Get your hands off me, perv!" She flinched away from Ross. Her volatile, angry eyes flashed around the group. "You can all go on and pretend," she spat. "Like a bunch of fucking little babies, playing make-believe. Like what, so everything's gonna be peachy now? Is that it?" She flung a finger at Graham. "Now those men with the guns'll be after you, won't they? So you're putting all of us in danger, so why don't you just do us all a favor and fuck off!"

"Yeah!" somebody else spoke up.

"Don't be so bloody stupid!" Sheilagh shouted. Enough punch in her voice to bring a large dog to heel. "Are you really so blind that you can't see what would've happened to us all in that place if Graham here hadn't done what he done? D'you really think in your wildest dreams that you would've gotten out of there otherwise?"

"Uh, yeah?" said the girl, as if Sheilagh was a complete moron. "They couldn't've shot us *all*!"

"Then you're stupider than that fuckin' hair makes you look," Sheilagh stated.

"Seems to me that men with guns are going around doing whatever they damn well please," Ross suggested.

"Anybody else see that guy wearing the red dress?" Mike asked. "What he was doing?"

"Yeah," groaned Sam, the guy with the wounded shoulder. "I saw him. Tall and thin, with a big head of thick black curls. I'd still be lying on the floor of that damn building if I hadn't seen it." With his nose, he indicated his injury. "We couldn't run when everybody else did. He was pointing people out for the gunmen. And it wasn't a dress he was wearing, son, it was a cassock, a priest's robes."

James and Tribe shared another glance. James wondering if Tribe felt the same weightlessness he did.

"Pointing at people, telling the guys with guns what to do." Sam's sweaty face turned towards the lamplight. "People who weren't wounded, they were being hauled up, taken away. And the wounded ones…the wounded ones…" Sam shuddered, unable to finish.

"They were shooting them!" Astrid cried, shaking her fists in outrage. "No hesitation, okay? Just bending over, putting bullets in their heads!"

Sam had his head back against the wall, eyes cinched shut. "That's when we knew – we had to get the hell out of there. No choice."

"We ran for the door." Astrid's voice was thick with tears. "They shot at us. I didn't think we'd make it, I thought we were dead for sure – but we got out. Thank God, we got out!"

"And what about the ones who weren't wounded?" Ross asked hesitantly, as if being forced to ask.

"Well, what d'you think?" Sheilagh snapped.

"Dragged off," said Mulligan with a cynical smile. "As slaves. I saw them being corralled outside, tied up."

"I can't believe that!" Ross spat. "*Slaves?*"

"You look to be in your sixties," said Tribe.

Ross nodded. "Sixty three. So what?"

"Around the time you were born, the Nazis had hundreds of thousands of slave laborers all over Europe. Why couldn't it happen now?"

Ross frowned, raising his hands in the air, as if to test for rain. "Well God, shouldn't people know better by now?"

Mulligan guffawed, shaking his head. "Know better? Know better than what, man!" The note of derision in his laughter irritated James.

"Look now," said Sheilagh, sounding cross. "It doesn't matter why any of us are here, except that we've all survived terrible things. I think that goes without saying." She paused, perhaps for emphasis, her sharp blue eyes whipping around the group. "Hard as it is, you've got to put that behind you and move on."

James was impressed by her command of the situation, the way she sized things up.

"Since we're all here together right now," she continued, "we may as well share what we know."

This was greeted by silence so tense that James found it rude. Only the hiss of the Coleman lamp could be heard.

"I don't know anything," said Mike it a small voice.

142

"Alright, then: what are the true priorities?"

"Food and water," said Tribe immediately, sparing another withering glance for James.

"Precisely. Any of you who've tried the taps knows the water's out. Now that everything's gone to hell, we find ourselves in the middle of a fair sized desert."

"But how can that be?" the cell phone guy piped up hysterically. "How can the water just stop? I mean, it just doesn't make any *sense*!"

Mulligan blew out another incredulous snort. "Dude, where's the lake?" And before the cell phone guy could answer, "It's down there." Mulligan pointed south. "Okay? Follow me so far? Good. Now – how does the water get from the lake down there to the tap right there?" Now he pointed at the sink beside the microwave.

"Just…I dunno, comes up through the pipes, I guess."

"Pumps, dumbo. *Electric* pumps." Mulligan's connect-the-dots tone made James's skin break out in gooseflesh. After what had happened to Allistair, he wanted to warn him: go easy.

But the cell phone guy just went back to fiddling with his little plastic talisman, tongue poked into his cheek.

"Why don't we head for the lake then?" Mike suggested. "Lots of water down there."

"You don't wanna be drinking Lake Ontario water over any length of time," said Ross. He had a way of regarding whoever he was talking to through half-closed eyes. Maybe calm, maybe subtly aggressive.

"Problem is this," Graham spoke up. "We can be down on the lakeshore tomorrow morning if we want, with more water than we'd know what to do with, sure, but then what? Seems clear the city's not exactly hospitable just now. Besides which, water's damn heavy. We won't be carrying much of it very far."

"Tribe and I have hand pumps and filters," said James. "For what they're worth, at least. They should be enough to make Lake Ontario potable enough not to kill us."

"So that's it? Now it's share and share alike?" the girl with the red hair squealed.

"You didn't seem to mind the food," Astrid mumbled from behind her.

The girl with the red hair was perched on a wheeled desk chair. She kicked the floor, spinning around to Astrid. "Fuck you!"

Astrid's lips compressed to a thin, white line. She smacked the girl's face. Hard enough to turn her head over her shoulder. The girl looked shocked, clutching at the red hand mark on her cheek.

"Shut up, you little beast!" Astrid hissed. "I don't know who raised you to speak that way, but I won't put up with it. Now – you can start behaving like a human being. Or you can leave. Your choice. One thing's for damn sure, missy: I've gone through about enough in the past three days without having to deal with your bullshit!"

The red-haired girl jumped up, sending the chair rolling backwards. She snatched up her black bag and scrambled for the door to the alley, throwing it open and taking off.

"Good fucking riddance," Mulligan growled, lighting yet another smoke. All of them had their lucky charms.

There was an uncomfortable silence. The guy with the useless cellphone calmly jockeyed himself into the abandoned chair. Astrid rubbed the hand she'd used to smack the girl. Her eyes had lost their stony gleam. Now she stared into the lamplight, stoned with exhausted fear. "I – I'm sorry," she muttered. "I don't know – I'm sorry…" Sam rubbed her back.

"Sometimes violence is the only proper response," said Tribe. "In times such as these, particularly."

"Doesn't make it right," said Sheilagh, giving Tribe a deadly look. "I know why you did it, Astrid, but it doesn't make it right."

James watched Sheilagh carefully. Something about this woman with the thick Irish accent. The way she'd already memorized all their names, calling them so confidently. As if she'd known them all for years. Authority coalesced in her hard, bright eyes. Almost angry, almost brutal. But appealing at the same time.

"So we've got the damn lake," she continued. "What about food, then? There are stores around, but without refrigeration, any of the perishable stuff'll be off by now."

"There's still canned goods," said Astrid hopefully.

"I'm getting out of the city," said Mulligan. "All of us are here tonight either because we're far from home, or our places are gone. There's a couple million people who'll be competing for the same food supply, I mean clearly. Then there's the gangs…"

"The crazies," Mike added, almost wistfully.

"No shortage of them," Ross agreed.

"Right, so it's out of the city," said Sheilagh. "Any disagreements?" Her request was met with silence. "Alright, we seem to be agreed on that, but where?"

"We're going northeast," said James.

"Why? What's up there?" Mulligan asked.

James shifted on the floor. "I don't know, I'm not sure…"

"Great!"

"Well we sure to God aren't going back west," said Astrid. Her husband had fallen asleep now, still sitting up against the wall.

She patted his leg absently. "It's hellish out there."

"I'll second that," said Sheilagh. Something in their voices was enough to make the rest of them understand that whatever they'd seen in the west end was too awful to be described. "Besides, it would mean crossing back through the downtown core, and that would be madness." She turned to James. "So what d'you mean you don't know why you're traveling northeast?"

A very strong urge to lie. Just as he'd always done in heated moments. Retreated behind his curtain. But he felt inexplicably connected to Sheilagh. Her alert eyes, her plump lips – so familiar somehow, yet far, far away. Her manner of regarding him, eyebrows raised. Frankly probing.

It occurred to him that she already knew. But how could that be? The feeling made about as much sense as a three-dollar bill. Or a guy refusing to believe his cellphone would not work. Or any of this shit.

What would be the point in lying to a woman who looked through him like a pane of glass?

James took a deep breath. "Ever since the pulse – whatever you want to call it…"

"Since the lights went out," said Ross.

"Yeah. I've been having…spells…going in and out of some kind of fugue states…"

"Yeah?" said Mulligan with biting doubt.

"Tribe here thinks I'm having epileptic fits. I don't remember what happens, not very clearly anyway, but Tribe tells me I've been speaking in some foreign language…"

"Well come on, come on!" Sheilagh prompted. "Out with it!"

"It's the Egyptian god Horus. He's commanding me to go northeast." The information spilled out of him now. "I don't know why, not yet, but I think – I mean I've got this impression that I'll know soon. It's like something just out of reach, like something I used to know really well, like a map that I've forgotten – I know how insane this sounds…"

"I hope you do!" Mulligan's smile was a curved vise grip in the lamplight. "Because that's the most crazy bullshit I've ever heard! An *Egyptian god?* Holy fuuuuck! Hey kid!" he called to Mike. "We got one of your crazies right fucking here!"

"Here now!" Tribe snorted. "You haven't been with him. I would be loath if I were you to toss about such careless accusations!"

"Alright, alright," said Sheilagh.

"I believe you," said Graham to James. Mulligan laughed, but Graham waved him off. "I do, mate. You're hesitant to say it, 'cause you're still playin' by the old rules. Oh aye, but I think it's fair to say the rules have changed just a wee bit." He peered at Mulligan. "Don't you, fella?"

"Ah!" Mulligan scoffed, crossing his arms.

Sheilagh looked deeply skeptical. Angrily so. James saw the look she gave Tribe, as if to ask him what the hell he was thinking, sticking in the company of a madman. She closed her eyes and took a deep breath. When she opened them again, she was looking at nobody in particular, but addressing them all. "Right. It doesn't matter why this is happening to him. It's not like we're signing our lives and souls over to each other. All we need to do is get out of the city. I believe that if we work together we stand a better chance of survival. Agreed?"

A general murmur of assent.

"Alright. We're already east of the downtown core anyway, so northeast seems as good a direction as any. I suggest a compromise. We head south tomorrow, to the lake. It's only a few miles, and we need water. A person can survive three weeks without food, but three days without water and you're finished. Then we follow the north shore of Lake Ontario. East. Out of the city. That way we've at least got the water we need. We'll forage for whatever food we can find on the way."

She looked at James, very directly. "I don't suppose your Egyptian god'll look askance at just a small detour, will he?" She winked, and then she smiled. A wide, toothy smile of delighted mockery. And James understood, as he would understand later, that it was the sharing of his food that had made the difference in her mind. That a simple act of generosity was the original foundation of the Group. And of all that happened afterward.

*

Another aching night on the floor. Even with the inflatable groundsheet, James's back and hips complained fiercely. His head pounded. His throat remained raw and sandy. A purely awful night, crowded with fervid visions. Rolling one side to the other, back again. As if the physical movement would take him away from the nightmares. Over and over again, Stacy with her waiting, engorged vagina, raising her hips to welcome him into herself.

And every time, he was fooled. That he was back in his own bed. The herbal scent of her gold hair. The saltiness of her undulating skin.

"Oh yeah," she'd groan. "Fuck that pussy! Fuck me harder!"

This smutty burble from the mouth of the mummy pretending

to be his wife would fill him with gulping dread. He'd rear back to see the distorted face of the woman he loved more than he loved himself. Purple-black, eyes jutting. Her mouth a tightly pursed sucking hole. No bigger around than a drinking straw, shrieking like a vacuum. Shrieking the same message:

Heru commands! Northeast! Go northeast! The Stone! The Stone awaits!

A dozen times through the night, these words jerked James awake. Disturbed by Sam's painful moans. But he'd slide back down into the same scenario again and again. Until livid dawn.

Everybody in the staffroom looked bedraggled, pasty. Wild-haired, puffy-faced. James could smell the body odor and bad breath. His stomach groaned, but there was nothing for breakfast. He knew what Tribe was thinking: robbed by generosity.

Sam's shoulder was bleeding again. There was nothing left to use as a bandage. Astrid had even stripped off her blouse at some point overnight. Sam's face, the texture of feta cheese. Astrid tried to hide her fear, but it was obvious that she was terrified. Equally obvious, Mulligan was irritated by her worry.

Sheilagh went over to have a look at the wound. "You need to keep up the pressure," she told Astrid. The hole was no bigger around than a pencil.

"I am, I am! It's not working – shit!"

Ross handed over his jacket. "Here, use this."

Astrid tossed away her bloody blouse and pressed the jacket over the wound. "I don't understand – the bleeding stopped last night – why the hell would it start up again?"

Sheilagh snatched up the Aspirin bottle lying at Astrid's feet. "Oh, *Jay*sus!"

"What is it?" James asked, stabbed by alarm.

"Aspirin makes it harder for the blood to clot!"

"So giving it to him last night made it start bleeding again?" Astrid wailed.

James held his head in his hands.

"Could be, Astrid. Just keep up the pressure, right?" Sheilagh put on a brave face, even managing a weak smile. She rested a reassuring hand on Astrid's bare back. "It'll stop again, pet. It'll stop."

*

They moved south in a slow column. Towards the lake. Of the twenty or so people in the staffroom last night, only nine joined James and Tribe. Astrid with one of Sam's arms across her shoulders, taking some of his weight. James had made a quick sling for his wounded arm, using a patch of curtain from the employee lounge.

Early morning quiet enveloped the streets. Fast food trash skittered along the pavement between cars. There had been lots of traffic on all the streets and motorways, off and onramps, at lights. Snarled up, bumper to bumper, for hundreds of feet. A few intersections had vehicles stopped in the middle, halted midway through their arcing left turns.

"Easy to see where the lights were red, eh dude?" said Mike, strangely bright.

The traffic lights, now blank and dead. One thing anybody could have counted on before. Any time, day or night, traffic lights merrily glowing red or green, flashing yellow. Not any more. Something creepy in their cold dark stares.

Mike peered at James. "Hey, dude? Easy, huh?" He poked James with an elbow and James leaped away as if stung. "Yo, take it easy, buddy."

James stared at his knife blade. Throwing morning sunlight as Mike tapped the flat edge against his thigh. Screw easy. He showed the kid his palms, shuffling out of arms length. Agitation only magnifying the whispering voice he heard all the time.

Heru commands you, Heru commands you, Heru commands you...

And other things, too. Something about a stone. A stone waiting for him, far to the northeast. It's true, he thought with a kind of eerie petrified glee. I really am losing my mind!

The landscape alone was enough to prompt doubts about his sanity. Wind chanting down canyons of office blocks, condominium towers. Cars overturned, vans smashed through shop fronts. Poles down, draping the street with snarls of black wire, like nests of hibernating snakes. It took great courage to approach those tented wires, to overcome lifetimes of warnings about the dangers of downed power lines. Enough power to fry an elephant. Climbing through one tangle, Mulligan waved a frayed end at Sheilagh. She flinched away, then told him to stop being so *feking* stupid.

They came across a corner store. Ransacked, heaped with junk. The funk of fermenting pop. Sweetly unclean. Gingerly scraping among smashed bottles to scrounge a few cans of soup, a box of crackers. They needed to heave a fallen shelf, James and Mulligan straining with the weight while Graham and Mike sprawled beneath. Sheilagh found some broken bags of pasta. On her knees, scooping up scattered penne with her hands.

"Hey look!" Ross, triumphant behind the counter. Two

chocolate bars in one hand, a rumpled bag of chocolate chip cookies in the other.

The summation of their joy: less food than might have been found on one shelf of an average larder.

*

"What day is it today?" James asked after they'd been on the move for a while.

"Today is Monday June twenty-eighth," Tribe pronounced.

Amazing how simply knowing this bare fact made the ground seem that much more solid. But the quiet street was starting to feel uneasy. He saw a curtain part in a window over a shop. A pale face in another. So still, eye sockets shadowed.

With dizzying clarity, James realized he was now a refugee. Homeless. All along he'd been labeling the people around him as refugees, but here he was. Carrying his food on his back, his stomach sore with hunger. His old life twisted away as easily as a skin tag. No certainty of where he'd be laying his head tonight. Nothing to look forward to now but struggle and stress. A daily scrabble for a hard life.

He heard Tribe groan softly, as if reading his mind.

"You alright?" James asked.

"Until the past few days I'd thought of myself as very fit," he said ruefully.

Graham made a biting laugh. "Not many people are really used to the weight of a pack."

"It's because you're so tall, yo," Mike offered playfully. "That's a lot of extra muscle you need to, like, keep you vertical, guy! How tall are you, anyway?"

"Just over six-foot-seven." Abruptly Tribe halted. Eyes wide.

"What—" James began, before Tribe waved him quiet.

"Do you hear that?" he asked.

"Nah," said Graham, then bit his lip. "Aye! Aye, I do hear it, right enough." The hands he raked through his Roman-cut hair shook badly.

"What is it?" Astrid hissed.

"Sounds like – like jingling chains?" said James uncertainly.

"I think we'd best get out of sight," said Tribe. He sounded scared.

They hurried off the street and crouched behind a panel van parked in a narrow alley. Peeking around the fenders, beneath the undercarriage, they waited.

Gradually, the clinking grew louder. Then they started hearing shuffling feet. A ragged column appeared, winding up the street. Men and women, heads down, hands fastened behind their bowed backs with plastic zip-ties. For what must have been half an hour, the column trudged past, heading north, overseen on both sides by a cordon of armed men. Many of them on horseback. Men in black jumpsuits and black berets. The Sicari.

Swaggering, smoking. Barking orders. *Move it! Hustle up! Keep them eyes down!* Hundreds of feet, pounding a relentless litany, kicking up echoes of ashen dust. Coughing, rattling with the chains binding them in pairs, the pitiful caterpillar trod past.

And accompanying them, taking up the rear, a short pudgy man, balding, feet kicking at the inside of his long crimson cassock as he struggled in the heat. He looked miserable, his face almost as red as his robes, swabbing his forehead with a handkerchief.

Astrid put her hands to her mouth, like she was trying to stuff them in. Stop herself from screaming.

James's thick pulse squeezing his face.

The stone! the Voice in his head droned. *The stoooone!* A deep resonance, as if amplified by soaring stone vaults.

Abruptly, the red-robed man stopped. Head cocked. The handkerchief pinched in one hand, poised a few inches from his sweaty face.

The stone! The stone the stonethestonethestone!

Who could tell how long the Collegian remained, statue-still on the street at the head of the alley. He looked like somebody trying to identify some half-forgotten tune. James held his breath for what seemed to be hours.

Finally, the red-robed man shook himself, peering around rather frantically. He hurried on, tripping over his robes, almost falling face-first into the gutter.

The slave column had passed out of sight, but the defeated pounding rhythm took a long time to fade out. The sound of an ancient, failing heart.

*

"Fuckin' hell," Graham kept saying, shaking his head. His puffy face creased with alarm. After they'd scraped together the courage to leave the hiding spot behind the van, the street was an open gallery, exposing every movement to the merciless penetration of a watchful eye.

The glaring *wadjet* of Heru. The hunting falcon.

"Betelgeuse." James's voice scraping concrete in his throat.

"Who the fuck are those assholes in the black uniforms?"

Mulligan asked.

Nobody answered. Not another word was spoken. All of them with alert, round eyes. Terrified of seeing more. As if the very act of looking around might summon them.

When they finally reached it, the lake seemed impossibly alive. Free. Vibrant with twinkling sun, every wave cupping ephemeral, fiery jewels.

The clean offshore wind whisked through their hair, pushing away the ashtray stink of the city. Green water slapped at the concrete of the Redpath refinery pier, inviting them to fill their water bottles.

Mike volunteered to go down the metal ladder set into the concrete, holding the hoses of the Outward Bound filter pumps in the water. James slurped back an entire liter, filled it again, and drank the whole thing down. He winced as the cold water struck his empty stomach with an icy punch. Slightly fishy-tasting, but slaking the horrible dusty flavor in his mouth and throat.

Then he splashed his face, using his hands to massage the coolness into his skin. Sinking into his pores, rinsing away the soot, the memory of those slaves. The haughty trot of the Sicari with their guns and cigarettes.

They found a spot away from the road, behind the hulking refinery building next to the water. Even with the food they scrounged, there was barely enough to feed everybody a single meal. They heated up three cans of soup, crumbling some crackers into it.

They sat with their backs to the ruined downtown, eating with their feet dangling over the edge of the pier, watching a huge rusty cargo ship drift with the waves, crosswise across the harbor. Amnesia, James thought.

He spooned the salty gruel into his mouth slowly, precisely. Enjoying every fragment of warm flavor. Careful not to drop even a crumb. When the plastic bowl was empty he used his finger to squeegee the dregs into his mouth. He couldn't remember the last time such fine detail of any meal had been penned so deeply on his awareness. For dessert, each of them was rationed one chocolate chip cookie.

When they'd finished the meager meal, they stayed put for a while, soaking up the midday sun. Digesting. Some shared tales of where they'd been when God called lights out. That was the phrase Ross used. "Lights out," he barked, sandy voice edged with the same tone people used to complain about income tax or irritating sales calls during the dinner hour.

Ross had been at a baseball game. Jays vs. Cardinals. When it happened, all the brilliant halide lights around the stadium burst in a final white flash, cascading brassy sparks over the crowd.

Astrid and Sam had been passing through town on their way to visit their daughter, who was taking summer courses at a community college west of the city. They'd stopped for a quick coffee. When it happened, a Bunn coffee maker exploded, spraying boiling water over the girl behind the counter.

"I was on the subway," said the kid with the kinky hair. His eyes bulged. "Total, complete darkness. Like – like Hell." It was all he would say. When Mulligan prodded him for his name, the kid just gave him a queer look. As if Mulligan had asked him to discuss his first sexual experience.

When gunfire erupted again away to the north and west, they shared some uncomfortable glances and reluctantly got to their feet. James watched uneasily as Sheilagh and Ross repacked their remaining stock of food. Five cans of beans. A few crackers. Three cans of tuna. Half a bag of the chocolate chip cookies.

"I'd give my right nut for another one of those," Mulligan groaned as Sheilagh shoved them into James's pack.

"Stale though," said Graham miserably.

They'd also grabbed four squashed bricks of butter, but it was a greasy, sloppy mess. A few considered sniffs told them it was rancid, so they left it behind. That was it.

James took Tribe aside as the rest were getting ready to go. "That's not much for eleven people to survive on."

"I told you not to be so damned generous with our supplies."

"Aw, Jesus, Tribe, don't say I told you so – don't do that."

"But I did!"

"What difference does it make? Feels like I'm dead already."

"Well you're not," Tribe snapped. "Stop being so stupid."

James lowered his voice. "We should tell them about Lichboegh, the Sicari. They deserve to know."

"I disagree. We don't have any proof that they are after us."

James gave him a skeptical look. "Don't kid a kidder, man."

"I'm not kidding. How would they have tracked us to that warehouse?" Tribe put a firm hand on his arm. "That slave column was just the latest sign of what Dr. Rivers told us: Lichboegh was prepared. They're scouring the city – and why not? This city is the richest concentration of potential slaves for hundreds of miles. Which is why we need to get away. No?"

James winced at a gunshot nearby. "There are lots of good reasons to get away."

"Let's assume you're right: somehow they tracked us to the warehouse. If that was the case, why then did they not track us to the store last night? Or find us in the alleyway this morning? James! What is the matter?"

"You remember how that Collegian guy stopped."

"What of it?"

"It was like – it was like he could hear what I can hear."

Tribe snorted. "You're deluding yourself."

"Look – we should tell these people the truth."

"To what end?"

"What do you mean, 'To what end'? The truth – that's its own end."

Tribe gave a condescending snicker, shaking his head. "You seem to be a reasonably intelligent fellow—"

"Gee, thanks."

"If the Fates have decreed that we are to be stranded with these people in this hellish situation, then so be it. I don't see the point in causing them undue panic over something that we don't even know to be true."

"You think this is gonna last forever?"

Tribe made a face. "Forever, twenty-four hours – what's the damn difference to us if we're killed by a mob? Or captured by one of Lichboegh's slaving squads? Think only of today – today we survive! Tomorrow, same again." Tribe took a deep breath through his long, flared nose. As if scenting a bouquet of damn flowers. "I feel freer than ever before in my life! Come on!" He pounded James on the back and stalked ahead to join the column of their new compatriots.

"At least I'm not the only one going insane," James muttered, following along.

*

Keeping their eyes on Sam and Astrid, they marched east in short stages. Sam was on his feet, moving under his own power, but his pallor was bad.

It was hard going. As the afternoon wore on, the group found itself but a small part of a swelling pathetic parade streaming away from the downtown core. Behind them, smoke-veiled office towers and condo blocks boomed and resonated, crackling. Intermittent but unceasing, the rattling breath of urban combat.

People peering back over their shoulders, stealing peeks at the city. Unable to believe. They'd all heard those sounds, many times in fact. Witnessed from sofas, from bedrooms, televised news reports on civil wars across the world. Now there was no buffer.

The Eleven stuck together. Hardly more than strangers

themselves, they avoided contact with anyone unknown. In a tentatively defined group, outside human contact was risky. Keeping in mind the thin ration in James's pack. Their all. Precariousness burning now like the hard sunlight on their inflamed necks.

People all around with huge ad hoc packs, precious things jumbled into bulging blankets tied with twine and electrical cord. An antique mantel clock that tumbled out of a woman's bundle, smashing on the pavement. Wailing, the woman went to her knees so that they needed to move around her.

They stalked past a smoky junked out backdrop of smashed shop fronts, dark and hollow, only hinting at the jumbled, wind-flapping chaos within. Block after block. A wedding dress signaled surrender around the jagged edge of a broken window, quivering with the fear of whoever was waving it – but there was no one. Just a tattered rag on a dismembered mannequin.

Heru commands you, Heru commands you, Heru commands you... the Stone awaits, the Stone awaits... the Stone the Stone the Stone!

Ever swelling in James's mind. Eroding his sanity as surely as termites boring through a wooden beam.

A commotion ahead. A thin swarthy man pressing through the passing throng, accosting people, reaching into their space, making them reel back. As they passed him, his bony pleading fingers fidgeted against James's hands.

"Excuse me, excuse me, is it gonna – is it gonna rain? Is it?" In a whiny childlike voice, pawing for alms. "Please, is it gonna rain? Excuse me, excuse me…"

James pulled away so suddenly he bumped Sam's wounded arm. Sam swore through teeth.

"Excuse me, excuse me, is it gonna rain? Is it gonna rain?" Fading into background noise as they left him behind.

The skirling wind shifted around behind them, and it started snowing. A grey blizzard of ash swirling down. Tufting on their shoulders and packs. James swiped at a sudden burning pinch on the back of his neck. It felt like a wasp. His fingers came away sooty. A hot ember. Burning snow.

By the time their gaunt shadows had crept out before them, their legs were weary. They started looking for a place to spend the night. There was a broad park with large trees north of the road. Cool shadows beckoned. They agreed to stop, and James heard Astrid whisper "Thank God, thank God." A resigned quietude, sore in his ears.

They wove their way between knots of people who'd already

staked claims to the grey-powdered grass. People sitting on blankets. Like an outdoor concert, James thought. Except everybody was dour. Faces sagging with exhaustion, grim women clutching befuddled children. Children grown furtive, wary.

James longed to hold Jen and Sara. To tell them it would be okay. All okay.

Searching for a place to bed down, James spotted her. Bursting ripe in his throat, panicky joy.

Horus, hurry! Announce to the gods of the East and their spirits: He comes indeed, this James, an Imperishable Spirit! Whom he wills that he live, he lives. Whom he wills that he die, he dies!

Her back against a huge maple tree, her face turned away from him – but he saw her straight golden hair, and he knew it was Stacy.

"Stacy!" he called hoarsely. He ran for her. "Stace! Where are the girls!"

Chapter 9

Lilac Taylor

When Betelgeuse struck its blow, Lilac was waiting for a streetcar, homeward bound from a particularly shitty date with Pete. Thinking of her friend Wendy. Wendy, who always said "Never chase after a man or a streetcar. There'll always be another one along." How true, Wen, how true.

The city rushed light and air around her, the fecund urban energy turning itself on for the night. Just fifteen minutes before, she'd pulled the plug on dinner with Pete at the Peartree Bistro. So much for her latest male accessory. Gleeful, naughty Pete and his meaningful, pregnant leers. And what was that he'd said about her? Um, Pete, would ya care to do a repeat? Gore whore. That's what he'd said about her. *Gore whore.*

Their third or fourth date, depending on how one counted the sweaty funk of date number two, which had turned into a full-on weekend under the sheets.

That evening at the Peartree, spooning crème brulé, they'd gotten into it over climate change. He'd dismissively called it a myth. She'd corrected him. Bitchily. Sure, she could admit it. Then, his retaliation: *Gore whore.* Pete's little comment was so childish, so amateur-hour, and that's really what set her off because Lilac just couldn't have it. It wasn't just rude. It was a pisspoor thing to say to anyone, let alone a friend.

Then, only to make things even worse, Pete responded to her stony look with waggling eyebrows: "Like, Al Gore, right? Get it?"

I mean, gawd. *Gore whore*? Was that the best this guy could do? Lilac knew she was over-reacting. Even as the tears blurred her vision, she told herself to stop, just hold it together girl, but her legs propelled her up, she grabbed her bag, and she was moving. And moving felt good. Better than sitting, pretending to enjoy that shit.

Off she'd marched, and Pete tailed her out onto the humid sidewalk.

"I'm sorry," Pete pleaded. His lean athletic face pathetically pinched. "It was a really dumb thing to say and I apologize. Don't go, okay?"

And right then she'd known: Pete wasn't trying to atone for hurting her feelings. No, hardbody Pete with the six-pack and the stockbroker credentials was still trying to close the deal.

All at once she'd laughed. Even as she swiped away tears, she was snickering at his pretense. "Y'know, Petey," she giggled, "you're not the first to call me a whore, but you might want to ask yourself, is that the best strategy to get your little dicky wet?"

She turned and strutted away, hearing him shout "Oh nice, real nice!" Feeling powerful. Flushed with honest pride.

A quarter of an hour later, her iPod died, right smack dab in the chorus of Ani Di Franco's 'How Have You Been.' She'd been grooving to the wavy-gravy horns, and suddenly the music was gone. Hitting the triangular play symbol over and over because she'd just recharged the buggery thing last night, so why wasn't it working, damn it!

The traffic accelerating through the green light along Dundas glided to a standstill. Lilac wondered why everybody was stopping. A fluey shiver trickled down her spine. Goose walking over your grave!

All around her, people were saying "Hello? Hello?" Jerking their cell phones away from their heads to glare at them in the gloom. "Are you still there? Hello?"

Gloom. Yes, everything did seem very dim. Then Lilac saw the lights in the streetcar were out. Bringing to mind a crippled submarine, a dark tube trapping shadows. Sinking into deep, deep black. Something about the shifting dim entrails of the dark streetcar probed into her pelvis with chilly dead fingers.

Car doors were opening now, people climbing out, gaping.

"Yours is dead too?" she heard somebody call out.

"Isn't this weird!" A frightful giggle, swollen with worry.

A shout. And then another. She was alarmed to hear those voices echoing. Sound smeared around the edges, like a child's finger-painting bleeding over the lines. Echoing the way they might in some lost, empty wilderness.

This was no longer an urban landscape, but a twilit maze-trap. More and more hollow voices, calling, questioning. Car doors booming closed, resonating like bass drums.

She heard a swelling babble, thousands of voices. As if she'd suddenly been gifted with the cursed ability to hear the thoughts of the entire city. Claustrophobic within a frantic crowd miles wide. Gobbling, gabbling.

Why can I hear all these voices?

Chickens.

She shuddered at the sudden intrusion of an unwelcome childhood memory.

The voices were just like the chickens Thousands of chickens. The memory, a charcoal rubbing off a grave marker, buried in her consciousness. She'd forced herself not to think about the farm for a long time.—

That's when she saw all the people lying prone. All around her, flat and limp on the sidewalk, on the street. A guy with a mullet and ratty red Converse high-tops. On his back in the gutter, arms and legs unbearably twitching. Wide sightless eyes staring into nothing. Unblinking. His mouth working, very slowly opening, closing. She saw his delicate cheeks flex and bend, just like the gills of a dying grouper.

"Look out!" somebody screamed behind her.

Lilac had to dodge away from a small East Indian girl. She was whirling. What the freaky hell was she doing? Whirling with her arms out, faster, faster, making a manic gibbering whine that made Lilac think she was being electrocuted. Faster, faster, like a siren. Careening back onto the sidewalk, she crashed through a shop window. The glass cascaded in jazzy xylophonic notes and the whirling girl went down with it, sliced to ribbons, spouting blood all over, still twitching, tinkling in the broken shards.

Lilac cried into her hands. Her eyes felt distended, desperate. Jolting horror in the failing light. Suddenly she felt herself engulfed by the silence. Only now it occurred to her why every sound was resonating, as if in a distant gorge. Why every voice was magnified. Gone – the comforting rushing hum of the city, the coursing energy of motors, machines, the dissonant clef of speed – all vanished into a creepy void. A desolate throat gulping her in.

She ran then. Forgetting her iPod. Letting it drop, the ear buds tearing free, opening her ears to the vibrating fullness of her own runners slapping the concrete. From far away, a rumbling explosion. Every sound, drowning in silence. The city deadened. Darkened, slipping into absolute nighttime.

Running through what seemed a dim forest of stumps. They were people, of course, she knew that. But the creeping shadows milling in the streets terrified her. Later when she struggled to explain the sensation to the rest of the Circle, she could only define the terror by saying that the shadows seemed dead to her. Shades.

She barely remembered getting back to her own apartment. Sweaty, she scooped Helga into her arms and sat under a blanket by the window. Lit some candles. Thought, why not put on some music? Then collapsed in a heap of hysterical giggling when she realized what a stupid idea *that* was.

Still, she did expect the power to go back on. Didn't they all, at first? Like Tom Petty said, the waiting is the hardest part. Hiding. The strained sense that she must not be found. Clenching her hands around her face at the screaming and hooting in the night. Gunfire.

Worse, far worse – that great gobbling of voices she'd heard. The city a mind effervescent with lunacy. Anything, *anything* never to hear that sound again.

Waiting. Fear metastasizing into gnawing fright. She nibbled her fingernails until they bled. Waited for some kind of news. Something. But dreading whatever cruelty it would bring. The dark blank TV screen a mocking grin. Eventually she needed to cover it with a pillowcase, unable to stand the sense of pregnant imminence.

Very badly, she wanted to call somebody. Her friends Wendy, Jesse. Anybody.

Even Pete?

Gore whore.

Yeah, Pete. Exactly. You go that way if you want. I'm done with snide.

I don't want to know, she thought defiantly, staring at the little television that now looked like a Klansman effigy. What good could more knowing possibly bring?

But why – why the hell wasn't anybody *doing* anything?

She tried to do some work on the sweater she was knitting for Jesse. Even burying her hands in her wool stash was no comfort against consuming paranoia, the sense of wily, unseen forces trapping her tight.

She sought Helga's calico implacability. Helga the wise. Helga the noble. Steady eyes, as yellow, as green as halved avocados. Only the rise and fall of her purring was familiar enough to ease the twist in Lilac's guts.

The Sunday morning after the power died, she was startled into wakefulness. Waiting to hear what had disturbed her sleep.

Complete silence.

She crawled out of bed for the first time in – well, she didn't know exactly how long, now that it came to it. Enveloped in her own musky odor, needing a wash. She peeked through her drapes at the empty street. The sunlight seemed pale and thin. A moribund sepia stain.

She was very thirsty, but when she turned on the kitchen tap nothing came out except a fading gurgle. What a shitter that was. Enough to prick her eyes with tears. Almost out of food, too. Even if the eggs were still fresh – which she knew they couldn't be, not in this heat – she had no way to cook them. And most importantly, Helga was giving her the keen, skeptical look peculiar to cats: she knew her Whiskas was gone.

"We're out, girl!" Lilac's strained voice sounded sad, bereft in the stuffy apartment.

Only one thing to do. Sunday was shopping day, after all.

Later, in hindsight, relating her story to the Circle, she'd be able to see that shock and fear had doped her mind. But that Sunday, the third day after the stoppage of the world, she sat and carefully made her list. Obsessively stroking Helga's arched back, she chewed up a piece of bread and peanut butter, planning her excursion. Her linen shopping bags, she'd need those. Wallet, check.

The nearest supermarket was at least seven miles away. Lilac had always taken the streetcar. "I think that option is poo-pooed," she told Helga. "Gotta walk it. The air'll do me some good anyway!"

Runners, check.

"Okay, yup, money. Don't think credit or debit'll do just now, Helga." And then singing the tune from Cabaret:
Moneymoneymoney! – moneymoneymoney! – moneymoneymoney! hoo!

Luckily she always kept a few twenties under her futon. Tucking the bills into her sweats, tying her shoes, grabbing her shopping bags, she gave Helga a pet-pet, told her she'd see her soon. But she stopped then, catching a peripheral glimpse of herself in the mirror by the door. She looked cross. She went back down the hall, scooped up Helga again, and dropped her in one of the shopping bags. Helga gave a bitchy mew, but Lilac scratched her head.

"You thought you'd get out of it? No way, buck-o!"

Then she was out the door, down the stairs, into the street. It never occurred to her – not even an inkling – that she'd never make it within miles of the supermarket.

Terrified of that crowded gobbling noise, she stopped just outside the door on the street. Mouth open, listening for the gabble of ten thousand panicky voices rising in a sudden crescendo. So much like the vast chicken pens, the clotting choke of ammonia—

No, no. No, no, no.

Thousands of harried chickens with their frantic little beady eyes. Ever alert but utterly doomed to slaughter.

No, damn it!

Nothing to hear, anyway. Just restless air whistling. Still early, balmy. But the air stank of burning rubber and plastic. The street was deserted, which only gave her the creeps.
> *If you happen to be rich and you find you are left by your love*
> *Though you moan and you groan quite a lot*

She'd only gone a few blocks before she saw the hanged. Five of them, swinging from the lowest branches of a few maple trees. Lilac heard the yellow nylon ropes creak and thought she was listening to the sound of her own descent. Devolution into something else. Something less than human.

When you haven't any coal in the stove and you freeze
In the winter and you curse to the wind at your fate!

Nothing but rustling leaves and rope creaking under the weight of corpses.

"Hey!"

She froze. The voice coming from behind her. Its merriness, its full-throated sociability sank hot nausea into her core.

"Hey, I said! Don't be shy!"

She ran, and they chased her. Whooping and screeching, gaming. Her breath was just starting to give out when the toe of her runner caught a lip on the sidewalk and she went down hard, scraping her palms.

Poor Helga screeched with fright. Kicking her way out of the bag, the cat was gone before Lilac could get her skinned hands around her. Gone. The closest connection she had with any living being.

She rolled over, cowering as her pursuers strode up. A gang of seven or eight. No more than kids. Streaked with filth, clothes ragged. One of them waving a machete.

"Now," he panted, pointing the blade at her with a jolly smile. "That was fun. But see, you gotta pay to be on our territory. So we're gonna have some real fun, bitchy!"

"Don't," said another voice. Off to Lilac's right. Deep and nasally. A tall, slouching man ambled up, just as if he was out to meet friends for a Sunday stroll. He held up something. A book. "Now, just don't."

The one with the machete drew sizzling breath through his teeth.

"Even more fun!" said another one, sliding one grimy hand down the front of his pants.

"Whatsoever you do to the least of my brothers," said the silver-haired man holding out the book, "that you do unto me." A Bible. Held out at arms length, a tiny shield of well-thumbed pages.

"Hey, if you insist," said another member of the gang. He had a thick coil of yellow nylon rope slung over one shoulder.

"You will not touch this young woman." The stranger hardly raised his voice. More a simple statement of fact than a threat, but the surety behind it was enough to make them pause. Just for a second.

"Dog," the kid with the machete laughed, shaking his head. "You trippin'."

Still laughing, he got down on his hands and knees. Reached

up, pressing the machete blade onto Lilac's face. Parallel with her nose. Lilac squirmed. Knowing even a small jerk of her neck would be enough to sink the keen edge into her skin.

"Don't be movin' now, bitchy!" Gripping her sweats with his teeth. Pulling them down.

They swarmed the man with the Bible, forcing him to his knees.

"You gonna do some prayin' for me, boy!" Even putting on the Deliverance accent. Yipping like hyenas. "And you better pray good!"

The kid with the machete luxuriated in tugging her pants off. Nuzzling her panties with his nose. "Whoo! You stink like chocolate!"

Then the kid spotted something, sat up. An explosion cracked down the street. Lilac heard a loud pop and then there was blood, lots of blood pouring all over her track pants, her runners.

"No!" cried the man with the Bible. "Aw, no, no!"

The machete suddenly leaped, clattered down on the pavement. Lilac gawked at the gaping hole in the kid's forehead. He actually managed to get to his knees, blood spraying out. Then the kid collapsed, hitting the ground like a sack of wet refuse.

Another sharp crack rent the air and the kid with the hand down his pants had his neck blown open with the sound of a giant rubber band snapping.

"Get away!" ordered a stern female voice, echoing from some way down the street.

For a moment the remaining gang members froze.

"You!" the female voice called. "in the blue tracksuit. You're next!"

The kid in the blue tracksuit, a curly-headed baboon with a paper-white face, flinched and ran. Suddenly they all scattered, the sound of their shoes smacking pavement, echoing away.

Lilac stared intently at the kid lying at her feet. The hole above his distorted left eye still spouting. And I can feel the warmth of his lifeblood soaking into my socks, she thought. His body's warmness mingling with my own.

Numbed by shock, only barely aware of being dragged away from the kid's corpse.

Moving through deadened streets full of bleak wonders: a klaxon-voiced man pogoing up and down, screaming "Yee-haw! Yee-haw! Yee-haw!" Even long after they'd passed him, she continued to hear his echoing screech chasing them down the street canyons.

She saw a dog hanging from a telephone pole by a large spike through its head. She was struck by its pink slug tongue. A totem of the future. But so immediate.

Unlike these frozen moments, Lilac only blearily registered her companions. The man with the Bible who said his name was Asshole. But no, that couldn't possibly be right. Could it?

The butchy woman with the rifles was called Amy. She'd shot the kids. Bathed Lilac in blood. More murder in her eyes. She scared Lilac.

Amy forced them to move fast, on and on for hours, until Lilac's legs ached, until she begged to stop. It never occurred to her that she could simply stop moving of her own volition. Amy was a woman who demanded. They stayed in a bus shelter for the night, bedding down on old newspapers. So this is what it's like to be homeless, Lilac thought to herself.

Amy had them up at grey first light. No food, no water. Only more hours of panicked trooping, wary as criminals on the lam. By that afternoon, the Bible man complained about his arthritis. "Can't go on," he gasped through his clenched dentures, leaning on a garbage bin. "Can't we stop?"

Amy revealed herself as a Darwinian. She wanted to move on, leave him behind.

Faint with hunger, Lilac insisted on stopping. There was a park across the road. They settled by a huge tree.

It was her fear of the guy sprinting headlong towards her, shouting about the kids, the kids, the kids that jolted Lilac back to full awareness for the first time in almost forty-eight hours. Yuck – her track pants and runners were stiff with blood! Disgusting!

That's right, the kid who was about to rape her. Shot through the head.

She turned defensively towards the guy running at her. He was filthy and sweaty, lean and tall. With both hands he flung his brown greasy hair off his forehead. Looking at her face seemed to affect him like she'd just hoofed him in the balls. He gasped and groaned. Stumbled back as Amy raised her rifle.

"Sorry…" he panted, surrendering with his hands. "Sorry – I thought – I thought you were…"

His voice trailed off into a pitiful moan. He sunk to his knees and elbows, completely done in.

Quick on his heels, a towering man in black, carrying a sword.

Chapter 10

The Dispossessed

Stacy turned towards James as he ran towards her. Sat up, lifting her back away from the tree trunk. He saw her face, the face that wasn't Stacy after all. A forehead mottled with shadowed worry. Hard distrust.

Jesus Christ, she didn't look a thing like Stacy! Except for the hair. Not even close, with her button nose and her pursed frowning mouth.

His legs weakened. He sank to the grass. Hope ground under an iron heel. "Sorry. I thought you were somebody else."

Her keen gray eyes kept at him, tweezing. Then he heard the sharp metallic snick-snack of a bolt action. A stout woman standing nearby, holding a rifle mounted with a huge telescopic sight. It wasn't aimed at James but he could see the probability on her wide face. One finger stretched over the trigger guard.

"Now, now," said a cotton-haired man, sitting cross-legged on the grass. He had a book open on his lap, reading glasses gripping precariously the very tip of his long upturned nose. "Relax, Amy. Take it easy."

The rest of the Eleven had come up behind James. For a few moments, all of them staring dumbly at each other. The woman with the gun worried by their number. James saw it in her pout, her eyes that kept roving to Mike's knife. Tribe's scabbard.

Astrid helped Sam ease himself down with a groan, sitting against the bole of the tree on the opposite side from the woman James had taken for Stacy.

"Don't often see a man with a sword on his belt," said the cotton-haired man. A wryness there, playing with the possibility of imminent death.

"One doesn't often find a man sitting with an open Bible," Tribe responded dryly. "In the midst of social calamity."

"I'm wondering if you can think of a better time to be sitting with a Bible." Behind the glasses, his eyes challenged him with jocularity. A diagonal crack across the left lens, a frozen spark. "I'm Athol."

James blinked. What did he say his name was?

Sheilagh stepped forward. "I'm sorry – what was that?"

"Athol." He spelled it out with a mild smile. Perhaps knowing

164

full well what James was thinking. Mulligan too, judging by the smirk on his face.

James caught Mulligan's quizzical glance. Both of them snorting together. Graham's full lips contorting, twisting. Mulligan didn't even try to hide his laughter. One of those situations when giggles catch on. Trying to smother them, they were stoked into blazing full-blooded guffaws.

Ridiculous! James thought. His eyes filled with tears and his lungs emptied of air. Athol. No, no, no. It couldn't be real – no way. This ragged-assed band, the Eleven, with dirt-streaked faces and outrageous bed head, the lot of them. Bleary-eyed, the stupid blink of early morning. Except they'd already kissed the afternoon goodbye!

And now. A Bible thumper. Named Athol.

"Dude," Mulligan managed. "I mean, sorry about the lisp, bro, but stop being so hard on yourself!"

James laughed until his breath squeaked in his throat. Desperate laughter, only a symptom of despair. Stacy still gone from him. And the girls.

Mulligan hacked like a kid. His even white teeth blazing in his purple face. Graham turned away with a hand over his mouth, pretending to cough.

Sheilagh looked pissed off at their rudeness. But Athol put out a big calming hand and a crooked smile. "Don't worry about it, miss. I believe I'm used to it."

"I'm Sheilagh," she said. They shook hands.

Once again, names dealt like Tarot cards. Athol did the honors for his side. "The lady with the guns is Amy," he said. A slow speaker. The sloppy intonation of a drunk. But James could tell he was perfectly sober. This was just his manner. *Athol.*

"Never been much of a *lady*," Amy muttered. Her face remained taut, impassive. Round, somewhat babyish. But stony. Supplely olive. She was a short woman, big-boned. Hard and soft at the same time. Shifting her weight back, propping the butt of her rifle on her hip. A Western maverick.

Now Athol's steady hand indicated the blonde woman James had taken for Stacy. "This is Lilac."

James choked. "You must be fucking joking!" His laughter catching in his throat like a stalk of dead grass.

"Does it look like he's fucking joking?" Lilac spat, lancing him with disdain.

And how unlike Lilac she seemed to him. The Lilac of his imagination was tall, dark and angular. She never would have used such profanity.

This Lilac hugged her knees to herself and James saw her shoes and pant cuffs were thickly painted with dried blood.

"Pull up some turf," Athol invited them amiably.

James saw Amy roll her eyes as she shifted her weight. Jesus, she had another rifle slung across her back.

Awkwardly, James's group all slumped to the earth. Finally surrendering to the gravity that had ground their joints all day. Closed-eyed, open-mouthed gasps of relief, of pain. Arrayed around the maple tree's bole, an organism that must have stood in that spot for two hundred years, the setting sun firing its leaves in a ceramic glaze. For a long time none of them spoke. Each lost in their own moment, relationships budding too new, too fragile to risk even small talk.

Athol broke the propriety. This man with the long, wide face, shining pink in the heat. He was very curious about them, peppering them with cheeky questions delivered in a slow cadence. Where were they from? Where were they going? It turned out Amy was leading he and Lilac to her grandmother's place a ways east of the city. Motes in the current of those fleeing the chaos.

James, trying not to lose his shit. Staring at the inscribed stela of the maple's huge trunk. He thought he'd come so close to finding Stacy, reclaiming something subtly like hope. Hunger, exhaustion fissuring his emotions to the consistency of weathered shale.

Mulligan ended up sitting next to Sheilagh, who was sticking close to Rohini. "What's her story?" he asked, indicating Rohini with his chin. His skeptical tone as whiny as James's grumbling stomach.

Rohini swayed zombie-like, her arms hanging limp, hands turned palms-up on the grass.

"I don't know. Found her wandering in this state, what, three nights ago now? She's not said a word since, 'cept tell me her name."

"You think she's...you know..." Mike stammered.

"One of them? What was it you called them Mike? Crazies?" Mike shrugged defensively.

"I don't know, to be honest. I just feel – it's just that I need to take care of her. Just that."

"Who says she's not one of them, though?" Mulligan asked in his pointed way. "Who says she won't strangle us in our sleep?"

"Nobody says that," said Sheilagh shortly. "Who says *you* won't?"

"Oh sure, turn it around. Okay."

"I just think you need to be a bit more understanding of things, Mulligan. You can't know what's going on in poor Rohini's head.

And here y'are, talking about her as if she's not even here!"

"Looks to me like she's not!"

"Ah, go on!"

James had his arms bridged between his knees, his forehead resting on them. Staring at black ants struggling through a jungle of grass.

The Stone beckons! Beckons the Stone! Northeast, northeast! Unto the will of Heru! Peret nefrew Heru! Behold the splendor of the perfect Horus!

Leave me alone, he thought. Please. Let me be.

*

They warmed the soup. No more than a few spoonfuls each. A few crackers. Half a cookie. Amy, the woman with the rifles, offered to trade for some venison jerky. None of them had the energy to debate, now that the smell of warm food teased their noses. Slow deliberation, the sharing of bowls, of spoons. Passed back and forth with such care. Even a drop wasted would be enough to crush their spirits.

"Nothing like eating *al fresco*," Amy remarked.

All around them, the fixed attention of the starving. Desperate people tugged by aromas. Their need pawed at the group, flaccid but insistent. James and the others closed circle around the maple's clasping roots. Fourteen now. Somehow communal in the tilting shadow of the mighty tree.

"Spare some?" A groveling man with two skinny children in tow.

"We've just finished all we have," said Tribe uncharitably.

"I'll lick the bowl!" squawked an elderly woman with a quaking face.

James saw Amy holding her rifle ready. A soldier now. "Back." So quietly spoken, the only word. Her even eyes casting the throng away.

"Assholes," the man snarled, dragging his children away.

James huddled over his bowl. Thinking, *what an apt description*. Wondering if it was possible to plumb the exact degradation of his spirit. A beautiful downward arc. Natural as breath.

Already, James thought. This is what we've become.

Perhaps it was shame that shut them all up. Not a word. Furtive glances, sure. Easily mistaken for resentment. Unfocused sidelong, never meeting the gaze of another.

The flavor of his meal clung to his mouth. A membrane, more

real than the food itself. He wished he'd eaten more slowly. Savored those few bites. Saliva still flowing, his glands anticipating. Demanding.

The southerly breeze shifted west. Cooling down. James put on his anorak, hugged it to himself. The trees seemed to be smoking as the wind blew the ashes from their leaves. He longed to be indoors, away from the chilly whispering air that stank of burning. Whispering that enveloped, that held you, crept into your pores.

Peret nefrew Heru! Behold the splendor of the perfect Horus!

"Jimmy?"

James, wrapped so firmly in the Voice that he didn't react. Then he heard Amy say "Back," saw this time she was actually aiming her gun.

"Jimmy! Fuck sake, tell this bitch to lay down!"

James looked up. A still figure in a dirty blue shirt stood over him. A squat colossus. "Massimo!" he shouted, jumping to his feet, embracing his friend. The smell of his sweat, the scratch of his beard on his neck. "Where did you come from?"

Solid assurance, a taproot to the time before. Nerves coursing, alive to Massimo's big calloused fingers. James held him at arms length. He laughed.

"Jesus Christ! Haven't had this kinda reaction since ma squeezed me out!" Massimo smacked James on the back hard enough to make him cough.

"It's damn good to see you, you big ape!" James introduced him all around. Acting ridiculous. Gushing, but not caring. Even Tribe seemed very happy to see Mass again, giving him a firm hug.

"Eh, but where's Dr. Rivers?"

James broke into tears. Still smiling, rasping a sob.

*

They needed water. James gathered all the bottles and canteens. Candy-hued plastic jugs. Dented stainless steel torpedoes. He and Massimo carried them south out of the park, across the wide expanse of Lake Shore Boulevard. Like some ancient contest ground now abandoned. The wind playing among the dead cars, minivans, SUV's and trucks lining the road. Whooping its impetuous answer to their muted engines, joyously loud. Mocked for a hundred years by petty machines. The wind that had played among waves of water and rock for a million millennia before life first stirred. What was a century to this thing? What did it mean for the wind to be patient?

The beach was on the other side of a wide parking lot. James beginning to see how much their civilization had gestated according to the DNA of wheels and motors. His and Massimo's shoes scraping across acres of pavement spotty with oil. The seminal leakage of virile machines. I knew about the car, James thought. Or thought I did. Only in the context of effortless speed.

And now?

What was it Maggie had always said? The fish are the last to see the water.

They stood on the shore, a heaving, breathing membrane between earth and lake. Water and sky. Way out, from just beyond the curve of the earth, a massive tower of black smoke roiled into the atmosphere.

"Gotta be ten, fifteen thousand feet, min." Massimo's robust mouth open, his head back to see the cloud's uppermost extremity, blurred by high winds.

They filled the bottles one by one. Taking turns with the pump, their arm muscles forcing cold arterial flow. Without a pier to sit on, their feet and pant cuffs were soon soaked through.

"This is harder than it looks," said Massimo after the fifth bottle.

"What? A big boy like you?"

Here, with their backs to the city, they might have been on a continental edge. The very rim of the known.

Abruptly, James stripped down to his underwear and charged into the waves. The water was bitingly cold, but it felt rejuvenating to wash the sweat-clotted dust and ash off himself. The first time he'd bathed at all in days and days.

After James put his clothes back on, they sat for a long while, staring at the jade waves foaming in. Seated in the till of rounded bricks and limestone, smooth glass giblets like foggy emeralds. The Great Lake's waves inscribing the shore with antiquated tales. Written in an eroded alphabet.

Gulls tossed on the offshore wind, brittle bone kites. Strung from James's spirit. Their weightless screech needling the hollow thundering waves.

When Europeans first came inland far enough to lay eyes on this lake, they beheld an inland sea. Stunned to taste sweet water instead of salt, ladling eager hands into a body so wide they could not see the far side. They must have felt wonder tinged by dread. A place so vast as to be unfathomable.

Now dirtied by centuries of such intercourse, the lake divested itself of partly digested junk. A huge, gentle mockery of ephemeral humanity.

This water was what pumped through their veins, their tissues.

Animated by cool wind smelling of fish and dank lake weed. This was sealed in their eyeballs, the pallet upon which the world painted itself.

"We are nothing," James whispered.

"Huh? What'd you say?"

James told him about Allistair. About the collapsed building. Finding his home burned. The soot of his collapsed home forming dark moons under his fingernails. The warehouse. He left out his vivid hallucination, the man with the dog's head. The Dog Man. No, that was not to be related.

Massimo shared his story in return. He never made it home. He was rounded up, stripped of his gun, hands zip-tied behind his back, roped in a chain of slaves driven by men in black. The Sicari. Of a tall thin man with black curly hair, wearing a crimson cassock. He'd been the one directing the operation. Calm, self-assured. A gentle smile.

James remembered what Astrid and Sam had talked about. In the warehouse, a man in red robes, directing the Sicari to haul off the able-bodied, and shoot the wounded. A tall, thin man with dark curly hair.

"They marched us south." Massimo's voice had the quiet, ineluctable quality of a hypnotic state. "Maybe a hundred of us. The way they were treating us, shit, it was easy to tell nothing good was gonna come. Nothing good."

"What happened?" James prompted after a moment.

"A few of us guys, we start whispering to each other, back and forth, up and down the line. Sayin', we gotta do something, we can't let this happen, right? We gotta risk it. The idea was, we'd rush the guards in a wall, use our numbers, bowl them over and take off. But of course, there's these bitches crying, moaning: 'They'll kill us, just do what you're told,' blah, blah, blah. I was like, are you fuckin' stupid, or what?"

According to Massimo, it was the whining and crying that alerted their overseers. The priest (which was how Massimo referred to the one in the red cassock) snapped his fingers, whispered to the lead guard.

Ten or twelve of the guards stepped up to the slave line. The wailing reaching a crescendo now. Men and women begging please, please don't do it.

"That asshole in the red dress, still with that faggoty little grin on his face, he just nods. Calm as fuck, right? Like a waiter just asked him, does he want a refill on his bottomless fuckin' coffee."

Facing every tenth slave, staring right into their eyes, the guards each shot one of them in the head.

"Guy beside me, he bought it. My right ear's still fucking ringing like a bell from the shot. That's how close it was. BAM! and down this guy goes. Like a fuckin' flag when the wind dies. So – but I'm tied to the guy, right? So he pulls me down and I'm on top of him and I can't move away because the rope's too fucking short, and I seen the blood, just pumping outta that guy's face, Jimmy."

Massimo's twitched. "Like – like a red drinking fountain, that's what it looked like. And all I remember thinking is, 'Jesus Christ, this guy's heart's still beating!' Right? Blood still flowing in his veins, but he was just meat. And I can feel this guy's chest heaving, Jimmy! He's still fighting for breath, and my weight's on him, my weight's crushing the breath outta him…"

Massimo punched his thumbs into his own eyes, wracked with sobs. As if the wind were singing sound over his mouth, the breath of a flautist.

"You are completely expendable," the lead guard had hollered at them. "You are surrounded by millions of replacements. *Millions!* We don't need you, but you need us. Am I clear?" He pressed the muzzle of his gun against a woman's cheekbone and she tried to shrink away, but the rope only gave her a few inches. Begging, crying. "Am I clear?" She managed to make a noise approximating an affirmative response.

As further torture, they were left splayed on the street. The corpses, the living. Interchangeable. By the time the guards cut the ropes holding the corpses and retied the line together, flies had already begun crawling into noses, into ears. Feasting on the thick ketchupy blood draining into the gutter.

Massimo's tale was finished. James put his arm around his friend's shoulders, jostled him as Massimo sobbed. James had never seen him cry before. And then Massimo did something which amazed him, and alarmed him a little, too. Massimo put his head on James's right shoulder. And so they sat. The shifting weight of Massimo's head against his collarbone. James rocking him like a baby.

For a long time, James gauged the slip of their shadows, sneaking around south as the sun descended. Using a rusty stone with an off-center hole through it as the point of reference. A brick worn down to a medal. What Jenny called a lucky stone.

Massimo sniffed and lifted his head. "You must think I'm some kinda fag."

"Yeah, Mass, that's exactly what I was thinking," James snorted, shaking his head. "How did you manage to escape?"

"That's the creepy part. I don't wanna tell you."

"You have to tell me."

"Yeah? Why do I have to?" Massimo wiped his nose on his sleeve.

"You don't, then you really are a fag, alright?"

Massimo's chest jerked his shoulders up. A silent, rueful smirk. "They'd just finished retying the ropes, getting ready to move us out. Then that priest with the curly hair comes up to me. Chinese-looking, this guy, with a weird long face, friggin' chin a foot long."

James got the sense he was listening to a confession. That Massimo had done him some grievous harm. Gearing up to make an excuse, build a rationale for whatever he'd done.

"He gathers up his robes, sorta squats down beside me, and I'm thinking shit, this is it, this is the end. 'Cause he's lookin' at me with this crazy expression. Like he's just realized I'm some kinda rare specimen, okay? I'm ready to piss my pants, that's how scared I am. He's whispering to himself, like he's friggin' praying, this priest. And I'm not kidding you, Jimmy, he was speaking the same language I heard you speak. The night the power went down, and the day you led us out to Markham. Like I said, Hebrew, Arabic, some shit."

"Ancient Egyptian."

"Yeah, whatever. Finally, he's like 'Your friend.' That's all he says. 'Your friend,' just like that, like he's singing a fuckin' love song. Still with that wacko smile on his face. Psycho casual. 'If I release you, you will see your friend again. Yes. Yes, you will!'" Massimo shook his head. "He called a guard over and ordered him to cut me loose. It was like he knew, man. Knew I'd run into you again, like he could smell it on me. How the fuck do you explain that, huh? How could it be?"

James shrugged off the chill in his limbs. "Coincidence." Even to his own ears, the word was bland, insipid. He turned his gaze back to the grey plain of water. Flecked with whitecaps, serpents white as clouds twisting into visibility, then swallowed by waves.

Just now, just this was enough to convince James of ephemeral magic, of arcane mysteries deeper than anything Massimo could imagine.

"Do you remember," said Massimo, and now his voice was very quiet again. Prayerful. "On campus, the night all this went down, that bald freak—"

"Hermes," James whispered, and the wind seemed to reach into his chest cavity, open his lungs to the cold.

"Right, yeah. Same red robes. Right? Those red robes, the attitude – I'm telling you, those guys are Satanists."

"Come on, Mass."

"Hey, can you explain it? Huh? That Chinese guy tells me I'll find you again, and here we are! Hermes, I heard him tell you, you'll be the one, the one to find it. Any idea what that was about?"

Something challenging in Massimo's sideways glimpse. For a second, James held Massimo's dark eyes. Then Massimo turned his gaze away. Hiding something. Shame there. Hesitancy. Unlike him. Then again, James thought, we are all becoming unlike ourselves. Growing strange, monstrous.

"It's some kind of stone. That's all I know. It's calling me, drawing me."

"So it's like some voice in your head?"

James nodded.

"That's fucked up."

"I think it might be called schizophrenia, in more normal times."

"Ignore it, man." Massimo grappled James's arm. Urgent now, hinting at desperation. "Just, like, pretend it's not there."

James tore his arm out of Massimo's grasp. "That's like telling me to ignore hunger. It's that deep. It already feels like it's as much a part of me as my teeth, or my ears."

"Okay, I say that Hermes creep did this to you. Some kinda hypnosis, some shit. I don't get how a stone could be calling you."

"Well it is."

"Come on! You're gonna friggin' walk for what? Days? Weeks?"

"I don't know." Then James reconsidered. "Weeks, I guess."

"*Ma donna*, weeks on foot, sleeping outside on the floor, starved, and what? You're gonna get wherever it is, and find a piece of gravel on the side of the road? And it's gonna say what? Thanks for coming!" Massimo snickered. "A fuckin' pet rock?"

James smiled coldly. "Maybe it'll have a cool fossil in it."

"Yeah, okay." He proffered a handful of beach stones at James. Round, smooth as eggs. "You got all the friggin' stones you need, right here! How bout this one? This one's pretty, ain't it?"

Abruptly, James felt a stab of resentment. Defensive, as if Massimo had just implied something inappropriate about Stacy. "You don't have any idea," he snapped, vociferous enough to make Massimo peer at him. "A stone of power. A seeing stone. I could use it to end all this! Can't you understand?"

The stones slipped through Massimos's fingers, clacking onto the shingle. "What? You're saying you could use this stone thing to turn the power back on."

Massimo's sardonic tone riled James even more. A vicious contempt boiled in his mind. "What do you know?" he sneered, bitter venom spurting on his tongue like a cardamom seed crushed between his teeth.

Suddenly he was standing over Massimo. Bearing down on him, and a voice thundered from James's throat. Fell and spooky, the voice of another being. *"IW DIDIN I NEFERT!"*

Massimo cowered away from him, raising a forearm over his face, as if shielding himself from some blinding light.

What am I doing? James wondered. Earlier he'd imagined termites consuming his sanity. Millions of minute bites, cumulatively huge. I know what a tree feels like, he realized. Being eaten from within. Dense hardwood reduced to dust. Filling with the excrement of parasites.

But power surged through him. Feeling obscenely good, seeing Massimo shrink onto the shingle. And he knew he was being granted a small foretaste of what was to come. What power the Stone could offer!

And yet – and yet at the same time, James experienced dread so heavy he thought he might never heave it away. Powerful, yes. But black. A black thing scraped from the depths of a drain. Masquerading as an Egyptian god. Horribly alive, swollen with cunning.

*

His nightmare that night.

Standing on a sidewalk. There are Jenny and Sara on the far side of the street! Holding hands, walking slowly. Looking sad, looking downcast. He waves to them, calls out. But his voice is plugged, muted as if by water. They can hear him, but barely. He waves and waves, so frantic to get their attention his arms grow strained.

He calls until black spots teem in his vision, until his throat feels split, raw as a blister. Jenny and Sara look to him. He smiles. But they don't smile back. Daddy's here girls, Daddy's come back, and he tries to go to them but his feet are cemented into the sidewalk.

He waves, he calls with his far, far away voice. Screams. Don't be sad, don't be sad, just come to Daddy!

But Jenny and Sara only stare. Grey, too grey for little girls. Gazing across the street, open-mouthed.

They don't recognize me! Huge crushing grief. An ocean's weight. My daughters don't see their Daddy. Can't hear his voice screaming out to a tiny pinpoint. A mosquito in a silent room. The girls are crying now. Mouths churning, gulping pain.

Then Maggie is on the street. Creeping up behind his girls. Pointing at him, laughing. Hideously preening herself with chortling joy.

Her thrusting mocking finger.

James clenched awake into wicked black nighttime. Nothing but the delirious wind.

The Stone. Taking him over.

*

Dawn came overcast. This was the first morning that he could not see Betelgeuse pierce the morning sky. Surprised to find he missed it.

The damp cold of a night on the ground in the open air had screwed pain into James's neck and spine. The counterfeit voice of Horus in his head, growing ever louder, prodding and prodding. He felt the itch beneath his sternum. The growing impatience of the Stone. Until even lying prone he felt himself subtly tugged across the grass. Inching northeast.

James and Tribe had offered their pup tent to Astrid and Sam. James saw Astrid helping Sam out of the tent, and he knew that Sam wasn't in good shape. His face an ashen, sweaty mask. At one point, he put out his bad arm to support himself and gasped in pain. When Sheilagh unwrapped the bandage, it was obvious to James that the wound was infected. Hot red, oozing.

Astrid wept. James was so ashamed about giving Sam the Aspirin that he didn't have the nerve to say anything. Once or twice he met Astrid's desperate gaze and he had to look away.

They were all keeping to themselves. After their confrontation on the beach last night, even Massimo was avoiding him. Hungry and fatigued. One long conversational lull.

Tribe had kept Allistair's bottle of penicillin. They gave Sam a couple of the capsules. Waited blankly for Tribe to boil the last of their food: plain pasta. Not even any salt.

"Tribe, Jesus," said Amy through a mouthful. "There's *al dente*, and then there's raw."

Massimo snorted. "This is what happens when you let a cake cook!"

"I never made any claims as a chef," Tribe growled. "If you want to volunteer, be my guest."

As they ate, James saw this group as the pivot on a huge wheel. The great tree as an axle. Fifteen of them now, including the kid with the kinky hair who still refused to tell anybody his name. James had started to think of him as Sideshow Bob.

Almost everybody in the park had slipped away in the morning. The turf around them clotted with trash. Empty cans, smoldering fire pits. Plastic bag tumbleweeds. The cloud cover stained everything a drab monochrome khaki. Beyond the Fifteen was the outside, the Other.

As if to confirm this, a group of people getting their things together about twenty yards away peered darkly at them, muttering ugly things. A hatchet-faced man in a long leather coat boldly strode up. He pointed an aluminum baseball bat at Sam. "You'd best move that nigger outta here," he squawked.

Sam tried to get up, but couldn't manage. Astrid burst into fresh tears, covering her face.

Amy hopped to her feet, brandishing her weapon, but it was Tribe who got the stranger's attention. Rising very slowly, eyes ablaze. He drew his sword. Emerging from the scabbard with an angry cat hiss. Pointing it, the tip just a few inches off the bat.

"Would you care to press your point?" Tribe growled. The wind blew his long hair in thin tarry whips across his glowering face.

The stranger spat on the grass. "Best watch yerselfs, all's I'm sayin'." He backed away, and marched off with his own group, all of them casting wicked backward glances.

*

East of the park, they found themselves on a boardwalk, a boundary line. To the south, the beach, the leaden lake. Elevated lifeguard stations, gaunt as labor camp watchtowers. To the north, the Beach neighborhood of spacious 1920's bungalows with wide porches and gently sloping rooflines. Shady streets overarched by the massive limbs of huge maples. Here, it might have been a quiet ordinary Sunday morning.

But distantly, carried on the wind, they started to hear shrieking. Cries of pain. Despair. Vague words, too far away to understand. Threads of terrible omens.

James and a few of the others shot glances at each other.

"What now?" Ross muttered.

In one of the streets sloping up from the beach, the screaming and yelling amplified. On plastic play sets, splashing in inflatable kiddie pools, dozens of children frolicked up and down the street. Shrieking, sure, but in *glee*.

James stopped, feeling swamped. Breathless. Even in the midst of catastrophic collapse, children still must play.

Far up the street, he saw a group of boys battling with hockey sticks over a bright orange ball.

Further down, a beach ball floated and bobbed above splayed, reaching hands. Still more kids climbed on porch banisters and in the trees.

Both sidewalks were lined with barbeques and coolers. The inner, backyard lives of families spilled out into public space. Neighbors and friends banding together.

Eerie, James thought, how normal it seemed. A July street party. The lifted tones of kids whining that so-and-so had done some outrageous thing. Only in the stillness of the adults, their closed-in poses, arms clutched tightly across chests, could any evidence of the crisis be seen.

James and Ross, Lilac, Athol, Astrid and Sam remained, staring at the scene. The others had trooped on a hundred yards down the boardwalk.

Easy to tell who had children, who did not. The resonance of children's voices, bitterly poignant. Athol and Ross were both old enough that they might even be grandparents. This music created more longing in them. Athol seemed to be tonguing something out of his teeth. James realized he was fighting not to burst into tears.

"What is it?" Amy called back at them.

By now, folks on the street were peering, pointing at the band of dirty interlopers who'd stopped on the boardwalk. James saw a group of men marching down towards them. Gripping baseball bats, crowbars, hammers. Their eyes hidden in the shadows of worried brow ridges and baseball caps.

He noticed then what he hadn't apprehended before. The clutch of five cars lined up bumper to bumper across the foot of the street. Not parked. Heaved, sweated in place. A barricade.

Behind it whistles blew, the shrill alarm of children's names called. Mothers and fathers, arms out, herding them out of sight. It was like watching a meerkat colony that had just spied a hawk. In seconds, the street was bereft of children, of laughter.

"Move on!" A beefy guy in a red baseball cap waved his bat at James and the others. "Get outta here! You're not wanted!"

"We don't mean any harm." Athol's voice wavered, hardly loud enough for the men on the barricade to hear.

The rest of the Group came back along the boardwalk. James saw the dude in the red cap gape at Amy's rifle. He and his comrades stirring, scared.

"Just move on, alright?" The tone modulated now. Anger doused by fear. "We don't have anything."

"Nothing!" another of them yelled.

"We wanted something, we'd of taken it by now!" Massimo

shouted.

Jesus! "Shut up, Massimo!" James spat.

Behind the barricade, a plastic basketball net fell over with a whack. Even from fifty yards, James saw the men on the barricade jump. He felt very sorry for them.

"We're sorry to have disturbed you," said Ross. Mouth pulled tight, shoulders hunched, he turned to move on.

They all did. Before they'd taken ten steps, one of the guys in the barricade called out again. "What have you heard?"

"Sweet fuck all!" Mulligan retorted.

Lilac held back the longest, teary eyes fixed on a beach ball slowly rolling down the gutter.

Delicately, James touched her shoulder. "Come on."

*

Enormous impulsion drove the Group. Fifteen strangers, strung out in a tenuous line. Every day, a few hours of rigorous marching. Until Astrid begged to stop, Sam unable to go any further. They'd find a spot that seemed safe enough to spend the night. The floor of an insurance office one night. A baseball diamond the next. Scrounging whatever food and equipment they could use along the way.

On the march, James noticed how Amy tended to stick a few paces behind the rest. Presumably so that she could get a clean shot at one of them if she needed to. Holding her scoped rifle like she was in a combat zone. Her cold distrust left James with a prickle down the back of his neck.

Often, James felt his head grow cloudy. Gloomed the way a room becomes by swift thunderheads. He knew it was the Stone. An octopus wrapping its tentacles around his consciousness. Just keep moving, he thought. Don't hold these people back.

Sleeping on a groundsheet night after night left him weak with fatigue. He knew most of them felt the same way. Too much exercise, not enough food. Constant paranoia. Quailing at the chatter of gunfire all around. All keeping fearful watch for squads of men in black. Men in red cassocks. Slave gangs. Exhilarant fear, the Slough of Despond.

Sure, James thought. And I'm a pilgrim with no clear idea where I'm going. That, and I'm not making much bloody progress.

His nightmares grew vivid, more intense. Terrible things about Stacy, about Jenny and Sara. No more than a few hours of sleep a night. Then, either lying rigid in his mummy bag, eyes wide in the darkness, or sometimes he'd force himself to get up and join whoever was on watch.

Usually it was Athol. Arthritis in the ol' hips makes it hard to sleep on the ground, he'd drawl. Athol sitting at an insurance adjuster's desk with his feet up. Or pacing the baseline between first and second. A crooked shade cast by the waxing moon. He and James would talk out the night, summoning pale dawn. If they were outside, they'd tend the fire with whatever sticks of wood they'd been able to scrape up. Athol would invite him to pray and James would bow his head, fervently hoping for his family's safety.

James lost track of the days that passed. The grinding sameness of shop fronts, apartment buildings, streets littered with the detritus of a civilization. Brown paper bags and cups and wrappers stuck in sewer grates, familiar fast food logos wrinkled like tattoos on bog bodies.

All painting over his mind with a cracked, blistered blindness.

Until Sideshow Bob announced that it had been a week since the lights went out. "One week today!" Oddly chipper, still brandishing his fucking cellphone. As if he'd just seen the date on its little screen.

It was another tired food scrounging mission. A sullen gray afternoon, perspiring humidity.

"Been longer than a week," Mulligan grouched.

"No, he's right," Tribe confirmed. "It was one week ago today."

This fact oozed disbelief around them all. Could it really be true?

"Lord, it seems like a lot longer than that!" Athol sounded weary.

"A lifetime, buddy," Sam murmured. His sweaty face seemed always to be twisted in pain now.

"So your group seems pretty tight," said Lilac.

Sheilagh gave a dour laugh. "You serious, Lilac?"

"Just trying to make some conversation."

"James and I, we worked together," said Massimo.

"We're friends," said James resentfully.

"Alright, alright." Still, Massimo would not meet James's stare. Since that evening on the beach, Massimo was treating James like he had a contagious disease. Fair enough. James felt diseased.

"The rest of us only met like, a few nights ago," said Mulligan.

"You guys have any kind of plan?" Amy asked, clearly with the assumption that they didn't.

"Look, I'm getting sick of craning my friggin' neck to look back at you," Mulligan snapped. "Why don't you walk up here beside us, and we'll tell you."

"Just walk beside me and be my friend," whispered James.

Keeping her finger on the trigger guard, Amy obliged. They told Lilac and Amy and Athol everything they'd discussed that night in the electronics shop. The trek northeast, their scheme to cooperate, at least until they were out of the city.

Out of the city, James thought bleakly. Just that phrase, the idea of being away from this sweltering maze of ruin and pain, was enough to deliver a tonic.

Amy listened to what they said without interrupting, her round face tense and serious, reserving comment. James sensed that something she heard resonated with her. When they were finished talking, she seemed more at ease. Maybe their honesty had been enough to win her over. For people depending on each other to survive, the truth of their words became a code, shared nourishment.

Whatever it was, James hoped his intuition was correct. They could use somebody who knew her way around a gun. Based on what Athol had told him over the past few nights, she was a deadly shot.

As was becoming common practice, they shared stories of where they'd been when the lights went out. Amy had been twelve hundred feet in the air, flying a two-seated Cessna, on her way to the hunt camp she ran with her father. When the power quit, she'd just managed to glide the machine down on a stretch of suburban road north of the city.

"Holy shit," said Massimo.

"Got that right," she said.

"Hey, where's your family from?" Massimo asked.

"There's a question outta the blue." Amy examined Massimo with cool detachment verging on distaste. "The west end."

"Nah, I mean where in the Old Country."

"Lazio."

"Ah, central Italiano," he grinned. "Mine, they're from Sicilia."

"Explains a lot, right there."

"Hey, watch out," he teased. "You don't wanna piss off a southerner."

James rolled his eyes. Even on just a few mouthfuls of sustenance a day, Massimo could still manage to shift into stud mode, lathering on the charm.

"You must be a superb pilot," he said very earnestly, "to land a plane like that."

"All I can say is, thank God for cable-connected, manual controls," said Amy, ignoring him. "Any of that automated aileron equipment, and I would've crashed and burned. Still, there were no instruments, no lights, it scared the shit outta me."

"Christ, I would guess so!" said Ross.

"Figured I'd be best off coming down here, getting home, which counts as the number one stupidest mistake I've ever made."

"Now I'm insulted," said Lilac without much enthusiasm.

*

They'd been lulled into delusional complacency, not having seen any burned areas for days. Even the stifling ashy miasma seemed to have abated. They bedded down in an abandoned lot on a windy afternoon. Late that night, James, Athol, and Sideshow Bob were sitting up. They spotted dawn. Redder than blood, veining the low clouds with molten light. Growing, climbing. James had just thought to himself that it seemed to be getting light awfully quickly when Athol jumped to his feet.

"Get everybody up!" he shouted, jostling the prone cocoons of the sleeping bags and blankets. "Everybody up – move!"

"Athol!" Sheilagh muttered, all groggy. "What the hell're you doing!"

"Jesus, Athol, stop!" James demanded.

"James!" Athol's bared teeth distinctly visible now in an unearthly orange glare. He flung an arm at the glowing sky. "That's north-west! Help me, help me get these people up!"

Constellations appeared, red and orange and yellow. Shifting, reforming against the clouds. James felt a rush of hot air. Suddenly burning embers cascaded down on them, bouncing across the turf in swirling sparks. One landed on Mulligan's blanket and it was instantly alight, Mulligan shouting awake, kicking free as it caught in a whoosh.

"God!" Sideshow Bob called.

"What the fuck!" Mike screamed.

The whole sky, alive with burning coals. Glowing reptilian eyes, seeking more to burn.

Amy shrieked as one struck her head. At last James shook from his stupor, ran to her and threw his coat over her head, smothering her burning hair.

They scrambled, shouting panicky gibberish. Torn from sleep to find themselves in monstrous light suffused with malevolent living shadows.

Rohini screamed and screamed, standing bent at the waist, clutching the hot air. Her face open to the flames, an ecstatic terror. Sheilagh tried to drag her away, but Rohini fought her off until

Tribe grabbed her by the waist, hefting her away as she kicked and wailed.

A garage next to the lot exploded with a great *WHOOF!* that yanked the air from their lungs. Gasoline fumes washed over them, sickeningly sweet.

A window on another place blew out, vomiting flames.

James frantically grabbed whatever lay to hand. Two packs, damp sleeping bags thrown over his shoulder, running with the rest of them down the street, away from the fire. But as fast as they could move, the greedy flames outpaced them.

Thundering flames four stories high, brilliant tornados raging from windows and doors all around. Shockingly loud, like rampaging herds. Pounding deep into James's ears. Hot radiation blasted their faces. Air that hurt to breathe, scalding the throat, the sinuses. Stifling, steeped in burning plastic, chemically revolting. They coughed and retched and spat.

Tribe was shouting, but James couldn't hear what he was saying.

All they could do was run.

Terrible, horrible things within the garish flaming jungle. Dogs, cats, people on fire, sprinting until they fell. James saw a woman stumble and fall, her smoldering dress catching flame even as he watched. She writhed and curled into a funeral pyre.

Lost now in a burning maze. A netherworld of dense, hot smoke. They sacrificed their precious water supply, dumping their canteens over their heads, soaking tee-shirts to drape across their necks. The shirts were dry in minutes.

The smoke so dense, they didn't realize they were on a bridge over a ravine. They double-timed it back to the edge of the ravine. It was one of the river basins that dissected the city from north to south, emptying into the lake. The Rouge River, James thought. They slipped, fell down the steep slope. Tripping over roots and rocks until they crashed into the river.

They waded upstream, heading north, peering skywards through the lacy treetops, black against the false dawn. Mercifully cool and dark, but jaggedly etched. Even down here, the sound of the fire pounded like a freight train. Coughing, hacking, bleak suggestions of life. An eye socket like a waning moon. A hand gripping a branch, wetly pale as a subterranean creature. The slick surface of the river twisting thin light, mimicking flames.

Crackling above. The treetops were catching fire, sprinkling them with nomadic sparks that hissed into the water.

Sam slipped, going completely under. Astrid and Ross pulled him sputtering back into the air. "What do we do?" Astrid wailed, leering at the flames overhead.

"The wind's blowing south-east!" Graham, speaking so quickly James had trouble understanding him. "I say continue north, until the fire's burned out on the western side, then climb back up the way we came."

"Back into the fire!" Sideshow Bob screeched, outraged.

"He's right," Amy barked. "Back where we came from, there'll be nothing left to burn. The wind'll carry the fire across the ravine and we'll be separated from it."

"We can't wait long," said Sheilagh. "This whole valley's going up."

"Least down here we've got the water," Ross gasped.

Just voices, ragged with fear. Shivering. In a brief flare of light, James caught Ross's face, hard breath distorting his drawn lips, ballooning them out. A bloated gargoyle, withdrawing into its dark lair as the light died.

"We have come to Gehenna," Athol moaned.

*

They received a blessing. As true dawn glowed, the wind subsided. The trees smoldered but never caught fierce light. They filled their canteens in the river. Like troglodytes they struggled out of the ravine. Lending each other hands scorched red by the heat. Mirroring each other's gazes of forlorn disbelief.

Above the ravine, heaps of fuming rubble, jutting with timbers and beams. A purgatorial wilderness stifled with sere smoke, robbing their mouths of vital moisture. Insistent wind prowled through the hulking ruins, humming hungry incantations. The sun glimpsed as a molten bronze disc through yellow-brown fog. Nuclear summer, James thought. All over, burned out vehicles, exposed like the skulls of prehistoric beasts. Blackened ribs encaging crumpled, smoldering rags that had been human beings.

They moved furtively, squelching shoes and boots spitting muddy water. Following the edge of the ravine, eyes wild for signs of fire. On the other side of the ravine, the sky was black. Smoke tortured their seared lungs with spasms of dry coughing.

Finally, perhaps an hour north of where they'd climbed out of the ravine, they came across streets remarkably untouched. Except for the fog of smoke, the stink of incineration, James never would have guessed there had been a fire at all.

They collapsed on the lawn of a municipal government building.

"We did it," Lilac shivered. Sitting with her arms tightly

clasping her knees, rocking. "We did it, we survived. We did it, we survived. We did it…" Each word bringing a sob closer to the surface, until she dissolved into tears.

Rohini shook as if she'd been stranded in a blizzard. Sheilagh edged close and put her arms around her shoulders.

Sideshow Bob, phone out, babbling like an adolescent girl. "We were lucky – damn lucky! You remember them bushfires in Australia, couple of years back? I read the fucking fire burned so fierce it sucked the oxygen right out of the air. Yup! People died, trying to flee cause their cars quit. So little oxygen in the air, the gas wouldn't ignite in the cylinders!"

"Would you shut the fuck up!" Mulligan shouted in his face.

The plastic clasps on Sheilagh's pack had warped in the heat. She couldn't get them undone. To get the pack open, Tribe had to cut the straps with a knife. Sheilagh had a tube of ointment for the blistered burns on Amy's neck and Mulligan's legs.

They ate what little food they had. Some crackers, a few bags of chips. Everything tasted smoked. Ashes and exhaustion clotting their tongues. Faces filthy, caked in soot, spitting black mucus.

The day before they'd scrounged three cans of soda. Two ginger ales, one tonic water. Sheilagh popped the tabs and they passed them around. Even warm, the sweet liquid fizz exploded fresh down James's throat.

"Hey, don't hog it all!" Sam gestured for the can. He looked limp, barely able to hold himself off the ground.

Small chatter flickered, as empty, as insipid as anything overheard at a cocktail party.

Awful humid. No rain – not even a drop for days and days.

Uncomfortable, manic giggles.

Remember that guy in the crowd asking if it was gonna rain? Freak.

Tribe's long fingers tapping Morse on the pommel of his sword. Astrid silent, eyes larger than saucers in her filthy face.

All their voices seemed very far away from James. Fumes obscuring his mind, as if the fire had found a chink in his skull. A flare oozing white smoke, twitching above a river that tugged him firmly down into its cold current. He abandoned himself. Drowning and not caring.

Chapter 11

Amanda Muir

It is the first time Maggie passes Jamie a joint. That lazy Sunday afternoon, sunshine pouring molten gold onto the back porch. Hot enough, bright enough to drive off the mosquitoes. The June before his twelfth birthday.

Maggie on the mildewed old couch they'd hauled outside ages ago, with her bruised white calves tucked under herself, a paperback Sylvia Plath anthology and her own spiral-bound notebook in her lap. Jamie settles onto the fusty cushion between her and the rusty splotch that dribbled over the edge, a relic of Uncle Randy's overindulgence.

But today there are no uncles around. Just the two of them. The house whisper-quiet. Jamie has edged out through the torn screen door, careful not to let it bang closed behind him. Needing to hear the subtle hum of life coming from the forest surrounding the little house. Warblers flitting through branches inundated with glowing emerald. Patsy Cline fading in and out of static fog on the old radio that never tuned properly.

A vague memory flits across his mind. Of flight. Of burning buildings. Jamie shakes himself, watching Maggie's nimble fingers crumbling pot onto the waiting rolling paper.

"D'you know, Jamie my son, that there is a club called Mensa?"

"Nope." Jamie squirming, hearing the taut tone in her voice. It tells him Maggie is working up a good head of frothy offence.

"Neither did I, my young buck. Check this shit out!" She flings a magazine at him. A wrinkled copy of Time she borrowed from the Wilberforce library last winter. "So this club, Mensa, they won't even let you join unless you're smart! Can you imagine that?"

Jamie looks down at the magazine. It shows a picture of a chubby man in glasses, standing against a backdrop with the Mensa logo on it. He looks nice enough, Jamie thinks. Unsure now how to placate her, Jamie knows to keep his mouth shut. When she gets going like this, it's best to stand back.

"C'mon now, Jamie! That seem right to you? Bunch of elitist arseholes in their ivory tower! Eh? Telling me whether or not I can join their little party? Their little *branch*. Who are *they* to tell *me* what I can or cannot do!"

She pauses then, as she often does. Gazing far, far away. *Peeking over the horizon*. She sucks her lower lip under her big front teeth. Unmoving for several minutes. Just a hint of wind creaking maple and hemlock limbs. The back lawn, long since gone to seed, swaying gently, gently.

Suddenly her body jerks. She is back. "Screw that horseshit! I'm joining! If they don't find ya handsome, Jamie, they may as well find ya handy!" She inserts the joint between her lips and slowly pulls it out. Regards it thoughtfully.

"You always say that," Jamie says.

"Young man," she replies, mocking stern. "Don't be insolent." She winks and lights up. Inhales. Lets the pale breeze tug the smoke out of her mouth and nostrils, staring at the trees, her head tilted left. "*A living doll, everywhere you look*," she recites.

> *It can sew, it can cook,*
> *It can talk, talk, talk.*
> *It works, there is nothing wrong with it.*
> *You have a hole, it's a poultice.*
> *You have an eye, it's an image.*
> *My boy, it's your last resort.*
> *Will you marry it, marry it, marry it.*

What d'you think of that?"

"Did you write it?" he asks.

"No! That's Sylvia Plath, Jamie." She sucks on the joint.

Jamie considers. "What's a poultice?"

She snorts, ejecting smoke. "Guess."

Jamie frowns. "I dunno."

"Well try at least, silly billy!"

"I guess…like a chicken?"

She stops, looking perplexed. "Oh, because it sounds like *poultry*."

"Yup."

Maggie nods very seriously. "I like that, Jamie. I like that image a lot. But a poultice is a kind of bandage."

"I still don't get it."

"You will," she says, winking at him. Then, to his astonishment, she reaches out, handing him the stub of the joint.

He hesitates before taking it. Afraid she'll be mad. But she doesn't say a word. Inhaling only makes him cough a little. Already he's been exposed to more second-hand pot smoke than most people twice his age. After the toke, he goes to pass it back. He's seen the ritual enacted countless times.

But she waves it away, telling him to finish it. Abruptly flinging herself off the couch, the porch floor accepting her weight with a chirr as her bare feet rub the plywood in a loose-limbed flowing dance. With her head way back, her arms pouring out and down on the breeze.

Suddenly she seizes the book from the side table and bounds down into the thick savannah of the lawn. Still turning, dipping, spinning, she flips through the pages with her thumb. "Listen to this, Jamie:

I am the ghost of an infamous suicide,
My own blue razor rusting in my throat.
O pardon the one who knocks for pardon at
Your gate, father – your hound-bitch, daughter,
friend.
It was my love that did us both to death."

"Scary," he remarks as the drug hits his brain and the porch, the lawn, the forest, all swim. Several screeching blue jays have landed in the towering hemlock at the foot of the yard, furiously screeching *danger! danger! danger!*

"Mmmm…" Maggie clutches the open book to her breasts, as if nursing the poetry. "You mustn't ever think of the past as frozen, Jamie. It's not…" Her little hand poises in the air, groping for the next, perfect word. "Unalterable; no, the past…is as much subject to change as the future."

She beams at him. Eyes sinking into inebriated slits, lips peeling back like curtains going up on her crooked teeth, her long gums. Impressed with herself. An endearing, goofy smile, girly and winsome despite the stripes of brown tartar.

Jamie claps. She does a low, hammy bow.

For a long time they both zone out. Maggie slowly pacing, pulling her knees up high, extending her legs above the grass fronds, a creeping villain. Plucking orange and yellow hawkweed flowers. Jamie charting the course of innumerable motes inflamed by the boiling sunlight. Tiny midges, seed tufts, tumbling, turning, lifting, falling. A blizzard of images, thoughts inundating his brain. Restless, atomized fire.

It is the thought of fire that jerks his memory. The aftermath. Ashes and soot. Right, yes! the city is aflame, and here he is. No, no. Here he *isn't* because he isn't really here. This, all this has already happened a long time ago. Not a dream, either. Not even a *bright* dream. Something brand new. A vivid simulacrum of a time sixteen years before the city would be set alight by crashing planes. For him as an eleven year-old boy, the city is but a distant unknowable image. He's never even been to the city. But that is where he *belongs*.

"How was church this morning?" Maggie asks, startling him

back.

"Alright, I guess." Hearing himself now, speaking the words he'd spoken on that day in his prepubescent squeak. Hearing them from the perspective of his later self. Remembering what Maggie would say next: *Just alright?* Scared of what his response will be. Knowing he'll say it. Knowing how she'll react.

"Just alright?"

No, no! Don't! But Jamie can't help himself. The past might not be unalterable, but it still must follow a patterned weave. He still must say, "I dunno. Mrs. Gritzner's a bit of an old fart."

"James Herbert Muir! Don't you speak of her that way!"

She stomps back up the porch steps and thumps his crown with the meaty side of her fist, hitting it hard, and the pain in his neck drives the truth into his mind, a bruised bone. Severed hawkweed flowers sprinkle in his lap. This really isn't a dream! No, he actually is back here, actually eleven years old again, feeling the pulmonary burn of his first joint. A sensation of weird disassociation rents the scene like a clash of cymbals.

Maggie bends low at the waist to glare at him in the eye. "All that woman has shown you is love and support, little man. You'll show her the respect she deserves. Everybody deserves respect, period. I won't have you searching that common ground. So common, Jamie. You are better than that."

Jamie pouts, crossing his arms. But even as he does it, he sees traces of Jenny in his own mannerism. Jenny, the daughter he will not have for another twelve years. Now he begins to shake. What the hell is happening?

"You hear me, Jamie?"

"Yeah."

"Pardon me?"

"Yes, I hear you."

This is not Maggie. Sure, this is what she'd said and done that day. This – this day. But something is dreadfully off.

As she flops back onto the couch and picks up her book, Jamie watches her out of the corner of his eye. A near-perfect facsimile of her, right down to her habit of biting her lower lip as she reads. Dragging her lip out from under the tight-pressed teeth, so that the skin whitens as it squeezes out, for just a second, until the blood flushes back in. The margin between the rind and flesh of a ripe watermelon. Over and over, until her lip starts bleeding. She only does this when she feels the writing tickle, as she calls it.

Her, and yet *not* her.

Jamie experiences a vivid crawling sensation at the base of his spine. This thing wearing Maggie's skin. A fat horsefly drones in, lands on the back of his neck, but he hardly notices to bat it away. Instead, he reaches out and touches her cheek, just to be sure, just to know that the flesh and bones and heat of this woman are real. And they are.

And again, he really did do that. A super-cautious eleven-year old, stoned on his own mother's homegrown weed. As the horsefly feasts on his blood, his fingers ease into the softness of her cheek. Feeling the shift of her jaw muscles as she smiles again, rears back in an easy way, giggling, "Jamie, what're you doing, now?" Taking his hand in her cool fingers, kissing his knuckles.

"What are you?" he asks, just as he had then. Pulling his hand away.

"Silly kid, don't you think Maggie's real?"

Yes, yes, this is a buried seed from his early life. Maggie still reminded him about it all the time, trying to irritate him, because she knew so well that he hated being reminded of any historical tenderness between them.

But hold on, hold on, that is – no, that is from another life, his later life with Stacy and Jenny and Sara. An attenuated relationship with Maggie, stretched thin through a phone wire. Reduced to tiny electronic pulses. Nothing more.

"But how can I know all that if I'm only eleven?"

"You're so Jamie." She ruffles his hair. "Such a Jamie and a half."

He knew very well this was all the dizzying work of some Byzantine trance, a worn nub unearthed from the distant reliquary of his childhood memories. And yet somehow rendered *real*. Renewed.

"This…this is really fucked up," he says.

"Yup." Just that simple. As if she's responding to a question about what's for dinner.

"You're not real," he says, renewing his visual inspection of Maggie. Of her eyes.

"Oh, stop."

It is almost perfect. A ninety-nine point nine percent duplicate. Still and all, a forgery. The eyes. All the wry twinkle and naughtiness of Maggie's, the directness. But too still. A lingering gaze that isn't Maggie. Not at all.

Jamie shrinks back, away from her. From *it*. "What are you?" Drawing his knees to his chest, curling inward. "Tell me what you are!"

The thing pretending to be Maggie hisses. No longer making much of an effort. "Oh, Jamie, but I almost had you!" Even without pretense, it still does an incredible job of imitating her. The way it tosses Maggie's bob of chestnut curls, coquettishly defiant. "I did almost have you, didn't I?"

Jamie tries to run away. Leaps from the couch, dashes for the screen door. Grabs the handle. Feels the pain of the aluminum frame skinning his knuckles. Flings it open—

But all at once he is back on the couch. Just like that. Like a skip in a DVD. And here is Maggie handing him the joint all over again...

"No!" he screams. "No, stop it, stop it!"

"Don't be frightened," it says, doing Maggie's pout with Maggie's lips. It tokes on the joint, wincing.

But Jamie does feel badly frightened. An eleven year-old's displaced drowning fright.

"You're very strong," it says in Maggie's quick cadence. "Very strong, Jamie. It would have been far preferable to use Stacy this way, or your girls, but you wouldn't allow it. All those terrible dreams of them – your doing, not mine. Such resistance! But now it's all settled!"

"Tell me what's happening!"

"Wonderful things, Jamie. Lovely things! I'm here to help you. Now, listen carefully. *Heru commands you northeast to the Stone, Jamie. The Emerald Tablet awaits! Ir quin'k ar ib'k meh'k quin'k im herdew'k zin'k hemat ma'k per'k! Nin hikr'k nin ibi'k – If you are brave and control your heart, you shall embrace your children, you shall kiss your wife, you shall see your home! You will not be hungry, you will not be thirsty—*"

Chapter 12

Scavengers

James snorted and was back. On the road. Blazing sunlight. Beside him was Tribe, who tried to steady him, grabbing his arm. Still, James stumbled, his pack dragging him down to the pavement. He put a hand to his forehead, blinking as if just presented with a life-altering conundrum. Which, of course, he had been.

"How long this time?" he asked groggily. Maggie still with him.

"A few hours," said Tribe.

Sheilagh, Mulligan, Graham and a few other dirty faces gathered around.

"Shit," Mulligan drawled.

"Do you see now?" Tribe asked him, giving James his hand, pulling him to his feet. James tottered. His head swam.

"You're awfully pale," Sheilagh told James. "Do you need a few minutes?"

James shook his head. But he felt giddy, seasick. His head splitting. Graham handed him a canteen, and he took a long pull of warm stale water.

"Just as well," Mulligan snapped. "We need to get the fuck outta Dodge, dude. We still headin' in the right direction for you?"

"Alright, alright," James drawled.

"Hey dude, don't get snippy with me. We're the ones waiting for you!"

"Hey mate," said Graham in a low growl. "Lay off, yeah?" Roughly, deliberately, his fingers screwed the lid back onto the canteen.

For a second the two of them locked glares before Mulligan backed down, muttering and grumbling to himself.

*

Sam was in a daze, barely able to walk. Astrid kept him moving, gripping one of his arms across her shoulders, struggling under his weight. Sam's sweaty head lolling forward, back. His hat kept falling off. A while after James came back from his vision, Tribe took Astrid's place. Against her protests, he needed to physically intervene between them. Sam was a large man, and

Tribe's height helped.

The compulsion throbbing in them now, to keep moving. Behind them, a wall of black smoke obscured the western horizon. They couldn't get caught in that again. An urgency fired by the people running past them, outpacing the Group's flight.

Mulligan kept stopping, maybe a hundred yards ahead, turning back to wait, huffing impatiently.

"What's wrong with Sam?" James whispered to Sheilagh. His own voice odd to himself.

Sheilagh stabbed him with her eyes, accusing him of idiocy without verbalizing it. Even as he asked the question, James knew it was bone headed. But things were blurry to him. The vision state still intruded upon reality. *This* reality. He felt he'd been away with Maggie for a long time, that he hadn't seen these people for years.

"It's the fucking shoulder wound," Sheilagh snapped at him. "It's badly infected. I'm sure splashing around in that filthy water last night didn't help. That bloody...!" It was an effort for her to control her voice. "The penicillin isn't working," she said quietly.

"How could it not?" Graham asked.

"It doesn't work on everything. And even if it did, it was too little, too late. We should've started giving it to him right away."

When Sam could go no further, they stopped at yet another park, with a plastic jungle gym in the middle. Turf bright with dandelions, partly obscured by ubiquitous dusty ash.

In a low groan, Sam said something. Astrid put her hand on his sweaty neck. "Sam? Sam, honey, did you say something?"

Briefly his glazed eyes flickered to her face. "Whole universe," he moaned, loudly enough for everybody to hear. "Not just the world. All worlds."

Disquiet beset them all, keeping their eyes on the towering black curtain to the west. They were exhausted – truly so, their limbs numb, wooden.

Wonderful things, Jamie. Maggie's voice jealous for his attention. *Lovely things! I'm here to help you!*

"You heard what Sam there said." Graham kept his voice low, relaying a dire secret to James. "Whole universe, like?"

"I heard," James muttered.

"You think that's true?" Ross asked, wiping his mouth. It was impossible to keep out the ash. "The whole world?"

"I'd say it's a fair bet," said Tribe.

"But we don't know that for sure," Sheilagh reminded them.

"Could be the whole bloody world, though, couldn't it?" said Graham.

"We don't know that," Sheilagh insisted. "Let's just go by

192

what we know, right?"

Graham smiled bitterly. "Aye, but it *could be*, you have to acknowledge that, Sheilagh." The lilt of his accent. Questions into statements, statements to questions.

"You damn northerners," she snorted. "Such contrarians, like!"

Graham cackled. "Sure, and you republicans, you're always ready to make accommodations, right."

"You don't suppose – it couldn't be just all in our heads," asked Astrid giddily. Dismissing her own question as it came out of her mouth. She'd taken Sam's hand, gently rubbing the back of it.

James saw Graham wince. They'd meant to keep their voices low enough that she wouldn't hear.

"Some kind of collective hysteria?" said Sheilagh, responding to Astrid.

"We've all seen what Mike's been talking about." Astrid sounded hesitant, as if revealing something embarrassing about herself. "The crazies. Maybe we're all somewhat crazy now."

"I doubt that!" Mulligan laughed. "Not all of us!"

"You doubt that, do you?" Ross snapped. "You seem to doubt everything!" His voice was rough and bossy. He had a habit of squeezing his bulbous nose like he was about to sneeze.

"Far as I'm concerned, it's almost impossible to be too cynical." Mulligan drew his long hair back into a ponytail, slipping an elastic around it.

"Son," said Ross with strained patience. "I don't see how your cynicism is helping us at all."

Athol seemed to find this exchange very amusing. He peered at them through his cracked reading glasses, his head slightly tipped back.

"You can rest assured it's not all in our minds," said Tribe, stretching his arms over his head. Exorcising from his muscles the ghost of Sam's weight. "At least, not entirely."

"Yo, it's so obvious that it's not just in our heads!" said Mike. "I mean, check it out – the sun's like, a different color even!"

"The fuck're you talking about, dude?" Mulligan jeered.

"Can't you see? It's like, redder than it was before!"

"Well, of course it's red!" Mulligan snorted. "It's setting through a screen of fuckin' smoke!"

"Setting?" said Lilac. The sudden intrusion of her sassy voice into the debate made all of them pause. "That's a stretch! Can't be later than six or seven." She drew her feet closer, grasping her knees.

"Yeah?" Mulligan blew out a sardonic hiss of cigarette smoke. "Gotta watch?"

Lilac scowled at him, her short fingers flicking at the bangs in her face. As if angry at the hair.

"How can you smoke?" Amy asked Mulligan. "After last night?"

Mulligan stared hungrily at the cigarette, hefting it like a dumbbell. "It tastes so sweet. So sweet."

"Ultimately, it doesn't matter what's happening on the other side of the goddamned world," said Ross, mopping his high forehead with a handkerchief.

"It doesn't?" said Mulligan.

"No," said Ross pointedly. His cross sidelong glance at Mulligan showed him out as a parent, James thought. Programmed for shutting down insolence. "Does anybody know what the hell is going on?"

"Like, what in God's name is that?" Astrid asked, pointing up at Betelgeuse.

James was about to answer her. Wanted to, even. But all at once he couldn't summon the energy. It just seemed too much.

Tribe cleared his throat. Began to retell the tale. Nourishing them with lore as he set up the camp stove.

When he'd finished, Mulligan spoke up. "Beetlejuice. Wasn't that some kinda crap movie?"

James smirked as he put his canteen to his mouth. His repressed laugh spurted water.

"No movie I ever heard of," said Mike. "What if all this is – like, some kinda alien attack, or some shit?" Still absently tapping his knife against the outside hem of his jeans.

Tribe smiled quizzically. "You weren't listening to what I just told you."

Ross raised his eyebrows. "At this point, I'd be willing to believe almost anything." He caught a piece of Mulligan's glare, then added, "Almost, I said."

"Yeah," said Mulligan, "what's that old expression? Close only counts in horseshoes? Almost is as good as close, bud, with that kind of bullshit talk."

"Bullshit talk!" Ross almost yelling now. "Is that so?"

"Exactly which *bullshit* are you referring to?" Amy asked. "Alien attack or exploding star?" She had a closed, clipped way of speaking.

"Whatever." Mulligan crossed his arms and lay back on the grass.

"If somebody had told you last week that electrical current would stop working, just like that, what would you have said?" Ross asked.

"I don't deal with hypothetical garbage," Mulligan snorted at the sky. "Look, dude – I don't know what the fuck is going on. *Obviously*. But nobody does. Except it's like living in the seventh circle of Hell."

"Well I think we'd all appreciate it if you showed more understanding for other people's needs," said Ross sharply. Clearly done-in, at the edge of his tolerance horizon. "I don't suppose it's occurred to you that some of us might be comforted by news – any news at all."

Mulligan shrugged, beaming sardonic amusement. "You wanna kid yourself, man, you go right ahead."

"I heard some guy the other night talking about fire falling from the sky, shit like that," Mike insisted.

"It was a meteor!" Sideshow Bob shouted. Part of his mane had been burned away, giving his head a strange lopsided look. Incredibly, he still had that fucking cellphone pressed against his ear. "It was! I saw it too!" A flashback to those inane, irritating people who always seemed to be yammering on cellphones, in line-ups, on the bus. File that one under things James didn't miss.

"There was no damn meteor," Mulligan scoffed. "I mean, *fuck sake*!"

Mulligan failed to understand, James reflected. These people were starving for something more than food. Information junkies of the digital age. All in severe withdrawal. Inoculating their fear with bizarre replicas of familiar meaning.

"I know a good meteor story!" Athol enthused. His slow, steady hands flipped through the Bible's onionskin pages.

"Here we go," Mulligan muttered.

"Revelation 8, verses 10 and eleven: 'And the third angel sounded, and there fell a great star from heaven, burning as it were a lamp, and it fell upon the third part of the rivers, and upon the fountains of waters; And the name of the star is called Wormwood: and the third part of the waters became wormwood; and many men died of the waters, because they were made bitter.'" Athol's voice, perfectly modulated, perfectly pitched. Scripture transubstantiated into prose poetry.

Mulligan, still lying on his back, rocked his head back and forth with a fixed, tired stare. "My gawd," he smirked.

"As you said, a good story, and that's all." Sheilagh's voice was sharp.

"I'll second that," said Amy with a withering look at Athol.

"Oh, I don't know," Athol responded. "Sounds to me like a darned good blend of what Mr. Tribe and Michael here had to say."

Tribe stroked his beard. "Was it Picasso who said that art is a lie that makes us realize the truth?"

"It's Mike," Mike shot back.

Athol nodded. "I apologize, son. Mike."

"What about me?" Sideshow Bob whined.

"Oh come on, there was no bloody meteor!" Sheilagh's whole body shook with indignation.

Athol smiled at her. The way a highly skilled therapist might smile at a troublesome patient. But he spoke without rancor or condescension. "I find it's interesting how skeptics become so agitated over something they claim has no weight of truth. After all, if scripture is simply a story, then what's the harm in reading it?" His speech remained slow and easy, but judging by the light James saw in his eyes, Athol liked a good debate.

"You make a good point," said Tribe. He was having trouble keeping a match lit in the breeze, so James shielded it with his body. All they needed now was to run out of matches. Ironic, the potential to be starved of fire while surrounded by an inferno.

"Because certain people stubbornly insist that it represents eternal truth," said Sheilagh. Opening James's pack, the angry whip of tie cords through Gortex as she unfastened them. "When there's absolutely no evidence that your sky god even exists."

"Right, and for certain people, eternal truth is what they need," said Ross.

Mulligan sat up. "Eternal truth: without food, we'll starve. That's all I need to know right now.

"Right on!" Restlessness in Mike's ropy adolescence. Thumbing that damn knife, sunlight angling from the blade. And it was reddish, tinged with the blood-filter of smoke, reflecting in his face like an emergency light. *Sin-sin-sin. Sin-sin. Sin-sin-sin.*

"What've we got left?" Graham asked in a tentative tone that told them he wasn't sure he wanted to know the answer.

Sheilagh laid out four tin cans. Corn. Kidney beans. Peach slices. Chicken soup. One by one, longingly. An offertory ritual.

*

The next morning glowed fiercely on their cold faces, the eastern sky drenched golden-red, the glorious promise of rain.

At some point in the night, Sam had slipped into a coma. There was nothing they could do. Too much blood loss, and now the infection had seeped into his bloodstream. Astrid slumped on her knees, gripping his limp hand. "I can't wake him," she kept repeating. "I can't wake him up."

As bleak overcast blocked the sun, a sense of numb urgency

befell all of them. Fidgety. Mulligan muttering what most of them were thinking: we need to move. We can't stay. Come on, come on.

He's right! Maggie insisted. *Think of your priority: the Stone, Jamie! The Stone the Stone the Stone...*

"We can't just leave 'em here, all alone," said Graham.

"I should have stitched the damn wound," James heard Sheilagh whisper to Tribe. "What was I thinking?"

"You were busy thinking of survival," Tribe retorted.

James rolled his eyes. Only Tribe could dress up comfort as a rebuke.

"How long will it take?" Mulligan asked, keeping his voice low.

A pause. The measure of his meaning.

"To die." Sheilagh, putting her hand to her forehead. "That's quite a question, Mulligan."

"Yeah, 'cause it's the most relevant one," he said. "We agreed help each other get out of the city. We can't just sit here!"

What a jerk, James thought.

"*Jaysus*, I don't know. I'm not a doctor, I don't know."

Athol joined Astrid, mumbling scripture. Lips and tongue and breath forming syllables, consonants not originally written in English. Hebrew, Aramaic, Greek. For much of the morning he sat a hapless vigil beside Sam's body – because although he was still shallowly breathing, it was hard not to look at the slack lividity of Sam's face and not think of him as a body. Until finally Astrid told Athol to shut up. Quietly but forcefully. Shut up, get away from us. Awkwardly put out, Athol acquiesced. Slouched back to his spot on the other side of the playground.

Sam's condition deflated their dwindled energy. Depression caught up to them, a hopeless lonely sorrow. Finally, Amy called them all around. All except Astrid, who remained beside Sam. "This is ridiculous," she said, giving them all a no-nonsense look. "We need food, we need water, and supplies."

"Aye, like good packs, proper footwear," Graham added.

"Right. Instead of sitting around feeling sorry for ourselves we should break up into pairs and threes, start scrounging for what we need." Amy's girly voice was so at odds with her direct manner. The aggressive way she threw her chin into her words.

"It's not safe," said Lilac. Jittery, rubbing her upper arms. "We ought to stick together."

"We'll be together, just in smaller groups," said James.

"I agree with Lilac," said Ross. Nibbling on the edges of his thumbs. They were starting to bleed. "We said we'd keep moving. That's what we need to do."

"But we can't keep moving on empty stomachs," Graham
responded. "And I still say it'd be callous as fuck of us to leave
Astrid and Sam behind."

"Won't do us any good if one of those slaving gangs comes
down that road." Mulligan had a knack for expressing what seemed
to be on everybody's mind.

"Ah," Ross scoffed. "We've left them far behind."

"You certain about that?" Athol asked.

"Not much point in being in a group, is there, if we, like,
abandon each other," said Sideshow Bob, into his cell phone.

"We've got a better chance of finding what we need if we split
up, as Amy suggested," said Sheilagh.

"But what about those guys with the guns?" Mike whined. "I
don't wanna run into them again."

"Quit it!" Tribe bellowed. "You're acting like moles, damn it!
It's the time to act like cats. We are not the hunted, we are the
hunters!"

"Right on!" Mulligan smiled, but he was mocking Tribe.

There was more discussion and debate until they decided to
have a show of hands. Everyone except Lilac and Athol agreed with
Amy. Rohini seemed to be coming out of her stupor, her eyes
following the conversation, but she didn't vote, so Sheilagh counted
her as abstaining. It was a moment, a thread of vital energy that
coursed through them, sewing them together.

James ended up detailed with Massimo, Amy, Lilac, Mulligan
and Sideshow Bob.

They'd been assigned to investigate the area north of the park.
Suburban streets of broken shop fronts, burned out restaurants. The
weary trudge of refugees. Several overturned cars had been set
alight, now smoldering, still ticking with heat. A city bus had
jumped the curb and torn through the front of a bank. Across the
windshield of an abandoned Toyota, somebody had scrawled in the
grey dust: BE WARE THE DARKSIDE!

All around were strange noises. Sudden metallic wrenching
that dropped a heavy stone through James's bowels. Echoing
shouts: *No! Please!* Twice Amy whirled around, raising her rifle,
only to see a distant figure scurry away.

They heard indignant squealing and shrieking. Rounding a
corner to find a swarm of gulls wheeling and flapping, fighting to
peck apart a corpse lying in the gutter. James tried not to look, only
getting an impression of a shredded face, eyeless sockets. Disgust
shook through Lilac's body, tripping over her own feet to get away
from the curb. None of them commented, keeping their eyes on the
sidewalk as they passed. The way we used to treat panhandlers,

James thought. The danger of contagion.

They snooped through several stores and restaurants, rooting through the piles of junk left behind. Not much to find. A broken-open bag of egg noodles. A rodent-gnawed box of crackers.

Then creeping up the dark backstairs above a wrecked hair and nail salon. A surreal experience, knocking on doors in the black hallway. In the light of Mulligan's hissing lighter, hearing screams within two of the apartments. *Fuck off! Leave us alone!*

"Let's get out of here," said James, feeling goose bumps.

The others studiously ignored him.

No response at the third door, so they kicked it in. Not as easy as it might have seemed. Each of them taking turns, battering the door with kick after kick until it splintered enough for Massimo to ram open with his shoulder.

They found blankets and sweaters in the tiny apartment. Two pairs of running shoes. Amy made Lilac try them on to replace her bloodied flat-soled Converse sneakers, but they were far too big for her. James tied the laces together, carrying them looped over one finger.

There was a poster on the wall showing a satellite photo of the city. A vast cancerous growth, spreading around the western end of Lake Ontario. James traced his finger along the north shore of the lake. The land entombed under arid concrete and pavement for a hundred miles in every direction.

"Long way to walk," he mumbled, aghast.

Long way to get to the green that dotted the edge of the paved execration like lichen speckling limestone. Beyond that were trees, were fields and farms. But so what? Say they managed to traverse this paved desert – then what? A food-filled Eden. Right.

"Shit," he said, and turned away.

"Good clothes in here," said Amy, bending over double, digging through the detritus at the bottom of a closet.

Massimo gave James an elbow, raising his eyebrows at Amy's plentiful ass. Mulligan made a wicked grin, sticking out his tongue and motioning with his hands as if he was caressing two bowling balls.

"Let's just get this over with," James muttered. It seemed obscene to be joking around while they took other people's stuff. A desecration.

Amy backed out of the closet with an old dusty backpack in one hand and a pair of pants in the other. "You can all forget about it," she said, tossing her head to fling the hair out of her eyes. "I bat for the dark side."

"No way!" Massimo's jaw dropped.

"What? You think nice Italian girls're too *hot* to be bull dykes?" She threw the gear at Massimo, who caught it awkwardly. "You guys are supposed to be helping Lilac in the kitchen. Get to it."

James knew they were buoyed by the act of doing something, anything, to improve their odds. But he couldn't join in the banter. Scrounging, they called it, but they were intruders, thieves. The eyes of the kids in the framed school portraits on the shelf next to the window, narrowed at James in accusation. James found his fingers playing with the little glass bell he'd found in his apartment. What happened when these people found their things gone? Things that these kids would need? He felt sick.

Massimo put a hand on his arm. "They're probably dead anyway," he whispered, close enough for James to smell his stinky breath.

"How do you know? What if they're not?"

"No I won't!" Sideshow Bob screamed into his cellphone, and they all jumped. "You'll never find us! No, never!"

If the shared truth nourished them, then that kid was the extra helping at the end of a large meal, just enough to induce regretful nausea.

James hung back as the others left the apartment. He found a pen and a scrap of paper and left a hesitant note under the dead phone:

> *Please forgive us for plundering your home.*
> *We need supplies.*
> *Almost everything I own now is stolen.*
> *James Muir*

*

James remained in the gloomy street while the rest of them trooped up to investigate another floor of apartments over a vacuum store. He didn't have the heart to go on with it.

Jamie! Maggie's voice resonating in his head like a warped bell. *Jamie, you're in danger! Danger!*

"You're not Maggie," he muttered.

It began to rain. Dime-sized dots spattering on the pavement. James didn't notice the color until a woman passing by shrieked, holding her hands out like a preacher. But in loathing, disgust. "My God, what more must we endure?" Black streaks stained her white blouse, ran down her face. At first, James imagined they were somehow emissions from within, as if her body was hemorrhaging black blood.

But then a drop struck James's arm. Another hit his thigh. More and more. Like being spat on by a chorus with mouthfuls of coal dust. Opaque, black as oil, infested with the soot of a burning city. Stinking, acrid rain come to pollute instead of wash away. Crawling over cars, greasy down shop windows, replacing the dry grey talc of ash with unctuous ink.

"Christ," James gasped, at the horrid stench, the growing black snakes slithering into the storm sewers.

He slouched in a doorway, peering skywards at slate clouds, pregnant with cremation. Pouring now.

Then, like a demon summoned by this hellish rain, the Dog Man rounded a corner down the street.

James froze, feeling such intense fright that it actually pained him. A vicious jagged stab of adrenaline low in his abdomen as the Dog Man turned straight toward him, jerking the pump action on the shot gun. The sound through the splattering black rain like a thin dry bone being snapped twice.

The Dog Man was already painted mostly black by the rain, but the asymmetrical red eyes remained incandescent, the white pupils avid, angry, pinpointed on the spot where James cowered.

The cramp of terror jutted from his belly to his spine, shook his stiffened body. He'd convinced himself this apparition had only been a hallucination, contrived by the discovery of his home in cinders. Donnie's body, wearing a malformed fabric dog's head. Harbinger of unspeakable cruelty.

"How can it be?" James's voice, a faint rusty squeak.

Gone was the Frankenstein toddle the Dog Man had shown when James had last seen him. Now he – *it* – strode with purpose, boot heels clocking with military haste down the asphalt.

Straight at him. No more than fifty yards away. Closing. Fast. What could he do?

The door, you idiot! Maggie shouted. *Get inside. Quick!*

He turned and yanked on the door, but his fingers pulled free. Locked tight. Shit! He'd stood in a different doorway than the one Amy and the others had used. He cursed his own idiocy.

The woman in the white sundress, now drenched black, dashed from a doorway across the street, screaming. She'd seen the Dog Man too.

The Dog Man raised the gun and shot her. The blast seemed to collapse the rainy air. She flew off her feet, torso torn apart. Tumbled behind an SUV.

The Dog Man, almost abreast of James now. Jerking the slide again, ejecting a smoking red shell.

Run – run! his frantic brain told him. But he remained fastened to the side of the narrow doorway. Gagging terror. Unable to breathe.

Donnie. Donnie beheaded and resurrected. The stretched holes in the neck skin, cinched tight by the cords attaching the dog head, reminded James of an H. P. Lovecraft collection he had, the cover showing dismembered bodies suspended on hooks. Donnie's body seemed more bloated now, the greenish belly swelling under the hem of the soiled undershirt.

Running into this thing again was no accident, no pale coincidence. The voice not of God, but a malevolent deity, demonic and confident. Hunting him.

Abruptly, James was running through the downpour. Without even being aware of commanding his legs to move. Boots splashing through the dark mucky rainwater. He dashed up the street, away from the Dog Man.

Others ran too. A teen in a red shirt. A thin old man with his hands over his head.

No more than a few strides before James collided with somebody. Knocked off his feet, sliding across the slick sidewalk. It was Sideshow Bob. Kinky hair matted with oily rain, still shouting into his cell phone.

"Look out!" James screamed, seeing the Dog Man looming behind him.

"Don't you dare!" Sideshow Bob shouted. "Don't you dare – don't you da—"

James saw the muzzle flash. Another explosion. Sideshow Bob's head burst apart. The crown of his skull landed scalp-side down on the sidewalk. Three feet from James's straining, astonished eyes. A hairy bowl filled with gleaming red jelly, rocking, rocking.

"What the fuck!" It was Massimo, diving out of the way just as another shotgun blast pulverized the corner of the doorway beside him. The Dog Man aimed at James.

Amy appeared, her rifle shouldered. She fired. One of the Dog Man's burning eyes disappeared in a burst of white stuffing.

The Dog Man shook, meaty arms jiggling. It stumbled backward, but didn't fall.

Amy reloaded. Fired again. The shot went wide.

James saw she was freaking, eyes bulging, teeth clenched. She fought with the bolt action.

The Dog Man pointed the shotgun at her. They were no more than forty feet apart.

Amy fired first, no time to even shoulder the rifle. The recoil jerked her sideways.

The shot ripped the Dog Man's right biceps wide open, forcing the shotgun high. It blasted an apartment window above them. Impossible to tell if it felt any pain. It jacked the slide again, ejecting another smoking shell. Pointed, pulled the trigger. But there was only a click this time. That shell had been its last.

Amy fired for the final time, severing one of the Dog Man's ears. It turned then and did a lurching lope up the street. Running away.

James stared as it receded. Cold black rain stinging his eyes. Sooty rills creeping through the contours of Sideshow Bob's mangled brain.

*

Congregating back at the playground, black rain lashing down now. All of them sopping wet, their faces inked with black pulsing veins of filth. James saw the looks the others gave each other when they told them about the Dog Man. The ones who hadn't been there, harrowed with doubt.

Lilac screaming, "It shot Sideshow Bob! It shot him!"

Ross asking who the hell was Sideshow Bob.

"Right," Graham snapped. "Time to get out of this manky weather."

Frightful urgency in the Group, just to get out of the stinking downpour. Gaping around for the reappearance of the Dog Man. They'd put Sam in a shopping cart that Mike had scrounged, propped on packs, his calves dangling over the edge. Tribe, Ross and Mike took turns pushing the cart while Astrid trotted alongside.

They were on a narrow side street now, tiny clapboard houses crowded up and down both sides, squeezed close to the sidewalks. No sound but the effervescent hiss of rain. Graham chose houses without vehicles in the driveways, hopping up the front steps and rapping at the doors while Amy covered his back. It seemed an interminable wait, shivering with cold, until he finally found one that was unoccupied.

They battered in the door, piling quickly into the narrow front room. Tribe, Graham, Massimo and Mulligan struggled with Sam, laying him on a couch. At first they all simply stood, numb, dribbling black puddles on the carpet. Fifteen people. Enough for a decent-sized Christmas do, James thought bleakly.

No, wait. Fourteen. Sideshow Bob was gone.

Such a relief to be out of the horrid inky rain, but lost within this strange dark space that belonged to none of them. And yet possessed now by all of them in common. Dreadfully quiet and dim.

A small calico cat slipped warily into the room, scenting the air. It meowed a welcome. All at once, they melted. Unslung their packs, pulled off their coats and jackets. Groaning, gasping at the clamminess of wet clothes. Everything – their clothes, their packs, the tent. Soaked through with soot, stinking.

As was becoming the ritual, Tribe set up the stove and got it lit. They kept as close to it as they could, facing its faint blue light. Warming their hands over it. The kitchen behind the living room was well stocked with dried and canned goods. They lit candles to ward off the gloom. Very little was said except the bare minimum necessary to get things done.

While Tribe warmed some instant soup and a few cans of brown beans, Mike and Mulligan, Amy and Lilac raided the upstairs closet and dresser for dry clothes. Then they all took turns using the bathroom to peel off their soaked garments, heaping them in the bathtub, changing into whatever they could find.

Written on the wall behind the toilet was the inscription:
A woman without a man is like a fish without a bicycle.

Soon they were sitting in the living room around the hot camp stove, sipping soup, gulping beans. All of them dressed like the same person. Tribe awkward in a shirt and slacks that were far too short for his rangy limbs.

"George A. Linton," Mike read off one of the envelopes piled beneath the mail slot.

"A senior citizen, I'd say," said Sheilagh, looking around at the thin sweaters, brown polyester slacks and blue oxford shirts they were wearing.

Graham found a well-stocked drinks cabinet. They busted out a bottle of Johnny Walker.

"Well I say we should offer some thanks to George Linton, whoever it is," said Ross. "Or was, I guess."

A moment of solemn silence.

"To Sideshow Bob," Lilac mumbled. Then, answering Ross's quizzical look. "The weird guy with the cell phone?"

A general grumble of assent.

George's calico cat had jumped into her lap. Desperately, she stroked it, as if in the act of petting the animal she could efface this horrid afternoon.

James recognized that the ones who hadn't seen the Dog Man with their own eyes still doubted the story. Suspicion there, the sense that James and the rest might be losing it. He understood their reluctance to believe. But one look at Amy was enough to convince anybody that something empirically terrible had happened. She had changed. Drained, not as haughty anymore. Her battle with the Dog

Man had sucked away some of her vital energy.

"Thanks to Amy," he rasped. "For saving our asses today."

Lilac burst into tears.

*

They waited out days of foul weather at George's place. By the next day the rain was no longer black. That was something, at least. The clouds flushing themselves clean. Enough to convince them that maybe – *maybe* – the Dog Man had been conjured by the black rain, and was now gone.

Every available spot in the house had drying gear hung on it. Doorknobs, the backs of dining room chairs, the shower curtain bar. They took down picture frames to use the hooks. Tribe was careful with his sword, removing it from the soaked leather scabbard, gliding a whetstone down its length and applying a sheen of oil. Amy disassembled both her rifles and oiled all the moving parts. Both of them showing the precise fervency of those who required their tools to keep their hearts beating.

They shared out all the stuff they'd managed to scrounge. Sheilagh had bagfuls of makeup. Mulligan scoffed, but she and Lilac and Amy pounced on it, applying lipstick and eye liner, spraying their faces with spritzers that promised refreshment. And delivered: their morale skyrocketed. Even Astrid tried some eye shadow, her eyes gaining depth to mask the hollow dolor.

Rohini got a pair of cross trainers to replace her Birkenstocks. The shoes were inscribed with the promise of a Dynamic Forefoot Cradle. Rohini smiled vaguely when Sheilagh had finished putting them on her feet. "There's hope for you yet," Sheilagh grinned, patting Rohini's cheek.

Massimo showed off a good hunting knife. Graham was impressed. "A sharp knife. A decent tarpaulin. It's those things that mean the difference between a wee bit of comfort and bare-arsed misery, like."

Seemingly insignificant things, too. A small traveling chess set with missing pieces – Tribe used a button for a black pawn. A small rock for one of the white rooks.

Playing cards. Matches, hats. A few bars of soap.

Sheilagh spent some time organizing the kitchen supplies. A decent amount of food, but fourteen people would go through it in just a few days.

"Not enough for more than two meals a day," she declared.

"Thin ones, at that," said Ross.

"Share it fairly, but don't take a slice of my pie," James sang.

Pink Floyd: always good for an apt quote.

He, Tribe, and Massimo were on the first squad to fetch water, with Amy on shotgun. Around the corner was a creek, one of the tributaries of the Rouge River that had saved their asses. Not much more than a few thousand yards' round-trip, but being out in the open ignited in James a sense of danger so extreme his own skin seemed dense, confining. After the first water run, the creek beckoned. Each squad would take a few minutes to bathe and gasp in the cold water before they collected more for drinking.

By the time they got back to the house, their arms were shaking. A shocking heaviness to water, an immensity even in a bucketful. Graham had managed to find razors and shaving cream. After they'd heated the water on the camp stove, James luxuriated in a shave. The clean feel of the shaving soap, of his smooth skin after so many days! Despite everything, he left the bathroom whistling.

Tribe bitched about their dwindling stock of methylated spirit for the stove, but Graham told him not to worry. "That kinda stove, it'll take anything for fuel. They give them things to air force pilots, right, in case they need to bail out, cause apparently they can even use jet fuel. Years ago, I was hill walking with a mate of mine, and we'd forgotten to bring fuel. We used voddy in a pinch. Almost cried, perfectly good booze going up in flames!"

Lilac arranged a schedule for who would do the washing up every night, prepare meals. Athol was happy to provide a New Testament quote: "'The multitude of them that believed were of one heart and of one soul: neither said any of them that ought of the things which he possessed was his own; but they had all things in common,'" he read in his slow, easy pace. "'…and distribution was made unto every man according to need.'"

"Acts?" Tribe guessed.

"You got it." Athol winked at him.

"Yeah?" said Mulligan. "And I guess we're the *multitude*, right? What are we supposed to *believe*, huh?" He slid his rook along a row.

"That we must do whatever we can to ensure our survival," Tribe answered.

"Sounds good to me." Ross scowled at Mulligan, spooning some soup into his mouth.

"Funny," Mulligan leered in the amber candlelight, "but I don't see God. Not anywhere."

"Me neither," Mike snickered.

"You can't see God, but you can see where he's been." Athol smiled, placing his queen. "Checkmate, by the way."

*

After a few days in the house, spending most of their time sleeping or just lounging around, allowing the weight of fatigue to drip away, they became restless. Searching, scratching into the crevasses of George Linton's life. Despite Tribe's injunction to be cats, they became moles after all.

Until Mike found a street guide in George's telephone desk. They used it to systematically scour the surrounding area, street by street, block by block. Every day a party would set out, bringing back reports to Amy, who marked points of interest on the map.

James and Tribe, Sheilagh, Graham and Lilac found a big Bass Pro outlet twenty five blocks northwest. A bonanza. Even in the ransacked dregs, they found everything they needed. Sleeping bags, tools. A stout ten-person tent, rain gear. By the time they left George's several days later, every member of the Group had been fully kitted out with top notch gear.

What a boost it gave them. Christmas, Mike called it, as they sat around sorting through the pile in George's living room. So much, it had taken three trips just to get it all.

The smell of fresh Gortex and rainproof vinyl. A newness that soothed away some of the jagged edges of their splintered spirits. Tribe claimed a pair of aviator sunglasses and Zeiss field glasses.

"Hey, Captain Studly," Lilac cackled cruelly. "Turn this way, let me have a good look!"

Sheilagh broke out into spasms of breathless, honking laughter. "Ah, that's brilliant, Lilac! Captain Studly! Brilliant!"

Tribe played along, standing in a statuesque pose, modeling the shades for them. "How about from this angle? How about now?" Until they were all laughing so hard they begged him to stop.

All except Astrid. James saw her wan smile, kneeling by the sofa, holding Sam's hand.

Then Ross pulled out a coil of yellow nylon rope. Immediately, Lilac's laughter was snuffed out. She stared at the rope as if it might rear up and bite her.

Predictably, the Bass Pro shop had been picked clean of every firearm in stock. Ammunition too. The display cases all smashed, hungrily empty. Chilling to think of all those thousands of cartridges being loaded into weapons all across the city.

You might be able to see where God's been on occasion, James thought staring at the empty shelves. But you can clearly see where other things have been too. Not necessarily devils, but close enough to send a shiver down your back.

Mulligan managed to find a slingshot that the looters had missed. He spent his time standing on the patio behind the house, using rocks to knock empty cans off a chair.

Amy found a library. The only public space they'd come across that had been left intact. Their turn to be the first raiders. Stealing beloved favorites, or books they'd never gotten around to reading. James found a battered copy of Conrad's *The Secret Agent*. Sheilagh scrounged several field guides to wild plants. For the rest of their time at George's she had her nose buried in pages of taxonomy. Most of them spent every free moment poring over text, brows furrowed, sating their greed for words, phrases, stories.

Tribe recited passages from *Metamorphoses* by Ovid. Narcissus by the pool, stunned by self-pity, self-longing, unable to possess the object of his utmost desire. The lyrical beauty of Ovid's prose painted intricate scroll work on their minds.

"There is more that one holy book in this world," Tribe told Athol.

*

Food was scarce. One afternoon, Amy appeared carrying a fat Canada goose by the neck. They built a crude fire pit in the backyard and roasted it. The .30-06 had done a lot of damage, but there was still plenty of meat to go around. Lilac refused to eat any, announcing that she was a vegetarian. Evidently so was Rohini, because she'd shake her head whenever Sheilagh tried to give her some. The rest of them gorged themselves on succulent goose flesh. But then, the next day, they were short again. A constant need for replenishment.

They scouted far and wide, but could only find corner shops and bodegas, all of them thoroughly scoured. McDonalds, Burger King and the like. Massimo found a bag of soggy fries that had been frozen but were now dissolved to mush. They made an attempt to roast them on the camp stove, but the result was so mealy and disgusting they could barely bring themselves to swallow the mess.

Lilac cross-referenced the map book with the Yellow Pages. It seemed the closest Sobey's was over seven miles away, nearly a full day of solid hiking there and back.

Tribe, Athol and Ross stayed behind with Rohini, Sam and Astrid.

The rest of them got lost, Lilac turning out to be a lousy navigator. When they finally got to the Sobey's, bewildered, hungry and tired, they found it swarming with hundreds of desperate freaky people. A gargantuan warehouse, so large that being inside meant groping in low light. They hadn't thought to bring lamps or candles.

James got swallowed in a boiling melee of spastic limbs, sweaty snarling faces. Cans, bags of lentils and cornmeal yanked from his hands as soon as he pulled them off the shelves. Dim pandemonium, shattering glass, rice and pasta strewing from packages torn in vicious tugs of war.

He struggled to tear a sack of flour away from a screeching woman. The sack split, spraying flour all over. In his eyes, up his nose. He couldn't stop sneezing, stumbling half-blind through the mad scrum.

In the disorder he became separated from the others.

The shrieking crowd wanted to smother him. Hands clawed at his face until he wrenched them away.

More and more people piling in, climbing over shoulders and backs, tumbling, a frenetic contest. Almost impossible to move, jostled and wrestled by the humid clutch of wiggling bodies pressing from every side. Panicking, he used his fists and elbows and knees to break out.

Shelves crashed over. Screaming and wailing. Then gunshots rang out. The crowd dove down as one organism, hurling James to the floor so hard he saw stars. Just a glimpse of Mulligan, hair flying, leaping across huddled backs to swipe at cans literally flying off the shelves. A blowout sale.

When they reassembled in the windblown parking lot, James was scratched and bloodied. He'd managed to pull out three jars of jam, two strawberry, one apricot.

Mulligan strutted out grinning, triumphantly pumping a shopping bag crammed with cans of creamed corn. "Whoo!" he caterwauled, as if he'd just slammed the mosh pit at an Iron Maiden show.

Lilac stumbled out, one eye blacked. Total haul: Mulligan's corn, the jam, two bottles of grape drink – not grape juice – grape *drink*. Three mashed loaves of bread and a bag of pre-sliced bagels. A single can of black beans, a tin of instant coffee and a bag of sugar. The bag was ripped, and didn't look to be much more than half full.

The experience finally convinced Amy to lend her spare rifle, a Ruger .30-06 bolt action. "It's not going to do us any good on my back," she said, "so somebody might as well take it. Besides, I'm getting sick of going out on every goddamn water run."

Massimo jumped at the chance. Amy told him he'd just disqualified himself. Mulligan disqualified himself when he took the gun and immediately put his finger on the trigger. She gave him a mirthless grin, waving her fingers for him to return it. "You don't touch that damn trigger until you've acquired a target and you're ready to shoot. An accidental discharge, that's the last things we need."

Sheilagh and Lilac both looked disgusted at the prospect of carrying a gun. Tribe flatly refused. "I don't handle firearms," he sniffed, as if rejecting the possibility of contracting an STD.

"Never fired a gun in me life," said Graham. "Though, I must confess to having accidental discharges now and again." There were a few giggles.

James refused. He'd been in the cadets and army reserve in high school, so he'd had firearms training. But he didn't want the responsibility of carrying a gun. Not now.

"Alright," said Ross reluctantly. "I was in the army, about an eon ago. I'll take it, if nobody else can."

"Believe me, it makes you a good candidate, that you don't want to take it. Keep that butt tight into your shoulder. It'll give you a big kick. Chances are, just the bang will be enough to scare the bejesus out of whoever needs it."

A pulse of silence passed among them like a ghost. James sensed what Amy and some of the others were thinking: not if the Dog Man comes back. Not if we run into another slaving squad. Not if…

*

Their third or fourth night in the house. Dark of night, the room candlelit. The Group sat around the living room, broken up into several smaller conversations. Tribe and Athol bent over a chess match. Massimo dozing in one of the dining room chairs. The room respiring with rising and falling chatter. Amy, Sheilagh and Lilac were leafing through a photo album they'd found. Occasionally, they'd take out a photo and pass it around for everybody to see. An athletic man, darkly handsome, square-chinned. Black-and-white shots of him, dapper in an air force uniform. George A. Linton. Lots of photos of him with a tall woman with direct eyes and an open smile.

"Must've been her that wrote that Gloria Steinem quote on the bathroom wall," said Amy.

"She must've died," said Lilac. "George is a widower."

Mulligan picked idly at a guitar he'd found in an upstairs closet. It only had three strings, but he'd gone through a great show of carefully tuning each one. He sang 'Redemption Song.'

"Love Marley," said Lilac drowsily.

James felt the dizzy tug that he knew presaged another fugue event. The Voice taking on a commanding tone, pummeling him. *The Stone! The Stone! The Stone!* Maggie at a peak of pique. Alright, he thought, closing his eyes. Just go with it now. Don't fight it.

To James, floor fell away. As if he was on a plane in severe turbulence. He forced himself to be aware. Not to have his consciousness blotted out.

When somebody began to chant *The Stone THE STONE! the Stone the Stone the Stone*, James opened his eyes, peering around the room. All the conversation petered out. All eyes flicked to him. Uncomfortable expressions, quizzical, even derisive.

The Stone the Stone the Stone the Stone...

"O-kay..." Lilac turned to Amy, raising her eyebrows.

Massimo was suddenly alert. "Jimmy?"

James realized with a shock that it was his own voice chanting. That he could not stop. He had a view of the entire room as if he was stuck on the ceiling. He saw himself, bulging eyes swiveling, his body swaying from side to side. Face morbidly slack, a loose mouth that did not seem to be forming any words. And yet...

The Stone the Stone the Stone THE STONE! the Stone– Hor-shn imy-khent ankh jit hery-sshta...

Horus the Divine, he who is foremost, living for all time, master of secrets.

Like the chanting of a Buddhist monk, a rhythmic hum pervading the room. The candle flames seemed to be pulsing in time with the hymn.

Nobody else said a word. Athol, frozen over the chessboard, a white knight pinched in his fingers.

It's hypnotizing them! James realized. Casting a spell.

All except Lilac. He saw her look around with alarm, shaking her head. "I won't stand for this," she snapped, getting to her feet.

"Oh yes you will, Lilac Taylor!" A powerful female voice blared from James's drooping mouth. Maggie's voice. "Do you wish to hear the babbling voices again, like the clucking of a thousand chickens?"

Lilac stopped halfway between sitting and standing. She slumped back down, shocked. "How could you possibly—"

"Sit and listen," Maggie's voice proclaimed. "Listen and sit! You wish for answers. Ask then, and you shall receive. Your *good book* knows, Athol, does it not?"

The bishop fell from Athol's fingers, rolling across the board and tumbling to the floor. "Am I hearing the voice of God?" He sounded asleep. Caught in a nightmare.

"No, no, no!" Maggie irritated now, the tone of voice James dreaded as a child, the precursor to a smack. Drool oozed from James's lower lip, falling in syrupy strings. "Ask then, and you shall receive!"

And still, pulsing beneath these cryptic statements, a ventriloquist chant continued. *The Stone the Stone the Stone the Stone...*

"That thing James calls the Dog Man," said Amy in a shaking voice. "What is it?"

"There are those who will go to great lengths to stop James from completing his quest. Yes, they will."

"So you're telling us that someone *made* that fuckin' thing?" Massimo asked.

"Many made it. Crafted. Conjured. Yes."

Massimo reached into a pocket. Pulled something out. Reverently laid it on the floor at James's feet. The Dog Man's severed ear. A thin blade of grimy rubberized plastic. A relic.

Amy hissed, actually forking her fingers at it.

"Made by whom?" Tribe snapped.

"Nguyen."

"Nguyen," Tribe repeated, uncertain. "Why does this Nguyen wish to stop James?"

"That is all I will say." Maggie being coquettish, saucy.

"I don't believe it," Sheilagh stated flatly. "It was a man wearing a costume head. That's all." Yet the fiery impetus was excised from her voice.

"Yeah, well you weren't there," Mulligan replied. "It was gunning for him!" Thrusting a finger at James.

"Why does James feel compelled to travel northeast?" Sheilagh's question.

"He seeks the answer of answers."

"What the hell is that supposed to mean?" Ross grumbled.

Then Maggie's and James's voices merged. "*The Stone the Stone—— Hor-shn imy-khent ankh jit hery-sshta— THE STONE! the Stone the Stone...*" Disharmonic buzzing.

"*The Philosopher's Stone. The Emerald Tablet!*"

For a while, there was nothing to be heard but the rhythmic drone: *The Stone the Stone the Stone THE STONE! the Stone—*

"Will my husband survive?" Astrid cried.

Suddenly almost all of them were shouting at James. Demands about loved ones, wives, parents, siblings.

"Fourteen there are here," Maggie moaned, and they all shut up. "Soon to be but nine. Five shall not survive."

Distress gripped the room. Sharp glances ricocheting through the Group.

"How?" Mike queried. "How will they die?"

"One shall die twice!"

"What a load of tripe!" Sheilagh threw her hands in the air.

"All must trust in all. Alone, all will surely fall. Together, most will find the way. Yet one shall betray all."

Tribe sat up straight. "Who? Who will betray us?"

"Too soon to tell, so soon, so soon. One in this room. He or she, she or he? Who can tell, who can tell?"

Christ, James thought. It was like hearing Maggie as a young woman precisely mimicking that Hermes freak!

He woke up lying on the floor.

"It's called glossalalia," he heard Tribe intone. Then something about somebody named Montanus.

"A portent from God!" Athol kept raving. "A portent from God! 'To one person he gives the ability to speaking in strange tongues, and to another he gives the ability to explain what is said!'"

Mulligan snickered. "Maybe he's just fucked up. Did you think about that?" And then he chanted, accompanied by jangling guitar notes: "He's just fucked up! He's just fucked up! He's just fuuuuucked uuuuuup!"

Somebody had put James in the emergency position. Judging from the ache in his ribs, he'd been there for a while. But he lay still, kept his eyes closed. Momentary solitude in a room full of bickering people. A cushion for his extreme embarrassment.

"Everything comes back to religion for you, is that it?" That was Amy. "Everything!"

"Can we concentrate on what's important?" Tribe shouted.

"What should it come back to?" Athol's nasal voice, smiling devilishly. "Your *sexuality*?"

"He's given us valuable information," Tribe insisted. "If we are attentive—"

"You heard him!" Massimo whined hysterically. "You heard what he said! Somebody in this fuckin' room is gonna stab us in the back!"

"Ach, don't be to sure about that," said Graham.

Sheilagh was one of the angriest. "I don't believe a word, damn it! He's having seizures, pure and simple. You lot are paying attention just because you're done in, you're stressed out— "

"Fair play, Sheilagh," Graham interrupted her, "but listen – listen, if that's true, what about the woman's voice, then?"

On and on they argued. Amy told Athol he was a stubborn old

prick. "O-ho!" Athol enthused, clearly enjoying himself. One of them – maybe Amy, maybe Lilac – told Tribe to shut up.

But hot as the arguments became, Mulligan didn't leave. Sheilagh didn't storm off. Already, a rudimentary team. Pulled together by a gravitational force they were only just beginning to comprehend.

After a while, the fight ebbed to a skirmish. Tiredness creeping in, stealing their enthusiasm. As James opened his eyes, Ross added the punctuation mark: "All of you need to relax. It's not the end of the world."

The irony melted through the group. Mild smiles, breath huffed through noses. Weary nods, acknowledging the joke.

*

Sam never regained consciousness. Astrid too, more and more withdrawn. They were the only ones who never left the house. The foundations, in a strange way, as the rest of the Group came and went, stomping through the living room to the kitchen delivering fresh buckets of water or showing off some paltry bit of food found on a scrounging mission. More or less ignoring them. Discomfort that none of them knew how to deal with. A dying man on the couch.

Tribe offered to lift Sam up to one of the bedrooms. Astrid thanked him, but refused. She didn't want to disturb him. James wondered if she was afraid that being hidden away upstairs would marginalize him. That the rest might forget about her husband.

When Sam began to smell, Sheilagh brought back packs of adult undergarments, latex gloves and baby wipes. Discreetly, they would all leave the living room, giving Astrid some measure of dignity and privacy she needed to tend to her husband.

Sheilagh kept changing his bandages, and it was hard not to notice the blackness of the shoulder wound. As if the polluted rain had seeped into the tissue. After several days, Amy and Lilac insisted that Astrid take one of the beds upstairs. They'd drawn lots to determine the order of who got a bed, but Astrid had spent the entire time sleeping on the floor next to the couch. Often holding Sam's hand, even in sleep.

"Get some real sleep," said Lilac, firmly enough to make Astrid listen. "Amy and I can watch Sam tonight."

It took some persuasion, but Astrid finally stumbled up the narrow stairs, sleeping for more than a day straight through.

James spent a lot of his time sitting on George's front porch. Keeping his eyes on the incessant rain. So much the better for keeping a look out. The Dog Man, out there somewhere, hunting.

He listened to the shots echoing all around. Horrifying echoes, like hoarse wailing. TOMB! they seemed to thunder. TOMB! TOOOMB!

Tribe and Graham joined him, leaning on the rail.

"This is the way things were for hundreds of years, you know." Tribe stated. "When a relative died, they died in the house."

"First of all, Sam's not a relative," James responded. "I shouldn't have given him that damn Aspirin." It had been the fecal smell that drove him outside. Even when Sam had been changed, the memory of it lingered. A marker for his own shame.

"Aw, James, but what're you gonna do about it?" Graham implored him. "What's done is done, man."

"He's embarrassed," said Tribe, toeing James's foot with his boot. "At being the center of attention the other night."

"Wouldn't you be?" James asked.

"D'you remember anything of it?" Graham asked.

"No," James lied. He didn't want to discuss it.

"He's lying," Tribe announced.

Somewhere a few blocks over, a voice shrieked a long lament, dying off into pathetic whimpers. James saw that Tribe and Graham felt the same panicky flutter he did. The way they both looked around, clenched their jaws. No getting used to the human voice shredded that way. Rage? Terror? Impossible to tell.

"Everybody thinks I'm a freak," said James.

"They do not!" Tribe's eyes flashing indignantly.

"We-ell," Graham rubbed his chin, "I think they sorta do, Tribe."

"Thanks, man." James couldn't help but smile at Graham's attempt to keep a straight face.

"Who gives a damn what they think?" Tribe boomed.

"They're dealin' with it, James," Graham shrugged. "It's gonna be some time before everybody digests what they heard."

That bloody Northern Irish accent of his. He pronounced time *tie-yem*. Digests became *dee-jeyests*. Just hearing Graham speak lifted James's spirits.

"Glad to see I'm gettin' through," said Graham, giving him a punch on the shoulder.

James sat up. "People coming."

"Steady," Tribe muttered.

A few men and women stopped on the sidewalk, peeked out from under dripping umbrellas and the cowls of raincoats. A pale, pinched woman wearing too much bright makeup stepped forward. "We live here, on the street," she said tentatively. "You guys, like, buy this place from the old guy that lived here?"

James, Tribe and Graham gave each other a pained look. "We're visiting from out of town," James stammered.

"Joe around?" asked a small pink-faced man.

"George," Tribe corrected him.

"Huh?"

"Your *neighbor*," said Graham sharply. "His name's George. And no, he's not around."

"Got any food?" queried another, his voice pitched high with longing.

"Have you?" Tribe retorted.

Without another word, the little search party moved on down the street, looking for all the world like one of those Monty Python animations.

Graham shook his head. "Fuckin' bizarre, wasn't it? I'm wonderin', who are the neighbors, who're the strangers 'n all."

"Welcome to North America," Tribe growled.

*

At dinner time, James noticed Ross sitting by the kitchen window, utterly rapt. After a couple of hours, Ross was still in the same spot. He hadn't eaten. He'd hardly moved at all, legs crossed, hands folded at his chin. Glaring concentration.

James crept up to Ross's chair and stole a peek at the object of Ross's fascination. A thermometer on the side of the house.

Ross jumped, looking over his shoulder.

"Sorry," said James. "I didn't mean to startle you."

Ross shifted, re-crossed his legs, rubbed the silver stubble on his wattled chin. "It's gone down, couple of degrees in the past while." He sounded defensive, but far off.

James realizing what Ross was staring at. *Functioning technology*. How awesome to see something that still worked. A device still providing tidbits of data. Teardrops of the gods.

*

They drew lots for the toilet, using stalks of grass. James pulled the shortest. By the time his turn came, the toilet was so bad, even going into the john was enough to make him gag.

"I am become Pele, the island maker," he muttered, glaring at the atoll of shit rising from a lagoon of piss.

After each of them finished, he or she was supposed to dump just enough water down to flush it away. Of course there wasn't nearly enough water to spare, so by the time James went into the bathroom, the bucket was empty.

To top it off, the seat was speckled with piss. James wondered bitterly who was responsible for that. He put his money on Mulligan.

"Shit," he spat, gagging again. And that's about what it amounted to.

James was desperate. He'd avoided this for two days. Now he could feel the weight straining behind his testicles. He had seconds, not minutes, but there was no goddamned way he could bring himself to come in contact with the streak-stained abomination of this throne.

He jogged downstairs, through the back door of the house. Through a gate at the rear of the backyard was a narrow alleyway bordered by rusty chain link fencing. He pulled down his pants, squatting in the midst of bloated garbage bags. A loose slurry poured out of him in gassy burps and wet snorts. A lifetime of toilet training almost betrayed him, as he stopped a dribble of pee just before the stream really started going and soaked the seat of his trousers.

Just a few yards in front, at the head of the alley, people slumbered past in both directions. This is what's become of privacy, James thought with a ridiculous smirk that forced out another juicy fart. Thus, the death knell of middle class pretension.

He waved at a disheveled, grizzled old trooper. The old guy stared, almost walking headlong into the steel post at that end of the fence.

It was only then that James realized he'd forgotten to bring out the fucking toilet paper.

*

Sam died on the sixth day at George's. James went inside, met by the rest of them, ashen, downcast. Astrid doubled over, hands clawing through her hair, moaning, heaving sorrow. Lilac went down on her knees by the couch, took Astrid in her arms. Astrid clutched at her until the worst of the terrible tremor had passed.

Rohini edged up with a box of Kleenex.

"I'm so sorry about your loss," said Athol very quietly.

Terrible, shuffling quiet in the room. A sense of being shut in tight together, unsure what to say, even how to move.

James was shocked at how the chocolate shade of Sam's face had drained to yellow-gray. He chided himself for ever thinking of him as a body while he still breathed. This was a lesson he would never forget. That life always bequeathed something noble. Ross lifted the sheet, covering Sam's face.

For some time they sat a vigil with Astrid. She told them how Sam had enjoyed bass fishing. An anecdote about an expedition when Sam had fallen out of the boat while he was trying to pee over the side. Astrid giggled and sniffed, shaking her head. It seemed immensely cruel that she should be denied the comfort of hearing relatives and friends reminisce. It reminded everyone of how alone they were now. This was their binding.

As the morning light angled into afternoon, Mulligan came in from the kitchen, soaked to the skin and smeared with mud. James hadn't even realized he'd been missing.

"Mulligan, are you alright?" Sheilagh asked.

"I – uh…" He screwed up his face, shifted his feet. "I took the opportunity, to dig a gr—uh, a resting place?"

It took a moment, but Astrid rose stiffly from the floor, lurched to Mulligan and threw her arms around his neck. "Thank-you," she sniffed. "Thank-you so much for this."

They used a clean bed sheet for a shroud. Stripped Sam of the sheet he'd lain in on the couch, smelling of illness and death. It was very hard work, maneuvering the body so that it was wrapped properly. They pinned the edges of the sheet so that it wouldn't fall off. Athol, Ross, Tribe, Graham, Massimo, Mike and James all lifted Sam's body, struggling under the weight through the kitchen into the backyard. Mulligan had used a mattock and spade to pry up the patio stones and dig a good, deep grave. Hours of hard labor there.

They buried him beside George's bed of lilies and penstamen. Astrid stood between Lilac and Sheilagh, gripping their hands until her fingers turned white. Each member of the group took turns putting spadefuls of earth in the grave, until it was full.

Athol came to the front. "I could tell you all that God works in mysterious ways, that the Lord giveth and the taketh away, but I know that doesn't cover this. Not at all. I will say this, though: I have seen some terrible things in the past two weeks. Awful things that have tested my faith in an omniscient, benevolent God. I've felt my faith wither, not sure it would survive this crucible. But I've also seen a group of scared people who've lost almost everything. And I've wondered at their willingness to sacrifice all they have left for each other – for strangers." Normally wry, Athol's voice broke now. "And it's been a wonder. Truly a wonder."

They went back inside, out of the rain. Lit candles. Raided the last of George's liquor cabinet. They spent the night drinking quietly, suffused with their own thoughts, their own wishes.

Ross talked about his wife, waiting for him at home, about seventy miles east of the city. Like George, Athol was a widower. He had a daughter doing aid work in Kenya. Another at law school in London. He wondered if he would ever see them again. Like James, Mike had walked home from work on the night the lights went out to find his home gutted by fire. His family nowhere to be found.

Memories stirred by the telling. Irrevocably altered, like a well-tended garden disturbed by tramping feet.

Mulligan picked at the guitar and Lilac sang 'Tomorrow is a Long Time' very softly. The cat arranged on her lap, sleeping poised like an Egyptian figurine.

"I've been thinking a lot," said Astrid. "It's the one luxury I've had these past few days – the time to ponder. Being here in George's place…it's been strange. I imagine a group of total strangers, you know, squatting in our home. Going through our things, eating our food." She paused, gazing a thousand yards. "I need to go home now. But first, I need to find my daughter. She's at college, west of the city."

Sheilagh and Rohini squirmed.

"I know," Astrid replied to them. "It'll be bad. But I need to be with my daughter."

"What's out there, to make it so bad?" Mike asked.

"The airport." Sheilagh's voice was husky. "All the planes, right? Coming in to land, they all went down. All the fuel stores. Everything – everything was on fire."

Rohini whimpered, hugging herself.

"But that was two weeks ago," said Astrid. "It can't still be burning by now. Can it?"

Nobody answered. None of them willing to even contemplate moving through such an area.

"My daughter, she's the only family I have left now. It's not a choice for me. I feel badly enough that I spent so much time coming east with all of you." A slow smile distorted her thin mouth.

Her lazy eyes made James realize she was drunk. So was he. More calories in the booze, no doubt, than in the food they'd eaten today.

*

The earliest, sickly pallor of dawn. Restive rain ringing in the eaves troughs, tinnier, more tremulous than notes on Maggie's old ill-tuned piano. A maddening clamor of birds singing compline teemed into James's head, disintegrating sleep like sand slurped seaward by a strong undertow. His legs kicked at the restraint of his sleeping bag, tossing, sweaty despite the chill. A maddening cocoon from which he would never emerge, never more than a squirming churning grub. Infected by the Voice, Maggie's now, the Horus charade now sloughed away like a snakeskin. *If you are brave and control your heart, you shall embrace your children, you shall kiss your wife, you shall see your home. You have been chosen, Jamie. You will find the Emerald Tablet!*

"Shut up," he muttered. He groaned, rolled over again. Close beside him on the floor of the tiny room, Tribe slept on, one long arm thrown over his eyes. On the other side, Massimo, snoring luxuriantly. Lucky bastards.

James sat up, reached to the foot of his bag for his trousers. In the left-hand cargo pocket, the wallet he'd kept. Functionally useless, but containing something precious. With urgent fingers he slipped out the photo he kept in there. Stace, Jen and Sara, all grinning and tanned, hair damp from their last swim in the lake. He'd taken this last summer at Mare's cottage. An anchor delicate enough to be blown away by a gust of wind.

Far, far from this dank, dusty room with its thin cat-smelling carpet.

He pressed the image of his lost family to his forehead. Lay back and said a silent prayer for their wellbeing. Wishing that one day – one day – they might be reunited.

That damned ancient Egyptian aphorism about seeing his home, embracing his children, kissing his wife if he was brave. He didn't believe it. First off, there was patently no longer any home left for him to see. But James wanted to believe that if he fulfilled his quest, if he actually managed to find this Stone, this Emerald Tablet, whatever, wherever it happened to be, he might be rewarded pricelessly.

One faint beam of light in all this. Now that it was Maggie – or at least *his memories of Maggie* – giving the instructions, James was determined that from here on in it would be a dialogue. That he would start talking back.

*

Later that morning, everybody getting kitted out to leave. A cog had rolled, a notion common to them all without having to be spoken. The road beckoned with all its menace and possibility. Everything you needed on your back. No more, no less.

Amid the clink of equipment, zippers, cords whipping taut, feet stamping down into boots and shoes, anxiety gripped the stomach. To know that your life could depend on getting things just right.

Their faces were grim, lean with concentration. A hardness beginning to carve itself into muscle and bone.

Graham had given them instruction on the right way to pack. Using a waterproof liner to keep things dry. Sleeping bag on the bottom, then spare clothes, toilet kit. To economize on space, they'd all agreed on only four sets of clothing: warm and cold weather articles for the march, and two sets for wearing at rest in camp. Heavier equipment on top, including water. Making sure their rain gear was always easy to access. Graham advised them to keep a good supply of sugary foods handy to eat on the march. Good for boosting energy and staying warm.

They'd put together a kitchen pack, agreeing that each member of the Group would take turns to carrying it. It contained the camp stoves and fuel, all their cooking gear, salt and sugar, the water pumps, and their soap. Each one of them carried an equal portion of their scanty food stock. Since Tribe was the first to carry the kitchen pack, James's pack also contained Tribe's spare clothes, his groundsheet, and their tent. It was a damn heavy load. He told himself to get used to it.

James saw Lilac fumble with something that fell to the floor. Her key ring. No point in her keeping it now, and yet. Like his wallet, and the little glass bell in his shirt pocket, fetishes of power.

Lilac snuggled George's calico cat, whispered that she wished she could take it along. But she couldn't. She left a whole bag of cat food open in the kitchen.

Graham had a final look at their gear. "You've got a kickin' pack, there, James, but the straps are all done up wrong." He adjusted the shoulder and waist straps with clean jerks, the rugged efficiency of a sergeant inspecting troops. It worked. Immediately, James felt relief in his shoulders, in his lower back, the weight held higher now, snug against his spine.

Before they moved out, they formed a circle in George's living room. A ceremony for a man they'd never met who had given them so much. After a moment of silence, Sheilagh spoke of their need to work together, of her pride in their resilience. There is nothing we can't do, she said. Athol said a short prayer.

Outside, the clouds had cleared off. The morning sparkled with fresh new sunshine. They said good-bye to Astrid and wished her luck.

James took her aside and apologized about the Aspirin.

Astrid shook her head, her sharp features softened by something like gratitude. "You helped me bury my husband." Her voice cracked. "I owe you a debt that I can never repay, James." She looked him straight in the eye. "I need to know if my daughter is alright. Do you know? Can you tell me?"

"I wish I could," he said. "It only tells me what it wants me to know."

She nodded ruefully and moved off, west down the street. The rest of them headed east.

Chapter 13

Hunger

James walked alone. Sometimes Tribe and Graham would fall back and join him, but he preferred the time alone to ponder this strange new world. Nobody else was willing to come close. Perhaps frightened of having their fortunes told. Even Massimo remained distant and cool. Ironic, James mused, how being with these others had separated Massimo from him, as much as any stranger. Their friendship dissolving in the solution of the Group.

Moving into the suburbs now. Wider roads bounded by plazas, strip malls, car dealerships. Perched on phone lines all around them, crows congregated like stooped ministers in glossy black vestments. Harshly cackling, celebrating the curing of human meat. If they had lips, they'd be licking them, James thought. Avatars they seemed, more akin to their distant dinosaur cousins. Sleekly cunning, merciless.

Corpses littered the streets, sidewalks. Many had obviously lain there since the power had gone out. Bloated, greasy clothes stretching tight. Fly hives.

Others fresher, bloody and raw. Animals too. Mostly dogs, but the odd cat as well. Feathery bundles of dead birds sprinkled beneath trees. Coons. Even a coyote or two.

"Ugh!" Ross cried in frustration and disgust. "These damn flies!"

The difference between the living body and a filthy sack of corruption was tissue thin. A tiny step. The body longing to fall, return to the soil.

Amy and Lilac tried tying handkerchiefs over their faces. They'd sprinkled Chanel No. 5 on the fabric. Still, their eyes watered in the blowing fetor. A smell so potent against James's gag reflex, so pervasive, he thought he'd never be rid of it. Imagining his nasal cavities stained the same blue-black as decadent skin.

Mike shrieked like a little girl, pointing just so they could all look in time to see a cadaver shaking its head at them. Undead disapproval. Then a wet rat slithered from the rocking mouth.

Mike and Lilac, both dancing with disgust.

The rat perched on the corpse's forehead, sleek and hunched. Stared resentfully at them, contemptuously cleaning itself.

"Just move on, forget it," Sheilagh muttered, waving at flies.

Mike gripped his mouth with a white-knuckled hand. "Yo, I'll *never* forget *that*, yo!"

Amy smiled bitterly. "Kid, you can bet your ass you'll see lots more."

"Revolting!" said Rohini thickly.

"It's just doing what we're all doing – struggling to live," said Sheilagh, already moving.

"*Nasty*, yo!"

In a great swaying column of ragged refugees they marched. Shuffling slow and wary through the gray sludge that was the excrement of fire and rain. On they trudged past dogs tearing flesh, dragging corpses along the pavement.

The view reminded James of a war documentary. Endless straggling columns of civilians, fleeing ruined cities. Compelled to keep moving. To leave behind all they'd known, to escape memory.

"'What are the roots that clutch, what branches grow, out of this stony rubbish?'" Tribe muttered under his breath.

"T.S. Eliot, the Wasteland," said Lilac.

"Well done," said Tribe.

Lilac bared her teeth. "I'm not just another pretty, vapid North American face."

Disheveled ogres were sticking lengths of garden hose into the gas tanks of cars and trucks. Fellating them until the odiferous fluid spilled into their puckered mouths and they spat, quick with spouting hoses into buckets, into jars, old water jugs. Hectic whooping down the garbage-choked streets, galloping away with their prizes of golden fuel.

Sheilagh smiled, but there was nothing in it but venom. "Interesting, isn't it? We've barely enough food to keep going. Plenty of petrol around, though."

James remembered the garage that exploded in the firestorm. Gasoline. The way the air itself seemed to ignite. Everywhere they went, hundreds of vehicles all around. Every one with ten or twenty liters of fuel in the tank.

"Nourishment for machines," Tribe grunted. "None for people."

*

The food they hauled from George's lasted three days. More and more time spent on desultory scavenging missions: bringing in less and less. For days they wandered without finding anything. One afternoon, Mulligan came back to camp wearing a self-satisfied smirk, swinging a half-empty white bucket of mud-colored doughnut dough.

They scooped the mold off the top, and each of them had a few spoonfuls. The consistency of modeling clay.

"I think it's supposed to be chocolate, yo," Mike suggested with a queasy look.

Clustered around it like cattle at a feed pen. Cutlery clattering in the scrum.

"Hard to believe I used pay to eat this shit," said Ross, scraping a mouthful off his fork with his front teeth.

A few days after that, they were rooting through the remains of a scattered, smashed health food store. The floor near the cash registers caked with torn magazines. Impossibly brilliant colors, brilliant teeth. Plasticized bodies. SHRINK YOUR BELLY! hollered one headline, tattooed across the sculpted abs of a wanton model.

James swayed, looking at that. Fuck. Well, shrink the ol' belly, alright. We call it the Collapse of Civilization diet. More of a regimen, really. Just a few mouthfuls of food a day combined with rigorous summer-weather hikes. I'll be the first to attest to the success of COC. Why, I've managed to pull my belt in a whole two holes in just over a week!

James giggled. A hoarse sound more like a sob, echoing from the steel rafters. COC, right. Fucking cock-up.

Athol exalted at five shriveled potatoes he found behind a tipped produce display.

"At least they're *organic*," Ross sneered at Lilac.

With the attention of pilgrims building a reliquary, they steamed them in the billy can, literally wiping away the drool as the earthy dank smell wafted into their noses. The potatoes weren't even cooked before they scooped them out, serving them by the slice.

Graham went around the circle, muttering "Body of potato," as he dispensed one slice at a time. Some of them laughed, but their intense focus was on when their next turn would come. No more than five slices each, savoring the starchy sweet crunch of half-cooked potato. Delectable.

It was the only sustenance they had for almost two days. Dissolution creeping into their aching, tired muscles. James noticed a constant flow of saliva, pooling along his bottom gums until he had to spit. His spittle strangely flocculent.

Somewhere, Ross found an orange. James almost cried when he saw it in Ross's liver spotted hand. A miniature star the color of sweet joy. It seemed miraculous that Ross had brought it to share instead of secretly wolfing it down.

They sat, intent as dogs, watching Ross's dirty fingernails tear the leathery hide. Mulligan's painful hiss as juice spotted the sidewalk. Then, a succulent dripping section of fruit for each of them.

When he'd swallowed his morsel, James felt a surge of nausea. Within a few minutes, a heady delicious glow. The sugar leaking into his bloodstream, electrifying his brain.

Untold days after that, they came across a corner store. An angry swarthy man posed outside the door with a sawed-off shotgun. Automatically, James assumed the swarthy man was the owner. Only gradually did the vague notion seep into his hypoglycemic mind that he could just as easily have been some thug who'd killed the owner.

"Please," Ross mumbled, lurching at him. "Please help us!" He seemed to have forgotten about the rifle slung on his shoulder.

The man shouted obscenities, aimed the shotgun at Ross's chest.

"Please..." Ross fumbled in his pockets. Twenties, fifties fluttering down. More clenched in his shaking fingers. "I'll give whatever I have, *please*..."

Across the street, Amy raised her rifle. Shouting, shouting.

"Just shoot the fucker," James heard Mulligan groan. "Just shoot him."

"I'll kill him, yes I will!" screamed the man with the gun pointed at Ross. "You leave now, you leave right now!"

"Ross," said Sheilagh weakly.

"Please," he sobbed, stumbling drunkenly. Still proffering crumpled bills.

"Amy!" Lilac shouted, the way you yelled at somebody to wake them from a night terror. "Amy stop! You gonna *murder* this guy? Come on!"

Minutes, hours. The standoff frozen that way, a diorama fissioning desperation. The guy with the shotgun, his eyes flicking back and forth, back and forth. Sweat rolling off his unshaved chin.

Finally in his peripheral vision, James saw Amy lower her weapon. Mulligan, looking shocked.

Tribe was the first to move on. He just turned on his heels and strode off.

"Come on!" Massimo cried, incredulous. "You can't – just—" He threw his hands in the air, exasperated.

Sheilagh and Rohini crept up behind Ross. Put their hands very gently on his arms. Slowly led him away. He was weeping. They all followed Tribe.

*

As if speaking a eulogy, Mike told them how at his high school there would always be food discarded in the hallways. Every afternoon, sandwiches, fruit, callously left by kids for the custodians to sweep up and throw away. How he longed for just a bit of that food now!

At night. The lapping glow of fire. The liquescent chant of Athol's voice. Summoning the creak of an ancient stylus tracing ink across papyrus. "'Five times received I forty stripes save one. Thrice I was beaten with rods, once I was stoned—'"

"Big friggin' deal," Amy's weak voice drifted out of the dark. "I've been stoned more times than that."

There were a few snickers. All they had now was humor. Humor and scripture. The only things to lift their hunger-dimmed spirits.

"'In weariness and painfulness, in watchings often, in hunger and thirst, in fastings often, in cold and nakedness.'"

"Yo Athol, you got a funny way of trying to make us feel better!" Mike's voice, lacerated by mirth or anger.

"Son," said Athol, dryly implacable, "why do you think Paul wrote down this narrative?"

"Dog, I got no idea. I'm *done*, yo."

"I think maybe to show how going without is like a test. We are in a desert, Mike. Lost, wandering. The point is that the desert is a place of death, of suffering, sure, but it's also a place of life. It's where Jesus went, and being tempted by the Devil wasn't the only thing that happened there. His mission was born there."

"Right," said Sheilagh. "Look what ended up happening to him."

"Dude," said Mulligan, all snide. "If this shit we're going through is supposed to redeem us, then we must be the most redeemed motherfuckers around."

Athol smiled his slow smile, eyes twinkling with captured fire. "Well, if that's the case then maybe St. Paul was right, after all."

"There was something unseemly about the society we lived in," Tribe growled. "Too much plenty. Entitlement for more, always more, more, more."

"For you, maybe," said Amy.

"Well I'm not about to speak for anybody else!"

"You're saying that you prefer things this way?" asked Lilac, incredulous. "It's like you and Athol think we deserved this!"

"Of course I'm not saying that. Just that there can be virtue in denial, abstinence. The ascetic ideal."

"What a load of bollocks!" The words heaved out of Graham. "Really! Our culture was drenched sarcasm, in irony. Easy when most of us had more than we needed. Did you know that 'irony' comes from a Greek word that means pretending to be ignorant?" Tribe huffed. "I hardly think that anybody needed to *feign* ignorance. There was plenty of that going around."

Graham nodded reluctantly. "Point well made, point well made."

"I have lived too long in a place where I can be reached."

A strange new woman's voice, that. A slow cadence, sadly poetic. James searched the faces around the fire. Caught Rohini's gleaming eye. She had spoken. For the first time, definitive words.

"I always wondered what Rumi meant by that line." Rohini's steepled fingers caressed each other. "I agree with Tribe. On a certain level, there is something...holy about loss."

"Don't know lucky you are until it's gone," Lilac whispered.

"I guess that's just another way of putting it," Rohini responded.

"It's really only when we've lost," said Athol, "that we realize the truth of things. We take the time to stop rummaging through the junk heap. Sit. Contemplate. Mourn."

"Ecstasy means 'ex stasis,'" Tribe added. "Coming out of mundane daily routine, escaping the static to achieve something our distant ancestors knew intimately: the terrible fear, the exhilaration, of myth."

"What is this, Tribe?" James spat. "Do you need to show off?"

"Wish I'd had you as one of my teachers," said Mike.

"Glad I didn't," Mulligan snarked.

"It's the essence of humanity," said Athol. "The moment of first human consciousness, the realization that we're doomed, that we're not really in control at all. The birth of religion."

"Spirituality maybe," said Sheilagh flatly. "Not religion."

"Athol, you're thinking of religion as a positive step," James added. "Just by virtue of itself. I don't think that's necessarily true. I mean, I don't think religion is all bad, but take a second look at your book there. What about Deuteronomy, what about Leviticus?"

"What about them?"

"Isn't it Deuteronomy 19 that says it's perfectly alright to stone your children to death if they disobey you? Or that bit where God invites the Hebrews to take sex slaves in war. Sometimes that sense that we're doomed only turns people into raving assholes."

"I saw more than my share of that at home," said Graham.

"Besides," said James. "I'm not sure you want to stretch the analogy with St. Paul too far. D'you think he would have looked kindly on us stealing what we need?"

"Yes, alright," said Rohini. "I'm not a Christian, but that

doesn't mean I can't see the need for rituals and songs and, like, dance. Like the old stories from our grandparents and great-grandparents, the ones that filled us with awe and even dread sometimes. Not necessarily pleasant, but human."

"All my granddad ever talks about is how crappy things were when he was a kid." Mike grimaced. "Like, how the Japs treated them all like shit."

"Mike, please," said Sheilagh. "It's Japanese, not Japs."

"Hmmm," said Rohini. "I used to wonder what stories I'd pass on to my grandkids. When the time came, what would I have to offer. And it's like something's gone dead in me. I've forgotten almost all of them."

"I know what you mean," Amy nodded. "When I was a kid, there were celebrations. Every few months, my Nonna and Nonno used to hold these massive *festas*. All the aunts and uncles and cousins got together, right? There'd be dancing and music and tons of food. That came from the old country. People needed to stick together. To survive. It was hard there. But they were so full of life!"

"Even before Lights Out, those rituals were going extinct, and it makes me sad." Rohini's hands came to rest in her lap. Her black eyes, exhausted and rapturous.

"All it is, we need different things now," said Massimo. James could tell he was trying to sound placatory, but he came across as stubborn. "I mean, things can't stay the same forever, right?"

"No, you're right," Tribe snapped. "They must always improve. Always, without fail." He jumped to his feet and stomped off.

A long moment of uncomfortable quiet was broken by Mike's gasping.

"What is it?" Sheilagh asked.

"I just realized, shit – I might not ever see my granddad again, my parents…" Mike's voice shattered into sobs. "It's just not right, yo, not right."

*

A ratty clapboard house beside an elevated highway, under a huge billboard sign carrying a booze add that advised James to *Demand Only the Very Best*. Nobody home. One acquired a feel for such things. Just to be sure, he knocked. No answer. He waited for what felt like a long time. Hammered the door again. Just the other day Mike had opened a door and faced down the muzzle of a shotgun. You didn't want to make that mistake more than once.

He smelled it as soon as he was inside. Skunky-sweet and rank. The rooms dusty, empty of furniture. The entrance to the basement bolted with a thick padlock, but it didn't take much to kick his way through. Below, on trestle tables rigged up with hoses and wires, foil-coated halide lights, dozens of pot plants loomed in his candlelight. Wilted, drooping after days spent in total darkness. Spears of buds as big around as his forearms. He laughed and got out his knife.

*

Hunger was all James could think about. His mind infected with his aching belly. No longer even groaning. A still, desolate grave pit moldering at his center, radiating its rot down into his legs. Stupefying the muscles. Difficult now to raise his feet off the ground. Footsteps stretched into dry, husky scrapings of his heels along the pavement. His head felt very heavy.

Last night, getting ready to bed down, James had unlaced his left shoe and pulled it off. Then he'd done the same with the right. Only when he'd started tightening the laces did he realize he was brainlessly putting the left one back on again.

The hunger leaping back and forth, thumbing its nose at him. *This is what I'm making you!* it sneered. At least it wasn't Maggie's voice. That, at least, had gone silent for the moment.

Instead, he was tormented by slavering fantasies: glistening cornucopias of grilled meat, of steaming mashed potatoes soaked in butter. Pork and fatty lamb, dripping salty juice from its plump pink flesh. Sausages so fat just the touch of a fork burst the casing in spurts of amber oil.

"I have to stop," Lilac groaned behind him. "I need – to rest. Please."

"Right," said Sheilagh. "A few minutes, then."

A collective sigh went through them all. A ghost whose scream can only be faintly perceived by mortal ears. Arthritic with bitter hunger, they eased themselves down onto the curb on the shady side of the street.

Behind them, the sign over a Chinese restaurant cruelly promised ALL YOU CAN EAT. As had become habitual, two or three of them crept inside to sniff out any sustenance. This time it was Massimo, Mike and Ross.

A few ragged groups of strangers ground past them. Sticking to themselves, keeping their distance from anybody else. Safest to avoid eye contact, pretend anybody who didn't belong just didn't exist.

James felt the twinge of his salivary glands, unable even to moisten his foul, glutinous mouth. Even the breath in his nose seemed to scrape. The gritty stink of inedible things: sunbaked asphalt, his own sour body, and faintly – always now – rotting meat.

He'd become so accustomed to seeing only languid movement that the suddenness of the commotion up the street startled him. Two men leaped from a doorway and hauled down a solitary woman. Two savage hatchet-blows to her head. Then they half-carried, half-dragged the limp body, disappearing back through the door.

Jesus Christ! It happened so fast that none of the others seemed to notice. The refugees around the predated woman hardly reacted. A brief, limp scramble away from the doorway, then back to their pathetic shuffle.

*

To Jamie, who is only ten, being woken by Uncle Randy's roaring rage makes his skin feel like it is being stabbed by a hundred needles. A very loud crash down the hall in Maggie's room. He shivers, clutching his own arms even though it is very warm in his room. Uncle Randy's voice sounds broken.

Jamie is able to piece the story together over the next few years: Uncle Randy had showed up at midnight without calling. He'd been down at the Legion hall all night. With a head full of beer, he'd decided it might be fun to surprise Maggie. When he'd found Donnie in her bed, he'd gone berserk.

Donnie and Maggie screaming too. Jamie opens his bedroom door just in time to see Randy and Donnie, faces contorted, wrestling each other down the length of the hall. They tumble down the stairs, crashing into the bookcase at the bottom.

In the morning, Jamie would find Maggie's copy of The Female Eunuch, *cover half-torn off, stamped with a muddy boot print. Randy's print, because Donnie had been naked. Next to the book, one of Uncle Randy's teeth.*

Somehow in the commotion the door of the woodstove creaks open, hellishly painting the living room. Donnie and Uncle Randy grapple as angular shadows, punching and kicking. Jamie roots for Randy as Maggie snarls at him to go back upstairs, goddammit, get back into bed!

Randy is the better man. Randy let him help with his tools when he fixed stuff. He even taught him how to use the splitting maul. Now he'd show Donnie the door. Donnie would be gone for good.

But Donnie is bigger. Shorter, but thick and solid. Jamie shakes his clenched fists, fervently wishing Uncle Randy strength, endurance. Then Donnie lands a solid right cross to Uncle Randy's chin. It sends him sprawling. Now Donnie can catch his breath. Flexing his fingers, he swaggers to where Uncle Randy is lying.

"Donnie, that's enough!" Maggie shouts, but she sounds really scared.

Donnie kneels astride Uncle Randy's chest and lays into him with measured, brutal punches. Inflicting maximum damage. He even lines up Uncle Randy's slack face a couple of times with his left hand, like a photographer posing a customer. The striking sound of his fist is horrible. Uncle Randy is already knocked out. Jamie can see that. His body so limp, it makes Jamie cry. Sure he is dead. Donnie will not stop hitting him until every bone in Uncle Randy's face is pounded to mush.

Finally Maggie flings herself at Donnie. Literally jumps on his back, screaming and crying to stop it, stop it, just stop it Donnie!

Donnie rounds on her, flings her down. The expression on his face lances Jamie with an emotion he's never experienced until this moment. Fear, yes, but a crazy kind of fear. Painful, quailing. Hope in him sickening and dying. Donnie bares his teeth, eyes headlamps in the firelight. In his plosive panting, James hears the clear probability that Donnie will beat them all to death this night.

"Get me a fucking beer, you fucking whore!" he bellows.

Uncle Randy survived the terrible beating. Gone by morning. Just blood-sprinkled foot holes in the snow down the driveway. Word in town was he needed reconstructive surgery on his face. James would see him only once more, several years later, just before leaving Wilberforce for good. In line ahead of him at the local Foodland, a withered bent stick of a man. His face altered so viciously that James didn't even recognize him. Until the clerk returned his change and said, "Alright, so long, Randy."

*

Massimo, Mike and Ross emerged from the Chinese restaurant with a flaccid rice sack. A few handfuls they'd managed to sweep off the kitchen floor.

They got moving again. So dizzied by his vision, James barely remembered the attack he'd seen on that woman. He saw red pulp smeared on the pavement. *Fruit!* his desperate brain screamed at him. *Watermelon!* Two succulent lumps, translucent in the sunlight, bright with juice—

Something like nausea crawled from the deep grave pit behind his navel. His abdominal muscles cramping against nothing, a horrid retch of bile onto his throbbing tongue. Already a fly had lit upon the bits of the woman's brain in the street. He felt such overwhelming jealousy for that insect that he laughed. A sparse bark, ripe with pain. Athol looked back at him, an expression somewhere between concern and loathing.

*

The smell attracted him first. Vaguely meaty. Warm oil, endearingly viscid. James stopped, raising his nose like a bloodhound.

Mike smelled it too. Both of them slaking themselves on scent.

"What is it?" Sheilagh barked back at them. Cranky as all of them were, spent. James and Mike were delaying the rest. James knew it seemed an intolerable offence.

"I smell food," said Mike dreamily.

The smell lured James and Mike down a narrow alley. The rest followed into the next street, full of beleaguered hope.

"Aw, naw! Naw, no way!" Graham griped, stamping his sneaker.

A pet food shop. The Backyard Dog. Even from a distance, it was easy to see that the shop had already been gone over. Torn bags of dog and cat kibble spilled across the window display.

They remained in the middle of the street, unable or unwilling to go any closer. To James, it seemed that another step forward by any of them would have been an admission of something terrible and irreparable. That desperation had finally denuded the last of their precious niceties.

For himself, James was shocked at how appealing the idea of a fresh, moist can of cat food seemed. He kept trying to make eye contact with Tribe or Graham, avid for permission. Tribe had his face set in a stony scowl. His jaw working back and forth, bending his chapped frown.

"James, you can't be serious, pal." But Graham's eyes kept darting towards the shop window.

"Holy shit," Mulligan rasped, raking his fingers through his hair. "Holy fucking shit." Giggling bitterly, he was the first to take a step forward. The first to acknowledge what they all knew for certain.

Mulligan had already reached the shop door before James followed. Then Mike. Slowly the rest of them shuffled after, dejected. Lilac, Rohini, Massimo and Ross remained on the street.

Inside, it quickly became clear that humans had not been the only looters. Most of the bags had been gnawed open, and there was a good deal of mouse and rat shit scattered among the strewn kibble. The smell seemed overwhelmingly inviting. Not pleasant, not exactly, but full, somehow. Whole.

It was food, damn it. Provisions! And for once, without the cloying quality of rot and decay.

"You'll want the canned stuff," said Sheilagh thickly. "You can rest assured all the bags've been contaminated."

James went through to the back, hearing the scurry of rodents. Shelves and shelves of food, so heavy they'd never be able to carry it all, even if they'd wanted to. Christ, why hadn't this occurred to them before? The agony they could have saved themselves, a salve for the jagged tear deep in his guts!

Mulligan shouldered him out of the way, grabbing for cans so greedily that many clattered to the floor. On the shelf and wall behind, roaches scattered in fast curlicues. Mike came up as well, holding his shirt out like a basket so that Mulligan could sweep cans down into it. When they had all they could carry, they jogged back out to the street, smirking.

"Whiskas or Fancy Feast?" Mike giggled, weighing the cans in his hands.

The cans had peel-off lids that struck the concrete like tiny bent cymbals.

Mulligan smelled the food, playing at being a connoisseur. "*Magnifique!* I highly recommend the Whiskas, *monsieur*. Hundred percent pure chicken. Says so right on the label."

"I can't believe you're even thinking of this!" Lilac was so revolted she had to turn away.

"Food is fucking food!" Mulligan yelled, clearly still convincing himself.

He dipped his spoon into the can, then put the food into his mouth. They all waited, hardly breathing. Mulligan chewed thoughtfully, slowly nodding. He swallowed with a slight grimace. "Fuck me, that is absolutely revolting!" he shouted. "But kinda deliciously revolting, if you know what I mean!"

James opened his own can. Mulligan was right. It really wasn't that bad. James supposed that if he'd been served this food without being told it was for cats, he probably wouldn't have turned up his nose at it. His main objection would have been its cold sliminess.

"Needs salt," he said after a few minutes.

"Youse are manky fuckers!" said Graham. But he got out his spoon, coming towards James.

"Get your own can!"

"Ach, come on, mate!"

James twisted his body so that it came between Graham and his precious can. His grateful stomach now churning and mulling over the first food he'd swallowed in almost two days. He felt very dizzy and wondered if it was due to the blood rushing from his head to his gut.

"Definitely got some mouthfeel issues," said Mike around a bite.

"Here, try this." Mulligan held out a spoonful of Tuna Delight.

Mike took some, but he made a face and spat it back out. "Yuck! Too fishy!"

James saw Tribe off on his own, unwilling to be seen partaking in this degrading spectacle. Still, he was tearing the lid off a can. Sheilagh edged up beside him. Asked for some.

James couldn't help but laugh at the horrified expression that came over her face, eyes cinched shut, her mouth pulled into a taught grimace. She retched, covering her mouth with her hand. Again, Tribe held out the can. Hesitantly she took another bite. This one she managed to keep down, but it was all she could force herself to eat.

Ross sat on the curb off to one side, simply refusing to take part. Muttering to himself, shooting loathing glances back over his shoulder. Massimo stood defiantly several yards away, arms crossed. Fuck them, James thought with a pang of feisty relish that felt drunken. If they'd rather stand on principle and go hungry, that was their problem, not his.

The more James ate, the better it seemed to taste. The bitter unguent quality of the processed meat and whatever other crap they added, all that faded into a kind of tasty background noise. Under his ribs, a tingling nausea gave over to warmth. A comfortable weight. He gobbled the second can even more quickly than the first. Lingering over it spoiled the illusion of satisfaction.

"It's bloody awful!" Graham choked.

"Tastes like this German meat spread my old man used to eat on crackers," Mulligan proclaimed. He sat on the curb with his elbows on his drawn up knees, squinting with satisfaction into the bright street. Spoon in one hand, empty can in the other. "Shit, I always suspected pets ate better than some people. Now I know it."

"Stop it!" said Rohini. Quietly, but still they heard it from the far side of the street, where she and Lilac crouched on a bus stop bench.

Mike giggled. "Yo, always figured I'd be eating this shit eventually. Guess retirement came early, eh Mulligan?"

"How can you degrade yourselves like that?" Lilac called sadly.

James saw Mulligan's freckled forearms tense. Then he threw the empty can at her. It only rolled hollowly into the gutter. But the effort was enough.

"Here now!" Tribe growled. "No need for that."

"Listen up, lady!" Mulligan shouted. "You wanna choose to stay hungry, that's your biz, but don't, like, tell me off for surviving, alright!"

"You had a cat, didn't you?" James asked, knowing the answer. Knowing why she no longer had a cat. Daring to use what she'd told him against her. "This stuff was good enough for Helga, I take it?"

"It's just like you self-righteous vegan organo-friggin-Nazi hippie freaks," Mulligan sneered. "It's never good enough, not for you, not for anybody!"

"I'm not vegan, I'm vegetarian," Lilac responded. Pedantically, James thought. "And here's a newsflash for you, James: you're not a cat!"

"Exactly my point!" James yelled. "I think a human being deserves more consideration than a pet, don't you? You think I feel great about eating this shit? Do you?" His voice broke. "I don't need that kind of crap right now, I really don't, and it seems to me, *vegetarian not vegan*, that we've got a few more important things to worry about than how finicky some choose to be about the bravery of others!"

"Yeah!" said Mike defiantly.

Lilac smacked her knees. "So eating pet food is bravery, now. Right!"

"Will you stop it!" Sheilagh roared, stalking to a point midway between Lilac and James. "Stop it, all of yis! Lilac, I don't like it any more than you do, but for fuck sake, we've got to eat, don't we? And you!" She turned on James and Mulligan. "What makes you think you're so special then, eh? Spooning that shite into your gobs and then yis have the nerve to bark about it like yis deserve a fucking medal! Shut up! Shut up, all of yis!" Shaking with rage, Sheilagh stomped a ways down the street.

For a long while they all stewed in the tense silence. Nobody looking anybody else in the eye. Strangers still and all, unable to reconcile what they felt with what they needed. James took a long drink from his water bottle, trying to rinse away the cloying aftertaste.

"Gotta admit, Sheilagh's right," said Graham, half to himself. "You were sorta barking, like. Woulda thought there'd be more meowing than barking, given the crap food."

James smiled dully. Graham winked, shuddering as he

swallowed the last of his food, tossing the can away. The littering bothered James. Before he remembered that it didn't matter any more. Not at all. Shit, what did?

He took a deep breath, and for once the air seemed to energize his blood. He got up, traipsing to the bench where Lilac and Rohini sat together in the cool shade. He stuck out his hand. "I'm sorry for the remark about your cat. It was a stupid thing to say."

For a moment he thought she'd just ignore the gesture, leave him with only her anger-squinted eyes. Then she sniffed, and her moist palm met his. "Me too," she mumbled. "You're only doing what you need to do."

"I think I'm just jealous," said Rohini. "I'm so hungry, my own leg's starting to look good. Anyway, you've started a trend."

James turned around, seeing dozens of people fighting their way into the store. Shit! So much for supplies.

It was already mid-afternoon by the time they'd loaded their packs with cans of cat food they'd managed to scavenge, by bullying the crowd. Amy even fired a couple of shots into the air, scattering them.

The Group bunked down in the seats of several cars in the roadway. Like many areas of the city they'd passed through, it seemed eerily empty of people when the sun went down. Disquiet quiet, as Graham said.

Chapter 14

The SuperCenter

They found the SuperCenter two days after the pet food store. Forty-eight hours of Whiskas and Fancy Feast had been more than enough. Even Ross and Massimo had caved and eaten some. The fuller they all got, the more disgusting the cat food became. Rohini and Lilac looked on in satisfaction as the rest of them were taken by disillusion.

Then, in a wide suburban plaza built around a vast parking lot, the SuperCenter. By now they'd become experts. Could plainly see the miracle: the store remained unlooted. A gigantic building. Full of food.

They ran down the sloping parking lot, ululating, cheering, happier than kids hearing the last bell before summer break. There was a semi-circular barricade of cars set up about thirty yards from the front entrance. A few dozen ragged people, a few holding broom handles with white shirts tied to them, gaped up at a man atop one of the cars. He was shouting at them, a politician on campaign. People in the crowd were shouting back, thrusting fists in the air. Keeping their distance, though. James imagined their caution had something to do with the ten or so other men atop the barricade, each one sporting a rifle. A few more looking down on them from the roof of the building.

"My kids are starving!" screamed a purple-faced man.

"We're *all* starving!" screamed a woman, as if in rebuke. "Just let us in, goddammit!"

The cacophony of shouting that followed made it impossible to catch any specific words. The man on the barricade waited for calm, holding his hands out like a priest consecrating the Eucharist. He was small and wiry, hatchet-faced. "What assurances do we have?" He raised his voice above the noise, but still managed somehow to maintain a mild tone. "What assurances do we have?" Now his hands gestured around the parking lot. "When the attacks stop—"

"It's not *us* that attacked you!" somebody hollered.

"Why are you punishing us for the actions of other people?"

James had been so overjoyed at seeing the SuperCenter that he hadn't noticed the bodies strewn about, supper for noisy starlings and crows. Bodies had become commonplace, it was true. But the corpses scattered across the parking lot told a definitive story. Of people trying to get into the SuperCenter. Of people inside the SuperCenter using their guns to stop them.

"I've made my position perfectly clear!" shouted the hatchet-faced man. "When you people come to terms, we're more than happy to continue our food dole!" With that he jumped down, striding into the huge building.

James saw Amy fighting her way to the front of the baying crowd. "Hey!" she called to one of the armed men. "Hey! We got—" The crowd knocked her side to side until she swung her elbows, knocking a few people back.

"You heard it!" a gaunt man in a John Deere baseball cap shouted at her. "Nobody gets in!"

From behind the barricade came a sharp finger-whistle, loud enough to get everybody's attention. A tall white-bearded old man stepped nimbly over the cars. He said something to the gaunt man, who reluctantly waved at Amy. "Alright," he said. "C'mon, then. C'mon, c'mon!"

One by one, against the mania of the raging crowd clawing at their clothes, at their packs, they clambered over the barricade and jogged inside.

*

They entered a fecund garden overflowing with food. The produce section, crammed with celery, carrots, lettuce, cucumbers, broccoli, corn, green beans, potatoes. The colorful profusion burst into James's mind. A scrawny kid with a rifle had been assigned to keep an eye on them. He laughed at James, probably at the rapturous expression on his face.

They engorged themselves. Dogs they'd become, unknowing, wolfing against the instinct warning them that very soon the food would be taken away. Bags of baby carrots, "Perfect for dipping!" screamed the bright green lettering – tearing them open, dumping them out, fishing for the few precious edibles in a rotten orange slop with the pungency of fresh pumpkin. Ripping apart mildewed heads of cauliflower, stuffing it down raw. Over in the deli department, whole containers of humus, of babaganouj, scooped into gluttonous mouths by the handful. Blocks of cheese torn from packaging, gobbled in huge bites.

Musty apples, wrinkled and soft. James had gobbled down several, cores and all, before he saw the label stuck to the geriatric browning skin: Royal Gala – Product of New Zealand. New Zealand, Jesus! Incredulous breath escaped his nose. This fruit had sunned and watered on the other side of the mother-luvin' Pacific

Ocean!

That this thing had been moved intact over that immense distance! Huge refrigerated container ships. Whole fleets of transport trucks. Hurling tons and tons of stuff across the planet.

Lord, it had taken them days and days to move just a few dozen miles. Those miles had sapped them, drained them of fat and sweat and hope.

Determined now to enjoy this precious gift, James closed his eyes and bit into the apple. Fluid drawn from the living earth by the fibrous roots of a tree somewhere in the Antipodes dribbled onto his tongue, down his chin. His jaw worked the soft, mealy flesh. Not so long ago he would have scorned the quality of this fruit. Today, his heart fluttered with the cool pleasure of its sweet nectar.

Suddenly the apple was slapped away. He was startled by a grinning face close beside him. It was the hatchet-faced man they'd seen on the barricade. With exaggerated ease, the hatchet-faced man caught the apple he'd just smacked from James's hand. He tossed it back. James fumbled and it fell to the floor.

"Good afternoon to our fair visitors!" he called out. "My name is Hal." He was a sleek man in camo hunting gear, wearing a sidearm at his hip, with an unshaven vulpine face, dark hair oiled back.

James was reminded of the wet fur on the rat they'd seen crawl out of that corpse's mouth.

"Against my misgivings, Grandpa Clay deemed it prudent to invite you inside." Hal's PR smile was jarring.

"Your misgivings," said a dry voice, quiet as murmuring sleep. James turned to find the tall white-bearded man in a long gray greatcoat, standing next to the deli counter. "I trusted, sir, that two additional rifles would be welcome, given the situation." Clay looked to be well into his seventies, but iron-spined. An uncommon gaze from his black eyes. Placid and wild at the same time, a blaze of sunlight glinting hard from a still lake.

There was a resonant boom. They jumped. Something had struck the front of the building. Several loud rifle shots came in reply. The Group shifted uncomfortably, cheeks stuffed, still chewing.

Hall seemed not to notice. "Twelve days ago, I and fifteen others commandeered this premises. I was honored to be elected leader." Hal threw his arms open song-and-dance style, expounding loudly enough to echo his voice. "Fact! The average food product travels just over twenty-five hundred miles to get to your local supermarket. As I'm sure you'll all agree, the situation has changed just a wee bit since all this food was trucked here. Thus, our divine mission: to protect the remaining available food stock."

"Divine?" Athol muttered.

"Okay," said Lilac. "I get that you're protecting it from the people out there. But for what?"

"Ah, the lady asks a germane question. This hysteria we're witnessing at the moment can't last forever. Eventually those poor people outside will be too tired, too hungry to continue their senseless attacks. Then we'll be able to make them see reason. Our plan is to wait until then, and start rationing out the food stock in a reasonable, organized manner." Hall grinned. "For the benefit of all."

"Meanwhile, you're shooting the people outside," said Rohini. "Very reasonable and organized."

Now Hal's smile was thinner than a razor. "From this time forward, we ask that no foodstuffs be consumed without express authorization from Ted, here, who has selflessly volunteered to be our rationing officer." He indicated a lanky man with glumly staring eyes and a face as pink as a Highlighter marker. "This is especially true of our water and other fluid supplies. I assure you, nobody will go hungry or thirsty."

Sheilagh cleared her throat. "Wouldn't it make more sense to just give the people out there the food they want? Wouldn't that calm them down?"

"You will all be assigned tasks," Hal announced as he strode away.

Against the front of the building. another loud boom. This time, accompanied by the sound of shattering glass. More gunfire.

*

Until their bellies were full, their starved brains had perceived the stink of the store as appetizing, somehow. Now their noses caught the rot of meat gone grey-green, of fish slimy with its own decaying fat. Heaps of produce concealed withering fruit and vegetables, suffusing the fetid air with mold. Glass freezer closets dozens of feet long, stuffed with soggy boxes of thawed pizza and lasagna.

"Ugh, smells like dirty socks," said Amy through her hand.

"Yeah, with the feet still in 'em!" Lilac canted.

"Bloody awful!" said Sheilagh.

Graham laughed. "We've no choice now." He dipped his chin at the kid with the rifle. "Fuckin' smorgasbord jail, isn't it?"

The kid with the rifle rocked from foot to foot. Edgy fingers clasping and unclasping on the stock.

"Easy, son," Tribe soothed. "There will be no harm done to you. Not by us."

Dozy with orgasmic fullness, they followed Clay through the produce displays, past the empty deli counter and refrigerated meat chests, into the vast shelving section. Shelves seven feet tall, lined up row after row down the length of the huge building.

James stopped in his tracks. So did Lilac and a few others. Starry-eyed. A vast quantity of food, a volume to cripple the mind under its morbid weight. Tons. Literally, tons. And they'd been measuring their sustenance by the handful.

Some cans were scattered across the floor, some bottles lay broken in dried tacky pools of juice and soda. Forensics of the frenzy before Hal's gang took control. But most of it remained intact, regimented on the metal shelving. James saw the cadaverous Ted and a couple of others holding clipboards, tallying the food supply.

"I notice most of the meat's gone," said Ross.

"Yes," Clay murmured. "It was going off. Hal ordered it to be distributed among the outsiders. The same with the deli meats. This happened a number of days before I arrived here. Then the outsiders grew bolder, and the barricade was built."

Clay showed them through rubber swinging doors into the gloomy warehouse. "This is the safest part of the facility," he explained, his soft voice desert dry. James felt a warm tingle on his neck. A voice yielding to quiet, solitary sadness the way powdery sand yields to the foot of a nomad.

A terrier trotted out of the shadows. A white dog with a brindle head. Clay bent to stroke it. "This here's Hood."

Through the open roll-up door of the loading dock, they saw a narrow alley behind the building. On the other side of the alley was a concrete barrier, perhaps fifteen feet high, above which peeked the roofs of suburban townhouses.

Hal's crew had barricaded both ends of the alley, posting riflemen. The attackers had so far concentrated their assaults on the barricade out front. Sentries on the roof blew referee's whistles to signal battle stations.

That was the term Clay used, speaking directly to Amy and Ross. *Battle stations*.

The attacks had come in waves, several a day. Growing fiercer as the outsiders gained men and their desperation grew. The last had been yesterday afternoon, and was only beaten back with many losses on their side.

"Most of them are not armed," Clay rasped. "But the outsiders are becoming inventive."

"I still fail to understand," said Sheilagh smartly. "Why don't you just start dolling out the food again?"

Clay turned his black eyes on her. Not aggressive, but powerful enough to make Sheilagh look away. And if there was one thing James had learned of her, it was that she did not back down easily. "Miss, from what I have seen here, that would not go well."

"For the outsiders, or for us?" James asked.

"What are they gonna do?" Lilac's voice was strident in the dark, quiet warehouse. "Just keep shooting anybody that comes to get food for their kids?"

Clay straightened his shoulders. "If strife and war are to take the place of brotherly love and kindness, I shall mourn for the welfare and progress of mankind."

James and Graham exchanged a glance. What the hell was that supposed to mean?

*

Days passed without attack from the outside. Ominous, impatient stillness. The adrenaline spike deep in James's belly corroded, leaving behind an aching canker. Sore, but bearable. The tension was eased by the consumption of easily-gotten food. Hal was true to his word. Ted provided daily rations that filled their shrunken bellies, though there was little water. They drank warm juices and sodas that did little to quench thirst, but pumped sugar into their blood to deflate hunger like salt poured on a slug.

They bunked down in the warehouse, inside a small square between stacked cardboard boxes. Even with good sleeping mats, cold concrete was not conducive to restful sleep. Neither was the smell of souring milk or the constant scratching of mice hidden all around.

The lingering presence of the kid with the rifle assigned to keep an eye on them didn't do much for their nerves. Not much older than Mike, his face still spattered with adolescent acne. His name was Dave, but that was about all he'd tell them.

None of the Group spent any time interacting with Hal's crew, who bunked at the opposite end of the warehouse, near the stairs that led up to the manager's office. Every so often, Hal would deign to come down for a grinning, twitching inspection of the operation.

One thing impossible to ignore was the wide-necked linebacker with a shotgun and a pistol in his belt who was a permanent sentry at the big steel door of the meat freezer under the manager's office. Always on guard, always scowling.

Lilac put it best: "Hal and his guys give me the creeps."

Nothing to do every day but lounge on their sleeping bags, wander around the store. James found himself jittery, unable to sit still. Entranced by the sheer volume, not only of food, but of everything. Cutlery, chinaware, table linens, kitchen gear, detergents and cleaning supplies. The order, the regularity of it all astonishing after weeks of being lost amid chaos. The mind-blowing montage of labels perfectly aligned, an Andy Warhol hallucination.

A library, James thought, strolling up and down the sixty-two aisles. A careful archive of what this moribund civilization had needed and wanted. By now, it was starting to seem foreign.

He drifted into the produce area. Paused with his hand on the cool rind of a watermelon. Seedless, the label promised. Product of Mexico.

He remembered a time last summer when he'd handed Jenny a slice of watermelon with seeds. "Eeew!" Jenny had exclaimed. "What's this black stuff?" Getting a little freaked out, even. His child, so divorced from natural realities that she'd been unable to recognize seeds in fruit.

"We were becoming so civilized we were well on our way to going bush."

He found Mike sitting on a stool in the canned fruits and vegetables aisle, neatly lining up the cans, turning labels face out.

"It's called facing," he told James. "What I was doing when the lights went out, yo. Used to hate this job, so boring, but dog, check it out, here I am doing it in, like, my spare time." Mike shook his head. "*Facing*. Like a habit. Shit."

James joined him, starting at the other end of the shelf. "It's comforting," he said after a while.

"I guess. Sorta seems wrong, y'know, seeing it disorganized. All this good food. It's like, I wanna…take care of it." He stood up, stretching his legs. "That old dude is something else, huh?"

"Clay?"

"Yeah. Can't tell if he's gonna start crying, or, like, punch me, y'know?"

"There's something odd about him. Every time he opens his mouth, he sounds like he's eulogizing his dead mother."

"Still," said Mike, "it's wacked, cause I feel kinda…I don't know, easy when he's around."

James smiled. "Yeah, I know what you mean."

He wandered to the front of the store, to the waiting cash register lanes. His fingers longing to hit buttons, interface with softly lit touchscreens. The caress they needed, of grey rubbery keypads on the credit card readers. Supple as artificial skin. Hit them as hard as you could, and still the only sounds they produced were fleshy little taps.

At the self-serve checkout lane, he saw his own image darkly reflected on the convex screens. Still smeared with fingerprints, the oily ID of whoever had been the last person to use this machine.

He considered the phrase *touchscreen*. The way it rolled around in his mind, an ice chip shrinking to frigid water. Devolving. *Touchscreen*.

The intimate nexus of human consciousness and machine logic. The squeeze of finger pads against light-warmed images. Icons. Meant to be caressed. Fulsome in blessing. Touch the right ones, and out you went with more food than you could eat. So much food that a lot of it just went in the garbage.

Instantaneousness had been lost. It had been an illusion, anyway.

Now gone. Struck down like a heresy.

*

One afternoon several days after they'd arrived, they were startled by blasting referee's whistles. Immediately, James heard loud impacts against the façade. Gunfire. James and Tribe followed Dave, running out to the front.

Black roiling smoke within the barricade. Strong gasoline fumes. Something sailed over James's head with a sound of a flag in full wind. It exploded in a fireball against the SuperCenter sign.

All of Hal's men were on the barricade, firing rapidly.

The parking lot sloped up from the store, about two hundred yards to the road, which was probably a good thirty feet higher than the store. Up there, the besiegers had set up large slingshots.

Tribe was watching them through his field glasses. "Shit," he spat, handing them over to James.

The slingshots were made from hooked-together bungee cords. James saw them stretch the bungees back, put bottles and jars against the elastic. The bottles were burning.

"Molotov cocktails," he said. Not believing the words as he spoke them.

The cocktails flew at the store. Many landed short, bursting into burning ponds in the parking lot. But many found the mark. The store's façade was a torrent of yellow flame.

James shifted the binoculars to see something Tribe was pointing at. His stomach wobbled. Another team of perhaps a hundred outsiders was manhandling a dump truck into place using ropes and chains. Lining it up with the barricade.

"Fuck!" said a rifleman to James's right. "Heads up on that damn truck!" he hollered, barely heard over the din of firing guns. He had straight red hair tied back into a ponytail. A weak-chinned face, with a forehead rounder than a bowling ball. He took careful aim and fired.

Through the field glasses James saw a man beside the dump truck jerk and fall. "Jesus, what a shot," he mumbled.

The rifleman betrayed no emotion except a slight ripple in his brow, as if he'd just remembered some neglected chore. Again he sighted his Garand, and fired.

Holes appeared in the truck's windshield and hood. Its side mirrors shattered. One of its tires blew. James gave the field glasses back to Tribe. He didn't want to see any more of this.

"No!" Lilac screamed, running up and grabbing one of Hal's men by the shoulders. She heaved him off the barricade. "Stop it! They're just hungry! All they want is some food!"

The rifleman wrenched himself out of her grip and shoved her down.

"Get her the fuck out of here!" Hal snarled at them.

James saw Amy and Ross standing awkwardly with their weapons. As frozen with fear as he was.

The rifleman with the red ponytail was reloading his magazine. He punched Ross's shoulder. "Hey! You wanna give us a fuckin' hand here, buddy?"

Another gas bomb whooshed past, spraying fire across a good portion of the pavement behind the barricade.

Lilac had jumped back up, kicking and punching the rifleman.

"Come on!" Sheilagh screamed, yanking her towards the store.

"Get back inside!" Ross yelled. "Go on, go on, go on!"

"Holy fuck!" somebody shouted.

James looked up to see outsiders giving the dump truck a running push, rolling it toward the barricade. Both front tires had been shot out, but it accelerated, barreling down the steep slope. The hopper and cab were crowded with men and women gripping Molotov cocktails, all of them screaming war cries.

"Bastards!" one of the riflemen exclaimed, his voice quaking with fear.

"Hold your ground!" Hal ordered.

Suddenly there was a very loud metallic crunch and the truck's engine roared to life.

James couldn't believe it, even when he saw blue smoke jet from the stacks. The motor revved and the massive vehicle leaped forward, hurling itself at them. He caught a glimpse of an astonished face behind the wheel before the truck smashed into the barricade.

Incredible momentum, shoving the cars aside, throwing James and several others to the ground. The huge truck growled into their midst. Its curled fenders like the muzzle of a huge attack dog.

Outsiders aboard the truck maniacally whipped gas bombs down on the defenders. Rifles cracked. Bullets sparked off the truck's steel armor. Men screamed. James saw Clay in the midst of it all, a revolver in each hand, popping off shots like an old west pistoleer.

Holy Christ, a rifleman near James was suddenly consumed in flames, shrieking in pain, twisting, turning.

Until the one with the red ponytail shot him through the head. Only then did his expression harden into something like angry dismay, glaring open-mouthed, as if smelling something deeply offensive.

James felt lost. Witnessing all this from a hundred miles away.

"Don't just stand there, asswipe!" The red ponytail threw James the rifle that the immolated one had just dropped. Still hot, its wooden stock scorched. "Get in the fuckin' game!"

James spotted a wild-eyed woman atop the truck's cab, a gas bomb raised over her head. Staring straight at him. Even after a lapsed decade his reserve army training kicked in. He raised the rifle and fired. Shocked at the bruising kick to his shoulder. The woman pitched backwards into the truck's hopper and suddenly it was awash in flames. Attackers leaped over the side, many on fire.

In just a few minutes they were all dead. Set upon by riflemen. Shot down. Clubbed with rifle butts. The last was a gaunt sunburned man in red jogging shorts who managed to make it through the smashed glass front of the store, scrambling through the checkout lanes before a bullet caught him in the back. He collapsed against a display of apple juice cans. The cans tumbled down around his sprawled body, sounding like the snare drum taps of a firing squad.

Above, a bright yellow sign announced a sale. Just ninety-nine cents per can.

Lilac came running back out of the store, her pack over one arm, closely followed by Sheilagh and Rohini. It was unclear to James if they were trying to stop her or hurrying her along.

Hal jumped down in front of Lilac, barring her way. "What? Leaving so soon?"

"Get the hell out of my way!" she shouted in his face. Jogging to her left to get around him, she almost tripped over a blackened corpse.

"Lilac—" Rohini began, but Hal held up a hand, cutting her off.

"I can understand how upsetting this must be." He chuckled, the sound of a chopping knife mincing a carrot. "Believe me. I've been here for a lot longer than you have, missy."

Lilac scowled. "Don't be calling me missy."

There was sniggering among the riflemen that scared James even more than everything he'd just seen. "I can't just allow you to leave," Hal keened, mocking self-pity. "Why, who's to say you're not one of *them*?"

"Them?" Sheilagh asked.

"Them!" Hal insisted, suddenly stony. "An *outsider*! Huh? Come in here to *spy* on us!" His glare crinkled into another chilly grin. "Now hear this!" he called out. "Nobody leaves. By order of…well, of me. We're all staying, gentlemen! None of you is going anywhere. We've got a sacred duty to protect this vital resource against those who seek to destroy it!"

Another gas bomb arced in. Everybody ducked as it exploded against the side of the dump truck. Everybody but Hal.

"Look, sweetie, you really want to go back out into that?" Hal winked at Lilac. "C'mon, get back inside, we'll get you some supper, and you'll feel all better. K?" He clapped his gloved hands. "Now get these bodies cleaned up! Jesus H. Chrysanthemum, what a mess!"

*

"Holy shit, what have we gotten ourselves into now?" Lilac gasped, holding her face, rocking.

It was later the same afternoon, the Group in its spot at the back corner of the warehouse. Sitting on their sleeping bags with their backs against pallets of cardboard boxes. Paper towels and Kleenex. In this windowless cinderblock prison, the light was so low they could hardly see each other's faces.

"Quite the quirk of fate," Tribe commented. "Now that we have all the food we need, we're trapped."

"Oh, shut up, Tribe!" Lilac snapped. "All this is just the upshot of your 'anything necessary to survive' bullshit!"

"Oh, I agree completely!" Tribe growled. "For attackers and defenders alike."

"Yeah, okay, but who's who?" said Massimo.

"It doesn't matter!" Tribe snapped. "What we saw today only shows how bold we need to be to outfox this Hal."

They all shut up at the approach of footsteps. A figure stepped into the opening. The one with the red ponytail. Everybody tensed as he unslung his rifle, Amy raising hers. "Relax," he said in a deep voice, crouching down. "I'm not here to shoot you."

"Strangle us, then?" said Sheilagh.

He shook his head. "Name's Gord. There's a few guys who want to talk to you. Just give it a few minutes."

Clay appeared next, carrying a glowing hurricane lamp. Hood the terrier jaunty at his heels. Then Ted and a couple of others, including Dave, the kid with the gun. He looked like James felt: panic-stricken. Gord took him aside, told him to keep watch.

Ted brought two shopping bags containing that day's ration of food: two heads of broccoli, a bag of carrots, a bunch of oranges, a block of cheddar, two boxes of crackers, a bag of bagels. Each of them received a can of tuna. Except Ross and Amy.

"You two don't get a ration for today." Ted's huge Adam's apple bounced with his glum words. "Hal's orders, okay? No fighting, no food."

"What kind of bullshit is that?" Amy asked.

"I was wondering the same thing out there," said Gord, "waiting for you two to fire your weapons."

Ross sat up, thrust a finger at Gord. "I got my fill of shooting people in Vietnam, before you were an itch in your daddy's pants!"

Clay showed Ross a placatory palm. "Hal is going insane." He was terse, but there was no hiding the weight in his words. "Quite insane. We know it. That is why we are here."

"Now keep your fuckin' voices down," Gord whispered very seriously. "You can bet we're being watched, so we don't have all fuckin' day." His implacable face went around the Group. The kind of smooth face that betrayed nothing of what was going on in the brain behind it. "It's just a matter of time before the outsiders break in. I don't wanna be around when that happens. They're getting good with them fucking slingshots. If the front of the store wasn't faced with precast concrete, we'd be finished already."

"Hal has men posted at all the exits now," said Clay. "Originals. Men who were with him when he first commandeered the store." He snapped a match with his thumbnail, lighting a cherrywood pipe.

"When he said nobody's allowed to leave, he meant it." Gord lit a smoke with the same match, and Mulligan leaned forward to light one of his own.

"We want to find out what your plans are," said Ted.

"There's something I don't get," Amy interrupted. "I mean, we've been in lots of stores. Every single one's been totally ransacked, right? This place, shit, looks like it's still open for business. Hardly anything's outta order."

Ted pursed his ample lips. He and Gord stabbed each other with an uncomfortable glance. "We've been here for ten days now, and we can't get a straight answer. I'll say this, though: that meat locker at the other end of the warehouse. Hal's got a guard posted there for a reason. Only time he pulls him off is when we're under full attack. Okay?"

"What's in the meat locker?" Athol's voice scraped like sandpaper.

Ted shrugged. "Hal says it's frozen meat. Wants to keep it preserved as long as possible. Okay?" The doubtful silence between Ted's pronouncements seemed to speak more than his words.

"Hal says he's been here for twelve days," said Gord. "By my count, that means he took over this place two weeks after the blackout."

"So he wants us to believe that this place stayed almost untouched for two weeks?" Mulligan asked. "No fuckin' way."

"Hal has a cadre of fifteen men," Clay rasped. "Who will follow any order he gives. Unthinkingly."

"Like killing starving people?" Rohini asked.

"Lot of that going around," Lilac muttered.

"Look," said Gord, sounding angry. "I'll do whatever's necessary to defend myself. When I got here, Hal and his guys were still handing out meat and chicken to those people. But then the meat and chicken started running out and they started attacking. I'm not gonna just stand around and let a fuckin' pack burn me up. But I'm sure as hell not gonna let Hal suck me into some kind of suicide pact, either."

"Maybe they started attacking because the meat and chicken they were being given was already rotten," said Sheilagh. "After two weeks without refrigeration, couldn't've been too sound."

Ted shook his head. "None of that matters now."

"Well, it sure doesn't to the ones who're dead!" Lilac exclaimed.

"Keep your fuckin' voice down! You wanna be dead too?" Gord's face in the lamplight, glaringly sardonic. "I'm telling you, that's what's gonna happen, if we don't figure out a way out of here. We don't have more than a few days. The outsiders, there's more and more of them all the time. Every bullet we fire means we have one less." He shrugged. "You decide."

"Even if we could hold them off indefinitely," said Ted, "it doesn't matter. There's a decent amount of food in here, sure, but don't be deceived. It won't last forever. What we're short on is water. Real short."

"But there's shelves and shelves of it!" Ross objected.

"No," said Ted. "There are shelves and shelves of *fluids*. Juice, soda. By my calculation, there's about five hundred liters of water left. Think about this: once the fruit and vegetables are gone – and they will be gone soon – a lot of the food left over in here needs cooking. Potatoes, corn. Rice, pasta, noodles. What're we going to cook it in?"

"Alright," said Sheilagh after a moment. "Our first priority, as always, must be food. If we're gonna break out of here, we've got to plan on taking whatever we can."

"But how can we pack what we need without Hal noticing?" Rohini asked.

Clay nodded at Ted. "Tell them."

"It's covered," said Ted. "I've already convinced Hal to start moving food stock from the front of the store into the warehouse here."

"The warehouse is our keep," said Tribe.

"Right, exactly." Ted nodded. "The warehouse is our last stand. If the outsiders break into the store itself, we could barricade ourselves in here, hold out a while. Okay?"

"We *could*," said Gord, "but I don't wanna even think about what that would be like."

"I will go to Hal and propose that you ladies be confined to the warehouse," said Clay. "Hal doesn't trust you in any case. I'll also suggest we use you all as laborers to clear the shelves. That way, you can concentrate on organizing the food supply we'll take."

"That's good, that's real good," said Ted. "We play on Hal's paranoia. Okay?"

"Did any of you think of asking *us ladies* what we think about your little plan?" said Lilac.

Sheilagh gave her a sharp look. "So we spend the next few days stocking up," she said.

"But how're we gonna carry it all, when we bug out?" asked Ross.

James smiled grimly. "Ever read *The Road* by Cormac McCarthy?"

*

And so they spent the next several days following the plan. Working in gangs to clear the shelves, neatly stacking cans and boxes into shopping carts, hauling the carts into the warehouse. Hal assigned riflemen to oversee the work, but nothing seemed out of place to them, and they quickly grew bored. Even as Sheilagh and

Lilac and Rohini parked the loaded buggies in the warehouse, they were keeping a very careful tally of what the Group would take, and it all seemed to be the legitimate business of doing as they were told.

At night they whispered of the day they would escape. Bug out, Ross kept calling it. Rohini expressed fear. They all did, in their own ways. Silence, gritted teeth. Athol talked about how the god of the Hebrews halted the sun and moon to assist Joshua against the Amorites. In response, Tribe quoted Shakespeare: "These late eclipses in the sun and moon portend no good to us." Sheilagh asked him what had happened to his talk of feline bravado. Tribe muttered darkly about their narrow odds.

*

James, Graham and Tribe were working together in aisle 17: canned vegetables. When their overseer's attention flagged, James borrowed cigarettes from Graham. There were dozens of cartons of cigarettes in the store, and Ted made sure to dole them out very liberally. James emptied the tobacco from the cigarettes, and refilled them with the pot he'd scrounged. Even Tribe partook. It softened the blow of the mundane labor and the serrated fear that saturated this place.

It had been forty-eight hours since the last outsider attack. But in the half-light of the store, the silence was ominous. When the guard complained about the pot, James bought him off with a dime-bag-sized sprig. The guard went off and left them alone.

Graham took his cigarettes out of his pocket, and a folded piece of paper fell to the floor.

"A certificate of some kind?" said Tribe nosily.

Graham made a sour face as he lit up. Squinting in the smoke, he unfolded the paper and handed it to Tribe.

"You received the Duke of Edinburgh Gold Award!" said Tribe.

"Aye."

"What's that?" James asked.

"It's an award y'can get for doing a set amount of time at certain activities," Graham responded, all bland.

"A spare way of describing an incredible accomplishment, my friend!" Tribe's voice was tight with admiration.

"Ah, it's not that big a deal, not really."

"You're being falsely modest."

"How did you earn it?" James asked.

"Hiking, orienteering. Some basic outdoor survival.

Community work, shite like that. I keep it in my pocket as a reminder, like." He sniggered. "To stay hard."

"That's where you learned all that stuff you taught us."

"In part, aye. I met him."

"The Duke of Edinburgh?" Tribe asked.

"Aye. Presented the certificate to me and all."

"Really. What's he like?"

He's a dirty old bugger. Pinched my arse."

"Come on."

Graham cackled. He started stacking cans of chickpeas and kidney beans in a cart. "Truth be told, I don't remember a fuckin' bit of it."

"You serious?" said James.

"Dead serious, mate. Dead drunk at the time, so I was. Middle of a blackout, and there I am, shaking hands with the Duke of Fuckin' Edinburgh. Far as I know, coulda been asking him what sorta lay the wife was, y'know?"

James laughed.

"Me ma's got the photo hung dead center on her livin' room wall. Pride of place, like." Heavy silence followed that, the lance of emotion that hunted any statement about family, about friends. Dangerous territory.

They finished loading up their three carts and wheeled them through to the warehouse, straining to make the turns. Loaded with cans, the buggies were very heavy. It was quite something to see all the shopping carts, over a hundred of them, lined up side by side along the length of the warehouse, loaded with food. A sentry barked at them to get back to work, but Graham brazenly gave him the British-style v-shaped sign for fuck you. Tribe announced they were taking a break.

They sat in the open roll-up door of the loading dock, feet dangling over the edge, and split a few nectarines between them. Graham used his knife to halve the fruit and cut away the rotten bits.

"Tell me something," James asked Tribe after a time. "Why were you trying to kill Lichboegh?"

"He killed my Master."

There was a pause, all three of them sucking succulent juice from their fingers. "That's it? You're not gonna fill us in?"

"Malvern Lichboegh was a very skilled fencer in his time. Not a swordsman, mind you," Tribe said sternly.

"What's the difference?" Graham asked.

"Fencing is a sport with set rules, judges, and the like. The object of the sport is to score points by striking your opponent with your weapon. Needless to say, whichever fencer scores the most points wins the bout.

"Now, in a real duel between swordsmen the object is to kill your opponent by driving your weapon as forcefully as you can through his body. There is no room for error. In fencing, if your opponent strikes, he – or she – simply gets a point. You may get a small bruise. In a duel there are no points. If your opponent strikes you will be grievously wounded, and you will, in all likelihood, die watching your own lifeblood pump from your body." Tribe shrugged. "But this is the consequence you accept when you challenge an opponent, or accept a challenge."

"And this is the life you've chosen to lead?" James couldn't keep the shock from his voice.

Tribe chuckled. "Yes indeed."

"So any time, you could be challenged, have to face another man who's trying to kill you," said Graham, incredulous.

"Or woman," said Tribe pedantically. "It doesn't happen often. You must remember, we are an increasingly rare breed."

"I guess so, if you're spending all your time killing each other!" James shook his head.

"You two must remember that in choosing this life I am accessing a tradition of great antiquity and grace. You have a much greater chance of dying in a car wreck than I do dying at the hands of an opponent." Tribe winced. "Or, at least, you did..."

"You think it's graceful, killing people with swords, then." Graham leered at him.

Suddenly Tribe leaped from the loading dock down onto the pavement, whipping out his sword. James shrank away from the narrow, thin blade, an insect's steel proboscis. "This, fellows, is a rapier. You see no adornments, no jewels. This is no movie prop, made to impress with its beauty; this is a weapon. And yet, it is elegantly made. Master crafted specifically for my hand by the Spaniard Inigo de la Juerta, one of the greatest swordsmiths of the modern age."

The grip was enclosed within several slender gracefully curving bands, obviously designed to protect the hand. One of these curled around the base of the blade like steel smoke. James complimented the craftsmanship. Tribe said the bands were called quillons.

"And now that I have unsheathed my weapon, I'm afraid I am honor-bound to draw blood!" He fixed James with a murderous expression.

"Wha – what?" James froze until he saw the twinkle in Tribe's eyes. "Oh, Jesus!"

Tribe laughed heartily, elbowing James's knee. "That one never gets tired."

"Jesus Christ, I almost pissed my pants!"

"Just so, James, just so. I jest, but this is a weapon made to take seriously. Elegant but deadly. The rapier is specifically designed to kill. The product of centuries of technological and metallurgical development." Tribe gave them a show of muscular yet balletic swordplay. "Made primarily to thrust— " he grunted, leaping forward. "But also if necessary to cut, to splay, to cleave." The weapon whipped the air with loud swoops. "As you can see, the edge is razor sharp, and yet the steel is supple enough to flex." He grabbed the blade and bowed it. "With enough spring to leap back into shape!" He let go, and the blade did just that, twanging deeply, like a string on a bass guitar. "I submit to you that any endeavor can contain an element of grace. Yes, even violence."

"Okay, Tribe, I get it, I get it," said James. "I can admire it for what it is, I guess. But it's a huge step from admiration to making the decision to murder somebody with it."

Tribe stopped cold. "No! Not murder! A duel. A contest!"

"Sorry, but it didn't seem much of a duel when you attacked Lichboegh's men on the York Campus."

"Indeed! I ask you: is it my fault that Lichboegh is a coward and refuses to face me? Who hides behind a cordon of men with guns? I have made my claim of retribution! Honor demands that I avenge the death of my master, Carmino Dalla Rive."

"What happened?" Graham asked. "What did Lichboegh do?"

Tribe re-sheathed the rapier, as if afraid he might be tempted to use it after all. "Dalla Rive was a great and rare man. The kind of man who cannot help but impart greatness to all around him. It came off him like…the way bronze is worn from an ancient statue by centuries of pilgrim's fingers caressing it."

"Very vivid," said Graham.

"I do try, Graham. Dalla Rive was like a father to me. He taught me to fence *and* to duel. What little is good in me came from him. Malvern Lichboegh is a fine fencer, but he fancied himself an Olympian. He sought out Dalla Rive for instruction. Dalla Rive took the challenge, but after some time he did Lichboegh the honor of speaking the truth. Directly, honestly, brutally. 'You are no Olympian, and you will never be one.' Now, Lichboegh dresses up like an aristocrat, but he is not noble. Far from it. He is just thin skinned. Precious. He refused to accept Dalla Rive's verdict. When Dalla Rive told him there was nothing more he could do for him…"

James saw there were tears in Tribe's eyes.

"And did Lichboegh return Dalla Rive's honor? Challenge

him, call him out? None of it! Coward that he is – rodent! vermin! – he ordered his henchmen to gun Dalle Rive down in the street. Like a common criminal, like a mad dog." Tribe shook his head, yanked out a handkerchief and loudly blew his nose. "Rubbing salt into the wound, Lichboegh then proceeded to poach my pupil: Nicolo Alvarro."

"The captain of the Sicari!" James remembered the stocky, proud gunman. How Allistair had referred to him as the one with Bay City Rollers hair. "You were his teacher?"

"For a time, yes. Naturally, Alvarro's betrayal only deepens my desire for revenge." Tribe cleared his throat, and when he spoke again, it was as if he was talking to himself. "However, it is best not to desire vengeance too deeply. For, as the Italians are fond of saying, revenge is a dish best served cold. Alvarro has no honor. He is not a moral man. So, it is for the best that I am no longer responsible for his conduct." Tribe wiped his nose again, and put the handkerchief away.

"Let me ask you something," said James.

"Ask away. You're good at it."

"Now that you've sworn to protect my life, what happens if it's necessary to kill me to get to Lichboegh?"

Tribe fixed James with his fierce eyes, as cold as blue granite. "Let us cross that bridge when we come to it, shall we?" He laughed and slapped James on the thigh. "Your turn to tell me something," he said, hopping back up onto the loading dock. "Was your mother really a member of Mensa?"

James gave him a startled look.

Tribe chuckled. "You mentioned it to Dr. Rivers. Don't you remember?"

"That's right," he said, scratching his head self-consciously. "I'd forgotten."

"Well?" Tribe prompted. "Was she or not?"

"She really was," said James. "The idea of a group that excluded people, just based on innate qualifications, that really offended her sense of justice and fair play. So that was it, she decided to join, just to show them out."

"Just like that."

"Just like that." James laughed, with a bitter edge. "That's why I joined the cadets and the army reserve when I was in high school. The idea of her son in uniform, carrying a rifle, that really pissed her off. That fucking woman. She scored 154 on Sandford Binet, right? And she thought, by doing this, she was proving Mensa wrong – that anybody could join, so screw them. Meanwhile…" James's voice stuttered out into open laughter.

"Meanwhile, the very fact that she scored so high only proved she was well beyond ordinary," said Graham.

"Right," said James, rubbing his eyes. "A certified goddamned genius. Of course, the money she spent to take that damned test, and the Mensa fees, all that came out of the grocery budget. So we ate nothing but Kraft Dinner for a month. Never mind the fact that the town already had a lien on the property for back taxes. If there was such a thing as a test for fuck-ups, she would've scored even higher, I can guarantee you that. Guys, I'm not kidding when I say I've spent my entire adult life trying to get out from under all the shit she dumped on me. And now that I'd do anything – give *anything* to find out where my wife and my daughters are, I've got Maggie stuck in my head, giving me instructions on how to find this Philosopher's Stone. Some kind of Emerald Tablet? I don't even know what the fucking Philosopher's Stone or Emerald Tablet are! I mean, I don't want to sound self-pitying, but my God!"

"The Philosopher's Stone," Tribe intoned, "was the substance thought by alchemists to be the key to transforming base metals like lead into noble metals like gold. There was a widespread belief that there existed a so-called Emerald Tablet created by an ancient Egyptian alchemist named Hermes Trismagistus, which was inscribed with the instructions on how to produce the Philosopher's Stone."

"Why didn't you tell me all this before?"

Tribe shrugged. "My dear James, you never asked." He squeezed James's trapezius muscle. "Don't forget that all this is happening for a reason."

James snorted. "How can you possibly know that?"

"I can't. But I *feel* that it's true. Why else would you and Massimo enter the library to save my life?"

"Why were you in the library, anyway?"

"Where else would you expect to find me, James?"

"Well, Christ, it seems like a piss-poor place to make a stand!"

Tribe chuckled, but there was an edge to it. "James, surely even you must see that to my eternal shame I had failed. I remained on campus, hoping for a second opportunity at Lichboegh – which never presented itself. By the following morning, of course, the campus was crawling with Lichboegh's men, and I knew I was finished. I chose the library as the place to spend my last day on this earth."

"Shit, if you were gonna choose a spot to die, I'd think that concrete pile would be about the last on the list!"

"I happened to know that the York library was one of the only collections to contain a reprint of the seminal fencing tome

Academie de L'Espee, by Girard Thibault of Antwerp."

So I killed a man with a book about fencing, James thought.

"At that point, my fondest wish was to die, lost in its noble pages. But of course, *you* came along and buggered everything up." Tribe spoke this last sentence with a note of mock bitterness, and laughed.

*

The outsiders assaulted the store again the next day. The whistles blew, panicky shrill, and bombs began smashing the façade. A mob of men and women waving baseball bats, shovels, crow bars, pipes, were repelled by heavy rifle fire. The outsiders managed to get a VW station wagon rolling, but Hal's men shot out the tires and it came to a halt about two-thirds of the way down the slope. The riflemen jeered as the car's inhabitants fled, chased by whining bullets.

After the attack petered out, James, Tribe, Graham, and Mike joined Ross on the barricade.

"I don't get it," said Mike. "I mean, they've obviously figured out a way to get engines running again. Dog, that truck scared the crap outta me when they started it. Why didn't they just start the car?"

The dump truck still sat where it had rammed through the cars. A redoubt on the barricade now, riflemen standing in the hopper. James noticed the rags stuffed into the two big fuel tanks on either side. The last option. Before abandoning the outer barricade, Hal's men would light them and blow the truck sky-high.

"They couldn't start the car," said Gord. "Not without voltage. But that truck's a diesel. Diesel's don't use spark plugs to fire the fuel in the cylinders. Just pressure. You get a diesel vehicle rolling downhill like that, you pop the clutch, turn the engine over, you got action, even without electricity."

"Then why'd it stall?"

"Well, the engine don't use juice, but you need power to run the fuel pump, right? Without that, you got a few seconds of fuel, tops, before the engine chokes."

"Youse aren't supposed to be out here," said a slack-jawed thug, waving a handgun at them.

"Shoot us then." Tribe raised his eyebrows expectantly. His fingers drumming on the pommel of his sword.

"I got it, Merle, I got it." Gord barked.

The gunman backed off, muttering.

James scanned the outsiders with Tribe's binoculars. Hundreds now. Among them were dancers. Madness displayed as an enthusiastic tarantella. Knees sprung high, rigid arms swinging in high circles. Their sweat-soaked faces exuberant but terrified, bloated pink in the afternoon heat. Dancing themselves to death. To James, they seemed scarcely human.

"We have come into the land of fairy," said Tribe. Quietly, contemplatively.

"Yep!" Ross exclaimed. "They look like faggots to me, too."

James peered at Ross. Amazing the way the old world clung, endured into the new.

Again, James swept his magnified gaze across the milling crowd of outsiders. "Holy shit," he gasped. There was the Dog Man! Astride the hood of a car at the top of the hill, hoisting the shotgun high above the massive dog head, pumping it in time to the growing unintelligible chant among the hunger-crazed.

"What's the matter?" Ross asked.

"You see that blue Ford Focus up there?"

They all ducked as a gasoline bottle twirled down into a bleak whump of flames behind them. When James stood up again, the Dog Man was gone.

"Shit!" he yelled. "Where'd he go?" He searched back and forth, but couldn't spot it.

"Where'd who go, damn it?" Gord insisted.

"I saw it," Ross muttered, lowering his own field glasses. He turned his watery eyes on James. "I believe it now. It's come for you again. Only question is, what are you going to do about it?"

*

They lounged around their square in the warehouse, drinking California Merlot and smoking pot, longing for gracious oblivion. Anything to blot out the olfactory reminisces of gasoline. And burning hair. That stink carried peculiar memories for James. The night Maggie wrote Heart's Tongue.

They ate in the new fashion: carefully savoring, consuming everything. Carrot greens, pear pits. Ross even tried to eat a bit of orange rind, but he spat it out. Too bitter, he said.

James hesitated before passing a joint to Mike. "You're too young."

"Dog! I've aged, fuckin' thirty years in the past month!"

Ross uncorked the third bottle, took a long drink, and got it moving clockwise around the Group. Gord and Clay were there too, Hood happily gnawing on a chewbone.

"*Red, red wine!*" Lilac crooned. "*Stay close to me!*"

In his calm way, Clay began asking them again about their plans. Loosened by inebriation, the discussion turned towards who they were, how they'd come together. They decided to do a round of introductions.

"I'm Lilac Taylor. I'm twenty-six. I'm a kindergarten teacher. Was." She looked to Amy, on her right.

"Amy di Taranto. Thirty-one."

"You don't look thirty-one," Massimo crooned.

She rolled her eyes. "Uh, well I did a little of this and that. Ski instructor in the winter months. Helped my father run a hunt camp up north in the fall."

"Where'd you learn to shoot?" Ross asked.

"My old man. I also competed in the Nordic biathlon. Almost qualified for the Nagano Olympics."

"Stupid question," said Mike. "What's the Nordic biathlon?"

"Skiing and shooting."

"Massimo Faccini. Twenty-eight. I was campus security at York U."

"Graham McMann. Twenty-three." He shrugged. "I didn't do much of anything, t'be honest."

"Graham is a rare and brave man," said Tribe impatiently. "In the middle of a mad crowd, he saved our bacon."

James giggled. "I guess that means every *crowd* has a silver lining."

"Oh, come now…" Tribe groaned.

Graham chuckled, hunched over his cigarette. Even a little disquieting, that hollow-eyed laugh. "Dead on, dead on."

"Quentin Tribe. Thirty-seven. The only job I ever earned money at was as a fencing instructor."

"Eh, there, Captain Studly!" Sheilagh snickered. "Can ye build me a fence, then?"

Tribe made a face.

"Quentin?" Rohini asked. "That's not a name your hear every day."

"Well, I was my father's fifth son."

"Okay, so what's really with the sword?" Lilac goaded him. "Do you see it as, like, an extension of your penis?"

Tribe smiled. Just a slight roll of the eyes. "I'd never be so bold as to claim my penis is capable of killing somebody."

Lilac smirked. "Uh, yeah, that's why you need the sword. That's my point."

"Mike Chan." Mike was giggling uncontrollably at the banter.

"I knew I shouldn't have given you any," said James.

"What's your story?" Sheilagh asked.

"No story," he stuttered. "I'm – uh, I'm in grade twelve. I work at a place pretty much like this."

"James Muir. Twenty-seven." He hesitated. "Writer."

"A writer." Massimo smirked. "He worked with me at York U."

Massimo turned pointedly to Gord. "Alright," said Gord after a beat, "I'll play along." His hawkish gray eyes, pinpointed by sharp pupils that never missed. Never. Possessed by a fanatical light. These eyes were of the ilk that had beheld new worlds and raped them. "Gord Havercroft. Thirty-two. Uh, I was a garbage man, till I was fired a few months back." He frowned slightly. "That's it, I guess."

"Havercroft," Lilac twittered. "Switch around the a and the o and you've got a hovercraft!"

Rohini chortled, but Gord met the comment with a flat, frozen look.

"Ted Baxter. Forty-four." His deeply-lined face seemed to be made of nothing but sinew and knuckle. "Soil management engineer."

"My name's Clay." His teeth clicked on the stem of his pipe. An awkward pause.

"And what do you do, Clay?" Lilac asked.

Clay looked at her, stroking Hood's back. His bearded face gave the impression of immense history. He looked at Lilac headlong, but without challenge. Plainly. "Well…" He cleared his throat, as if addressing something uncomfortable. "I…uh, I do what most folks do, I s'pose." And that was it. Clay's steady gaze, the set of his mouth, wore the expression of somebody who had just been slapped across the face, hurtfully struggling to figure out if he should retaliate or apologize.

James started to wonder if Clay was suffering from dementia.

Lilac smirked uncomfortably, looking down at her busy hands.

"Ross Clinker." He was giggling too, as if at Lilac's discomfort. "Sorry, sorry. First time I smoked the wacky tobaccy in a long, long time. I'm sixty-three. Manager of a golf course, east of the city. Close to retirement." He ran a hand over his bristly curls, gray to the point where it was impossible to tell the original color, except that it had been dark. "Well, guess I'm retired now!"

"Athol Jones." So far Athol had been the only one who had refused to partake. Now the bottle came to him again, and he took a swig. Winced, stuck out his tongue. "That is awful stuff, just awful. I'll be sixty-five in just about a month. I'm retired now, but I was a criminal attorney. In another life."

"I'm sorry," said Massimo, "but I gotta ask. Where did your

folks come up with the name *Athol*?"

Athol offered one of his wry smiles. "It's a place in Scotland, where my maternal grandfather was born. Contrary to what you might think, he was actually a very decent man. Not at all an *Athol*."

That earned some giggles around the circle.

"Rohini Radhakrishnan. Um…ooh, I'm drunk. Do I really have to give my age?"

"Ah, go on!" Sheilagh goaded her.

"Alright, I'm thirty-three. I've done a bunch of stuff. Mostly of the dead-end service-sector soul-destroying variety. I'm between jobs, living at home again. You know."

"Sheilagh Navan, twenty-nine. I'm a student, on exchange. From Dublin, in case you didn't catch the accent."

"Student of what?" said Amy tersely.

"I'm a botanist. I came over here to do some field work. First time in North America, like. Stepped off the bloody plane twenty minutes before the blackout."

"You're damn lucky you weren't still in the air," said Amy.

"I know it!"

"Where's that Mulligan?" asked Lilac. "He's always disappearing!"

Ross giggled again. "If I didn't know any better, I'd say his parents golfed a whole hell of a lot, giving him that name!"

"We still don't even know whether it's his first name or his last," said Sheilagh.

"Ah, he's probably just taking a piss," said Massimo.

"Dude," Mike giggled to Tribe, immediately on his left. "I probably shouldn't ask you this, and there's no way I would if I was, like, sober, but can I see your sword?"

This provoked a good deal of laughter. Smiling, Tribe pulled the scabbard out. It was of intricately tooled black leather. He carefully removed the rapier and laid it flat across his palms to show Mike.

"In the movies there's always a kinda ringing sound when they take out their swords," said Mike.

Tribe chuckled. "Yes, well that is for dramatic effect. To make that sound you'd need to have metal inside the scabbard. In real life, that would only dull the edge."

Mike mangled the inscription etched along the blade. "Sorry, dude, I don't speak, like, Greek."

Tribe laughed. "It's Latin, Mike. *Audaces fortuna iuvat.* Fortune favors the bold."

"I've always preferred *Beati pacifici*." Athol's saucy grin, seeking the fun of a joust.

"'Blessed are the peacemakers,'" Tribe translated for Mike. "For myself, I've always found it interesting how much peacemakers benefit from the protection afforded by men of arms."

"Damn straight." Gord lit a cigarette.

"So, you've, like...killed people, 'n stuff?"

Tribe reared back from the question, bemused.

"How many?" Lilac asked, challenging him to answer.

"No." Tribe slipped the weapon back into its scabbard. "That is between me and the Fates." He took a long pull of wine, passing the bottle to Mike. "Now, what about that knife you're carrying. Do you know how to use it?"

Mike shrugged with teen insolence. "What's to know, dog? It's not like it comes with an instruction manual."

"You're very naïve. When we get out of this place, I plan on giving you instruction on the proper techniques of fighting with edged weapons."

"Hold on, hold on," Ross interrupted. "You're gonna teach a seventeen year-old kid how to knife fight? Isn't that a little irresponsible?"

"Quite something from a man carrying a rifle!" Tribe exclaimed.

Ross shrugged awkwardly. "Well, that's different."

"Is it? He's got the damn knife. Are you going to take it away? Do you have the right?"

"We've got the right to make ourselves safer," Lilac snapped.

"Of course! Teaching him to use his weapon properly makes us all safer, Lilac."

Mike snickered uncomfortably. "Um, I am sitting right here!"

Tribe turned to him. "But are you truly prepared to put this weapon into someone's body? It's not so easy as it seems, Mike. The body jealously resists. You'll be surprised at how much strength it takes, chopping through muscle, sinew, bone."

"Eew!" Rohini cringed.

"We must speak candidly of these things if we mean to do them. Mike, you're carrying that knife as a weapon. That means you mean to use it to butcher another human being."

"Dandy, Quentin," Athol intoned, "you should have been called *Dia*Tribe!"

"I'm only carrying it to protect myself!" Mike complained.

"Offence or defense, the principle is the same. To use that instrument to do harm. Hold out your arm. Stretch it out, now. There: that is the absolute maximum distance your opponent will be from you as you do it. You must *own* the act, Mike. You will possess it for as long as you keep drawing breath. I do not exaggerate when I say that I have seen murderers on their deathbeds, men who prided themselves on their ruthlessness, and the last thing they ever uttered were weeping laments, the names of those they killed."

Tribe's sonorous voice was inscribed with such stern weight that the entire Group was rapt.

"You will wear your opponent's blood. Believe it. The handle of your knife is of wood. The blood will soak in permanently. Do you understand what I mean? You will never get it out, not ever. Your mind is like the handle, Mike. Once stained, it can never be wiped clean."

Amy was listening very intently. "I can tell you from personal experience, butchering deer, elk and moose in the bush. Even then, after the animal is already dead, it's a mess. I've been doing it my whole life. It's not something you get used to."

James ruminated over that phrase Maggie had always used. "You mustn't think of the past as unalterable." He wondered about that. As if his thoughts had summoned her, her Voice began chanting in his mind. The first time in days. *The Stone the Stone the Stone...*

His head throbbed. Too much of that astringent wine. He retrieved his pack, dug through the top compartment for his Aspirin bottle. As he popped the lid, he saw Astrid's smeared thumbprint on the label, limned in Sam's blood. A sign boding nothing good.

Graham stepped past Tribe and Mike, sinking down on James's right. He pulled out a surreptitious bottle. Tanqueray gin. He raised his eyebrows, spurting a plume of tobacco smoke from his mouth, then sucking it into his nose. The way it vanished, inhaling cotton batten. A carnival trick.

Sheilagh: "Oh, Graham, you're going to get yerself shot!"

"Ah!" Graham scoffed, cracking it open. "I even got glasses, from the housewares section, like!"

Seeing the gleaming tumblers, James felt his tongue twitch. More akin to hunger than thirst. He and Graham shared a lascivious glance.

"Anybody else?" Graham's voice had taken on an exaggerated confidence.

Nobody responded. The Group discussion had disintegrated into several conversations. Tribe pontificating to Mike about edged weapons. Clay, Ross and Athol absorbed in quiet talk. Lilac, Rohini and Sheilagh were playing a card game. Crazy eights. Graham and James, oddly alone.

"I don't think that's a good idea, having any more booze

tonight." Massimo frowned at them.

Not totally alone, then. James picked up the drink Graham had just poured. He ignored Massimo. Fuck it, he thought. Just fuck it. He and Graham clinked tumblers and downed the gin. Room temperature, treacly on the glass. Perfume in his throat.

Graham's wide eyes burning with the same pale light as the bottle at his right knee. He kept it there, on the opposite side from James, protecting his claim. Smoke slithering up the length of the cigarette he'd just lit.

"To family," James croaked. Drank. Gagged.

"To electricity."

"Good one! To new friends."

"To old ones."

The booze slopping down, shot after shot. Already, James felt well and truly sloshed. Some part of his mind flickered a warning about mixing drinks. Even before the gin he'd been well on his way. "To the end!" he crowed.

"To the fucking future!" Graham snarled a laugh.

The alcohol unleashed James's tongue. What fucking future, he slurred. It was not knowing about Stacy and the girls that was driving him mad. That, and the prodding Voice urgently whispering, whispering. Tinnitus with an agenda. "And too boot, I've got my so-called mother's fuck friend with a dog's head sewn on his body, trying to kill me. I mean, what the fuck!"

"Too right, mate, too right." Graham's snickered. "Tinnitus with agenda. Nice one, pal."

"I just don't care anymore," said James, belching. "Let him find me. Just get it over with. Anything's better than living in this aftermath. I don't want this mission, I never asked for it."

Graham poured the next round. Only half of their elixir left now.

"Hey!" James shouted. "You're pouring yourself more! Stop the skimping! Top me up!" Sensing the appraising eyes of the others upon them.

"Your turn for a toast," Graham mumbled, doing as he was told.

"Can't we just drink!"

"A fucking toast, mate!"

"Alright, alright." James raised his glass melodramatically. "Fuck the Stone! There – I said it. Fuck! The! Stone! Horus, do your worst, asshole!"

Graham laughed.

*

James and Graham had just tossed back their last drink when Hal and two beefy riflemen appeared, dragging a semi-conscious, bloodied Mulligan into the little square. They dumped him, moaning semiconsciously on the concrete. Hal as chipper as always, sweaty from the exertion of pummeling their friend.

"What are you two doing in here?" he demanded of Gord and Clay.

"Keeping an eye. Sir." Gord dead pan, just a hint of defiance.

Hal's smile widened. "Well, given the fact that we found *this* one in the manager's office upstairs, maybe you need to keep more than one eye!"

Tribe leaped to his feet. "I for one don't remember any warning about staying out of the damned office!"

One of Hal's men yanked out a handgun.

Immediately, Tribe drew his sword. "Come on, then!"

Hal waved off his man. "He's right. I wasn't clear enough. It's the only reason this head banger is still alive." Hal gestured at Mulligan, winked lecherously at Lilac. "Now you know. Grandpa Clay!"

Clay stood deferentially. "Sir." But James saw blazing anger in his stare.

"From now on, I hold *you* directly responsible for the conduct of this crew."

"Understood. Some one among us needs to take responsibility."

Hal's paranoia-lacquered eyes narrowed. His Cheshire Cat grin frozen in the lamplight. "Two girls for every boy!" he suddenly sang, wagging his eyebrows at Rohini, snapping his fingers as he marched off. His cronies followed.

James and Sheilagh tended to Mulligan. As gently as they could, putting his sleeping bag under his body. Pouring wine into his bloody mouth.

"Mulligan!" Sheilagh scolded, opening her first aid kit. "What on earth were you thinkin'!"

Mulligan winced, wine spilling from his mouth. "Kept thinking. That fuckin' freezer. Attack this afternoon. They pulled that fat fuck guard outside. So I went in."

"What's in there?" Mike asked for all of them.

"Five bodies," he whimpered. "Four men, one woman. Bullet holes, backs of their heads. The woman is naked."

A pause. For a few seconds, all of them measuring the meaning.

James lit another joint, put it between Mulligan's split-swollen lips.

He inhaled and groaned gratefully. "Checked out the manager's office. Photos on the walls. Same faces. Mom, dad, three sons.

Rohini was crying. Lilac rubbed her back.

The sight of Mulligan's bloody face killed James's spirit. Already poisoned with booze, it expired. He got the impression the others felt it too. The stress they'd been desperate to stave off this night, erupting among them like a corpse bloating in fast motion.

Sheilagh and James went about aiding Mulligan, but their actions were the fruit of disconsolation, heavy dread. None of the cuts on his face needed stitches, but Mulligan cried out when Sheilagh palpated his chest. She thought he had a couple of broken ribs.

"Good pot, dude," Mulligan muttered. His left eye was swollen shut, the right almost as bad. Every movement made him grimace. "Their names were Khan," he continued dully. "The old man, store manager. Gun locker up in the office. Open and empty."

"Those goddamned bastards," Ross spat.

"Explains how the store stayed so neat and tidy," said Massimo. "This family defended it."

"Aye, until along came somebody with more firepower," Graham slurred.

*

James slipped into a fugue. Recalling only dimly the map they placed before him.

The Stone the Stone the Stone the Stone the Stone!

"What's with the Stevie Wonder impression?" James heard Gord from far, far away.

"He's pointing, he's pointing!" Mike.

"Jesus Christ, he isn't kidding when he says north-fuckin'-east!" Ross.

"That's gotta be a two hundred and fifty miles!" Massimo.

"As the crow flies, perhaps." Tribe. "Considerably longer on the road."

As if from a great height, James saw where his own hand was pointing. A web of red highway lines, brown regional roads, veins among pale blue lakes. He felt a twinge of familiarity, elusive and faint. Somewhere in there, a lake. An island.

"It's the back of beyond," Graham, despondent.

"That wildlife preserve just to the north." Amy. "I've been

hunting up there. I can tell ya, there's nothing around. I mean *nothing*. God's country."

"Where is he taking us?" Lilac.

Maggie's voice erupted from James. "A farm for nine! An island for three!"

"What the fuck!" Gord. Sounding truly frightened. James felt a pinch of satisfaction. What do you say about Stevie Wonder now, jerk-off?

"He already told us five of us were gonna die." Lilac.

"One of us twice." Mike. Still giggling.

"Four, now that Sam's gone." Rohini.

"Right," Mulligan gasped. "Whatever."

"The Philosopher's Stone! The Emerald Tablet!" Maggie's voice, raging now at preternatural volume. Clay's dog began barking. "You will assist James! You will accompany him! No choice, no choice! Wonderful things to come! Take him there and he will show you, he will show you the wonders of the Stone! You must prepare! *Wiben ra im put!* The sun rises in the sky! The final attack by morning! Stay and die! Stay and die! Stay and die!"

The Group shrank away from James, prey before the predator.

Suddenly Clay rose in righteous anger. "Enough of this!" he commanded. He seized James by the scruff of the neck, flinging him down onto the floor. It worked. It shut Maggie up.

James plunging deeper, deeper.

*

The aftermath of Maggie's epic thirty-fifth birthday party. The house is full of snoring reprobates, and there are many tents out in the back yard. Jamie is up early. There is an army reserve dress rehearsal this morning for the Canada Day parade.

He needs to press the shirt of his dress uniform, so he puts a little water in a pot, just so it won't overheat, filling it on the counter because the sink is crammed with dirty dishes. Post-party slumber, the house an wasted dream floundering in a Sargasso Sea of alcohol.

He sets the pot on the heating element. A favorite time of his, this gentle lull between noise and confusion and embarrassment. When he can let his mind be cleansed. While the pot of water calmly ticks he stands and listens to the sound of his own breath. Reminding himself that there is a life separate and distinct from the clamorous discord that kept him awake most of the night.

Then he hears an odd sound coming from the back yard. He peers through the open kitchen window. There is Maggie, buck-

naked, unconscious, lying face down in the dewy grass. The sound is coming from Donnie, still stuporously drunk, dragging himself across the back porch down onto the lawn. For some reason, Jamie's first thought is that Donnie wants to pick up Maggie, bring her inside. But Donnie doesn't do that. No, he unbuckles his belt. Stooping over her, his hips sway and wobble. Even standing erect is difficult for the bastard.

Jamie's mind cannot reconcile what he is seeing with what he thinks it means. Donnie's belt clinks and shines in the low sun. His clumsy hands tug down the fly on his Levis.

By the time Jamie runs through the mudroom onto the back porch, Donnie is already bare-assed, straddling Maggie's prone, still body.

"Leave her alone!" Jamie shouts.

Donnie hardly even takes notice. His loosely hanging mouth slobbers as he starts to grind his pelvis against Maggie.

Jamie jumps onto the lawn and sends a flying kick into Donnie's side, knocking him off Maggie. "I said leave her alone, asshole!"

Donnie gets to his feet. Very slowly. His face a taut mask of pure rage. He no longer seems drunk at all.

Never taking his eyes off Jamie, Donnie bends down to pull up his jeans. His bare chest coated in tattoo ink. A lifetime of hoisting tires and engine blocks has carved his shoulders wide and powerful.

"Okay, asshole," Donnie growls. So quietly, he growls it. "Okay."

Jamie's mouth goes dry. His knees feel unsteady. But he stands his ground. He knows the time has come. A time he has spent many long hours poring over in his rapid mind on those nights when he chases evasive sleep.

"Just go home, Donnie. Sleep it off." Jamie struggles not to sound winded, desperate.

Donnie puts his head back, jutting his square jaw at James. "I am home."

They circle each other. Coiled springs.

Donnie is cunning. "You just bought your mommy a big fat one up the ass."

While Jamie formulates a response to this outrage, Donnie charges him. Jamie puts up his fists in feeble defense, but Donnie's huge fists slam his face, his ribs, his stomach. Jamie is down in the wet grass. A hatchet of pain driven into his nose. He gasps for air and his ribs scream. He's choking. All he can hear is a high-pitched whine, like a boiling kettle.

Donnie sets in, kicking him barefoot. Excruciating pain.

Jamie curls up, regressing to a fetus. Thank Christ he's not wearing his work boots, he thinks. For sure, he'd kick me to death.

Donnie's aiming for Jamie's kidneys, but dislocates two of his toes on Jamie's spine. He backs off, hobbling, swearing.

Jamie can't draw a breath for the pain. Can't stop himself from writhing. A puppet of agony. He chokes and spits out a mouthful of blood.

Five feet away, Maggie stirs.

*

James had no memory of leaving the SuperCenter. A breezy damp night. It had been raining, but it was clear now. A bronze boomerang moon slicing the sky. His breath wisped. He was carrying a rifle. The same one Gord had handed him during the assault.

Find him, Maggie hissed. *Slay him. You must!*

Hands badly shaking, he opened the gun's bolt. Chambered a round. Levered the safety off.

The road divided suburban plazas, chain restaurants, movie theaters. A large mall on the right, a squat unadorned castle sitting amid an empty moat of a parking lot.

Anywhere, North America. Powerless.

This landscape of entitled luxury, appalled by darkness, dotted by spectral fire. Barrels, a large Dumpster, bonfires, a few vehicles, all in flames, illuminating spewing smoke. Edge-on faces traced in angry red. Roman candles were going off, spray-painting the darkness with twinkling, ephemeral sparks.

He didn't know what else to do, so he walked, wobbling as if his legs were diseased. Still feeling the buzz of alcohol, the drowsy web of a fading pot high. A stilt man among gyrating sultry wanderers. In the SuperCenter he'd imagined a twisted jungle of creeping leaping murderers. Leering psychos to gash his throat with broken glass and feast on his living limbs.

Here, he was surrounded by them. Crinkled mouths and eyes containing nothing but shadow. He had no idea how to get back to the SuperCenter.

Macabre noises split the dark. Chiming metal, tortured whines like nails prized from rotten wood. Stuttering shouts. Slouching shoulders in and out of firelight like mammoth moths. A whole world of heel-dragging mumbling vagrants.

He walked through an intersection. The crossroads. An adolescent boy crouched on a broken plastic chair holding an improvised wire snare. The loop lying flat on the pavement around a small pile of kibble.

"C'mon, kitty! C'mon kitty-kitty-kitty!" He chirped with his lips, his whole gaunt body jittering.

James saw a pair of glowing green discs creep up from the ditch to the boy's right.

"C'mon kitty! C'mon now!"

He could tell the boy was struggling to keep his words soothing, but awful panic tinkled behind each syllable. The cat crept into view. Warily slunk towards the wire noose. Hesitant, smelling danger. It's tail twitched as the boy coaxed it, almost pleading. The closer the cat crept, the tenser the boy's legs became.

"That's it," he cooed. "That's it, kitty-kitty-kitty."

Pathological rage there too. A prowling shark just barely rippling the placid waters of his voice.

The cat stepped into the snare for a sniff at the kibble and the boy yanked on the wire so hard the chair toppled over backwards, his skinny legs imploring skywards.

The snare caught the cat's foreleg. It shrieked, tried to run. The boy held the wire fast, but the cat fought, a demon in it, screeching as only cats can, an earsplitting warping. Leaping, twisting, thrashing until it was suddenly free and gone. Just a flash of tail into the shadows. The boy was left with an empty circle of wire.

Shaking with frustration, he sobbed. James hoped he would never again hear such desolation in a human voice.

The boy glared up at him, a face eaten raw by dim firelight. "He's in there!" he screamed. A ropy arm indicated the mall. "He's waiting for you!"

*

Struggling to control his breathing, James entered the mall through a smashed entranceway. Some vehicle had ploughed through, leaving swerved black streaks down the main concourse. Some poor bugger's clenched seizure, the moment the lights went out. Just ahead, an SUV sat jammed through the front of a menswear store, the front tires wedged on the display, so that the chassis remained angled off the floor.

Thin moonlight dribbled through the mall's skylights, coating the edges of things with pale urine-tinted varnish. That and the twisted glimmer of flames outside lent just enough light to see the detritus scattered everywhere: crumpled clothes, cheap jewellery, DVD's and CD's gleaming like crazy, leering irises. Cell phones, iPods, digital cameras, every imaginable device, scales molted from the body of some vast electronic reptile.

Worshippers had abandoned this temple, left it to its mendacious gods.

James pulled out the piece of the Dog Man's ear that Massimo had kept. "Donnie!" he shouted. "Missing something?" His voice boomed in the cavernous hollow.

From somewhere in the mall, the drumming echo of boot heels chopping the floor. The Dog Man. Coming for him.

James peeked over the banister of the atrium. Down in the lower level, a knife blade shadow flicked across a customer service kiosk.

Hot fear leaped in his throat.

Stamping up the dead escalator now.

The time had come.

James ducked beneath the SUV, its rusty guts bearing down on him. Propped on his elbows, he shouldered the rife, aiming for the top of the escalator.

But first to appear was a woman. Nude, the boniness of her body chiseled hollow in the low light. A human shield, a whimpering sacrifice. The Dog Man gripped her with a meaty forearm. Over her heart, Donnie's flexing heart tattoo. The shotgun erect behind her right shoulder.

The Dog Man's boot heels smashed and kicked and hammered, splintering junk as he strode towards James. No more than fifty yards away.

James's finger pressured the trigger. The gun's mechanism shifting against its spring. He couldn't aim properly. The sights refused to stay aligned. Jolting with his thudding heart. Abruptly he remembered Sergeant Mosley, who'd given him firearms instruction. Never until you used a gun to slay a man did you become truly aware of your own pulse.

Shit! If he missed, he'd kill the woman. The Dog Man would sight him, and that shotgun – that shotgun would come up—

Now! Fire now or it's too late – miss now, you'll never be able to chamber another round in time—

James clenched his teeth as the Dog Man's squalid snakeskin boots crunched to a halt just feet beside the SUV. Shifting, scraping as the Dog Man peered about. The woman's feet, torn bloody, skittering as the monster yanked her back and forth.

James smelled its rotting odor, pregnant with death. An undead parasite on the body of a decaying world. In the stretched holes around the neck, and the ragged gash Amy had inflicted on its right biceps, maggots churned. Tiny worms the color of lead, wriggling, spilling from the wounds.

*

Donnie is gloating over Jamie. Limping back and forth before Maggie's bleary, puffy face. Huffing through the pain of his broken toes. He goes in for another kick with his left foot. Jamie catches the cuff of his jeans and twists. For a few seconds Donnie fights to pull his foot free. Jamie hangs on, screaming in agony, bashing his fist on Donnie's injured right toes. Donnie shouts in pain, heaves over, landing on his side. A confusion of tangled, punching, kicking limbs. Donnie almost has him pinned. Groaning, crying, Jamie is flailing. He lands an elbow straight to Donnie's solar plexus. The wind sputters out of Donnie. Gagging, eyes bulging, Donnie can't hold on.

*

James aimed at the Dog Man's right boot. No more than a few feet away. He couldn't miss. Just as Sergeant Mosley had taught him, he let out his breath. Hugged the rifle tight into his shoulder. Gently squeezing the trigger.

Please don't let me miss.

The deafening explosion blew the Dog Man's right foot off. The poor woman was screaming. As the Dog Man tottered, she wrenched herself free and ran down the concourse, filling the mall with a gamboling wail until she was gone into the night.

The Dog Man tried to take a step, but tumbled hard as the stump of its leg squished on the tiles. The shotgun slid away. James's palsied hands struggled with the bolt action. Only dimly aware as he scrambled out from under the SUV that the rifle's mechanism was jammed.

The hideously deformed dog's face, one eye destroyed, leered at James. Then the Dog Man lunged for the shotgun, grabbed it, swung it up—

James leaped away as it went off. A fist-sized hole blown in the SUV's front fender. Knowing now his gun was useless, James swung the butt down with all his strength, clubbing the Dog Man's chest. He heard bone crunch. He must not allow the Dog Man to work the shotgun slide. If it got off another shot at this range, James would be torn in half.

With a desperate, agonized grunt, James kicked the shotgun. It fell from the Dog Man's grasp. Another clumsy kick sent it sliding out of reach. Overextended, off-balance, James tried for a club at the Dog Man's head. But the rifle butt just bounced on the fabric. The momentum of the blow pulled James down. He fell across the felt head, disgusted at the stench, its nauseating pliancy. The pressure of his weight spewed maggots from neck holes like squirming toothpaste.

James rolled away, losing the rifle. Utterly horribly silent, the Dog Man was already on its hands and knees. James saw it grasping for something at its belt. Even with only one foot, it managed to struggle up and now it had a machete in its right hand. It swung the blade savagely down. James just managed to roll out of the way. The machete clanged on the tile.

"No!" he screamed. "No!"

Hungrily aggressive, the Dog Man leaped at him, the gleaming machete zipping the air just inches from his face. Attacking, attacking. James sidled crabwise. The machete whooshing like a mute cough. James dodged, but the blade caught the right side of his head. Fierce agony, his blood pouring across the tile.

*

Jamie is on top of Donnie now. One hand gripping Donnie's throat, he punches the face again and again and again. Donnie turns his head side to side, the hammering fist opening his cheek, his forehead, splintering his front teeth. A fury in Jamie, blood foaming in his screaming mouth. Driving his fist down, his knuckle gashed on the sharp stumps of Donnie's teeth.

Then there are arms around him, around his neck, Maggie yelling at him to stop, stop you're killing him!

*

The shotgun! Maggie's voice, shrill and goading. *Get it! Get it quick!*

James felt his blood soaking his right shoulder, gluing his shirt to his skin.

The Dog Man above him. Both hands on the machete now. The weapon raised high. Dim light streaked along the notched blade, mingling with James's own gore.

The mall collapsed into a crushing singularity, suffocating him with fear.

The shotgun is right there! Maggie insisted.

He'd fallen right beside it. He grabbed it with both hands, raised it as a shield, the machete chopping into the stock like a hatchet. Stuck fast. James twisted the gun, swung it to the side, pulling the machete out of the Dog Man's hands.

He jerked the slide back. Saw the red plastic shell pop out.

Yanked the slide forward. Cutting his hand on the machete blade. The Dog Man threw itself at him. James jerked the trigger. The shotgun blast blew the Dog Man back. It landed spread-eagled on the tiles.

James bounded up, snarling, working the slide. A hole in the Dog Man's chest, bigger around than a football. Still, the Dog Man struggled onto its elbows, the plush head bobbling.

"Die you motherfucker!" James shrieked.

The Dog Man reached for him. He fired, obliterating its right forearm. Donnie's red heart tattoo erased.

Again James reloaded, but when he pulled the trigger there was only the snap of the firing pin. As the Dog Man dragged itself away along the floor, James threw the shotgun down, pinned the stock with his feet, and pulled the machete free.

A strained whimper simmering in his contorting mouth, James whirled on the Dog Man and went to work.

*

Dawn. The color of soiled linen. James in the midst of a massive assault on the SuperCenter. He raised his arms and the battle petered out around him. Shouting, gunshots, all silenced except for blowing flames. Gaping faces war-painted with soot, full of wonder, full of fear. Outsiders kept their distance as James marched toward the barricade, the Dog Man's severed head hoisted high. A totem of his power.

"Hold your fire!" someone on the barricade shouted. Clay. It was Clay.

Clay helped James climb over the barricade, surrounded by expressions of wide-eyed disgust. When he was inside the store, there was a gunshot. Suddenly the assault thundered again. Thousands of voices raised in screaming frenzy, a jagged fusillade.

The siege was over. That much was clear. The entire glass front of the store was smashed in, much of the interior ablaze. Dozens of outsiders had already managed to breach the defense, scrambling among the shelves.

A propane tank hurtled against a checkout lane, clanging like Vulcan's hammer, crashing into the magazine and paperback stands. It broke James's daze. He hit the floor, hearing a panicky whoosh as the propane caught, then an explosion that burst painfully inside his head.

"Mister Muir!"

Riflemen retreating all around them, chased by outsiders.

"Mister Muir! Come, now!" Clay stooped over James.

Grabbed his shirt and tugged him up. "To the warehouse, to the keep!"

Dizzying orgasmic madness. Outsiders piling on riflemen, beating them with clubs and pipes and bats. The Dog Man's head engulfed in flames. James let it go, gripped Clay's arm. They dashed for the rubber doors into the warehouse, pursued by a screaming mob.

Massimo, Amy, Ross, all of them pushing loaded shopping carts down the length of the warehouse.

"Jesus!" Massimo shouted at him. "What happened to your face?"

"No time, no time!" Sheilagh threw James his pack. "Where the fuck've you been?"

"Move it!" Gord turned and fired two quick shots.

They dashed past the stairs to the manager's office, the infamous meat locker.

"Where the fuck do you think your going!" Hal screamed at them, jumping down the stairs. He fired a few shots, so focused on their laden carts he was overwhelmed by a gang of outsiders. The last James saw of him, struggling in a mass of boiling limbs. Being clubbed, beaten to the floor.

Athol broke through an emergency exit. Back out into daylight. The alley behind the SuperCenter. Running so fast Mike's cart overturned, spilling cans across the asphalt. He actually stopped, trying to retrieve some of the food. An outsider jumped on him, fighting for a peanut butter jar. Tribe flicked his rapier, opening a gash in the outsider's arm. Tribe and Mike ran for their lives. A pack of outsiders descended on the cans. Dozens more chased after the rest of the carts. Catching up fast.

A bottleneck at the end of the alley, barricaded by two end-to-end cars. Just enough space to squeeze between the rear bumper of the right-hand car and the wall.

The roiling gang of outsiders, ten yards and closing.

Amy, Ross, Gord and Clay atop the cars, firing at them. Everybody shouting now, furious encouragement to keep moving, get the carts through.

Massimo tore Rohini's cart out of her grasp. She swore at him, but he told her to run. He reversed the cart's direction and shoved it at their pursuers. It worked. Most of the outsiders gave up the chase and attacked the cart in a wild melee. Massimo did the same again, taking Lilac's cart, giving it a running push. He and Tribe were the last to scramble over the barricade.

They ran left towards the road. Mulligan gripping his own chest, fighting to keep up. Across the sloping parking lot, the dump truck's fuel tanks went off with a hot concussion that slapped them, even from fifty yards away. A teeming torrent of outsiders scrambling, climbing, jumping into the burning store. Something droned over James's head. He ducked, still running. Zipping bullets whacking the asphalt. Riflemen on the roof, gunning for them.

He turned on the trot to give them the finger. Just in time to see a crowd swarm the roof, tossing the last riflemen over the side.

Chapter 15

The Horrors

"Oh, *jay*-sus!" Sheilagh hissed, peering at the side of James's head. The wound from the Dog Man's machete.

"Dude, it took off most of your whole ear!" Mike sounded fascinated. James wanted to smack him.

The stump stung wickedly. The whole side of his face lit up with pain, brighter than the corona of the exploding propane canister.

"Ah man, that's mingin'!" Graham wrinkled his nose.

"It's your fuckin' fault," Massimo spat at Graham.

"My fault!"

"Absolutely, asshole. I told you not to get into that fucking booze!"

"Ach, stick it up yer hairy arse!"

Massimo and Graham stood nose-to-nose. "Wanna go?" Massimo's tone suggested an offer to take Graham to a baseball game.

"Will the two of you grow up, damn it!" Sheilagh yelled.

"Mass, stop it for fuck sake," James chided him. "It's nobody's *fault*, man!" Massimo and Graham caught as they all were, a Sundance upon tenterhooks.

Massimo and Graham rolled each other through the mud by the side of the road. The spastic limb-tangled flopping of a real fight. Both of them wheezing profanities.

Lilac made a feeble effort to intervene, but Tribe told her to let them finish it.

Hood yipped and leaped around.

"Too bad we can't tell tickets," Mulligan laughed.

"Shut up!" Rohini sneered.

In a few minutes Massimo and Graham were too tired to continue, both of them scratched and sweaty. Graham had bloodied Massimo's nose, so Tribe announced he'd come out on top.

"My fucking ass!" Massimo panted, standing with his hands on his hips.

Tribe forced them both to shake hands.

"This is ridiculous, gentlemen," said Athol. "We've got to find a way to solve our differences, before things get out of hand."

"Things *are* way out of fucking hand," Lilac spat.

Tribe, Ross and Mike held James down. He shrieked as Sheilagh poured peroxide over the stump, dabbing away dirt with a cotton swab. Then she tied a bandage around his head. James's turn to start taking the penicillin. He fervently hoped it would be more effective for him than it had been for Sam.

He kept thinking of the prophesy: *Five shall not survive.*

Ross tore a bed sheet into strips. Sheilagh helped him bind them tight around Mulligan's chest. He was in too much pain to carry his pack so they put it in one of the shopping carts. Mulligan's face looked like some of the corpses they'd seen: piebald livid blue.

Gord reported Ted hadn't made it. Speared with a sharpened broom handle in the final assault.

"What about that kid Dave?" Rohini asked.

Gord shrugged. "Never saw him."

The SuperCenter had surrendered twelve carts of provisions. Every spare inch of their packs stuffed with Ziploc bags of nuts, sweets and dried fruit from the bulk food section. Sheilagh kept the Group on low rations, meant to squeeze as much time as they could get out of their stock.

They marched northeast. Using their maps to plan stages of ten miles per day. Thirsty work it was, too. The road exacted its toll in blisters and aching joints. The soles of their feet sore with heat. Graham taught them the importance of bathing their feet nightly. To carefully dry and powder them, using both hands to massage out fatigue.

"Watch here," he said, reaching for one of Hood's paws. Hood immediately jerked the paw back, staring at Graham's hand with predacious intensity. "Instinct, right? He knows even a small injury and he won't be able to keep up with the pack, won't be able to hunt. Basically, he'd be fucked."

They agreed to rest every few days, using the time to launder their clothes if enough water was available, air out their tents and sleeping gear. Rohini had taken sacks of cardamom and mustard seed, turmeric, cinnamon, ginger powder. She made them curries that filled them with warmth. These holidays beckoned with a fervency they could scarcely believe.

Always, always underwritten by the Horrors.

Spiritual fatigue that silently waylaid them. Especially on their off days, when there was too much time to contemplate. The Horrors.

Ross elbowed James, raising his eyebrows at Rohini. "Thousand yard stare," he whispered. "What we used to call that look."

Rohini's vacant eyes divined deep pain. Difficult for James to look at.

Ross spat into the dirt. James sensed he would not have done that a month ago. Forty years ago, perhaps. Reverting to an earlier incarnation of himself.

Weren't they all.

"Who's got a Band-Aid?" Athol asked. He had an angry open blister on his heel.

Massimo had one out for him immediately.

A rigid attention to detail enforced itself sternly on their field craft. For the seventh time this day, James went through a quick inventory of his supplies. So that his hand would fall exactly where it should when the time came: right side of his belt for his knife; insect repellent and sunscreen in his right cargo pocket. In the left, the Ziploc bag of leaf and moss tinder they all carried. A first aid kit with scissors, tensor bandage, surgical tape, gauze and antiseptic spray.

Like being on the job at York U. Living it. Gone were the days of absent-mindedly putting down his keys and then spending a few minutes finding them. That luxury had been banished along with weather reports and running water and automated air conditioning and refrigeration.

Their coffee and tea ran out after just a few days. And for days after that, they'd suffered through caffeine-withdrawal headaches. Sheilagh worst of all, her head wrenched by migraine.

On a rest stop, they tensed at two gunshots sprinkling sharp echoes. The first they'd heard in a few days. Half an hour later, Amy arrived back at camp, flushed and sweaty with effort, dragging a field-dressed doe.

Lilac was horrified by the animal's bloody nose, its lolling tongue. Rohini put her hands on its head, mumbling a short prayer.

"You two better step away," Amy advised, removing her belt. She stropped her knife on the leather before butchering the carcass, slicing the luscious meat into thin strips. They laced these on sticks, roasting them over the fire.

"Tasty!" Mulligan teased, dangling a piece at Lilac as if to hypnotize her.

"Outrageously delicious!" Mike enthused.

Clay tossed the dog the strips that fell into the coals. Then Hood got a bone to gnaw.

"I'd do something wickedly outrageous if somebody could just tell me the time!" Lilac announced, perhaps trying to take her mind off their fare.

Clay glanced at his wristwatch. "Five forty-four," he said. They all stopped eating. Staring at Clay as if he'd just spurted fire from his fingers. A real, functioning watch! An old winder. "P.m.," he added self-consciously.

Massimo grinned at Lilac. "You made a promise!"

Lilac hugged Clay, kissing his cheek.

"That'll do, Ms. Taylor," he chuckled. "That'll do just fine."

For the leftover meat, Gord built a makeshift smoke hut with the tarpaulin and some weathered lumber he'd found. Amy used green maple wood to cure venison jerky. Chewy stuff that stuck in the teeth, the smoke imparting an acrid flavor. But food. Scarce animal protein.

*

Of the Horrors.

Lots of spontaneous crying. My cup runneth over with saltwater, James thought, wiping his eyes. Sadness and loss, emotional dew points precipitating from red swollen eyes. How many tears to fill an ocean, he wondered. As many as the stars in the galaxy? Perhaps. Perhaps a number signifying an absolute horizon. Like the speed of light or the charge of an electron. Horrific inevitability with no recourse.

Rohini's brown skin glazed by riverine deltas.

She caught James staring at her. The meek tug of her mouth that might have been an embarrassed half-smile.

"You okay?" he asked.

"Nope. There's a debt to be paid. For the food we took from those people."

"What about Rumi?"

"What about him?"

"I just thought there'd be some fragment of wisdom, you know, to bridge the gap.

Rohini considered. "'When a seed falls into the ground, it germinates, grows, and becomes a tree: if you understand these symbols, you'll follow us, and fall to the ground, with us.' We need a new meaning, a new idiom. That's all."

"Hmm. Not sure I'm ready for whatever all this means, to be honest."

"Doesn't mean shit," said Mulligan sourly.

Now Rohini did smile. Tender pity there. "Everything means *something*."

"Sure. Just ask him." Mulligan indicated Athol with his chin.

"Nobody said you had to like it," said Lilac. "Doesn't mean it's meaningless."

The Horrors: lurching through the macabre empty suburbs.

Every wall, every surface defaced, beaten in. Plazas, homes, disemboweled, strewn. The demonic imprint of soot slashed over the glassless windows. Becoming mascara-daubed eyes.

To James, this was no mere resemblance – the windows *were* empty, staring eye sockets. Long sooty lashes raised, aghast. Demanding in the voice of the mourning wind, *how dare you besmirch me with your look. How dare you?*

At night, Rohini often screamed in her sleep. *"Daddy! Daddeeee!"* with the ferocious voice of a person tortured with red hot steel.

Rohini stayed far from the fire. Lilac sat so close, James was afraid her hair might catch. Huddled into herself, hands buried deep in her fleece jacket. Shivering, teeth chattering. Not with physical cold, he thought. Something deeper, chilling her with bone-jarring fever.

Amy sitting with her arms gripping her knees, fervent as a lover about to lose a partner. "I can't stand it any more!" she cried, "I can't take this shit!"

Sheilagh went over and sat with her. A self-conscious arm across her crouched shoulders. Whispering platitudes unheard by the others. An intimacy.

"No," James heard Amy keen. "No, no."

Spare platitudes. In this frowning labyrinth, a thread forever withdrawing, always just out of reach.

Sheilagh had moments too. Gazing a thousand miles. Fingers pressed to her lips. Still, so still. A vein in her forehead, a flaw in white marble.

Mike could not sit still. He told them why. A creeping sensation, his skin suddenly terrified of an enemy close behind. He'd turn around to find nothing. But convinced his eyes were blind to something clearly there. Grinning, waiting for the right moment to pounce.

Until he told the Group, Mike thought he was the only one. Becoming difficult to map out a place in that most precious of divides: madness or sanity.

James rarely slept the night through. He'd roll onto his severed ear and the pain would invade his dreams. The Dog Man grabbing for him, jolting him awake in the darkness. Hearing the heartbeat of some machine, far away but real.

He crawled out of the tent, eager to find out what it was. He saw Clay, who insisted on sleeping outdoors, only a thin groundsheet and his greatcoat for a blanket. It was Clay's wristwatch he was hearing. The night so quiet, even from thirty feet away James perceived the tiny gears working.

But the massive relief of that sound, as if in palliation of chronic pain. James's brain seeking machine noise the way a speed freak craved the next hit.

He couldn't get back to sleep. Too cold, too pure. Ross was on watch, but he'd fallen asleep, sitting against a tree. James lay looking at the fast face of the moon sliding above the rim of the east. Nearly full. How massive it seemed, a great round window above the porch of an ancient cathedral. Clad in amber instead of stained glass.

As it reached apogee, he was awed by it for the first time in his life: not a simple disc, a glowing pill. No, a gargantuan globe of rock looming over the earth. The porcine face of Hermes saying *Toodle-dooo!*, bloated with sallow light, leprous with shadow. The promise of decay.

James mourned then. For Stacy's breath under the blanket. Warmly odiferous, her nose full of calm wind. Linen the temperature of her body. Burrowing deeper, to breathe her in.

*

Graham came up with the idea that the Group should share their stories, their dreads, their beliefs. Before bed down, after supper had been cleared away, they luxuriated in a few chore-free moments before the bliss of sleep. Naturally at these times they sat around the fire in a rough circle. Usually more of an attenuated *C*, the open end turning as people moved out of the stinging smoke that shifted with the fickle breeze.

Even before Graham made his suggestion, there was something special going on. Most of them could remember mild summer nights gathered with friends and family around a backyard fire pit, or camping, mesmerized by its beauteous heat.

The Circle was sadder, more circumspect. And yet festive, James thought. Tiny things. Hot instant soup, stretching your tired legs. Every swallow of water, every minute spent sitting instead of marching, every mouthful of food. All these gifts they knitted together into cordial celebrations, purled with laughter, cabled with each other's company. No longer strangers.

Finally beyond the dreary strip malls and industrial parks of the city rim, into open countryside. Finally green instead of stained baking concrete and the foul brown of industrial lands polluted by hissing weeds. Away from the deafening clatter of urban guerilla warfare.

Despite a determined effort, James thought, human beings hadn't dirtied everything. Not yet. Nothing but crickets in the quiet dark around them. Protective rather than ominous. James saw the great *W* of Cassiopeia slipping over the trees. The calm turning of the Earth. He took a deep breath. Let it out, very slowly.

At conversational low tide, when all were wandering in their own thoughts and fears, Graham made his suggestion.

"Dunno," he mumbled. "Just seems we could all use this time to sorta share what we're feeling, y'know?"

"Sounds kinda touchy-feely," said Gord.

"I think it's a fantastic idea," said Sheilagh. "We all need a little therapy, don't we?"

Graham made a face. "Don't know if 'therapy' is the right word, t'be honest."

"What do we talk about?" Lilac asked, sipping tea. A couple of days ago, Sheilagh had discovered a patch of wild mint.

There was silence for a long while, all of them considering. The fire spoke its own crackling language. A stern mother *tsking* her child, sprinkling fierce embers.

"How about we describe what happened to us when the lights went out?" James saw Rohini shift uncomfortably. As if frightened the fire would hose her with pain. "Come on, some of us have already talked about it. Wouldn't it be good to hear all our stories?"

Mike grimaced, rubbing his stubbly chin. "You think? I kinda like just chillin', y'know? Talkin' about whatever."

"Yeah, I enjoy having a chat in twos and threes," said Lilac. "The way we usually do. It gives us a chance for a little anonymity. No offence, but the Group feels a little… *incestuous*, sometimes. I don't see why all our time has to be structured."

"Besides, talkin' about *the night of*, yo, that'd be hard," Mike added, sounding low.

"It ought to be hard!" said Tribe. His hard stare went around the Circle. "That's precisely the point. If we mean to form a firm bond, we must pay an ante."

"Dead on, dead on," said Graham.

"How much are we willing to share with each other?" Lilac's knowing half-smile was a dare. Flirtatious, but cold. "How far do we go?"

"We're not gonna get anywhere without being honest," said Amy. She was performing the foot massaging ritual, her whole body rocking with the effort. "Honesty, that's it."

"I agree," said Tribe. "Without frank discussion of the things that haunt us, our fellowship will remain weak."

"A fellowship?" said Mulligan, mocking. He flicked his butt into the fire, wincing at his ribs. "Is that what this is?"

"You got another name for it, we're all ears," said Amy,

looking up at him.

Mulligan and Gord glanced at each other. Their expressions were enough to tell James what they thought. That the entire discussion was more than a little *gay*.

"I used to feel that sharing my emotions would be a waste of time," said Graham. "Now, I'm not so sure."

"Think about what we're doing," said Tribe sharply. "Already we are living together, eating together. Already we each have assigned tasks, ensuring everyone's survival. Together we've shouldered some of the most extreme experiences imaginable. And by God, these are early innings! We need bonds."

"All for one and one for all?" said Massimo quietly.

"Damn right!" Tribe responded.

"That's what I meant by *incestuous*," said Lilac.

"Sounds like socialism to me," Ross muttered.

"So what?" Sheilagh demanded. "It's gotten us this far, hasn't it?"

"You didn't have a problem when Athol read about the fuckin' apostles living that way," Mulligan sneered. "You remember that, don't you Ross? At George's house? Acts, I believe it was."

"That's right," said Athol.

Ross frowned, stubbornly shaking his head.

"The only question is one of will," said Clay in his papery voice. No, James thought, not paper. Vellum. Dry sheets that have absorbed the wise ink of centuries. As always, his quiet voice seemed to embrace them all. He drew a burning stick from the fire pit, sucking the flame into the bowl of his pipe. "Fellowship or not, these are but semantics. The key point as I see it is for all of us to keep our principal task at hand."

"Which is?" Massimo asked.

"Why, to find a way to live on as human beings, Mr. Faccini. It is that simple, and it is that complex."

"Right," said Graham. "Except for hermits and other cranks, people have always needed other people, have they not?"

"Isn't that what society is all about?" Sheilagh asked.

"Aye, and I don't sense that any of us are the hermit types." Graham laughed. "Wild locusts and honey, my arse!"

"May as well be, fuckin' diet Sheilagh's got us on," Gord grumbled, and then they all laughed a little.

"So who'll be the one to bell the cat?" Tribe asked after a while.

"I'll go first," said James.

Hissing wood, sparks tumbling star-wards as Gord poked and raked the coals.

James was struck by a sense of enormity. The next words out of his mouth would be the most important he'd ever spoken. Words metered by the heart that moved his blood. He felt Maggie's presence. Tracing his words with a calligraphy he knew the others could hear. An incantation, drawing them to him.

Without these people he would die. Alone, bereft. A decadent bundle of stinking rags by the road. Like to many they'd seen.

"Time speaks tales for those who will listen. Circling stars, mercurial moon..." A tingle deep in his bones.

With that, he told his tale. Of waking on that final morning he would spend in his bed. The story assumed its own dimensions. Organic growth, maturing into something different than the one he'd intended to tell. Expanding like water assuming the shape of the vessel it fills.

He told them about the time he and Stace had gotten sloppy drunk on their anniversary. So drunk that when Sara woke in a fit of night terror he tripped jogging to her and split his bottom lip.

No shame. No, they were well beyond shame. They'd moved into something darker and more hallowed. Faces liquid in the firelight, bending, melting. As if reflected on a pool of black water massaged by night winds. The depthless river carrying them to the Emerald Tablet.

He told them about crying when Jenny had come down with pneumonia. So beaten with exhaustion he had prayed for respite from the braying cries of his daughter, too feverish to recognize him.

The fire hissed hot contempt. *You thought then you knew exhaustion! What do you think now?*

Screw the fire. By dawn it would be only warm ashes. But these compatriots would still be here to listen. To share their food and their laughter. Even their scorn. A crowd thrown together under an awning to wait out a sun shower.

All of them in turn would distill their tales, bestowing wishes upon each other and sowing magic deeper than whatever stalked them. Elaborating an ancient ritual. The fecund pulse of the numinous singing through them the way a hand resounds against the drum skin. Or a fingerprint rustles the pages of a tome once lost but now found.

"We are making something wonderful and terrible," he whispered.

Around the fire, the glowing faces of his new friends drew in and in. And it seemed their combined breath became the flames.

*

A beautiful, sunny rest day. They filled their bellies with Rohini's delicious *dahl*. Spent hours basking in a field lit with goldenrod and milkweed and vetch. Cherishing the massage of cleansing sunlight. It healed the weariness of weeks spent sleeping in cold damp tents on the ground. But by that afternoon, they were sunburned. Lilac worst of all, her skin purple.

Sheilagh made her drink as much water as she could stomach, and they coated her with enough Bactine to make her glisten like a basted turkey.

"Always found it telling," said Athol, creaking around the campsite to loosen his arthritic joints. "Damp and camp rhyming the way they do."

"Nothing good about camping, goddammit!" Ross squawked.

"No, no, Ross," Rohini chimed in, dumping a handful of dirt and dead leaves from the porch of her tent. "Constantly fighting to keep clean, I mean, that's living!"

"You can keep clean?" Mulligan smiled bitterly. "Shit! What's your secret?"

"Having brown skin helps." She winked. "Hides dirt better than yours."

By the next morning, Lilac was still in no condition to march, woozy and whining self-piteously about her sore skin.

Gord had no sympathy: "Your own fault that you're redder than a frigging lobster."

But they got another day to lounge and air out their tents.

As promised, Tribe drilled Mike in thrusting, parrying, footwork. He was a taskmaster. "No, Mike, no! How many times have I told you?"

Mike's flushed, sweaty face dropped to his chest. "Thrust, don't slash."

"Never mind what you've seen in the movies! Roman legionaries were taught the same lesson. A slash cut rarely causes deep wounds. A thrust penetrating only a few inches can cause devastating injury. Do it again!"

Sitting on his sleeping mat, James spotted a shadow flicking across the wildflowers. Looking up, he saw sharp wings streak from the brilliant sky, snatching a hapless sparrow in mid-flight. Soundless, a beam of darkness and gone. A few downy tufts tumbled on the breeze.

"Did you see that?" Mulligan exclaimed.

"I saw it."

"What the hell was it?" Massimo sounded aghast.

"It was a peregrine falcon," said James quietly.

"Frickin' *awesome*!" said Mulligan. "You ever seen anything like that before?"

James saw it every time he closed his eyes. The powerful *wadjet* of the falcon-headed Horus. The Distant One. Ruthless and beautiful. Just like Maggie.

"A sign," he said, squinting up at Betelgeuse.

"Eh?" Ross leaned forward. "What'd you say?"

"He said it's a sign," said Lilac, sitting close beside James.

"Sign of what?" Rohini asked.

"That a bird was hungry," said Mulligan, pulling back his hair into a ponytail. Sheilagh and Ross smiled.

"True," said James. But more. A sign of blood to be shed.

James wondered if this was what the Magi had experienced, following their star. Voices, visions. Hauling precious frankincense and myrrh all that way, braving bandits. A hunger-plagued quest, for what? For an impoverished family huddled in a stable. Censed by goat dung. An infant languishing in dirty straw. Gawping illiterate shepherds mouthing awed simplicities little removed from the noises of their herds.

And what did those saddle sore, parched travelers think? Sunblind, shaking dust from their wind-wrung robes. That the Hebrew god had played them, baited hooks for fish?

Star of wonder, star of light! Star with royal beauty bright!

How keenly the Magi must have longed to be back in their temple observatories! With their antique scrolls, their algorithmic charts.

Of course, they hadn't been driven from Babylon by ravenous antic flames. Nor been hunted by slavers armed with guns. Their disappointment surely blunted by the promise of returning home. To priest-kings eagerly awaiting their reports. Sumptuous verdant Babylon, tinkling with the music of sweet flowing water. Silken curtains breathing perfumes. Honey. Cloves.

What did James have as an offering to the hectoring beckoner marked by the silver flame of Betelgeuse? What collapsing bitterness awaited him?

The Philosopher's Stone.

Unlike the Magi, James could not even lay claim to wisdom. The object of his trek would be far more arcane, esoteric than himself.

*

Tribe's map told them there was a town nearby, and the next morning they strolled in to root out supplies. Wind moaning painfully down the dusty main street. Just a few people about, furtive as mangy foxes. Emaciated cargo cultists, waiting for businesses to reopen. Weak and frail, plainly despairing for the food in the carts, but careful to keep their eyes low when they saw the rifles.

A dissolute blank woman pushing a baby stroller. Vacantly cooing to the baby within. But one whiff of the dark space under the sun visor was more than enough to convince James her baby would never cry again.

Clothing and jewelry shops, two banks, a few antiques outlets. In a tiny pharmacy James found a few packets of fresh gauze for his ear. The two variety stores had long since been scoured, utterly empty.

Lilac found a small knitting boutique. Lilac and Rohini were awestruck, handling skeins of yarn with the tenderness of neonatal mothers, raving over textures and profuse shades.

"Oh!" Lilac moaned, pressing braided skeins to her cheek. "Rowan! And Donegal Tweed! Beautiful yarns."

"Sheilagh, what's wrong?" Rohini asked.

"Ah, nothin', I'm grand, I'm grand. It's just – me Ma's people're from Donegal, y'know? Y'said 'Donegal Tweed', and I wished I could have just one more glance at Donegal Bay."

"Lovely country," said Graham wistfully. "I've done a wee bit of hillwalking in the Darty Mountains. North of Sligo. *Sleeego*," he drawled through his nose, apparently imitating the local accent. "*Doneeegal, like!*" Sheilagh laughed, and the two of them were off on their own private romp through a realm the rest of them could never know.

Tribe was holding a long metal knitting needle, stroking its length.

"Need some time alone?" Mulligan cracked.

Tribe frowned. "I was just thinking that these could be used as decent thrusting weapons, in a pinch."

"Only *you* could ruin knitting," Lilac grouched.

Tribe grabbed handfuls of the needles.

Lilac helped herself as well. Crazily enumerating brands as she dropped them into a cotton sack: an Addi Turbo needle kit. Scissors and darning needles.

"I dunno," she said. "Cotton or wool?"

"The old timers back home have a saying," Graham's eyes still gleamed from reminiscing with Sheilagh. "'Cotton kills.' When it's cold, and you're wet, wool stays warm. Cotton gets cold, draws away body heat."

"Wool then! Noro, too. We're gonna need a ton of socks."

They were on the street listening to Lilac brag about how

much money she'd just dropped when the shots came. The plaster façade of the yarn shop spat dust with a loud SPRANG! before any of them heard the rolling crack of the shot.

They all dove for cover as another shot tore a ragged hole in the hood of a car.

"Where the fuck's it coming from?" Gord yelled.

Ross pointed up the street. A church bell tower, perched atop a hill overlooking the town.

"Jesus, it's gotta be five hundred yards!" Amy's voice, sore with fear and awe.

James heard a little girl screaming "Daddeeee!" He whirled around, slugged by heavy hope, but of course it wasn't Sara or Jenny. A bullet kicked the asphalt a foot from his face.

Amy dragged him back behind the car. "What the fuck's the matter with you!"

Across the street, a little girl stretched against a wall. Her hands pressed to her temples. Her face torn open at the mouth by screaming terror.

James was astonished when Tribe jumped out into the street, facing the distant steeple, arms stretched wide. "Come on!" he shouted at the top of his lungs.

"*Quentin!*" Sheilagh screamed. Bullets nicked the tar around his feet.

"Amy, Gord, Ross, put some shots in that damned tower," Clay commanded. "The rest of you, grab them carts. Soon as they start shooting, you move!"

Amy, Gord and Ross opened up and the spire spurted puffs of dust. Feeling as if every step would be his last, James got to his feet with the others.

"Move it, move it!" Massimo shouted.

James took a cart and ran. Looking over his shoulder for the screaming girl, but she was gone. Not watching where he was going, a wheel jammed into a sewer grate, and the cart toppled. Jars and cans rolled across the street, chased by cargo cultists. James halted to fight them off. A can of kidney beans exploded, struck by a bullet.

Tribe seized his arm. "Leave it! Come on!"

The main street abutted a shallow rocky canyon. They followed a paved path through a park, down into the canyon. Out of breath, they halted by a shallow, meandering river.

Ross's lips quivering, eyes twitching back and forth. "My daughter – my daughter Carly's wedding – it was just *six weeks* ago. *Six weeks!* Jesus, six weeks! My beautiful Carly's big show…"

Athol took his arm in his own shaking hand. "It's alright, Ross, it's gonna be fine now…"

Fine, James thought. As in a finely honed blade against the throat. He concentrated on taking deep breaths. Fighting with his own lungs, demanding that they work.

Tribe stuck a finger through a hole in the armpit of his shirt. A shot had come that close.

James did a quick headcount, realized Mike wasn't around. He trotted across the karst canyon bottom, finding him in a park overlooking the river, next to a copse of trees. Just catching a glimpse of him flinging something white into the brush. Mike was startled when James appeared. Red in the face, grinning ineptly.

"You okay?" James asked.

"Uh, yeah, okay, fine." Mike hurried past him, back towards the rest.

Then James realized. He'd tossed away his soiled underwear. Just a boy. Embarrassment stripping away haughty adolescence like the withered disc that peels from an old blister. Jesus. Poor kid.

A bullet had punctured one of their precious cans of olive oil. Everything in that wagon now soaked with oil. An unctuous baptism, James thought quizzically, helping to unload and wipe things down. Another cart's wheel had been damaged, so they abandoned it, dividing its content between the others.

His apology for losing the cart was met with awkward silence and furtive glares.

"No more fucking towns!" Amy demanded.

"Hear, hear," Athol agreed.

"It was my fault," said Tribe. "I should never have suggested it."

"Ah," Sheilagh scoffed, "how could you've known, Tribe?"

They followed the asphalt path that wound down the length of the gorge alongside the river. In the shade of maple woods on one side, a balmy breeze in their faces, it would have been impossible to guess they'd just come under attack. Except for the uncomfortable silence among them.

The gorge wall was defaced with graffiti.

"At least the graffiti of ancient Rome could be read, and understood," Tribe sniffed, casting a steely eye at the cartoonish cuneiform.

James snickered at him. "Nothing ever matches your lofty expectations, Tribe!" Among the colorful tags James could read some of it quite easily. "*No matter how good she looks tonight,*" read one line, "*someone somewhere is sick of her shit!*"

A few hundred yards further, "*Jesus Loves You!*" Below that, in different script, somebody else had added "*Make sure he wears a condom!*"

James pointed it out to Mike. When Mike snickered, James felt the load of his pack lighten. Just a little.

*

The diarrhea started with terrible stomach cramps. Athol got it first, then Ross. It spread through the Group with a relentless certainty. At first Rohini and Lilac were smug, assuming the illness had come from tainted deer meat. Two days after the rest of them had succumbed, they were squatting in the bushes too.

For five days they moaned, gasping at the painful squeeze in their guts. At the audacious the wet farting.

"Jesus," Graham gasped at one point, squatting behind a fanned ostrich fern. "Close your eyes, you'd swear we're on the set of an anal porn shoot."

Sheilagh started laughing, that half-stifled honk of hers, and soon all of them were laughing. Even Clay had a chuckle.

"Oh god, oh stop!" Lilac begged through her own hilarity, clutching her aching belly. Then dashing behind a tree, hands frantic to open her pants.

The sour stink of illness pervaded the camp. They tended a small fire, kept water hot for tea to keep up their fluids. All of them overcome with hopeless disgust at their own weak, pasty bodies. For two days, the weather was drizzly cold. They crouched under the tarpaulin. Dampness invaded everything, their sleeping bags, their tents. The camp devolved into a patch of stamped-down plants and mud. No comfort, not in anything.

Then Maggie began to cant in James's mind. *DANGER! DANGER! DANGER!*

Sheilagh read of a plant remedy in her field guide. She prepared a bitter tea of common plantain for them all to drink.

"Jesus!" Gord winced at the taste. "You wanna give us the pukes to along with the shits?"

"Stop your whining and drink it!"

The next day their appetites improved. They ate a few bites. But just a few hours later the meal was pouring from them again in wrenching spasms.

DANGER! DANGER! DANGER! YOU ARE NOT SAFE HERE!

Some of them began to think that they would never get over it. James saw resignation in Ross's downcast eyes. Graham and Massimo were grey effigies, modeling sallow endurance. Clay did his best to lift their spirits, trooping back and forth from a nearby stream to replenish their water, sitting with them, one after the other.

"Buck up," he told James. "Focus on how well you will feel when this blight passes. Because pass it must."

Rohini groaned, stumbled off into the ferns. They all heard the horrid watery pour. As she returned to her spot, nobody looked her in the eye, all of them sharing the mortification. A sense that with each diarrheic attack, a thread of their humanity was left in the dirt.

Horrible, but James felt this trial drawing them even closer together. Sharing in revulsion, they were growing united. Impossible now to hide secrets from each other. He saw Ross, bent painfully at the waist, immobilized against a tree. How Amy and Athol took his hands, guided him back to the fire. How Graham passed Mike his canteen when Mike's was empty.

PAY ATTENTION! WHO FOLLOWS YOU?

James called Tribe aside.

"We're not safe here," he whispered.

"What do you mean?"

James shivered. "I'm not sure. I just know we're not safe."

Tribe looked concerned, but said nothing. Every morning he roved out to scout the surrounding countryside. One morning he returned early, asked James to follow him. Tribe had found a ridge that afforded a clear view of the surrounding farmland. Concealed in a sumac thicket they lay in the timothy grass. Tribe pointed to a broken down barn shimmering in the haze, maybe a mile away. He gave James his field glasses.

At first James couldn't see anything. Then, he spotted a glint of metal along a road. A party of walkers. "Twenty at least," James whispered. Too far away to see many details. Except that the one in the lead was clad in a long, crimson robe.

"Shit!" James took a deep breath, struggling not to panic.

"Clearly I was wrong," Tribe growled. "This is no coincidence. Somehow, the Sicari are stalking us."

"But how the fuck do they keep finding us?" James cried, having another look through the binoculars.

"That is a question, now, isn't it?"

"We have to tell the Group."

"That is not a good idea."

"They deserve to know!"

Tribe shook his head. "I'm telling you, as things stand now, it will devastate their morale."

But James insisted on fetching Clay, Amy, Sheilagh, Gord and Massimo. The Sicari had moved down the road by then, but each of them got a good enough look to know.

"Those're the fuckers that had us trapped in that warehouse!" Sheilagh whispered, as if the Sicari were only a few yards away.

Massimo whimpered like a punished puppy.

They told Clay and Gord about the slaving gangs. Malvern Lichboegh's private protection squads. Men in black, led by men in red robes. One in particular, tall, with black curly hair.

"We must move," said Clay.

"But where?" Sheilagh keened. James was disheartened by the sliver of despair in her voice. It was unlike her. "I mean, they've tracked us this far—"

"They're heading east," said Amy. "It's like they know – they know what direction to find us!"

Massimo's eyes narrowed. "You remember what Jimmy said, back at George's house? One of us would be a traitor – he said that!"

James clenched his teeth, willing Massimo to shut it.

They headed back into camp, clouded with worry. Gathering round the fire, Amy got all their attention. "Listen up, people." She told the rest of them what they'd seen. The lugubrious atmosphere degenerated into despair.

Tribe gave James a look of smug anger. James gave Tribe the finger.

"I'm heading out at first light," Amy continued. "To my Nonna's place. Where I was heading originally, but…" She shook her head like somebody trying to explain a particularly bizarre dream. "I just sort of…forgot about going there. Fucking ridiculous! I mean, how could I *just forget* about my own grandmother?"

James felt their eyes on him. Massimo's, particularly. Not accusing, but close enough. Questioning. As in, *How could you do this to us?*

"You're all welcome to join me," said Amy. "Thing is, it's not in the right direction."

"What direction is it?" Clay asked.

Amy asked for the map. She examined it for a few minutes. "I'd say not much more than fifty miles northwest. With the state we're in, it's gonna take us a few days."

A collective groan.

"That is very wise" Clay nodded approval. "If these Sicari expect to find us east, it would be well to move west."

No! Maggie carped. *No, the stone awaits NORTHEAST! NORTHEAST is where you must go!*

"Fuck off!" James scoffed.

"What's that?" Amy looked at him sharply.

"Sorry, sorry." James waved her off. "Not you."

294

Chapter 16

Nonna

On the fourth day of their march, they came into a small town perhaps eighty miles north of the city. Huge trees, a sprinkling of homes across green rolling land.

Amy grew anxious, quickening her step, way out in front.

Thick, stupid lassitude gripped them all. James was especially sluggish. Maggie's strident nagging crumbling his sagging will. TURN AROUND! YOU IDIOT, YOU'RE GOING THE WRONG WAY!

Next to this nattering in his head, the silence without made James's ears ache as much as his hips and knees. He heard the tap of a robber fly lighting on his hat. The whiz of a crow's wings overhead.

"Mare's tails," Graham whispered as he looked up at the bird. He pointed at high bands of cirrus clouds, curled at the ends.

"So what?" Mulligan trudged past without even glancing.

"Change in weather on the way."

James heard a violin. Far off, a sad rippling tremolo, faint as the touch of a damselfly on a still pond.

"Bach," Tribe whispered, voice thirsty.

"Zio Albert!" Amy laughed and sobbed at once. She started running down the road.

Amy trotted up the driveway of a plain old split-level red brick house.

They followed her through a side gate into a backyard that stretched back hundreds of feet. Three people were sitting around a patio under an umbrella. Seeing Amy, a tiny old woman shrieked, pried herself out of her chair and clutched her fervently. It brought tears to James's eyes, seeing Amy holding her grandmother, rocking back and forth.

"Oh my God!" the old woman cried. "Oh my God, my Ameriga, oh my God! God brings a miracle! My God, my God!"

Another couple greeted Amy, beaming and crying. It was obvious she'd known them all her life. Quivering with excitement, she introduced the Group.

"These are my friends."

Her Nonna, gripping a cane in her gnarled hand, a dark woman with a wide face like Amy's. She hugged them all as if they were her lost friends. Surprising strength in her arms. She smelled of sweat and earth and wood smoke. Her deeply hooded iron-gray eyes direct and obstinate.

"*Ciao, la bella signora,*" Tribe intoned, bowing low, kissing Nonna's hand with a gallant flourish. "*Piacere di fare la sua conoscenza!*"

Nonna giggled, putting a small hand to her breast. Said something to Amy in Italian.

"Thanks a lot, Tribe," said Amy. "She says you speak Italian better than her own granddaughter."

"It is the tongue of fencing!"

"Yeah, well now I'll never hear the end of it!"

Albert was the violinist, a large bearish man with thick fingers callused like emery. He and his wife Mary were a decade younger than Nonna. Mary was plump, black-haired, with sun-browned arms. Albert and Mary had been Nonna's neighbors for longer than Amy had been alive.

Gasping gratitude, the Group loosed their packs and lolled in the grass. As Amy and Nonna wept and caught up, Albert welcomed them with several bottles of homemade wine. There was hard cheese, sharp and salty. Even fresh bread – fresh bread! Crusty, chewy, a groan-inducing marvel of nourishing goodness.

Albert grinned, sawing his violin with the bow as if the instrument deserved punishment. A stern man emerged from the house, small and lithe, about Nonna's age, in denim overalls and a ratty work shirt. Amy introduced him as Giuseppe. He was Nonna's boarder.

There was a flurry of festive activity. Nonna directed the proceedings with a sharp tongue and voluble hands. Giuseppe stoked a fire in a fieldstone oven. Mary sliced thick slabs of salami, pretending to be hurt when Lilac and Rohini demurred.

Sheilagh took Amy aside. "We can't steal all this food from your grandmother!"

Amy laughed. "Let me show you something." She led Sheilagh, James and Lilac into the house, down plank stairs into the basement. In candlelight, they saw hundreds of home-jarred peppers, peaches, eggplant, crushed tomatoes. Bags and bags of flour, sugar. Bottles of wine. Baskets of onions and potatoes and garlic. Strung from the rafters, several prosciuttos coated in cracked black pepper.

"These are my peeps," said Amy proudly. "It's like they've been prepping for this their whole lives. Albert and Mary, they got pear trees, they got peach trees. Chickens, rabbits. Combined, Nonna, Albert and Mary got like three acres of land cultivated."

Sheilagh laughed in amazement. "Jaysus, Amy! We should've

come here ages ago!"

"Like I said, I can't believe I forgot. Whatever that thing is inside you, James, it's got some kinda power!"

Sheilagh grinned, pinching James's cheek. "It's why we're still alive, eh Jimmy!"

They brought out jars and cans and bags of flour. Nonna set to work with the vigor of a woman half her age. Mary brought three eggs. James and the others gazing fascinated as Nonna cracked the shells, dropping the glistening yolks into a bowl of flour. A real miracle being performed.

Within the hour, Nonna and Mary had prepared a huge batch of fresh pasta, leaving it on sheets to dry in the sun. Then Nonna started the sauce, cooking on the stone oven. As she stirred and chopped, she spoke in Italian. Amy translated.

"She says it's been scary, not knowing what's going on. She misses her son – my father – but she knows he'll be alright." Amy stopped for a moment, wiping away tears. "She says, all this reminds her of being back in Italy. She was already thirty the first time she saw an electric light bulb. Can you believe that?"

"Sure," said Sheilagh, "it was the same in Ireland. My Poppa's place in Donegal didn't have any power till I was in school."

Nonna's yard laughed with flowers. Roses and Jerusalem artichokes, black-eyed Susans, sunflowers, hostas, Echinacea. Bees, wasps and flies danced among the blooms. Spread along the edge of the patio were many terracotta pots verdant with thyme, sage, mint, rosemary, parsley, basil and lemon balm.

"*Parsley, sage, rose-mary and thyme!*" Lilac sang.

Through a fence further back was a large shed and a huge garden planted with lettuce, tomatoes, cucumbers, peppers, beans, peas. The bed surrounded with bright orange plastic fencing to keep out rabbits and deer. Amy told them Giuseppe took care of the labor in return for his room and board. Amy's grandfather had died in a construction site accident when she'd been just a little girl.

"Always wondered if Giuseppe and Nonna have been getting it on." She giggled. "He's getting old, though, having trouble keeping up with all the work."

Beyond the garden, the lawn stretched away into a lovely meadow, overshadowed by large linden and ash. Hood frolicked among the trees, returning sticks tossed by Gord as he set up their tents. There were blackberries and raspberries in abundance. Strawberries, too. Rhubarb, mint and dill.

"This is paradise," James murmured. Even Maggie had shut up.

"This is my childhood," Amy laughed, watching them staring

at the berries. "Go ahead, take, take! That's why it's there!"

She retrieved a small basket from the shed and they filled it, bringing it back for everybody to share.

Nonna cackled at their naked delight. "One summer, eh, two year back, we pick forty pound! Forty pound raspberries!" Pride there, but gratitude as well. Knowledge rooted in the soil, aware of its charmed potency.

At a well in the corner of the yard, Giuseppe drew water from a hand pump, filling two huge pots. Massimo hoisted them onto the stove. Albert beamed as he and Mary showed off two rabbits and two chickens.

Lilac shrank from the birds. To her they might have been giant scorpions.

"Jesus, Lilac, they're *chickens!*" Ross laughed at her.

Rohini stroked one of the rabbits, cooing at it. "Aw, they're sweet!" No inkling at all of why Albert had brought them out until he reached to take it back and she saw his knife. "Oh, no, no!"

The feast Nonna prepared blanked their minds with sumptuous plenty. Athol led grace. They were all passionately thankful, panged by all the food. Deep feeling, for this day, for their lives.

The first time since Lights Out that James's belly ached with fullness instead of hunger. Delicious pasta with fresh Romano beans he'd helped to shell, a marriage of Nonna's light spaghetti with a peppery tomato sauce of garlic and onions and fresh basil. Asiago and parmesan cheese sharp enough to sting the tongue. Rabbit seasoned with rosemary, stewed in Nonna's sauce, with potatoes and carrots. Sage- and thyme-herbed roasted chicken, stuffed with under-ripe apples that had fallen from Albert's and Mary's trees. Succulent meat that tingled James's cheeks with indecent pleasure.

Albert bit a huge mouthful, grease dribbling from his wicked toothy smile. He mumbled through the meat, something that sounded to James like 'monica.' Whatever he'd said prompted uproarious guffaws from Nonna, Giuseppe, Mary, Amy and Tribe.

"He says it's tender, like the tits of a nun!" Amy translated.

The meal finished in the Italian fashion, a salad tossed in oil and wine vinegar. Lettuce, tomato and cucumber burst with the flavor of cool sunshine and rain. Vegetables that had still been on the plants just an hour ago, sipping from the living earth.

Not mere consumption. Sight and scent, labor, conversation, all immersed them in transcendent happiness. James felt light and razor-sharp. Blessed details. Ash leaves bending in the cool evening breeze. Swifts twittering high above.

Afterwards, they all helped with the cleaning up. Everybody

chatting and laughing, teasing each other mercilessly.

"Eh, I hope you know how lucky you are, coming back here!" Massimo eyed Amy, a jaundiced expression that worried James.

"Jealousy is a terrible sin, Massimo," said Athol with a wink.

As James scrubbed a saucepan, he felt the handle loosen. He thought he'd broken it until Nonna cackled and spanked his back. "I had them pots for fifty years!" she effused. "Some people, they say, always buy the new ones. *Ma, perche?* I no throw out good things. Never!"

Gord built a roaring fire and they all sat around until long after dark, their weariness replaced by drowsy contentment.

Tribe stood, wobbling. Sheilagh laughed and whistled. They were all feeling the effects of Albert's magnificent strong wine. "I wish to take this opportunity to offer our sincerest thanks to… to…ah, bugger Amy, I've just realized I don't know your grandmother's name!"

Everybody laughed and hooted.

"It's Stella," Amy called.

"You just to call me Nonna, like everybody!"

"Right. *Facciamo una brindisi alla nostra ospite meravigliosa!* To Nonna!"

"To Nonna!" they all roared.

"And to Albert and Mary for the rabbits and chickens!" Sheilagh called.

"Cheers!" everybody called, crashing cups together.

Then, as Albert stroked lovely tremulous music out of his violin, Athol read them the story of Simeon. Their vespers canticle for a night of long, deep slumber.

*

"I mean, check it out!" said Mike. "This garden's twice as big as my whole back yard!"

He, James, Graham, Gord and Amy were tending the vegetable garden. Pulling weeds, tilling in compost. Giuseppe supervised, intervening grouchily whenever one of them did something wrong. Which they apparently did often. In the trees above, cicadas droned hurdy-gurdies.

"Amy! You no learn nothing!" Giuseppe took his shovel and waddled off down the lawn, unable to stand their amateurism any longer.

"He's right," she admitted, stretching her back. "All those years, watching Nonna raising vegetables, all that cooking, all I ever did was mock how old-fashioned it was. I never really paid attention, never learned."

"You're learning now, right?" Gord, with a smoke in his hard mouth, shoveling compost from a wheelbarrow onto the soil. James and Mike were mixing it in with spade and hoe.

"Always thought, it'll be the old timers who'll survive the shite," said Graham.

"That's because they've already survived shite aplenty," said Tribe. He was standing beside the garden bed with Clay and Mulligan. "This has been a ghastly experience, but I'm sure the Second World War must have seemed like the end of everything to people like Nonna, and everybody else who lived through it."

"Second World War?" Clay looked confused.

Tribe blinked. "You've never heard of World War Two?"

James peered at Clay. What a weird dude.

"I remember a war." Anguish in Clay's shaking voice. "A terrible conflict that blotted a landscape much like this one. Farms littered with the dead. A long, long time ago. But I...I can't seem to remember what it was about." His white eyebrows twitched.

Mulligan frowned. "I always thought we take ourselves way, way too seriously. Right? Like we're so much smarter than people used to be, back in the day. When you think about it, though, if you got sent back in time, what could you really teach them?"

"Shit!" Mike smiled. "I'd teach them to make a Wii. Make a friggin' fortune, yo!"

"You couldn't do that!" Mulligan scoffed. "You don't know shit about how a Wii system works. How could you teach somebody how to make one?

"Me, I'm a computer geek, okay, so I could build one without too much trouble. *If* I had the components. If. But let's say I got sent back, like three hundred years. I couldn't do shit back then. Sure, I could use a quill or whatever and draw out the circuit boards and all that crap, but what good would it do? I'd be fuckin' dead in that world."

James leaned down and picked up a lump of black loam Gord had just shoveled on. Still warm, a living relic of the teeming community beneath Nonna's compost heap. Centuries of lore.

"That is the meaning of time, Mr. Chan," said Clay. "The past informs the future, not the other way around. Simplicity is always the truest teacher."

*

Just as the sky had predicted, the next day poured with rain. Everybody piled into Nonna's house, a big living room where they

300

could all stretch out on the floor. Amy said her Nonno had built the house with huge rooms to accommodate the big family gatherings he knew would happen one day.

Gloomy enough that they lit candles. Flipped through old magazines, played poker and chess.

Nonna's walls were covered with baby and school portraits of Amy and her many cousins. The odd experience of tracking Amy's development from bewildered infant to pink-frocked little girl in pigtails, face scrunched up smiling. Then, huge adult teeth protruding through early adolescence.

"Here's the Amy we all know and love!" Lilac laughed, pointing to a photo of her as a surly teen. Nonna laughed too.

"No, no," said Massimo. "This is the one you gotta see." A group shot of her in a wedding party. Sporting a fuscia bridesmaid's dress that looked like something out of a Disney fantasy.

"Ah Jesus, you look like you want to kill somebody!" Sheilagh giggled.

"Ugh," Amy shook. "My cousin Grace's wedding. I hated every minute of it."

Mike was grumbling about the rain.

"Eh!" Nonna protested. "You no likea the rain, huh, but you likea the food! Whatsa matter with you?"

"Sorry, Nonna," said Mike sheepishly.

She settled back in her chair, still lancing him with a disapproving look.

Before long they were bored, so Lilac suggested an activity. Mind calisthenics, she called it. "Everybody provides a metaphor or simile for the sound of rain."

"Christ," Gord muttered.

"I'll go first," she continued. "Tearing stitches. The heated pull of torn stitches, a black silken teddy torn in a boudoir."

"Does it have to be so elaborate?" Rohini asked. She seemed glum, slumped on the sofa sketching in a notebook. James peeked over her shoulder at drawings that looked like Edward Gory crossed with Salvador Dali. Lilac told her to just listen to the sounds coming through the open windows and use her imagination. "A snickering bird," Rohini said tersely.

"Rocks rattling in a jar," said Mike.

"Good, Mike! Next?"

"A squawking woman who won't shut up," Gord mumbled.

"Hey, watch it!" Amy growled.

"I don't see you offering any friggin' poetry!"

"Okay." Amy paused, listening intently. "Shit, I don't know! It sounds like rain, what else?"

They all laughed, even Gord.

"Tenuous," said Tribe. "Water trickling down a throat too weak to swallow." He was on the sofa, his long legs stretched out over the carpet, Sheilagh tucked in close beside him, holding his hand.

"The pattering feet of mice," said Athol.

"A laughing child," James suggested. That got some strange looks. He shrugged. "It's what I hear."

"Meat in a deep fryer," said Ross.

Mike groaned. "Stop it, dog! You're making me hungry!"

"Wind blowing through the trees," said Sheilagh.

After a pause, Lilac smiled. "It really does! I never heard it that way before."

"Aren't trees clever, Mike?" Sheilagh added. "Using the wind to call for the rain that keeps them green."

Nonna got up and hobbled into her kitchen. James heard her poking through a cupboard and she returned with a clear plastic bag of what looked like pot, handing it to Rohini. "This, it will make you feel better." Then, in response to Rohini's dumb stare. "The raspberry leaf, *ci*? You makea the tea, for the cramps."

Rohini looked embarrassed, but thanked the old woman.

"Not the diarrhea still!" said Tribe.

Now she looked even more embarrassed. "No, Tribe. Another type of cramps."

"Oh. I see."

"Nonna's right," said Sheilagh. "Tea made with leaves of the *Rubus* genus are a well-known folk remedy for menstrual cramps."

"Okay," Rohini huffed, "can we stop discussing it now?"

"Giving Nonna your scientific blessing, there Sheilagh?" James teased.

She seemed put out. "I am a trained botanist," she sniffed.

Graham laughed at her. "And you with them books and all!"

"Graham, y'can't expect me to know everything now, can ye? I'm into trees. All these bloody North American herbs, and their medicinal uses, they're doin' my head in!"

"Then why'd you come over here?" James asked, still snickering.

"More trees than back home. Why'd'you think?"

Nonna came back from the kitchen again, toting another plastic bag full of dried leaves. "The linden tea," she said. "Good for the upset stomach."

Both Graham and James gave Sheilagh an expectant, saucy look.

"The linden," she pronounced, fighting a smile. "Otherwise

known as basswood. *Tilia americana.* And yes, tea made from the flowers and leaves is supposedly a good digestive aid."

Nonna found this very amusing. She gave her high-pitched cackle, gesturing at Sheilagh and rattling off something in Italian. Even before Amy translated, James could tell it was a direct challenge.

Amy smiled. "She says there's an old saying: 'The blind man is a sage to one who is also deaf-mute.'"

"I guess that fella'd have some trouble playing Lilac's wee game," said Graham, winking at Sheilagh.

*

When the weather was fine they kept busy. James helped Gord dig a latrine in a secluded spot next to the garden shed. Sweaty work, but satisfyingly real. "We're the outsiders now," said Gord. "Gotta earn our keep."

They used Amy's grandfather's old hand tools and scrap lumber to build an outhouse. Gord sawed a hole in a plank, bolted on a toilet seat from an inside bathroom, and they had a rudimentary toilet. Now Giuseppe wouldn't have to haul buckets of water inside to flush.

Amy, Tribe and Ross labored at breaking a wide patch of turf adjacent to the existing vegetable garden. Amy's idea was to give Nonna and Giuseppe a hand up for the next growing season.

Gord found an old-fashioned reel mower in the shed, coated in dust. He spent several days sanding away rust, oiling the moving parts, filing the blades back to sharpness. He and Ross took turns mowing a patch a day, until all three acres were as neat as a golf green.

Tribe used the same file to sharpen the aluminum knitting needles he'd taken from the yarn shop. Using them like daggers, Sheilagh, Graham and Massimo were drilled until they were as sweat-soaked as Mike.

Then Tribe demanded more. "All the energy of the strike comes from the core portion of the body, thighs to sternum. What the Japanese call the *hara.* By far the strongest muscles in the human body. Your hand only directs the weapon – your legs provide the force that will send it through your opponent. Again please!" His students groaned.

James enjoyed sitting in the muggy afternoons, watching Tribe demonstrate leaping, turning, retreating footwork, the whipping rapier flashing beneath the white August sky.

The way Tribe and Sheilagh moved together in an enclosed

dance, Tribe standing behind her, gripping her hips, smoothly guiding her through a thrust. Lilac wagged her eyebrows, giving James a saucy look. "I think those two have the hots for each other!" She giggled impishly. "Hey Tribe! Can you dehumanize me too?"

Tribe pranced across the grass to fetch his water bottle, wiping sweat from his eyes. "People keep saying that violence is inhuman. It's as much a part of us as walking on two legs or building telescopes." He took a long drink.

Lilac rolled in the grass and laughed, patting Hood. "Tribe, you're too much!"

James wandered down the yard, reveling in the scent of freshly mown grass, the ash trees creaking in the breeze. He sat by a tree and picked a few blackberries. There was an insect on the plant, a malformed creature with stunted wings. Milky pale. Something from a dank, lightless hole. The poor thing mutilated by pollutants, probably, its wings no more than useless stumps.

He put his head back against the tree, losing himself in the resonant cicada song that plunged its tone deep into his mind. Deeper even than Maggie's voice, the pull of the Stone.

When he glanced down at the deformed insect again, he noticed that it had changed. The stubs flexing, stretching into iridescent wings. Wonders of delicacy traced with fine silver veins. He could see the body hardening, enameled green and rose, a knight girding for battle.

Flushed with amazement, James realized it wasn't a pathetic mutant after all. He was observing a cicada freshly emerged from its chrysalis, the final stage of its imminent splendor. It patiently grappled a blackberry leaf with its brand new legs. Utterly vulnerable, unable to fly or even crawl very quickly. After about half an hour it was ready. Its wings now longer than its body, lustrous capes full of strength and light. The transformation was so dramatic it didn't seem real. A droplet of the divine. The cicada took flight, suddenly flicking away to join its singing cousins in the treetops.

James reflected: how did it know to use its wings if they were new? Why did it not have to learn?

Sakh, Maggie whispered to him.

"*Sakh*", he said. The ancient Egyptian verb meaning to transfigure, to become a heavenly spirit.

*

Lilac told them her tale as she knit. Having yarn wound around her fingers, looping it over the needles, seemed to free her tongue.

"I don't get it," said Ross when she was finished. "What were those gobbling voices you talked about?"

"It was so quiet, because all the motors had just died, right? I was downtown, surrounded by thousands of people, so suddenly I could hear all of them talking to each other. Like thousands of gobbling chickens." She shuddered.

Her silver needles sped on, scissoring, looping. As if mesmerized, Lilac delved deeper, just as James had done. Told them about her parents dying when she was just two and a half. Spending the rest of her childhood in one foster home after another. At nine, being sent to live with a family who owned a factory farm.

James took her tone to be stiff, formal, direct.

Until Mike whispered in his ear. "She's terrified, yo." His voice wondering why.

Yes, James realized. For some reason, stiff with fear.

"Modern farms, they're nothing like most people think. That movie, about the baby pig."

"*Babe*," said James. It was Jenny's favorite flick.

"Right. *Babe*. That's a bunch of bullshit, okay? You can't understand until you've heard what ten thousand chickens sound like, all together in one pen. It's a terrible, famished sound. Like – like mass panic. Each chicken is stupid, but collectively, they know the slaughterhouse is their destiny, and they're crying for release." Lilac was shaking. "When I heard all those *human* voices, all around me, sounding *just the same*, instantly I was back in that barn, I was one of those ten thousand birds. Doomed." Silence for a time, just the crackle of the fire and Lilac's clicking needles. "What a bizarre night."

Perhaps sensing Lilac's tale was through, Albert started to play, joined by Giuseppe on accordion. Tremulous, pensive music. Everybody chatted and sipped wine, or just stared into the fire.

Lilac started singing along with Albert's playing. Unselfconsciously, eyes closed, in a sweet warbling voice. Unsure at first, too soft to hit the notes in their sweet spots, but with growing confidence, more breath. She sang 'Going Away for to Leave You'. Slowly, down-tempo.

Full of pale longing. Two verses in, she lost the plot. The lyrics broke down and she laughed. They all applauded. Lilac blushed, waving them off.

Her vulnerability braided with the brazen fiddle strings filled James with exquisite sadness. Feeling that somehow he knew a smidgen, a flash of what it was like for that cicada to transmogrify.

To lament the loss of what it had been.

Then Albert struck up a wildly up-tempo number, a tune for clapping and dancing. Giuseppe put down his instrument and took Nonna's hand. They trotted together smoothly across the grass, incredibly lithe and supple. Nonna had left her cane behind. The music infusing her with vitality.

Most of them were on their feet jumping and swaying around the fire pit, whooping and cheering. Ross did his best to show Rohini some slick ballroom moves. Mulligan boomed a beat on a watering can, driving them, filling them with joyous heat.

Giuseppe sat back down and took up the charge on the accordion. Faster, faster, music translated into the frenetic eloquence of whirling, leaping bodies. Finally, the rhythm broke and they all cheered and hooted, flopping back to the ground with panting smiles.

"Albert, you're amazing, you really are!" Lilac's face glowed with perspiration.

Albert grinned. "Not bad, not bad. My fingers, too thick for playing good!"

Playing at being surreptitious, Graham darted forward, threw his hat down at Albert and Giuseppe's feet, and flung a few coins into it.

Everybody clapped and laughed. Even Giuseppe managed to crack a faint smile.

*

Later, James blamed the wine. He'd just finished saying something about Maggie. Only instead of calling her Maggie, he'd used Donnie's pet name for her. Mandy.

"Wait a minute, hold on," Amy interrupted. "Your mother was Amanda Muir!"

Hearing that familiar wonder in her voice, James's face fell into hands. "Oh, Christ."

"Come on!" Lilac squealed. "Amanda Muir! I didn't even know she had any kids!"

"Neither did I," James muttered.

"James – she was my goddamned *hero* in university!" Amy was breathless. "I mean – I mean, her poetry, what can I say about it..."

"That it's derivative shit?" James exclaimed.

"James!" Now Amy looked angry. "Your mother – she helped create my identity as a woman, as a dyke."

"He's just full of sour grapes." Lilac smiled scornfully.

"Mommy's career took off, but his own never got off the ground."

James shook his head. Was she just teasing? He bit his tongue.

"I mean, Heart's Tongue—" Amy stammered.

"Omigosh, Amy! Heart's Tongue – it's like, there's more in that poem about me than any other piece of writing I've ever read!"

Amy laughed. "Hands off, bitch, cause it's all mine! '*Silent blade in rusty nighttime, slathering you in moontide blood.*'"

As Amy basked in memories engorged with the promise of forbidden Sapphic loving, James scowled at the image of Maggie setting her own hair on fire.

"So you must have witnessed her at work!" said Lilac.

"Amanda Muir?" said Tribe. "Sorry, but I've never heard of her."

"Almost nobody has," James said pointedly, glaring at Amy and Lilac.

"Yet another literary icon nobody knows about," said Ross.

"Exactly," said James.

"Lilac's right," Amy snickered. "You're just jealous."

James surrendered to the heat in his chest. "Every once in a while I run into some disaffected woman—"

"Hey now!"

"Some disaffected woman," James pushed on over Amy, "who took a few women's studies courses in university and had a vicarious love affair with Amanda Muir. *The Great.* I'll tell you something, I did see her at work. I watched her debase herself in ways that should make 'feminists' like you puke."

Amy snorted. "You don't know what you're talking about!"

"She was my fucking mother!" James roared at her.

"James—" Athol muttered, trying to warn him off.

"My childhood wasn't some comfy university tutorial." So angry now that flecks of spittle flew from his mouth. "While she was fucking around with her poetry, I was doing my homework by candlelight because she forgot to pay the hydro bill."

Up he jumped and stomped off into the darkness, away from their petty hero worship. Deepening dusk, when shadows precipitate from the trees. He smelled cigarette smoke, the mordant odor of scorched butts in an overflowing ashtray – and he knew what it was. So he closed his eyes.

*

When he opens them again, Maggie is splashed on the living room floor. So drunk and/or stoned she can hardly even sit up.

Maggie rolls over and topples the taper candle she's stupidly

*got going in a saucer. The candle falls against her hair and
suddenly it's alight and James pounces on her, ripping off his shirt
to smother the flames.*

*"Jamie!" she slurs, flailing him with her arms. "What the
hell're you doing?"*

*"Nothing," he says, just as he did on that night, almost two
years before his final showdown with Donnie. Wrinkling his nose at
the odor of burnt hair that she's too obliterated to even notice.*

*"Jamie, now that you're here – I'm glad you're here, cause –
cause I just finished this, and I want you to hear it, Jamie." She
fumbles with some papers. "Ah, here it is. It's called Heart's
Tongue." She clears her throat, blearily examining the sheet.
"Okay, here goes. Ready?"*

"Just read it!"

*"Alright, alright! Jesus, Jamie, what's up your bum? Shut up
and listen!" Her reading flounces, totally wrecking the meter:*

*Ocean's depth in which your seed was sprout
　I am
Silent blade in rusty nighttime
　slathering you in moontide blood
　I cut
Vomit a warm poultice
Your cold poultry flesh
　I devour
And you ask will my virus
　heal you
My murderer, my beloved
Plastering a honeyed wound
So that only you can know it
　I breathe.*

She grins crookedly. "Well, what d'you think?"

"It's total shit," he tells her with abrupt teenage disdain.

*She seizes the heaping glass ashtray and flings it at him.
Scarily accurate despite her inebriation, it strikes him in the
forehead, raising a stinging welt.*

*Now James does what he hadn't done in real life. This is my
chance, he thinks suddenly. I won't let this thing cow me!*

*In life he'd run sobbing to his room, his eyes clotted with filthy
cigarette ash. Instead, he vents his disgusted rage. He kicks her as
hard as he can in the stomach. Seeking to bruise the womb that held
him.*

"Fuck you!" he roars.

*The thing that calls itself Maggie glowers up at him, grinning
evilly. "That's not allowed!" it sings.*

"These are my memories!" James howls. "I'll tell you what's allowed!"

The thing in Maggie's skin seems amused.

"Tell me why was I chosen! Why me?"

Maggie laughs, snoring into her bent wrist. "Oh sweetie," she giggles. "Sweetie, sweetie! You weren't chosen, not at all! Maggie was the one. All along! The alembic in which your seed was sprout!"

James slumps on the stairs. "It's so unfair, that I have to relive all these awful memories."

"How do you think Maggie felt? Used as a vessel?"

"She knew?"

"How could she not?" Sighing, Maggie flings herself back on the floor, arms over her head. Her robe falls open, revealing one of her breasts.

Again, this thing shocks James: just exactly what Maggie would have done. Right down to her finger idly winding through her chestnut curls!

"What are you?" The first time he asks this vital question without a note of panic. "What are you really?"

"Just get on with finding the Stone!"

"I'll take all the time I want!"

*Maggie peers at him, giggling. "Will you? You're not paying attention to how short the days are getting. In six days it'll be September, Jamie. Before too long, you'll have all the time you want to freeze to death! You and your little friends. Goddammit, you've squandered enough time! Concentrate on surviving the quest. Then you'll find out what I am! I'll show you **everything!**"*

*

"James?" Lilac's voice.

He was still standing, one hand braced against an aspen, the leaves above rattling like glass beads. Branches intricate black against the glowing dusk.

"Over here," he called.

Footsteps rustled through the underbrush and Lilac materialized as a pale blue flame. "I heard you shouting. You alright?"

"I'm fine."

"Jesus, James, we were only teasing."

"Even before all this, I hated it when people realized I'm the son of that icon. You know what I mean?"

"She was no icon to you. I get that. Look at it this way:

something good did come out of all that drinking and partying and debasement. Your mother's poetry, it helped save my life. I guess Amy feels the same. It's not all bullshit, James."

He nodded. "Sorry for being a dick."

They stood quietly for a long while, watching the black branches and fluttering leaves paint the sky darker. A warm night. James had just spotted the first star when Lilac took his hand.

"Listen," she said. "I've been wondering how to broach the subject, but I've been dying for a screw—"

James kissed her and she kissed him back, hard enough that their teeth clinked and they laughed, struggling with each other's clothes, James pushing her against the aspen, relishing his hands squeezing her breasts, her hands yanking his belt open, clawing his ass. He buried his face in her neck, licking and chewing her skin that tasted of salt and earth.

Fighting to be naked, pressing their bodies together, sharing the excited flush. James, not used to her smallness. Stacy was tall enough that they could fuck standing up. Lilac's head barely reached his collarbone. As she stroked his penis, he had to hunch his shoulders to reach her clitoris. It was uncomfortable, so he knelt to her.

"Harder," she moaned, rocking her hips against his face. "Harder…"

They lay on the ground and she straddled him, hands on his sternum, every rock of her hips flavoring his belly, his thighs with sweetness, pulling it, sucking it, up and up until his pelvis quivered, his legs shaking beneath her.

"Fuck yeah!" she squealed as he bucked and rammed, feeling himself rush into her.

She lay her head on his chest. They dozed. A whining mosquito woke James. He was covered in fresh bites.

Lilac rose on her elbows, a smiling appraisal of James's face. "How you doin'?" she said, hamming it up. Perhaps imitating Massimo.

"Embarrassed. That was a piss-poor performance."

She got off him, grinning. "You're not expected to be Adonis for a screw in the soil. Extra points for going down, though, Jimmy. You're good at that – it was super creamy double-fudge dee-lish!" Then she squirmed, covering her eyes with her hands. "Oh gawd, I should be apologizing to *you* – my vag must be perfectly vile!"

James sat up looking for his clothes. She brushed the dead leaves off his back, sending delicious tingles over his skin. "Tell me the truth," he said. "The only reason you fucked me was so you could say you laid Amanda Muir's son."

She smacked him playfully. "Don't be a jerk."

He pulled on his shirt, lay back down beside her, cupping one of her breasts in his hand. Smaller than Stacy's, plumper. Her nipple erect against his palm. Waxing moonlight through the trembling leaves, flickering lace on her skin. Sheilagh was right. They did sound just like rain.

"I wanted to tell you," she said drowsily. "I really admire the way you opened up, telling us everything."

"You did the same tonight. You and I have a lot in common."

"How do you mean?"

"You're an orphan, I've got no idea who my father was. I've always thought of myself as a functional orphan. After that fight with Donnie, I left. Alone. Headed for the Big Smoke. Jesus, it's hard to believe I was only Mike's age."

"Why would such a brilliant woman choose to be with men like that?" Lilac sounded truly disturbed.

"Power," said James immediately. "She knew she was brighter, so she could hold the leash. Though, sometimes the dog bit back."

"Tell me the truth. Were you really writing a book with a character named Lilac?"

"She was the *main* character."

Lilac shivered. "It's just so unbelievable."

"Crazy to think, all the work I put into that project – *years* – is gone."

"Just a bunch of ones and zeroes," she sighed.

"Too much had been reduced to that – to nothing." He smirked. "Here's one for you – everything was *binarized*."

"Very good, very good."

"What's the matter?"

"*Seriously?*"

"Other than the fact that we're struggling to stay alive amid the collapse of civilization," he added facetiously.

"Oh! Other than that, everything's peachy."

"Tell me."

"Shit, James, it's not just the *collapse of civilization*—" She said it in a mock news anchor voice. "Some of the shit that's happened, especially to you – it's just mind blowing."

James nodded, encouraging her.

"And the fact that your novel's main character was named Lilac. Jesus, I just don't know what to think about that. I really don't."

"Then try not to think about it."

"Right! That shouldn't be too hard!" They zoned out for a few minutes, both of them lying quietly. "Do you think all of this was – you know, *meant* to be?"

He gave it careful thought before answering. "Yes," he said, feeling the weight of the word. "I do. *Meant to be* – I mean, the phrase had been cheapened, you know? TV, Hollywood. It's been made into an adolescent fantasy. So I resisted believing it. It seems ridiculous, to think of *us* at the center of some grand scheme."

"Who put the scheme together?"

"Or, *what* did." Another long pause. "Think about it this way: you know, frost forms on a window in regular shapes and patterns, right? But that doesn't mean that some intelligence created the pattern. D'you see what I mean?"

"You mean that some things just are."

"I guess. I don't know, Lilac. It's like we're the subject of some vast experiment." He didn't verbalize his next thought: that nobody remembers the rats that die in the lab to grease the wheel of progress. "As Sheilagh would say, it's doing my head in."

She smiled faintly. "That has got to be the worst imitation of an Irish accent I've ever heard."

He smiled back. "If she was here, she'd thump me for sure. You remember that woman, the one who said that coincidences are God's way of talking to us?"

"Yeah. Mrs. Gritter."

"Mrs. Gritzner. I asked her once when I was a kid, why aren't there any miracles any more, like you read about in the Bible."

"What did she say?"

"She said that miracles do still happen, but they happen in their own way, in their own time. That if you look for them, you'll never find them. She said it's like trying to see your own reflection when you turn your head away from the mirror."

"Okay."

"Well, I think what's happening is, something's shifted, so that there are more mirrors around us now. More opportunities to glimpse things that were always there. It's just that we couldn't perceive them before."

"Through the looking glass."

The wind had died and it was very quiet in the grove. The brooding calm of old trees. It felt very good to hold her, to be held.

"Maybe," said James. "Shit, Tribe was right about irony. You can't say anything about spirituality anymore without sounding trite. I mean, what does that say about us?" He withdrew from her. Sat up again, groping for his pants.

"Hey, what's your rush?" She stroked his back. "Let's go again."

"I feel a little guilty."

"What for? Cheating on your wife?" She guffawed, irritating him. "Come on, J, in the middle of this shit? I don't think anybody'd begrudge a little hanky-panky. Gawd! Lighten up!"

"I happen to believe that oaths are important. I just broke one I made to the woman who's my soul mate. It's not something I'm exactly proud of."

"That's sweet. In a kind of self-righteous – I don't know, post-Christian way."

"Jesus, Lilac – a promise is a promise!"

"Okay, now you sound like a kindergarten kid. Believe me, I know what I'm talking about. And how about a little *anal* to boot?"

"So that means being true to your word is – is *puerile*? You're really starting to piss me off."

Lilac pinched his side. When he turned around, she squeezed his face in her hands. "Stop thinking so much!"

"Thanks for the good time," he snickered, taking her hands.

She snorted. "I can honestly say I've never spent the post-coital moment engaged in a debate about the honor of an oath. Well done!"

"Next time it'll be a lecture on themes of morality in the works of Joseph Conrad."

Lilac peered up at him with a saucy smile. "Who says there'll be a next time, rock star? What happened to your almighty guilt complex?"

"You convinced me – you're right. Besides, didn't you just offer me some *anal* action?"

For a second she didn't get the barb, but then she squealed and reached for his penis. "You've got a way, J., you really do!"

*

James and Lilac went back to the fire. Nonna, Giuseppe, Mary and Albert had gone to bed. The rest of them clung on, as if unwilling to let this day go.

The moon went down and the temperature dropped. The fire died low. The sky blazed with colorful stars, scored by exotic meteor plumes. James felt himself whirling midcourse with them in the merciless cold majesty of the universe.

"Wow!" Mike breathed.

"Pretty spectacular," Lilac cooed. Honey in her voice that James wanted to lick from her lips.

"It's like being on a different planet," said Mike. "Seeing a new sky for the first time. Too bad about that cloud that's in the way."

James didn't know what Mike meant. It was a crystalline night.

"Where do you see clouds?" He heard Sheilagh lift her head, scanning.

"Right there, above us," Mike replied.

James smiled. "That's the Milky Way, Mike."

"Oh. Don't I feel like an idiot."

"Stop it," Sheilagh chided. "As you said, this is a new world for you. Growing up the city, the light pollution always blocked your view. How were you supposed to know?"

"Uh, now I'm really gonna sound stupid, but, like, what is the Milky Way?"

"You're looking at the arm of a galaxy." Wonder in Sheilagh's voice. "So many stars it looks like smoke."

Tonight it did look smoky, as if the fire had breathed it into life.

Mike laughed. "Yo, that is boss!"

"Stars played a very important role in the development of civilization," said Tribe after a time.

"Here beginneth the lesson," James muttered.

"The ancients of the very first cities used star calendars to determine when to plant their crops, when to collect taxes, when to start building projects. Kings wouldn't marry or fight or fuck unless the stars told them to."

"Come on!" Massimo scoffed.

"Every king had a private college of astrologers or astronomers – in the past, there was no difference. Even Galileo drew up horoscopes for the Medici. The Maya, the Chinese, the Indians – every culture spent a good deal of time and effort studying the cosmos."

"The Egyptians even built the Giza Pyramids so that when they were viewed from the air, they'd look like Orion's belt," James added.

"I didn't know that," said Sheilagh.

James smiled quizzically. Until this moment, he hadn't realized he'd known it either.

"And that star, Betelgeuse," said Massimo, "it's part of Orion, right?"

Of course, for the Egyptians Orion had been Osiris, first king of Egypt. Betelgeuse, the burning right shoulder of Osiris, who was murdered and dismembered by his brother Seth. Eventually avenged by Osiris's son Horus, who lost an eye in a great battle

314

with Seth, before casting him out into the desert.

James recalled what Allistair had said: Orion was a winter constellation. By December, Betelgeuse would be rising at night, bright enough to cast a shadow. Then he thought about what Maggie had said. Would any of them even be alive to see it?

"Even as we evolved," Tribe continued, "our distant ancestors roving the African savannah probably gazed up at the stars much as we're doing. For eons, whether they were starving or thriving, cold or hot, sick or well, no mater what, the stars always followed the same reliable patterns. Never changed in that entire time."

"So that means, if we were lying here, say, ten thousand years ago, we'd be seeing the same stars?" Lilac asked.

"Even a hundred thousand," said Sheilagh. "Really, it's only the past seventy-odd years that light pollution destroyed that view. Quite something to ponder – humans had three hundred thousand years of brilliant starry skies, only a few decades of bland, light-polluted rubbish."

"And that was what we thought of as the norm," Rohini added. "Until now."

"And in those seventy-odd years," said Tribe archly, "as our so-called society started spending more time staring at glowing screens instead of the heavens, what did we call the people we were gaping at?"

"Stars." James cleared his throat, as if the word had got stuck.

"Fuck me," said Graham.

"No way that's a coincidence," said Rohini.

"That's fuckin weird, that's all I gotta say," said Massimo.

*

Cool dewy mornings were the epithets for summer's dotage. Tribe and Lilac saluting the rising sun with athletic yoga, trying to outdo each other. Tribe always beat her out. His limbs were almost a foot longer that Lilac's, and he could achieve impossible poses.

Routine flowed into the whole Group's sinewy limbs: once the day's water had been drawn, garden plants plucked of bugs and caterpillars, vegetables picked and washed (at Nonna's and across the road at Albert and Mary's), laundry scrubbed, rinsed, wrung and hung to dry, pots and pans scoured, wood hauled and split and piled, ashes shoveled and spread in the gardens, the days were theirs. Deliciously idle evenings spent playing *bocce*, or lying in the grass, contemplating the clouds. Drinking the serenity just as their throats gulped the plentiful, cold water from Nonna's well.

After the feast on the first night, they ate plainly. Simple, tasty meals of pasta and beans. Knots of chewy dense bread flavored with aniseed called *chamella* that Nonna boiled then baked like bagels in the stone oven. Cheese and a little salami or *prosciutto*. Just enough to keep hunger quiet for a few hours.

Splitting wood was James's favorite task. Just as well: he, Amy, Gord, Sheilagh, Tribe, Graham and Massimo had felled and sawed by hand two whole ash trees, hoping to lay away enough wood for Nonna and Giuseppe to burn through the winter.

James knew from experience that even with the luxury of chainsaws, this work punished the muscles. Now it left his arms limp as rubber bands. Even wearing work gloves, his hands were sorely blistered.

Still and all, something immediately satisfying about using physical strength to make the splitting maul tear blocks of wood in half. Great way to work out frustration.

"Better get used to that." Gord gave James one of his level glares. Gord had the eyes of a carved Medieval icon. Chiseled holes. "I hear using wood for fuel is the latest thing."

"I'm reacquainting myself." James matched his cool tone. "When I was a kid, wood was the only heat we had. I was usually the only one around to do the splitting." He smiled to himself, remembering Uncle Randy teaching him how.

"Really," said Gord skeptically.

Gord had clearly decided James was a dilettante. Fuck him. "This stuff'll barely have enough time to cure before they have to burn it."

"It'll have to do." Gord was using some scrap planks and bicycle parts he'd found in the shed to assemble a makeshift rickshaw. It would be heavy when they loaded it with their food stock, but far more manageable over uneven, unpaved ground than the bungling shopping carts.

Seeing the rickshaw almost finished made James feel regretful. It was a sign that they must soon depart, and he didn't want to say adieu. Even the insistent draw of the Stone and Maggie's badgering were no match for the serene power of this place.

Often James and Lilac stole away for strenuous fucking sessions, growing into each other, learning to prolong the exquisite frisson before the final explosion. Lilac would slow her thrusting hips, drawing painful hissing moans from James, endearing herself to him with her impetuous open mouth and her swaying breasts. Afterwards they'd lie together on the timothy, their sweaty skins drying in the breeze.

Once as they snuck out of their little grove, they ran into Tribe and Sheilagh on their way in. All of them giggling like preteens.

The same excited tangle.

Whenever he got a chance, James wandered alone through the shallow golden dales behind Nonna's property. Wide timothy meadows splashed with white and purple asters, Queen Anne's lace and goldenrod. He'd found a mighty oak, a great fan of a tree, eighty feet high and almost as wide. He sat now at its huge foot, embraced by the wind, a riptide through the leaves. Such a perfect late summer afternoon. Clear and baroque. Yes, like the soft, hazy background of an antique painting.

Robins frolicked in the branches. Their songs and the rushing wind, the only sounds of the westering world.

Lord how he missed Stace and Jenny and Sara. The twitch of the Stone's eldritch intelligence now buried in his heart told him they were alive still. Somewhere. They did not die in the fire.

Alive, damn it, alive! Believe, he thought. Hold on to it. Send out those signals. Stacy and the girls, they'd catch them.

He still wore his wedding ring. Dulled, scratched by the rigors of this new life. Nothing could change the bond he'd forged with Stacy. Certainly, he felt *himself* changing. Shocked at how easily he was able to continue cheating on his wife.

The guilty pinch could not overcome the frightening exhilaration of being with Lilac. The quiver he got, just thinking of his hand caressing her lightly furred lower back as she curled and stretched over his pumping groin.

The plain truth was very ugly: he'd killed the Sicari soldier in the York U library. He'd shot that woman on the dump truck at the SuperCenter. Allistair's death was his fault, and he'd contributed to Sam's too. He'd hacked the Dog Man to pieces. Willful plunder and theft literally cloaked him and filled his belly.

On a scale of iniquity, sex with Lilac was a flea beside a blue whale.

Plangent robin song settled into his mind. Trills and clicks and tremulous whistles, fantastically arcane Mayan hieroglyphs rendered audible.

James took a moment to be thankful. Truly, heart-achingly thankful for survival. For the Group. For this outstanding afternoon.

"Please don't let me lead these folks into oblivion," he whispered to the guiding star that had granted him the visions, mapping their route northeast. As he watched, Betelgeuse sank beneath the horizon. Setting now hours earlier than when the lights went out in June.

*

James was with Ross, Giuseppe and Albert playing *bocce* – or, as Ross insisted on calling it, lawn bowling – when Amy approached him. She had an odd look on her face. Sheepish and little scared, as if about to break upsetting news that she knew he'd blame on her.

He decided she wanted to fell another goddamn tree. No question, that would have ruined his day.

"Nonna wants to speak to you," she said under her breath.

"What is it?"

As she led him away. When they were out of earshot of the rest, she continued. "She wants to talk to you about your ear. She calls *Il morso di cane*."

"What does that mean?"

"James, that's Italian for 'the dog bite.'"

James winced. "Geez, Amy, you shouldn't have told her that story, it'll only upset her."

Amy took his arm. "That's my point. I didn't tell her anything, James. She just knew."

James looked across the wide lawn to where Nonna sat, a tiny old woman in a folding aluminum lawn chair, caressing rosary beads as she gazed at her flowerbeds.

"My old man told me, years ago, back in Italy they used to call her *strega*, a witch. I don't know about that, but I'll tell ya something: you can't get anything by her. When I was a kid staying here, she'd know I was in trouble before I did. Know what I mean? She wants to help us. And she can – she can really help us. But listen to me, buddy."

James met Amy's no-nonsense stare. "Yeah?"

"Be honest. Don't try to deceive her. Don't hold anything back. Got it?" James nodded.

They approached her, and Nonna gestured at Amy's trousers, which were torn at the right knee. "No good!"

Amy showed her the waistband as well, which was missing the button to fasten it closed. "It's okay, Nonna, I'll scrounge up another pair."

But Nonna scowled at her, waving a hand that threatened a smack. "You no listen to what Nonna teach you! These, I fix it, no problem! Get the sewing basket."

Amy went into the house and returned wearing her second set of pants, carrying a laundry basket. In it were her torn ones and a few other pieces of clothing. There was also an old shoe box neatly lined with spools of thread. In one corner of this was a smaller wooden case full of buttons Nonna had saved over the years. She opened it, poking through the collection with a bent discerning finger, choosing the right one. Nothing precious in the button box, but still a treasure trove.

Nonna began mending Amy's pants, a calm but uncompromising expression set into the deep seams of her face. Grey hooded eyes focused on passing the needle through the fabric, pulling the thread, looping it into neat mattress stitches. She worked with precision and beautiful speed.

James and Amy sat on the grass at her feet. He told Nonna the truth. He spoke at length, leaving nothing out of his recounting. The Quest. The Voice in his mind and how it had co-opted his memories of Maggie to suit itself. The Dog Man. His fears and doubts about taking this fellowship of people into the dim unknown. Never, not once did Nonna even glance at him while he spoke. Occasionally her peaked eyebrows would rise, or furrow into a frown. Otherwise, she gave no indication she was listening at all.

When he'd finished, she sat quietly and sewed for a long time. Now patching a set of Giuseppe's faded overalls.

James had expected an immediate answer. That seemed to be Nonna's style – abrupt, quick-witted. But he was surprised at his own contentment, ready just to sit and wait, absorb the tranquility of this moment. The only sounds were Nonna's rough fingers against the fabric, the thread whispering as she yanked it tight. Amy lay back, her hands pillowing her head, staring up at the ever-changing clouds.

Nonna began speaking very quietly. A slow, relaxed cadence, as if chatting about pleasant weather. She spoke in Italian. Amy translated, keeping her face turned to the churning creamy vapor far above.

"She's more comfortable speaking in Italian," she said.

"That's fine."

"Um…okay, I've heard this story before, but to be honest I never understood what it meant."

"Okay."

"Pay attention, she says. Outside her village back home, there was an old woman who lived as a hermit in a stone hut in the mountains. The villagers believed her to be very wise, and they would go to her for advice on everything from, you know, health issues to marital problems. Even stuff like what crops to plant. So, there was this one guy, the miller he was, who went to this old woman far more than anyone else. Okay? Always complaining, whining, never happy with anything."

Amy smiled, shook her head. "Nonna says he was a self-pitying old son of a bitch. Being wise, the old woman was very patient with him, even when his bitter words chafed at her, even when his complaints began to fill her dreams. She always gave him her best advice, but nothing contented him. Year after year, this went on, and she watched the miller become older, his body bent by the strain of his own unhappiness.

"Finally, she had enough, right? I mean, this sour old bastard wasn't just ruining his own health, driving himself insane, he was filling the old woman's little stone house with, like…um, bad vibes, I guess you would call it."

"The *malocchio*, yeah I got that part," James interrupted. Amy raised her head to peer at him. "The evil eye. I'm not *that* much of an Anglo."

Nonna smiled devilishly, and gave his intact ear a pinch. "*Zitto! Ascolta!*" she demanded. Again, James got the gist.

Amy grinned. "That's what the old woman told the miller, too. Here's what she said: 'Is your cucumber rotten? Throw it out. If the path is thorny, find another way. That is enough. Do not go on and whine, 'Why were evil things ever brought into the world?' The wise will only laugh at you; just as a carpenter or shoemaker would laugh, if you found fault with the shavings and scraps from their work, which you saw in the shop. Yet they, at least, have somewhere to throw their litter; whereas Nature has none. That is the miracle of her workmanship: she's able to reabsorb into herself everything that seems worn-out or old or useless. Then she re-fashions it all into new creations. She never needs fresh supplies. For her, there is no refuse. All she requires are her own space, her own materials and her own skill.'

"Here's another way of saying it: spiders that bite, nettles that sting, illness, decay, all these things that we think of as unpleasant, they're just small parts of other things that are themselves beautiful and noble. So remember that everything comes from one divine source. All the ocean's waters are only a drop in the universe. Mountains are just tiny lumps of rock. Millions of years, just a pinpoint in eternity."

At this, Nonna brandished her needle at James. For the first time her resolute gray eyes fastened on him. Now she spoke with alert attention.

"Never forget," Amy translated, "nothing is unrelated. Everything is part of the universal whole. You need nothing that has not already been made a part of you." Nonna waggled her finger at him, squinting mischievously. It took Amy a few moments to translate the next phrase, her face flushed with an embarrassed smile. "She says you don't even need the drugs in your bag. There will be times when they make things easier, but they are not required. And she says Lilac is a nice girl, but remember: there's a very good reason why you feel guilty."

Nonna's stern, wrinkled face split then into a charmed smile and she tittered at the stunned looks on both their faces. "Not so easy to hide the secrets from Nonna, eh?" She laughed with a sharp note, both merry and devious.

James giggled uncomfortably. There was no way Nonna had any access to his pack. Not unless she'd been creeping around in the middle of the night. No, he kept it in the tent at the foot of his bag, done up tight. She couldn't have opened it without waking him.

She'd simply known about the pot. Just as she'd known about his ear.

His organs felt lighter within the sack of his body. Not altogether a happy feeling, but necessary. Somehow *true*. "*Grazie*," he said to Nonna.

She shrugged, making a face. "Eh! You ask, I tell you, that's it."

She couldn't push the needle through the thick denim seam of Giuseppe's overalls. Looking cross, Nonna picked through the shoe box, shaking her head. "Amy, I forget the thimble. Go back to the house, get it for Nonna. The drawer beside the bed."

Amy hopped to it.

Even before Nonna spoke, James got the impression she'd arranged this moment. She waited until Amy was in the house, then turned to James in a pressing whisper. "Listen, James, what I say. You must go, soon."

"Absolutely, Nonna, we've already eaten too much of your—"

"No, no, no. It is…how you say? The time, it has come, no? It is…uh…mean to be?"

"Meant to be," said James. Very quietly.

"*Ci, ci.* Now listen. Amy, she no want to go with you. She want to stay with her Nonna."

"Well, sure, of course—"

Nonna's gray eyes suddenly glowed. It was like watching storm clouds ignited by lightning. "*Stuzito!*" Then a rockslide of angry Italian. James knew she was swearing a blue streak, frustrated at his density. "James! You no listen! Amy, she no want to go, *ma*, she *must* to go with you, James! Amy, she cannot stay here with me. *Capisce?*"

"No, I don't understand – don't you want her to stay?"

"*Ma donna*," Nonna cried, and James realized precariousness of her mood. She was on the verge of hysterical tears. "No *my* choice! The time is a gonna come, you a gonna need Amy and she's a gonna need you. She must to go. I tell you this, so you can be ready, you and your friends. Okay?"

"What do you mean?" James asked weakly. "How will she

need me?"

"Eh!" she cried, giving him smack on the side of the head. "I no allowed, see everything. I only know, it is meant to be." Tears dribbled down her cheeks, following deep seams worn by a life of frugal diligence.

James felt awful. Now he was *meant* to steal this poor woman's granddaughter away from her. Her only family. In the midst of all this horror. It seemed so cruel and pointless, unnecessarily punitive. He wanted to ask Nonna more about this, try and figure out a way around it, but Amy was halfway back across the yard from the house.

Nonna wiped her eyes with a handkerchief.

When Amy saw the tears, she ran up. "Nonna, what's wrong?"

James saw Nonna's struggle, the fight in her to force a smile. And he thought he witnessed just a narrow measure of the burden that was her gift.

She took Amy's face in her arthritic hands, pulled her down to kiss both her cheeks. "*La bella mia*," she burbled.

*

A lugubrious feeling suffused the Group. The next day they would be leaving this wonderful place. There was little banter after dinner. Albert and Mary stayed home, so there was no music. They missed it sorely.

James went and sat beside Amy. He needed to speak to her about what Nonna had told him. "Amy, I don't want—"

Amy flashed him a palm, cutting off his words. "Don't. Just keep it to yourself. Nonna already explained it to me. It's not your fault, not even your responsibility, blah, blah, blah. I get it." She went to get up, but whirled to face him again. Her wide, frank face jutted into his comfort zone. "That fuckin' Stone thing better be worth it, James." Then, a parting shot at Massimo: "Lucky, huh? Kiss my ass!"

With that she stomped off through the aspen grove.

James watched his old friend frown, suck his teeth. It dawned on him that Massimo was having a very hard time. For him, the food and wine, the language, all of it must be reminding him of what he so sorely missed.

In this solemn atmosphere, Graham told his tale.

"Unlike Sheilagh, I came over here not of my own volition, but because me mother had decided I'd already made enough of a name for myself in my hometown as a drunken knob. Town of Ballymoney, Northern Ireland, population 9,000. She thought maybe a spell away'd be enough to dry me out. Then, see, me mate Doxie came over too. Couldn't avoid the lure of the North American consumption zone – consumption of nuclear proportions, aye?"

"Oh, yeah," said James.

"Fuckin' alcoholic dream state, isn't it? Vast gluttony. And cheap booze to boot. Far cheaper'n home." Graham took a deep breath, shaking his head. "Sorry, guys, sorry. Don't mean to be maudlin, like – I just feel this sudden…desire, right, to get all this shit off my chest."

"No sweat, Graham, no problem."

He told them everything, leading up to that day in the ruined warehouse. "My name is Graham McMann," he pronounced. "And I am an alcoholic." He blinked wondrously. "Never been able to say that before now, not so easily."

"First step," James said quietly.

"Oh aye. Square fuckin' one, so it is."

The chatter died low. Everybody disturbed by Graham's cryptic admission, James thought, taking a long drink of water. He'd done something horrible.

"Tell us about the girl on the subway," said Lilac. "What did you do to her?" Peering at Graham through the watery heat above the fire pit, challenging him.

Gord had just thrown some sticks on the fire. As they flared, James saw Graham's face, and got ready to jump between him and Lilac. Graham grinning murderously, leering eyes brassy hot. James was sure he'd attack Lilac for her impudence. She didn't flinch, though. Kept her attention fused to his, deadly serious.

"I don't want to talk about that," said Graham stiffly. A catch in his voice that transmuted James's fear into pity. Graham's rage wasn't directed at Lilac, but at himself.

"You don't have to tell us," said Clay around his pipe. "But you would bless us with it."

Graham bit his lip. "Ah, believe me, Clay, when I tell you it's no blessing." He gripped his own face, hands wedged in tight under his cheekbones.

"C'mon, fucktard!" Mulligan snapped. "All this *sharing* was your idea!"

There was a long tense wait. "I puked on her," he finally said, strangled by grief. Now he looked terrified, haunted by what he saw peering back at himself. "Oh, Christ!"

"Why?" Rohini asked, very softly. No accusation there, just gentle inquisition. "Why did you do that?"

"Ach, I don't know!" he shouted. For a moment he only

breathed, fighting against sobs. "No," he quavered. "No, that's a fuckin' lie. I know. To show her a fuckin' lesson."

"What kind of lesson?" Ross sounded disgusted.

"For being alive. Vicious, drunken, cruel *cunt* that I am! *Here's how the world really is, little girl! Here's your christening, here's your inauguration!* I knew I was gonna puke. I could have turned away, yakked on the floor, but I *chose* to do it to her. I saw them huge blue eyes staring up at me and they were targets and I actually shifted around to improve my fuckin; aim! Oh…oh Jesus! What am I like?" Shaking with the sobbing.

For a long while, nobody spoke.

Then, Clay's voice, so sharp and yet so calm. "You were wrong, Mr. McMann. You have provided an enormous blessing."

"How's that?" Graham croaked, sniffing.

"You have set the highest standard for honesty and candor I have yet seen."

Tribe jostled him. "I admire your bravery, Graham."

"Bravery! What a joke that is!"

"Listen, buddy," said Gord. "We've all done stuff we wish we hadn't done."

"I just think of that little girl," Graham quailed, looking up at the stars. "I think of her having to live the rest of her life with it, burdened with that weight. It's not right, it's just not right."

"Forgive yourself," said Athol. "That's the *real* first step."

"Graham?" Lilac waited until she had his full attention. "I need to tell you that you are not a cunt."

James had to suppress a giggle. Lilac was being so earnest, as if Graham had put all his heart and soul into his dream, and she was breaking the news that he'd never make it.

As Graham wiped his tears, James saw his mouth twist, fighting a smile. James was relieved, glad he wasn't the only one tempted by jocularity.

"Jesus Christ," said Mulligan. "Bit anticlimactic, I have to say. I thought you were gonna tell us you're some kinda pedophile freak."

There was a general release of tension around the fire. Like cool fresh air sweeping a stagnant room.

"D'you really think not?" Graham asked Lilac, playing along now.

Lilac grinned. "The fact that you feel so awful about it proves you're not. I mean, doesn't it?" Lilac gestured to the others for support.

"A trifle self-pitying, perhaps." Sheilagh winked at him.

"You need to move backwards a few inches," Mulligan

commented.

"How's that?" Graham asked.

Mulligan could no longer hide his smirk. "You're more of an asshole."

Ross laughed until painful gasps wracked his lungs.

"Nice," said Graham. But he was laughing too. They all were by now.

"Haven't you just done one of the twelve steps?" James asked after a bit.

"Aye, I have and all. Step 5: admitting to God and another human being the exact nature of your wrongs. I only wish I could go about making amends."

"Hey!" said Massimo bombastically. "You almost broke my nose a few weeks back. How 'bout makin' amends to me?"

Graham got to his feet, walked around the fire and gave Massimo a bear hug. Everybody clapped.

"I love you buddy," said Graham. Playing along with the frivolity, but James could see in his hunched shoulders that his admission had left him drained.

Cold was drawing ever closer, tasting their backs while the fire washed their faces and knees with heat. A cringing effort to pull back into the frigid dark to burrow fully clothed into clammy sleeping bags.

*

Morning dawned frosty. They were all up early, antsy to be away. The tents were left to dry in the sun. Gord's rickshaw was packed. A hearty breakfast of toasted bread, salami, cheese and a few eggs.

Then they were presented with parting gifts. Nonna had refashioned a pair of Giuseppe's overalls into a saddle bag so that Hood could carry some weight. Albert and Mary presented a laying chicken in a small pen, and a bag of chicken feed.

Amy strapped an old pair of her skis and poles to the outside of her pack. "Not too long now before these'll come in handy."

They lined up, taking turns to say goodbye to Nonna. "You remember what I tell you," she said soberly to James. "Soon, you gonna understand."

James didn't know what she meant, but left it at that.

Watching Amy say farewell to Nonna broke James's heart. He had to turn away. By noon they were on the road, receding footstep by footstep from a *strega* with her teary face buried in a handkerchief. Even from a hill two miles away, Amy could not stop herself from looking back through her binoculars, just barely able to see the tiny pale flutter of Nonna's waving bandanna.

Chapter 17

Pursuit

Days before the attack, James sensed the presence of furtive stalkers. Catching up with the Group. The swiftness of the Sicari. Even in broad daylight, clouded gloom seemed to loom. Maggie was eerily silent, but he became certain some malfeasance was at work upon his sluggish legs as they endlessly repeated the mute mantra of gritty footsteps. A marching cadence that levered into his mind like the most insistent of earworms.

A stiff Gordian knot in the cellar of his abdomen, tightened by the echo of Maggie's prophesy: *five shall not survive!*

It had been more that two weeks since they'd left Nonna's. Close now. So close to the end of the Quest. Despite its silence, the Stone plastered James with fleshy longing. Desperate urgency. The spot on the map he'd identified at the SuperCenter, no more than a hundred miles away. Perhaps another week of marching. His serves sang with anticipation. But the note was discordant, flat.

Amy reached into the chicken pen that morning and retrieved a guano-coated egg, pathetically small. "Whose turn is it?" she asked, cradling it.

"Mr. Clinker," said Clay.

Ross chose to boil it. Jealously, they watched very carefully as he cracked and peeled the shell. When he popped the entire thing in his mouth, he chewed slowly with his eyes closed.

Easy to see that this bird had lain her final egg. The last of the feed Albert gave them had gone into the cage yesterday.

The two lane highway rose and fell through rolling meadowlands thick with bush lots, acres rich with ripening timothy and wild rye. Hills rising towards the densely wooded highlands of the Group's eventual destination.

Tribe edged up to James. "What's the matter? Why do you keep looking back?"

James didn't want to deal with Tribe's agitation, so he said nothing. He hadn't yet convinced himself that his fears were anything more than twisted fancies born of exposure in these vast open spaces.

Broad daylight, indeed. How truly broad it seemed now, overwhelming his senses. The hazy horizon flung more than a day's march away. As if scenting the same jeopardy as James, Clay had kept up a grinding pace all through a hot, dusty afternoon. Thousands of steps, inching it seemed, feet punished by the stern upstroke of hot pavement. One-two, one-two, one-two…

"I long for a gas pedal," James muttered, half to himself.

"Oh yeah," Lilac moaned. "Just to get there."

Graham sniggered. "You lazy fuckin' North Americans!"

Early evening. The map told them there was a nature preserve nearby, so they left the road and followed a parched trail into a cool beech wood. The path led to a green pool, perhaps an acre in size, which was the reservoir behind a small earthen dam across a tinkling creek.

Everyone refilled their canteens, engorged themselves with water. Schools of tiny minnows flitted in and out of tree shadows as frogs hurled themselves through the bulrushes. All but Tribe and Clay stripped down to their underwear and lunged into the pond, which was surprisingly warm. For a while, the forest was filled with the gasping breath, the kicking splashes of bathing. James waded near the side, only his head above the water.

"Tribe!" Lilac called. "Come on in!"

Tribe smiled so faintly it was hardly visible through his beard. "Thank-you, no."

"Aw, Tribe!" Rohini teased. "The water's lovely."

"Yes, I'm sure it is."

"He can't swim," said Sheilagh. "He's too ashamed to admit it."

"It's the sword," said Athol devilishly. "It'll drag him down."

Suddenly a man on horseback charged out of the bush. Clay whipped out his pistols, but the man whistled, spurring his horse into a swift gallop that plunged him back into the trees. Come and gone so quickly, only a few of them even saw. The briefest glimpse of laden saddlebags, a rifle strapped on, a burly man in a brown Stetson. As they listened to the receding hoof falls, James reflected on how fortunate they'd been that the stranger didn't have any malign intent.

They got out of the water and started the camp setup protocol, each person working automatically at his or her task. Amy trailer-hitching a rope between two poplars. They hung their sweaty hiking clothes, donning their camp garments. In the chill of morning the clothes would be redolent of wood smoke, stiff with sweated salts, but at least dry.

Sheilagh and Rohini's fingers ringing the lids off cans of tonight's rations. Chickpeas and chicken soup, thickened with a few spoonfuls of flour. James's stomach groaned. Today had been a hard slog.

Still, another uneventful day. A blessing.

James and Graham were responsible for packing away the rickshaw. They were getting good at making sure it couldn't be seen. Three steps. First, choosing a spot. Not a simple matter, since by definition they were seeking a place that was hard to see.

Graham leered, taking a drag off his hand-rolled. He'd taken to smoking dry leaves. "Only we'd be searchin' for the fuckin' invisible, ya wanker!"

James snorted. "Story of my whole damn life."

Tonight they found a good spot behind a large lilac copse. Graham cracked a joke about hiding the wagon in Lilac's backside. Both of them sniggering. Stupid, puerile, necessary.

Second step: concealment. They cut down some boughs and stuck them in the wheels, careful not to bend the spokes. Christ, Gord would have their hides if they damaged it.

Third step: check and recheck. They went up the path and walked back, paying careful attention to the hiding spot, making sure they couldn't see even a part of the wagon.

This was a vital task the Group had entrusted to them: if the cart got stolen or badly damaged they were in a lot of trouble. All their food and supplies were offloaded nightly, but without the cart they wouldn't be able to carry it all.

Satisfied, Graham and James strolled back to camp, each hugging his own aching shoulders. That heavy-limbed feeling of journey's end. Dopy, not entirely unpleasant.

Amy took the chicken pen out of camp so Lilac and Rohini wouldn't be upset. She slaughtered the bird just as Albert had taught her, gutted and plucked it. The naked carcass seemed incredibly scrawny.

Gord was on his knees getting the fire started. An angry intensity. But empty, somehow. Same as the way he'd shot that man on the barricade at the SuperCenter. Impatient routine, as if reaching for his wallet or unlocking his front door.

Better with us than against. The best James could say. Not so long ago, Gord had been the kind of renegade that haunted James's imagination whenever he started a shift at York U. A hope, a prayer that he wouldn't have to face *that* guy, not tonight. Someone who might have a lot to lose but just didn't care.

What fueled his type? Impossible to tell. You might just as well ask a damn piranha why it swarmed with the others.

Gord coaxed fire from inert dead things, on his hands and knees, gently blowing, giving his breath to succor the fragile flame. Each and every fire was an offspring. Communion between his lips, his throat and lungs, and the tinder.

Rohini took a special interest in Gord's handiwork. Often kneeling beside him, concentrating, enumerating his recipes.

"Why do you prefer that kind of wood?"

Gord's responses terse and pregnant. "This here's maple. Better for building the coals."

"And this?" Fingering the brittle branches he'd gathered.

"Spruce. Don't burn long – not enough heat. But you'll need that to get 'er going." Gord sat back on his haunches, opened his hands at the materials. "You do it."

Rohini, almost bashful, an apprentice poaching the wiles of her master. "Oh, no…"

"Come on."

"But tat's your job."

"It ain't rocket science."

"No." Rohini's gentle smile, directed at him as solace. "It's lore."

Gord's wrinkled brow was impatient. "You'll never get richer than Bill Gates tryin' to sell it."

Rohini set to it, and soon a good blaze had risen. "Hard to believe this is the same thing that caused the firestorm…" She had to swallow some obstruction in her throat.

Gord seemed to consider this notion. "Well, it is."

"No. This is a tool. That was a monster." Her words were stalked by such grief, even Gord frowned. Aware, perhaps, that most of the Group was listening to their conversation. "Okay, add your logs there."

"But the first bunch is just catching."

"Flames're nice and high. What's your hardwood for?"

"To build the bed of coals."

"Yep. Coals give you your heat. Think of it like baking a cake, okay? You wanna bake your logs in the flames. Cook off the moisture in 'em. That way they'll ember nice and hot."

Rohini plopped the wood into the flames, jerking her hand away.

"Why're you scared of it?"

"It's so hot."

"Don't be a pu— " Gord caught himself, his face beaming crimson.

"A pussy?" said Rohini with sly humor.

Gord shrugged.

Everybody had gathered round now, stretching and yawning. Lilac was knitting. The shape of a mitten emerging from her needles. The fire, pale in the glowing dusk, rolling blue smoke that smelled of incense.

"Funny how people get so interested in the things that scare the shit outta them," said Gord. Looking sidelong at Rohini.

Amy chopped the chicken into pieces. They roasted them over the coals. When they'd finished supper and washed up, Rohini took a deep breath and began telling her tale.

She'd lived with her parents just east of the airport. Her father had been so proud of his accomplishment, living the immigrant dream. Born and raised in the slums of Mumbai, and now a bona fide home owner! She and her brother had teased him endlessly about buying a house under the main glide path of a major air terminal. They would turn up the TV when he went to the kitchen for a snack, until it blared loudly enough to be heard over the whistling roar of jet engines. He'd storm back in and shout at them not to be so bloody cheeky.

Rohini had just stepped outside into the postage-stamp backyard when Lights Out struck. A huge airliner glided overhead, the area of its wings much larger than her father's proud patch of grass. No more than fifty feet off the ground, a gargantuan machine that blotted out the sky in a loud *WHOOSH*! So low that Rohini went to her knees. No rocketing engine noise. Just the enormity of the air it displaced. It crashed just two blocks over. A fireball ploughed into the sky and she felt its menacing heat.

"You probably all remember, it was pretty windy that night. The wind whipped the flames into a frenzy. It was just like the night of the firestorm. Just like it. Burning embers flooded the sky. I couldn't believe what I was seeing. I was stunned – literally stunned. I just stood there, stupidly. My mother and father ran out of the house. My brother was out with friends. The sky looked like a freeway of rushing tail lights. Everything around us was catching fire. The grass, Daddy's garden, the roof. Before long the house was in flames. I don't know what I was thinking. I wasn't thinking at all. I ran into the house. Daddy screamed behind me, 'Rohini, don't go in there!' But I needed something, I just had this overwhelming reflex to get to my room, to my desk, to retrieve this small, petty thing.

"Daddy ran in behind me. To stop me, to save me. I didn't realize until after I was back outside. My eyes were full of tears from the smoke. Mommy was screaming, screaming a sound I couldn't imagine coming from her body. Then I realized: Daddy wasn't there. He hadn't come back out. Before I could stop her, Mommy ran into the house to find him. I tried to stop her, I tried…"

She stopped. Abruptly, as if about to utter some offense. "I saw one of them – not sure whether it was Mummy or Daddy – one of them on fire, whirling out of the door, a burning body that fell down the deck stairs. Right at my feet, okay?" Her voice broke. She waved her hands in front of her. She still felt the scorching heat.

Both her parents perished in the fire that consumed her house. Her father's pride and joy. After seeing one of her parents burn to death, Rohini could remember very little except intense heat and living light. Somebody dragging her out of the yard, into the street. A bunch of men opening a fire hydrant and forming a bucket brigade. Useless of course. The whole neighborhood was in flames. Everybody ran.

After she was finished her story, dusk had deepened to indigo. Later than usual for them all to stay up, but on nights when one of the Group told their tale, they all felt an imperative to listen without interrupting.

Even long after the last of Rohini's words faded, they sat and examined the play of hot colors. The wood she'd placed, transformed into its own essence, a tinkling, radiant mound.

"My condolences, about the loss of your folks," said Ross.

"Thanks," said Rohini. She screwed up her mouth and sighed. Not entirely sadly, either. They were learning how the expression of their own stories could exorcise great anguish. Not necessarily palliating the pain, but perhaps rendering it familiar. Distributing the burden among all.

"What did you go back inside to get?" Sheilagh asked softly.

Rohini blinked, coming out of a daydream. A dusk dream, James thought. "I'm ashamed," she said. "I feel responsible for the death of my parents – all because I went back for this – this scrap of paper." She pulled it out of her pocket. "When I was in university, I fell in love with an exchange student. He had to go home, to Iran, and I was heartbroken. He knew I was obsessed with Rumi – I was doing my undergrad thesis on him – so he left me these lines of his:

Burning with longing-fire, wanting to sleep with my head on your doorsill, my   living is composed only of this trying to be in your Presence.

Wine to intensify love; fire to consume. We bring these, not like images from a
        dream reality, but as an actual night to live through until dawn."

She shrugged hopelessly. "I don't know what got into me, I really don't. I was just – I needed to get it, like my life depended on it."

"And here you are," said Tribe, "still drawing breath. Maybe your life *did* depend on it."

As they readied for bed, the last enactment of their protocol was to spread out the embers. Raking them flat to prevent sparks that could catch on a fly sheet or their drying clothes.

They pulled apart the careful signature of the fire, blinking in the stinging smoke. Wincing at the heat. Until the coal bed lay round and thin before them. A hot orange galaxy glimmering in the dark, intractably vibrant. Holding out their hands to receive its heat, it was hard to turn away from its fearsome beauty.

"Incredible." Rohini sounded sated.

"Trees are so full of energy that it assaults you," said Sheilagh. "And all this heat, Rohini, where does it come from, ultimately?"

"I don't know, to be honest with you."

"From the sun."

Rohini smiled at Gord. "You see? It's miraculous, what you taught me to do, igniting a tiny star."

The vision struck James down like an arrow through his head. The words sun and star bursting pain behind his eyes. He reeled away from the coals that suddenly became the swollen, grinning face of Hermes.

The thin blade of Hermes's tongue flicked like a snake's. Hermes's mouth opened wide, revealing stumps of rotted teeth. Then a fist flew from the gaping maw. Lightning quick, it grabbed James by the throat, squeezing his windpipe, choking him to his haunches, pressing him to the cold soil.

"TAKE HEED!" Maggie's voice bellowed, and those who had gathered round to help him jumped back. "WHEN RA'S MIGHTY BOAT RESURRECTS YOU MUST SET AS HE SETS INTO THE LAND OF THE DEAD! YOU ARE PURSUED!"

"What the fuck're you on about?" Sheilagh demanded.

No response came but a weak burble from James. His arms and legs twitched and he lay still.

*

A long sleepless night spent breathless in candlelight, begging for dawn. Too frightened to sleep. Cold, but not daring to rebuild the fire.

With his head pillowed in Lilac's lap, her fingers running through his hair, James mumbled an explanation of what Maggie had said: Ra was the primordial Egyptian sun god, the forefather of creation, giver of life. Great-grandfather to Osiris, the first king of Egypt, himself the father of Horus. The Egyptians had envisioned Ra reborn each morning, crossing the sky in a great barge. Every night Ra passed into the underworld, the land of the dead.

"Fuuuck," Gord drawled. "Now we gotta bury ourselves?"

James told them about his fears over the past days, that the

Sicari were on their trail.

"Jesus Christ," said a male voice, so weary and desolate that James couldn't even identify who it was in the dark.

"There is a big culvert, back yonder," said Clay, pointing up the sandy path towards the road. "Come morning, I suggest we might find cover there."

At first light they hastily packed their tents and gear. Their supply of canned goods they half-buried and covered over with branches.

"What is this?" Ross groused. "We oughta be getting the fuck away from here."

"Come on!" Amy objected. "You think we're gonna pull that damn rickshaw fast enough to stay ahead of these guys?"

"I agree with Ross." A weak quavering in Massimo's voice. "We – we don't wanna stay around here. Not if those fuckers in black are coming."

"Okay, look," said Mulligan. "I don't like it any more than— " He stopped, eyes bulging, hearing what they all heard in the still morning. The approaching trudge of boots, the metallic clink of equipment. Gruff voices coming up the path from the road.

"Move!" Clay commanded.

Everybody grabbed what they could. They scrambled down a steep embankment overgrown with shrubs and saplings. At the bottom, a creek meandered through a large concrete culvert. They crowded inside. Peering upwards, as if able to see the approach of their predators as easily as they could hear them.

James closed his eyes. Breathed deeply. One passing above he could almost see. The one in the red robe. The tall one with curly black hair. Nguyen. Conjurer of the Dog Man.

Nguyen stopped.

"What is it?" snapped a voice sprung with hatred. Nicolo Alvarro.

Tribe bared his teeth, silently drawing his sword. Sheilagh put a warning hand on his arm.

"They are close. So close." Nguyen sounded like a man on the verge of an orgasm.

Massimo clamped a shaking hand over his own twitching mouth.

"These ashes are still warm," said another voice.

"You see? You see?"

"Your fucking hunches," said Alvarro disgustedly, "have led us on a merry chase. For nothing. This campsite could have been used by anybody."

"No," Nguyen decided. "No, this is it. I feel it. Back to the road!"

This prompted a chorus of swearing and grumbling among the Sicari until Alvarro ordered them to stop their whining and move.

"But wait!" Nguyen said suddenly.

"What—" Alvarro began, but Nguyen must have cut him off.

Silence. Nguyen frozen on the trail, just fifteen feet above the culvert where the Group crouched, hardly breathing.

He knows we're here, James thought with a fearful dry retch.

Many minutes passed. James sensing Nguyen probing, groping for him. Even the beat of his own heart seemed a blaring signal.

"Yes," Nguyen said delightedly at last. "Yes. They are very close, indeed! Back to the road."

*

They waited for a long time, unwilling to show themselves into a trap. Finally, Tribe swore under his breath and Sheilagh let him go. He skulked up the embankment, scouting the length of the path. The Sicari were gone.

Very quickly they packed up the cart and moved out.

"What do we do?" Mulligan asked in dismay. "We can't just keep going the same way. I mean, obviously. Those fuckers know how to find us."

"But how?" Sheilagh threw up her hands.

"That's not important just now," said Tribe.

"Bollocks!" said Graham. "Seems to me it's the key issue!"

"No, no, no!" Ross rebuked him. "The key issue is staying away from them!"

Graham laughed bitterly. "Right! Which means finding out how the fuck they're finding us in the first fuckin' place!"

Where the road crossed the next highpoint, Tribe stopped to scan the route with his field glasses. "Not a sign of them."

"That doesn't make me feel any better," said Rohini, clutching herself.

"It's better than having them on top of us!" Mulligan stated.

"Can you give all of us a frigging break!" Lilac shouted at him.

"Why don't we all just take a few breaths—" Athol started, having to raise his voice to be heard over the others, "—and decide on what we're going to do!"

"Why don't you give me a break!" Mulligan's smile at Lilac was sharp and hot. "The last thing we need is whining!"

James spoke words too quiet to be heard above the fray. Last night's vision had left him feeling hollowed out, as if he hadn't slept for days. His eyes just as glazed and unfocused as his mind. He spoke again. Again, nobody paid any heed.

Nobody but Clay. "Quiet," he said. And then "QUIET GOD DAMN YOU ALL!"

Like a flipped switch, silence.

"I know where they are," said James dreamily.

"What do you mean, you know where they are?" Massimo demanded. He sounded scared. Of them all, he'd obviously been affected the most by the proximity of the enemy.

"They're very tired," James continued, still staring off into space. "More tired than we are. Moving fast and hard, living very lean. Alvarro knows they need rest. Nguyen is nominally in charge of the squad, but Alvarro's the one the men listen to. They've set up camp. About nine miles…" He paused and turned in the right direction, pointing east. "That way."

They hunkered down in a ditch alongside the road and debated what to do next. Clay warned them sternly that he wouldn't tolerate any more damned bickering.

Gord kept digging at his left ankle, wincing in discomfort. "Some kinda fuckin' rash," he said when Sheilagh asked what was the matter. "Itches like a bitch. Just what I fuckin' need."

Sheilagh looked at it and diagnosed poison ivy. In a damp patch down the ditch she found a clump of jewel weed. She chewed up some of the leaves and applied the poultice to the rash, telling him it should help if he left it alone.

Eventually they decided to take James at his word. Tribe, James, Amy, Gord and Ross would sneak up to the Sicari camp, reconnoiter, and find out what they could.

They set out late that afternoon, so that dusk would hide them when they got there. A patch of bare earth where a meadow edged onto a small bush lot. James and the others crept up through the underbrush, the noise of their approach hidden by the rough gripes of the Sicari.

All they'd had to eat for weeks were energy drinks and protein bars. They complained of Nguyen's arrogance, that he was leading them too far from their supply base.

James was dismayed by their number. Almost sixty of them, stocky and well muscled. Several horses too, munching contentedly on grass. In the red firelight, men in black paramilitary body armor toyed with huge hunting knives and the actions on their submachine guns. Alvarro was among them, his Roman nose as sharp as the knife he was using to attack a stick, flinging wood shavings into the darkness. While he didn't join in the banter, it was clear from his manner that he was as sick of the chase as were his men.

At first James didn't see Nguyen. He was about thirty yards off, kneeling with another crimson-clad man, pudgy, middle-aged, balding. Both had their eyes closed as Nguyen chanted a prayer, droning like a muezzin.

"*Hotep-di-iw asir neb jidew khentyimentu netr aa neb abydew,*" he chanted.

An offering which I give to Osiris Lord of Djedu, Khentyimentu, great god, Lord of Abydos.

"Guide us, Lord of the Underworld," he sighed in English. "We serve only you, Great One, sower of the seed of life. Only through you are wondrous things possible. *Diwa wasir im pert'f nefert jit ir nehh.*"

Adoring Osiris during his wonderful procession for ever and ever.

"What an ugly language," Tribe whispered. "Spoken as though he's got a chicken bone stuck in his throat!"

Nguyen and the other Collegian got up and came back towards the Sicari. James noticed how they all shut up as he approached. Contemptuous of him, yes, but fearful too. Nguyen asked for a map and showed Alvarro and his men his plan.

"We know they are going northeast," he said. "There are only two possibilities from this area. Highways twenty and fifteen. Noldor here will lead half of you from the north, to where twenty crosses fifteen. I will lead the other half from the south."

"A pincer," said Alvarro with just a touch of admiration.

"Toady," Tribe growled very quietly.

Nguyen smiled. It was like the blossoming of a gruesome flower. "Our trek is almost at an end, gentlemen. This I promise you!"

Chapter 18

Nguyen's Noose

James and the reconnaissance party felt very good about themselves, stumbling back through the dark to find the Group. The plan seemed simple. If Nguyen and the Sicari were expecting them to follow highway twenty north, they would head south until they hit route seven, then head west from there and find another way north, describing a long loop around the danger. A time-consuming jaunt far out of their way, but they had no choice.

The next morning, Athol seemed very glum, withdrawn. He and Mulligan kept falling behind, Mulligan's sore ribs as much a handicap as Athol's arthritic hips. Athol would tilt his face towards the sun, eyes closed, mouth hanging open.

Once Graham hung back with him. They exchanged some words. Athol handed him his Bible. Graham waved it off, but Athol insisted until Graham took the book. Afterwards, Athol seemed much happier. As if he'd achieved some kind of catharsis.

As they moved south, the terrain opened up into flat sod farms. They decided to lessen their time by cutting across a large field, knowing they would hit Route seven eventually if they went more or less south-west. The road didn't seem safe now. Even with the rickshaw, it was hard to pull the weight of their canned goods across the dusty brown grass. As Gord pulled, Tribe and Massimo pushed from behind.

STOP! Maggie kept carping. STOP! YOU'RE GOING THE WRONG WAY! YOU DON'T UNDERSTAND!

Shut up, James thought viciously. *Just leave me the fuck alone.*

He concentrated on bobbing goldfinches, the way they folded their wings as they coasted down, then flapped to arc up again. Sailing the clear morning towards a bush lot on the north side of the field. Chattering merrily with every upswing.

No cover across the dying sod.

Mulligan coughed, forcibly enough to catch James's attention. James looked around, registered the blood dribbling from Mulligan's mouth. Mulligan dropped to the turf. Only then James heard the shot.

All along the road four hundred yards behind, men were trooping after them. Sicari! Something whizzed past, followed by the rolling crack of another gunshot. Men on horseback thundering over the field to ride them down.

He heard Lilac scream, he heard Sheilagh's roar: "*Run, damn it, run!*"

Terror punched him hard in the gut, the Gordian knot cleaved. His breath whistled. Gunshots aplenty now.

He ran back, knelt with Athol beside Mulligan, who was hiccupping blood all over his own hair, haloed around his head. "Don't – don't leave me…" Terrible gurgling from the hole in his chest. Athol gripped Mulligan's hand.

"Grab an arm!" James yelled. "We gotta get him to the trees!"

Athol reached out his arthritic fingers. "I can't carry anyone. Leave us. Get moving." His sad smile told James what he already knew anyway: Mulligan would not survive the sucking chest wound. Athol would never outrun the Sicari.

"Fuck that! I'm not leaving you!"

"You go!" Athol shouted. Behind his spectacles, his eyes were bright with terror. "You can't do anything here! Go, son. Run!"

James squeezed Athol's outstretched hand. "God bless you," he said. Rising to his feet, he felt as if his legs were only a foot long.

He ran.

Two hundred yards to the tree line. Minimum. Every stride an agony of time as bullets whizzed past.

One hundred and fifty yards.

Screaming at each other. *Come on, move it! Keep up!*

James saw Ross's sweaty face, his bulging eyes. Heard his panicky squeaking breath. The verdant wall of the bush lot creeping closer. Still more than fifty yards away.

Two horsemen came abreast of the wagon. Gord let go the bar and shouldered the Garand. Just before James lost sight of them, Tribe thrust his rapier into a horse's chest. The animal screamed.

James and Ross dashed headlong into the sumac of the forest edge. There was a horrid wet snap and down went Ross with a strangled scream. In the slanting morning sunlight, James saw a pink mist of his blood churning.

Horrible confusion as gunshots broke the air. Wildly looking around for the rest of them. Seeing nobody. A sapling beside him burst apart. He dove for cover.

Ross had been shot through the left wrist. Blood spraying all over everything. James had just enough presence of mind to clamp his hand over the wound, but the bleeding wouldn't slow until he dug his thumb hard into the hollow below the heel of Ross's thumb. The radial artery had been severed right at the point where the pulse is checked, where it hugged tightly to the inside of the bone. Almost impossible to squeeze shut.

Ross drenched in bright blood. His mouth worked at some word, face full of longing.

"Tell me about your daughter's wedding. Talk to me, Ross." An old trick Lars had taught him. Keep the victim talking. Distract him from the terror.

Ross's smile flickered and extinguished. His face tense with pain.

Sheilagh ran up, oh thank God. She crashed down into the bracken, digging frantically in her pack.

"Goddamn wedding," Ross rasped, barely heard over the gunfire. "Carly wanted a big show. She's our youngest, is Carly. Always gave her whatever she wanted. Spoiled her, plain and simple."

The blood had slowed to a trickle, but James's hand was getting strained, keeping up the pressure.

Sheilagh swore, flinging things away until she pulled out her little sewing kit.

James gave her an urgent look. Just shifting his weight, even a little, allowed a thin jet of blood from the wound, painting the arm of his shirt. Aghast to see the ground through the gaping hole in Ross's wrist. A pattern of grass and old leaves and twigs. As if his body were already starting to break down.

"Tell me more," James prompted, making sure to smile brightly. He felt woozy, couldn't draw enough breath.

"What a night," Ross whispered. "Carly's dress alone...two thousand bucks. She was a princess. Glowing. Under a spotlight. All night long."

Ross's eyes fluttered. Tension draining away from his chalky face.

"Put your pack under his feet!" James hissed. Sheilagh did. "Ross!" He smacked his face. "How – how many people were there? Must've been quite a crowd."

"Hmmm?" His slack lips worked.

Sheilagh's hands were shaking so badly she couldn't get the damn thread into the eye of the needle. "Come on!" she begged. "Come on!"

"Four seventy-five," Ross mumbled. "You believe that business? Mmm..."

"That's not a wedding, it's a small village, man!" James squeezed the wound and Ross winced back to semi-consciousness.

"Ridiculous, Teddy. But you know Carly. Shit, you were there, Ted, you saw it."

Finally, Sheilagh had the needle threaded. On her knees, bent over the wound. "Move your thumb, give me room!"

James tried to keep up the pressure, dragging his thumb down Ross's wrist. As soon as he moved, the blood started pumping. "Jesus!"

"Put more pressure on it!" Sheilagh dug the needle in, pinching the wound closed with her other hand. She pulled the needle through to the knot in the thread. Looped it around and through in a mattress stitch.

Blood flowing, meandering through the dead leaves, sinking into the deep loam.

"Hurry!"

"Jesus Christ, will you shut up!" Sheilagh bellowed. "Hold on!"

"I am fucking holding on!"

"Tighter, damn it!"

"Stop your bickering, you two," Ross burbled. "Frank, watch your mouth..."

Sheilagh made a second stitch. Then a third. The blood flow was slowing. But not because of the stitches.

Lord, James thought. I'm watching Ross's blood pressure dropping.

Sheilagh dug the needle in again, but she couldn't get it through. She bared her teeth, swore.

Ross's body twisted so violently he almost tore his wrist out of James's grip.

"Oh!" he cried, but faintly, so faintly. "Carly, you're hurting Daddy, sweetie."

She finished the stitches. Blood oozed through the sutures. Ross's flesh looked sallow, doughy. James wept. He'd seen that chalkiness too often. He smacked Ross's face again, shouted at him. No response. He felt for a pulse under his jaw. Just a faint, thready twitch.

A Sicari burst through the brush, tripping over Sheilagh. Still on her knees, she whipped out the knitting needle. She lanced his groin as he struggled to regain his balance. Jumped to her feet, thrust the needle through his throat. He screamed and she lunged again, plunging it into his stomach just below the body armor. The form, the function of Tribe's training in her frenzied strikes. The Sicari fell and she pounced on him, her face a rictus of disgust.

James picked up Ross's rifle and started firing at every figure in black coming across the field. So many of them! But he wasn't hitting shit. Panic and rage making him jerk the trigger.

Yet Sicari were dropping. He spotted Amy lying just to his left. Taking her time, lining up her targets on the reticule of her scope. She fired. A man across the field pitched over. Another shot. And another. Every bullet found its mark. Nonna had said there would be a time when they'd need Amy. That time had come. James counted at least ten kills. Making the Sicari pay dearly.

James saw some Sicari running back towards the road. He took a deep breath. Squeezed the trigger. Saw a man fall. A terrible, convoluted feeling: electric fear, revulsion. The intimate connection to a person shot down by a bullet that had just been inside the rifle.

Now the Sicari were the ones trapped in the open, under fire from the thick cover of the trees. Still, there was no way the Group could hold out for long. Not against dozens of armed men.

He saw the abandoned food cart and despaired.

James pulled Sheilagh away from Ross. "We need to get into the trees! Come on!" She fought him. "Sheilagh! He'd dead!"

They took off.

*

A narrow deer path wound downhill into the dark wood. Seconds in and James was directionless. His heart pounding hard. If he took Sheilagh the wrong way they'd run right back into the Sicari. Gunshots and shouting echoed all around.

He knelt in the damp soil. Tried to calm himself.

Thrashing saplings to their right. He took aim. But it was Amy. Mike, Rohini, and Lilac close behind. All shaking and crying. James hugged Lilac, gripping her body with enormous relief.

"Get your fuckin' asses down!" Amy hissed, wild-eyed. "They're comin' round behind us!" She knelt behind a tree with her rifle raised.

Pasty-mouthed, James took a position to her left. Without realizing what he was doing, he saw his own fist knocking the tree trunk. As if desperate to gain entry. The bark skinned his knuckles.

What the hell am I doing?

A squad of Sicari crept through a grove of saplings. Amy fired, the boom deafening in the trees. The lead Sicari was punched backwards. His comrades dove for cover.

A rider crashed through the undergrowth almost on top of Amy. Jesus Christ, they were surrounded!

Mike leaped from the bracken into the horse's path. He lunged with the knife. It was the bravest and stupidest act James had ever seen. The horse reared back, almost throwing the rider.

James fired at the rider. He missed.

"No!" Sheilagh screamed as the Sicari rider pulled his pistol and shot Mike through the forehead. All their voices earsplitting as

Mike collapsed.

Then Tribe bounded from the other direction, with Massimo. Emboldened, the squad of Sicari jumped up and fired.

"Come on, you bastard!" Tribe snarled, pointing his rapier at the rider.

The Sicari horseman galloped through the trees straight at Tribe. Tribe stood his ground. The rider fired several shots, but Tribe struck the horse with his sword. The shrieking animal somersaulted, catapulting the rider into the brush.

A gun battle raged. Two more shots and James's rifle was empty. Only now he realized he'd left the spare ammunition on Ross. Shit!

Then Clay jogged up behind the Sicari, gravely firing his pistols into their backs. The crossfire slaughtered most of the squad. The survivors fled into the trees.

James caught a glimpse of a flitting crimson robe. Nguyen had gotten away.

Amy stood, aimed and sniped one smooth motion. One of the men went down.

"Alvarro!" Tribe shouted. "Face me you cowardly son of a bitch!"

The stocky Captain stopped and turned, glowering. Drew his own sword. Amy aimed at him, but Tribe waved her off. "Today he tastes steel!"

Tribe and Alvarro did battle, leaping, turning, lunging through the greenery. Blades chimed and rang and whipped the air.

"Get him Tribe!" Graham snarled.

Tribe dueled with a falcon's glare, a dancer's grace. But brutally direct, unflourished. Alvarro's style was blunt and muscular, his blade tracing dramatic curves as he feinted and dodged.

After a few minutes, they separated for a breather. Alvarro snarled. "You can't win, Tribe!" he panted. "This wood is surrounded!"

"*Haaa!*" Tribe hollered. With an incredible burst, he charged twelve feet in one magnificent stride, parrying Alvarro's sword and slicing open his cheek in the same stroke.

Alvarro clutched his face, stumbled and fell. As Tribe descended on him Alvarro pulled a pistol and fired. Tribe jerked back, twisted down into the bracken. Sheilagh cried out. Alvarro ran. Clay fired at him twice, but missed.

"I'm alright, I'm fine," Tribe moaned as Sheilagh ran up to him. But as he stood back up he was clearly shaken. The bullet had torn the side of his jacket. He grimaced, holding his ribs.

Sheilagh and Lilac were on their knees by Mike's body. Breathless sobs, bereft of consolation. They wanted to bury him. Ross too. But Amy was stern. No time, she spat.

The wounded horse made a pathetic whinny, giving them the whites of its terrified eyes. Purple folded intestines swollen through the gash in its abdomen. Amy shot it in the head.

The rider remained tangled in a hazel thicket, curled over on his knees, his humped back heaving. Massimo punched and kicked as he hauled him over. The rider mouthed unintelligible words around a mouthful of blood. Sheilagh, her face twisted by sorrow, stumbled up. Tribe looked to her and she nodded. He rammed the tip of his weapon into the man's throat. Straight through to the ground it went, the rider making a gacking noise, convulsing to stillness.

Rohini shook and cried, hiding her face behind her hands.

Clay collected the rider's weapons and ammo.

*

They hastened deeper into the bush. Still heading downhill, the ground growing sodden, huge logs impeding their progress, velvety with moss. Climbing over one, Lilac slipped and fell into the black mud. James went back for her. They paused, panting, searching the dense green. Impossible to see more than fifteen or twenty feet. Sounds of approach hidden by their breath, their hammering hearts. The wind had picked up too, forcing ominous creaking in the trees.

"Hold on, hold on!" Massimo rasped. "Where the fuck's Graham?"

"And Mr. Havercroft," said Clay.

"Shite!" Sheilagh bit her lip.

They decided to wait for them. "Ten minutes," Clay muttered, glancing anxiously at his watch as they hunkered down.

"How will they even know which way to come?" Lilac groaned. "We gotta give 'em more time!"

"It's all we've got," Clay muttered.

They waited. Dismayed, forlorn, remembering their dead. Lilac seemed to have collected herself until she realized Mulligan was gone.

Her tears, moved by the wind across her cheeks. Drops of the sea breathed life by the urgent air. "Why am I crying?" She sounded helpless. "He was such an asshole. Why am I so upset?"

None of them replied. What was there to say? Sniffling faces broken by grief, bowed to palsied hands.

Amy leaned over and retched around her protruding tongue.

Saw Lilac's worried expression and sighed. "You believe before all this shit I'd never killed another person? Never."

Come on, Graham. Come on! James's foot tapping, adrenaline that seemed to fill his lungs with hot water. He thought about Athol giving Graham his Bible. Lord, Athol was *dead*! In his peripheral vision, Ross's blood on his sleeve flashed like a bicycle reflector. A third of the Group slaughtered in only a few minutes. He tried to calm himself, focus on sending Graham signals, helping him to find them.

"That's time," said Clay, almost guiltily.

"That wasn't ten minutes!" Rohini cried.

"'Fraid so." Clay blew his nose. Only then did James realize that Hood had disappeared.

Amy's glowering eyes shifted side to side, scanning the bush. "The longer we wait here—"

"We won't leave without Graham!" Sheilagh stated flatly.

Massimo was pacing back and forth, shoes squelching in the mud. Whispering to himself.

Twelve minutes.

"Sheilagh—" Amy began, but Sheilagh cut her off.

"We stay."

Suddenly, commotion in the thick bushy alders off to their left. All their guns aimed at Graham as he stumbled out into the open with Nguyen in tow, a leash of nylon rope around his neck, another loop binding his wrists. Gord took up the rear, the Garand aimed at Nguyen's back.

Massimo whooped with fright, shrinking back. Everybody else rushed forward, embracing Graham and Gord, offering congratulations.

"Brought youse all a present." Graham's face ashen sober.

Nguyen, rod-thin in his robe, almost as tall as Tribe. Black corkscrew hair matted with twigs and leaves. An ageless, sharply triangular face, high cheekbones and a chin so long and pointed it looked deformed. The face of a mantis.

The moment his almond-shaped eyes fell on James they filled with tears. His full lips parted in awe. As if seeing a long-lost lover. "You really are *the one!*" He fell to his knees and crawled to James's feet, clasping his pant leg. A pathetic mendicant.

James was acutely embarrassed. Not at all what he'd expected to feel. Up close, he could see the tattered hem of Nguyen's robe, the crimson fabric muted to rust by filth; he smelled goatish and cheesy.

"*Di iaw in wesir sent a in heru!*" Nguyen kissed James's shoes. Giving praise to Osiris, he'd said. Kissing the ground to

Horus. He peered up at James, simpering, his mouth now smeared with mud. "You can understand me, can't you? Amazing!"

"Get away!" Tribe growled, grabbing the rope and hauling him back.

"I say we just kill this fucker and get the fuck outta here!" Gord pressed the Garand's muzzle to Nguyen's head.

"No, no!" James pushed the gun away. "He can give us information."

"I can, I can!"

"Shut up, asshole!" Amy sneered. "He's only trying to trick us!"

Nguyen implored James with prayerful hands. "I'm sorry for what I've done to you and your friends. Believe the torment I've felt, needing to destroy you! But you must understand! Hermes cannot be allowed to possess her!"

"This is all an act!" Massimo cried, panicking. "I told ya, Jimmy, I met this asshole before!"

"What are you talking about?" James asked Nguyen. "Possess who?"

"You've been desperate to find out! I know, I know how you feel! She beckons to you, she won't let you alone!"

"You're talking about Maggie!"

"Maggie, I know not."

"How've you been following us?" Lilac asked.

Nguyen smirked. James saw his glibness sneaking back. "How do you follow a scent when you're hungry? Hmmm? How do you know what hunger feels like?"

Massimo picked up a rock and smashed it down on Nguyen's crown. It took Gord, Clay and Tribe to wrestle him away. Nguyen shook himself. From his hairline, a thin ribbon of blood leaked down his tall forehead.

"You must listen to me!" He begged James. "Our time is short, but we will meet again, oh yes we will! Short but long, long but short. Ten years is what I see lying ahead till we next lay eyes on each other, young one. Ten times one, one times ten, but a pinprick in eternity, and so long she's been waiting for you to find her! Five hundred years she has lain in wait!" He winked knowingly. "Mustn't think of the past as inexorable."

An involuntary moan escaped James, and Nguyen giggled. Massimo's blow seemed not to have affected him at all.

"The Voice," James snapped, "you mean Horus—"

Nguyen waved an impatient hand at him. "Horus, Porus, Morris. Might as well be Fortuna, Quetzalcoatl, Baal – just a moniker, young one, a label for the Stone – think of her as a beacon,

346

homing you in. Giving you a foretaste of what you will experience when you find her! Oh yes!"

"You're full of shit!" James shouted. "You created the Dog Man, you sent it to kill me!"

"You conjured that creature as much as I, James. Hatred and resentment are very powerful."

"Fuck you!"

"Many of us tried to halt your Quest. We failed. I was a fool to think I could thwart her will. Just a smidgen of the Stone under the fire of Betelgeuse allowed us to create the creature you call the Dog Man. Even prior to the supernova, a tiny fraction of the Stone allowed Hermes to predict the coming of darkness. Hermes is the great malefactor! He has spent a very long time studying, practicing his art, dismayed that she has never summoned him. When he possesses all of the Stone, he will be all-powerful. He will make terrible things, things to turn your eyes inside out, young one. He seeks to create an army of homunculi!"

"I thought the Philosopher's Stone was supposed to turn lead into gold!"

Nguyen hissed smugly. "You kids are so prosaic. That is just an allegory! You don't understand yet, but you will, oh yes, you will indeed! She is a *being*, summoning you. *You*, James. She possesses an ancient consciousness. Beware, young one!"

Nguyen grinned and jumped to his feet. Raised his bound arms and flung something to the ground. There was a blinding flash, a loud pop. White sulfurous smoke engulfed them. They shouted and screamed. When it cleared, Nguyen was gone.

Chapter 19

To The Last

With heavy feet they fought their way through trackless forest. Maple and beech gave over to dense stands of cedar and black spruce, grabbing at their packs, forbidding free movement. The ground grew ever softer, muddier until pale gray overcast oozed through the penumbral dark and they found themselves staring dumbfounded across a wide open bog. No choice now but to traverse it. They couldn't risk going back.

Tersely, Sheilagh told them to watch their step. This was a quaking bog, a thick mat of shrub willow and many other plants floating above deep waters. One wrong step and they'd plunge through to the bottom. To be mummified like the ancient bog bodies of Scandinavia. So well preserved their last ceremonial meals remained undigested in their crushed leather bellies.

The food stock was gone. The horrible truth of it tightened like a vise. James knew Nguyen had succeeded after all. Just as if the lot of them had been gunned down. Nothing of the Quest now but slow starvation, lost in a wilderness of pain.

James found himself wishing he would tread on a weak spot, entomb himself in the cold blackness below. Sheilagh's seething anger glowed from her, a presence between them more palpable than heat radiating off a stove. She wouldn't even look at him.

Rohini's foot went through the mat and she couldn't pull it free. They had to work for a while just to get her out. Then James suddenly dropped through to the waist, crushing his testicles against a root. Massimo and Graham pulled him up, but his legs were soaked to his aching crotch. Soon his thighs began to chafe.

Every moment, expecting the next volley of shots from afar.

It began to rain. Heavy drizzle at first, intensifying into a blowing downpour by the time they finally reached the far edge of the bog. Even in their waterproof jackets and pants they grew wet. Crawling into the black spruce, where at least it was a little drier than being out in the open. No space to set up their tents or even spread the tarpaulin over their heads. Hardly enough even to stretch out on their groundsheets. No fire, lest the smoke be spotted. A miserably cold night, water worming its way into every opening. Feet soaked and cold. Paranoid that the murmuring tapping showers hid the approach of the Sicari.

Tribe grimaced with pain taking off his pack. "Let's have a look," said Sheilagh. Tribe tried to refuse, but she fixed him with such a violent glare he was forced to show her the wound. Alvarro's bullet had grazed the latimus muscle under his left arm, leaving an ugly dark-purple bruise that looked like the livid lips of a corpse.

For Sheilagh to see it properly, he had to take off his shirt, revealing a pale trunk and arms covered in ugly brown scars. Especially his right arm, which looked like it had been splattered with brown paint. "The price one pays for apprenticing as a swordsman," he mumbled. Clearly trying to cover his embarrassment.

"All those times you wouldn't take off your shirt," said Graham, "I thought you were just a prude!"

"Here," said James, crawling over to Tribe. "Let me help."

"Haven't you done enough!" Sheilagh exploded. "Your god Horus or your fuckin' Stone or whatever it is – couldn't it have warned you? Eh? Saved Ross's life? Saved – Mike's life!" Her voice broke. A terrible, final sound.

"Sheilagh…" said Tribe.

"No! I won't shut up, not about this! What a fucking cock-up!" She burst into raging tears.

*

Moving deep in the hinterland now. Days passed without a sign of settlement, road, fence. Occasionally they spotted red and white communication masts poking defiantly above the trees and they knew they were near a road. But they dared not go nearer. The Sicari must be closely watching all approaches north and east.

The landscape reminded James of his childhood. Steep granite outcrops, the earth's bones jutting from sudden hills and sharp valleys, thickly wooded. Hard going, bushwhacking through mile after mile. Hiding with them in the forest's columned halls, boulders larger than SUV's, some the size of small houses, that had lain unmoving since glaciers had dropped them one hundred and fifty centuries before. Hairy with gray lichens and ferns.

Waking every dawn into temperatures hovering just above freezing, breath exploding in steamy plumes. Cold enough to ache the knuckles.

"You gonna have some gloves or scarves ready at some point?" Gord asked Lilac.

"Learn to knit and do it yourself," she snapped, crouching beside the fire pit, rubbing numbness from her hands.

James kept thinking of Mike. Of Ross, Mulligan and Athol.

All lying unburied, comfortless in the elements.

Not long before their store of nuts was depleted. Nonna's *chamella* was gone. After two days sickened by a diet of only candies, Sheilagh reluctantly showed them the dried legumes she'd secretly stowed. Her rucksack jammed with packages of kidney and black beans, chickpeas, black-eyed peas. She'd meant these to be their failsafe. Along with packets of potato, corn, squash and zucchini seeds she'd also taken from the SuperCenter, the Group's precious store for next Spring's sowing. Just now, next Spring seemed a distant corner of another universe.

Every night, Sheilagh measured out five cups of dried legumes with the focus of a pharmacist. These were left in Ziploc bags full of water through the night and the next day's hike, softening enough that with half an hour of boiling they could be chewed for supper. That was it. One spare meal a day, supplemented with hot teas of Nonna's raspberry leaves and linden flowers – tricking their stomachs with the illusion of fullness.

Amy spent precious energy stalking deer and moose. Tracks and scat tantalized them with the promise of meat, but she didn't see even one animal. After a few frustrating days she gave up.

One night, James rolled a joint, thinking it might dull the edge. They passed it around, but it only tortured them with salivating longing for food.

He and Lilac spent more and more time on their own, filling themselves with sex. Vigorous and desperate to punch vibrancy back into their bodies. Too chilly now even during the day to strip completely naked, grappling, kicking black forest loam as they fought together for release.

"We have to be more careful," she said while James dozed upon her belly. "Fuck, all we need now is for me to get pregnant."

"Or to end up with some juicy STD." His voice sounded distant, even to himself.

His head bounced as her stomach tensed in a faint laugh. "Nice."

"You don't have to worry," he mumbled. "I got the snip after Sara was born."

"So you're shooting blanks. Useless!"

He turned over to nip the flesh beside her belly button.

Golden leaves tumbled around them, swirling in a gust of wind that was an umbilicus stretched to the Arctic circle. The nutty scent of Autumn, and the equinox was still almost two weeks away. Every day, less sunlight. How many days till Winter then? Inevitable, the grinding patience of the planet suffering to have them crawling on its skin.

He began to caress her, enjoying the free intimacy of sliding his fingers below the waistline of her panties. The mushroomy odor of their unwashed bodies, their filthy clothes. She parted her legs to accommodate him, but when he searched her face she looked troubled. The way her forehead rippled, like the sea seen from the sky. The same as when she'd first laid eyes on him.

"Eventually we're going to run out of steam." Her voice was faint.

His fingers rested on the inside of her thigh. "Yeah."

"I just…I wonder how it's gonna happen, you know? I mean, will we just fall over? Or just not be able to get up one morning?"

James didn't want to talk about this. To face the swell of anguished guilt in his chest. But he let her go on.

"One way or another, it's inevitable. Like aging. I imagine it'll be a lot like getting old, y'know? It's weird, 'cause I don't even feel hungry any more. And I hear that happens to the elderly too, close to the end. They stop eating. I just feel…hollow. Like an empty clay pot on the verge of crumbling to dust. Like sometime soon, I'm gonna put my foot down the wrong way and my leg'll crumble and I'll fall into a heap of dry fragments."

Dizzy and weak, they meandered hand-in-hand back into camp to sit near the fire's heat that seemed to nourish them right through their skins. The billycans of chickpeas sitting in the coals, bubbling furiously. Speaking the accusation that no human voice dared: that James's dream quest was leading them to their doom.

*

That night James was ripped out of a dream where Nonna had been just about to tell him something vital, something to save them—

Screaming confusion, scrabbling limbs in the brush. Gord shouted some obscenity. A white flash gunshot exploded. Panicking, James pulled his knife and scrambled from the tent into gelid thick darkness.

"Where are they!" Tribe shouted.

Rohini and Lilac, both gagging sobs, babbling incoherently. James tried to make his way to Lilac, running into Gord with enough force to wind them both.

"What the fuck's going on?" Graham shouted.

"Rohini!" Sheilagh shouted. "Answer me! Are you hurt?"

"It came!" Rohini screamed. "It came – it came right through the tent!"

Clay flicked his lighter and got a candle going. Just a thin seam of light.

The tent Rohini and Lilac shared had been torn to shreds.

"It was a bear," said Amy angrily. "You were keeping food in your fucking tent, weren't you!"

Rohini hung her head low. "It was supposed to be a surprise!" she sobbed.

In James's arms, Lilac violently shaking.

"What was supposed to be a fuckin' surprise!" Sheilagh demanded.

Amy picked up a twinkling shred in the candlelight. Foil wrap. She sniffed it, flung her head back in disbelief. "Can you be serious! Fuckin' chocolate in your tent!"

"She told you," Lilac choked. "We were saving it, we wanted to surprise everybody!"

Amy put a hand to her own head. "What did I tell you about keeping food in your fucking tent, girls?"

"But it was still in the wrapper!" Rohini keened.

"Holy fuck," Gord snickered nastily.

"Jesus Christ!" Amy exploded. "Are you really that dense! Can it be? Rohini – that friggin' bear could smell that bar from five hundred meters away!"

"I for one don't buy that horseshit, that you were saving it for a *fuckin' surprise*." Calmness in Gord's voice, chillier than the night air. "My bet is you were hoarding it for yourselves."

"How can you say that!" Lilac shrieked at him. "How can you fucking say that!"

The problem with starvation. With exhausted despair. The power to unmake, rebuild anyone into a self-pitying, self-righteous fool. Forms transmuted, boiled into unforms.

*

The next day's hike was silent and tense. Sometime around midday, they came across a narrow bush road carved through the forest. They stopped, blinking dumbly up and down its length.

"Well?" Gord snapped at James. "You got the friggin' compass in your head. Which way?"

James turned right and the rest followed him north. It was little more than an ATV trail, dirt ruts divided by a rounded grassy hummock. Rocky, potholed, mean. Rising and falling, curving through the steep terrain, closed in on both sides by sheer hills of granite blocks tangled with large trees, ferns and shrubs. Plate fungi growths on tree trunks. Ugly, squashed gargoyles of rusty iron and pale marble. Knot holes that were mouths, puckered in terrific shock. Hushed, abbey quiet. The furtive rustle of curious chickadees through the branches. The clank of equipment, the groan of empty stomachs.

Such a relief to be on a trail, not having to fight their way through branches. But James noted the others, like himself, concentrating on keeping their footfalls soft. Lest the Sicari had also found this trail and were lying in wait. Or perhaps it was simpler: they lacked the energy to place their feet solidly.

"*The pack on my back is aching,*" Graham chanted in a low voice. "*The straps seem to cut me like a knife.*"

James had told Maggie to shut the fuck up, and sure enough she had. Sullenly silent. Only the sense now that he was moving the right direction. Just as Nguyen had described, following a delectable aroma that he could somehow sense with his entire body. Every weary footstep deepened the musk. Until he felt himself tugged along, an entranced marionette.

Something scrambled through the bush at them.

Amy, Gord and Clay leveling their guns at a tree just in time to see a black marten peek around the trunk.

James's stride didn't even slow. His own rifle, Ross's, propped mutely over one shoulder.

Difficult to track the course of the day in the trees, seeing no more than shards of sky. When gold started deepening to blue, they stopped, slumped to the ground. Nothing left. Not even enough energy to open their packs. James looked at Sheilagh's sunken eyes that stared off into nothing. Rohini, so limp she might have gone back into the zombified state.

He struggled to ignore the horrified wellspring in his stomach, the mounting certainty that he'd been tricked, was leading his friends to miserable death in the bush. For nothing.

*

It was a few minutes after Amy had gone off for a pee. Lilac had dug out her knitting, the needles twitching, rubbing like a fetish. Graham staring at Athol's Bible as if studying his own reflection on its rusty red cover.

As Sheilagh reached for her pack of meager provisions, James saw Gord thumb the Garand's safety. On or off? The decisive flick of his thumb, the way his lower lip protruded beneath his bottom teeth. His eyes on her pack, dead to everything but want.

Oh yes. No question. He'd just switched that damned safety *off*.

Enough in that pack to keep one person going for a while.

Long enough to find a hunter's shack or an old logging camp. This bush road must come out *somewhere*. These were the dire thoughts James read in Gord's callow, focused gaze.

"Don't," James croaked.

Gord blinked slowly. The bright turquoise irises focused on James.

But Tribe and Clay were already on their feet. Tribe with the rapier out, Clay gripping his guns. Both of them facing down Gord.

Only now did it dawn on the rest that there was something seriously amiss.

"Whoa, now," Graham whispered, "whoa, fellas."

"Why don't you put the rifle down a while," Clay rasped. His old fingers flexed around the butts of his guns.

"You can't be fucking serious," said Massimo quizzically to Gord.

"Oh," said Tribe, almost jocular. "He's serious, alright. You know you won't live," he said to Gord, "not more than a few seconds."

"Jaysus feking Christ!" Sheilagh bellowed, flinging her hands at them. "Is this the way it's all to end! Would you look at yourselves! Sure, I shoulda stayed back with the Sicari! Least I know what side *they're* on!"

A moment of awful weight. None of them moved. Finally, Gord bobbed his head with a bitter little smile. It seemed he was just about to say something when a deep, throaty voice called from the bush.

"Hope youse ain't gonna kill somebody on my property."

Impossible to tell where the speaker was. Sound acted that way in the bush, galloped through the trees like a panicked buck. Melting away, directionless. Before any of them could react, a figure in camo hunting gear stepped onto the trail thirty yards back. He carried a crossbow. It wasn't aimed at them, but James could see it was cocked and loaded with a bolt.

"Bin trackin' youse since this morning," he said calmly. "Since youse crossed onto my property." He pulled down the camo mask to reveal a ruddy, fleshy face, fully bearded. "Name's Remi. Bin expectin' you."

Amy emerged 50 yards down the trail, her rifle aimed at the stranger. She ordered him to drop the crossbow. Remi laughed, revealing teeth browned by a serious nicotine habit.

"Youse're the ones with all the advantages," he said. "Three rifles, includin' a semi-auto. Two pistols. One sword. Lotsa weaponry 'gainst one little crossbow." Still, he bent and put his own weapon on the ground. "Fuckin' good to see some faces, hear some

354

voices other thin my own."

"What do you mean, you've been expecting us?" Lilac asked.

He sauntered down the path towards them with a heavy step. He looked to be in his late forties. He had a beer gut. The rolling shoulders of somebody used to hard work. Amy shouted at him to freeze, but he just waved her off. As he drew closer, James saw the front of his dirty baseball cap was embroidered with images of fishing lures. The caption read *Support Your Local Hooker*.

"Don't s'pose any of youse got any smokes?" he asked.

"Just about to ask you the same fuckin' thing," Graham moaned.

"Aw, fuck." He scratched his head and adjusted the cap. "How 'bout we just sit awhile."

He'd had dreams of them coming. Ever since Lights Out. Or, as he called it, BFU: the Big Fuck Up. Dreams vivid enough to scorch his memory with their faces. He didn't know how they'd found the hidden way into his valley, but he supposed it was to be expected, given the odd circumstances and all.

Seven years ago, he'd quit his long-haul trucking business. Sold the rig. He and his wife had taken to the bush. "Waitin' for the shit to hit the fan," he chuckled. "And boy, didn't it just, eh? Gotta admit, didn't see it pannin' out this way, though."

He had two hundred acres of bush. Thirty cleared. Twenty planted with forage grass. A hundred apple trees, twenty plum, thirty head of sheep.

"*A farm for nine*," James whispered to himself. "*An island for three*."

"Yup," said Remi, glancing at him. "That's the way I heard it too. Way I see it, it's meant to be, eh?"

James saw Lilac shudder.

"Easy to see youse've been through Hell. Youse need food and a place to overwinter. Me, I need hands to replace the ol' John Deere. Gotta shitload of work to do before the snow flies. Apples and plums to pick and stow, hay to mow, get it all stored away. Time's runnin' out."

"So you've been up here all by yourself ever since Lights Out?" Rohini asked.

"Yup. Whole summer. Just me and my dogs. My wife Betty, she died when it happened. Just clenched up tight like a seized motor, eh?"

"How awful!"

"Well, it ain't easy buryin' your wife, that's for sure. Still and all, better she went quick, 'n all. Gonna be mighty thin this winter. Chances are it'll be pretty fuckin' bleak. 'Scuse the French. That's what I got to offer. Ain't much, but fuck, what choice do youse have?" He produced a manic, wheezy laugh.

*

They followed him up the trail, climbing a great rocky ridge that overlooked a broad valley. From the top they could see for miles and miles. The distant forest canopy a quilt of faint Fall colors. To their right at the head of the valley, they could just see a twinkling lake. Below that, fields of grass rippling with wind.

"Over a hundred years ago, buncha Scots farmers tried settlin' up here. Dirt-cheap land, eh? But it all hadda be cleared, ploughed. Real hard go. Most of 'em couldn't take it and moved off. But a few stayed on. Tough fuckers. This land was cleared by a guy named MacLaren. Lucky son of a bitch. This land, see, it was an old bog. I'm talkin' hundreds of years ago, eh. Coal-black soil five feet deep. MacLaren stuck it out, raised a big family. Eventually, they all moved down to the city, but they kept the property. I bought it from MacLaren's great-granddaughter. Old biddy, ninety-eight years old. I kid you not."

The trail fell steeply into the valley, fording a shallow stream at the bottom that Remi told them flowed down from the lake. They passed a corrugated steel barn, a large low sheep shed and paddock crowded with baaing sheep. On a hill above the paddock was a small two-storey stone house beside an enormous maple tree. Not tall, but massive. The trunk at least four feet through.

"Look," said Lilac, pointing at the tree. "It's an Ent."

James could tell she was desperate to infuse her voice with optimism. All of them, numb, hungry and very tired. Depressed, even.

They all froze as two huge wolfhounds galloped up to them growling and barking.

"Ah, shut up, you mutts!" Remi growled, bending down to scratch their gray wooly fur. He didn't have to bend far. They were enormous bloody dogs. He must have noticed the way James, Rohini and a few of the others shrank away from them. He chuckled. "Not to worry. They're stupid, but friendly enough. This here's Jackson, and this's Stuart."

As they neared the house, they could see a hump of earth beneath the maple, marked by a carved plank.

The house was warm and clean, but smelled of cigarettes. And it was tiny. After weeks in the bush, it seemed stiflingly hot. Plain walls, narrow rooms chaining their vision, preventing it from stretching out.

Through a damp mudroom into a small kitchen, Remi led them into a cramped living room. As they crowded in, James saw the looks on Sheilagh's and Amy's faces and knew they were wondering the same thing he was: how were all of them going to live in this space? Dependent now on a stranger, an unknown quantity. Remi threw some wood into the airtight stove, told them to make themselves at home. But they all just stood, slouching, hollow-eyed.

Finally, they had reached the end of something. But so many had not made it. Half the prophesy had been fulfilled. Yet there was nothing to feel but dull despair weighing more heavily than their packs ever did.

Chapter 20

The Final Leg

"'Spect you'll be headin' out before too long," Remi had said to James that first night, breaking the sullen quiet.

The Group hollow-eyed, shell shocked. Remi was sitting in a bent-back rocking chair, scratching Stuart's head. Or maybe it was Jackson. James couldn't tell the dogs apart.

"Ain't done yet, are ya?" James gave him a look. "Dreamed that too!"

Indeed, the next day James set out again. His legs felt leaden sore. He was bereft of energy, but the impetus lay beyond his will. Everything, everything orbited the Stone that grappled at him so impatiently.

He didn't ask anybody to come with him, but Tribe and Graham volunteered.

James was disappointed that Massimo didn't offer. He'd changed. Oddly silent, sullen. He'd been badly affected by the confrontation with Nguyen. Even since their time at Nonna's, Massimo seemed sour, resentful. James needed to sit down with him, but it would have to wait. Nothing more important than the final leg.

They borrowed toques and gloves from Remi. His long johns were too big around the waist, but they were better than nothing. They packed a few packages of dried chickpeas and a slab of home-cured meat that Remi called lamb bacon. Remi had managed to pick lots of apples, but they were too heavy to carry more than enough for a couple of days.

Sheilagh was weepy as Tribe tried to reassure her, tenderly holding his face in her hands. She sensed they would not see each other again. Lilac remained reserved and cool, unwilling to betray the agitation James noticed in her flighty hands. They hugged, they kissed, and then the trio was off.

Bushwhacking due north through mile after mile of solid forbidding forest that had never felt the axe. Thickets of hobblebush and buckthorn catching their trousers, stubbornly resisting each step. Dead snapped-off limbs of fir and spruce formed spikes sharp as nails, scraping and welting the skin.

Filthy strenuous work.

By the end of each day's hike they were stumbling tired, sweaty despite the chill. And next morning, the bones of their feet and legs still ached. Yet they took no days off. Tribe and Graham deferring to James's ever-swelling desperation to reach the end of his Quest. To find what he had been sent for.

James with a growing, gnawing sense of the exact direction, driven on like a whipped mule.

Up, up the land climbed in rocky shoulders, steeper than staircases. They clambered with hands as well as feet, gripping branches and roots. There was no sure footing. Rocks hidden beneath thick leaf litter, shifting beneath their weight, waiting patiently to break their ankles and snap their knees. Mats of moss suddenly giving way, slippery as ice. Only a panicked scramble of limbs stopping them from plummeting and being maimed against granite teeth thirty feet below. Just one step away from an excruciating death, lost in the bush.

Nothing. Nothing but tree and rock and river, a wilderness to maul a person's will. Fallen logs and branches to climb. Streams, waterfalls. All around them an immensity of stone. And the trees that hated the stone, prying and breaking it with their roots. All silently deriding their puny human softness.

Graham kept stopping and looking back. When Tribe asked him if he'd seen something, Graham shook his head.

"Assuming we survive this fuckin' business, we'll need to get back. There's an old method of way-finding called the 'look back' – turning round to take note of what your return route will look like, right? That way you've got a picture in your mind of what to look for on the return trip. I've heard that bees and wasps do it for the same reason."

"Really." Tribe sounded intrigued.

"Don't know about bees," James mumbled, "but I've just seen evidence of a WASP doing that trick."

"Hey, alright," Graham snickered. "Fair play, fair play. Good to know you're not a complete zombie, James."

There was no joy at camp. A small fire, a handful of bland, mealy chickpeas. A few thin slices of Remi's bacon. Beneath the ogival woven branches, they could hear approaching winds braying through the trees before feeling the blowing cold pinch their faces. Now fully, cruelly Autumn.

Even with their groundsheets lying on stones and knobby roots, they would fall into blank dreamless unconsciousness little removed from comas.

Ever closer, the Stone teasing James with its reticence, but the pull on his heart, his lungs was unbearable. A sickening, stroking sensation, terrible and quickening. The urgency of sex. Exploiting his most primal reptilian drive to yank him over every stony ridge.

Time and again the vector in James's brain brought them to a rock face forty feet tall, or a sudden cliff that must be circumvented. With aching knees they'd blow out their frustration and move on, trying to find a way down or around.

One night in the bush, their glowing domed tent puny among the silent black columns of trees. James stumbled into the ferns for a piss. Dark enough that he couldn't see his hand in front of his own face. Ominous, a sense of skulking presence in the black. Holding his breath, holding his urine, James was sure he heard breathing. Something watching him. A heavy snuffle that made him crawl back into the tent without bothering to finish.

He squeezed into his space between Tribe and Graham. Aware of every jostle and twitch of his compatriots.

"Blacker than a cold night in Hell," Tribe muttered after he'd blown out their candle.

"Tribe," said James.

"Yes."

"Nguyen said that Hermes wants to create an army of homunculi. What was he talking about?"

"A homunculus is a little version of a person. The alchemists were fascinated by the idea of creating artificial life. I think it was Paracelsus who gave a recipe for making a miniature man by baking human semen in horse dung for forty days in a retort."

They lay quietly for a time. James could hear the furtive snapping of their chickpeas soaking in Ziploc bags, popping open like living eggs. He shivered. What had Amy said to him, that night before they'd left Nonna's? *That fuckin' Stone thing better be worth it.* Could anything be? He felt giddy with guilty dejection.

"Graham?"

"Aye."

"You know how you told me, when we were at George's, that everybody in the Group just needed time to digest everything I'd said?"

"Aye. I think they have, don't you?"

"I don't know."

"Don't let Sheilagh get to you, mate. She knows it's not your fault. Tribe! Am I right?"

"Sheilagh's intellect will overcome her passion." And then Tribe added archly, "If not, I'll just have to have a little chat with her when we get back."

James smiled. "Right. Good luck with that."

360

"Think about it this way," said Graham. "You're the one who saved us all."

"Bullshit."

"It's not! It's you that led us to the farm. Nothing to be ashamed of, James." Graham paused for effect. "'Cept maybe that you've got no balls."

Tribe blew impatient wind through his nose. "What have I been telling him all this time?"

*

On the ninth day, the three of them stepped out on the rocky shore of the lake.

Many lakes they'd passed. This country speckled with water.

But this was the one they sought. Larger than most. Morose choppy water the same hue as the slate rubble clouds that plaqued the pale blue sky. An archipelago of treed islands about a mile out, withheld from shore like a collection of heirlooms venally guarded by a brooding old hag.

One island in particular. A granite wedge thrust from the irondark water like the prow of a half-sunken ship. Topped by a crown of pines. Grim cliffs on all sides except the south face, where the rock sloped down to the water. Perhaps just gently enough that it might be climbed with some effort.

Somehow James felt an echo. Almost five hundred years before, another weary trekker had stumbled out in this same spot. Absorbed this view with a mixture of dread and relief. To know that the malignant cargo he carried would soon be hidden. The world made safe.

James was about to betray that man, shatter that safety. The force of the Stone so strong he felt his ribcage bend towards the island. His blood gathering towards it like a tide.

Moontide blood.

Through cracks in the cloud he saw the blue-powdered waning moon, the golden sun. The left and the right eyes of Horus. Between them, more avid than the glitter of Horus's beak, the silver flame of Betelgeuse.

"Goddammit!" James shouted.

"What is it, mate?"

"I can't fucking swim!"

"You can't?"

"You believe that? After all this shit?"

Graham put a steadying hand on James's arm. "You don't want to be in that water anyway, James. It'll be bloody cold."

"Bah!" Tribe scoffed, tugging off his anorak. "It's an easy swim. I'll go."

"No!" James bellowed, as if at a disobedient dog. Tribe glared at him. "Sorry, Tribe. This is my task."

"What boy doesn't learn to swim?" Tribe retorted.

"It wasn't a priority in the Muir household, Tribe!"

Tribe and Graham told him to stay put. They would scout the shoreline. There must be some boat or canoe somewhere.

James was left alone, staring across the unfriendly waves. Finally, Maggie spoke again:

A man can drown in a bowl of chicken soup, sweets!

But he could not wait. The proximity was excruciating. He saw a big cedar log floating in the waves. He stripped off all his clothes. Everything, jacket and boots included, went into the waterproof bag lining his pack. He made sure to tie off the bag in a cinched, watertight gooseneck, just as Graham had taught him.

Naked in the wind, he was immediately shivering. He put his pack back on. Hesitated, staring into the depths of that dark water. He took a ginger step and slipped, falling into the lake, whooping at the cold. The freezing water clenched James's muscles, squeezed the air from his lungs. So like panic, his chest seizing to draw breath. His teeth started chattering.

He grasped the slimy log and started paddling towards the island.

Chapter 21

The Stone

Waves kept smacking his face, jutting into his nose, making him sputter and cough. The dark lea of each wave a black, serpentine creature peeking above the surface for a hungry look at its next meal.

Just keep kicking, he told himself. Eyes on the prize.

He felt he'd been in the water for hours, and the island looked barely closer than it had been when he was on shore. His body raw with cold.

As clouds scudded he caught glimpses of the sun. It hadn't shifted very far.

Once he made the mistake of glancing back. The shore was hundreds of yards behind him. Panic prickled through his numb limbs, forcing a deep breath. He inhaled water and choked, gagging, body jerking. His legs swung down perpendicular to the surface. He felt the yawning depths beneath him, yanking his body down—

"No!" he coughed, frantically throwing his arms over the log, mouth gulping at the sky. Forcing his legs back up to the surface, forcing himself not to think of the huge black space below. "Kick, you fucker! Kick!"

One thing he hadn't counted on was the drag of his waterlogged pack. The weight straining his shoulders against the buoyancy of the log, always threatening to turn him over.

But even the log wasn't as buoyant as he'd imagined. Sick with despair, he realized it was slowly sinking. His mass forcing it lower and lower.

Even worse, the wind had picked up, really roaring now, casting whitecaps that completely washed over him. The relentless pounding wrestled him off the log, swamping his face. He was underwater, struggling in the brown noisome blur to find the log again. His arms thrashed as the pack rolled him over, tugging him lower. He saw the metallic gleam of the surface above him and knew he would drown.

Then his hand knocked painfully against the log. He gripped the stump of a branch like a handle, summoning the strength to pull himself up to the top. Gasping, spitting water, he forced his body over, onto his front. For a few minutes he was wracked by painful hacking until white spots swam in his vision like glowing sperm.

Shivering violently, his legs so numb with cold it felt as if they'd dissolved.

The log sunk now so far that it was difficult to hold on and keep his face above the suffocating waves. Heavy rain pelted him, puckering the surface. The island invisible behind the gray shroud.

Desperately, he kicked.

It seemed an age before he finally touched the pebbled wall of the island. Pawing himself along the edge until he reached the slope on the south side. Beneath the surface, a sharp ledge of rock jutted, hollow beneath. Very difficult for him to pry himself out of the water, using only his shaking arms.

Gasping noisily he crawled on all fours up the incline until he was clear of the water. His fingers so stiff it was some time before he could get his pack open and untie the gooseneck. At least his clothes had stayed dry. He fought to get into them. Leaving his pack behind, he struggled up the slope to the pinnacle of the island.

It was an even smaller island than it looked from shore, perhaps only twenty yards long and half that wide. The pinnacle stood about thirty feet above the water, topped by an enormous pine tree that made sinister hushing sounds in the stiff wind.

James knew exactly, precisely where to find the grotto. Hidden behind a rock lip, so that it could only just be seen if one stood in the right spot. A narrow horizontal cleft partly blocked by the pine's thick roots. The entire top of the island was thick with rusty old pine needles. James scooped away several armfuls of the needles to access the cleft. Even then, the space was so narrow he had to wiggle through, lying on his back, wedging himself along with his elbows. Twice he felt himself get stuck. Only the desperation of reaching the Stone made him fight.

The grotto was a narrow hollow in the rock, sloping down towards the back. Just high enough to sit up in, no more than three feet wide and seven feet long. James's heart leaped in his chest. There, leaning against the back wall, dimly seen in the low light, were five clay urns. A sixth had split apart. Heaped beneath the clay fragments was a fine green powder.

The Stone!

His own breath hollowly loud in the narrow space. Something in his mind split open, and he knew it would never again be healed. From behind the split, a tangle of legs pulsed and twitched. This thing that had been waiting since his conception to be birthed.

Jenny and Sara's glass bell was in his hand. The talisman he'd retrieved from his burned-out apartment. He had no awareness of getting it out of his pocket. He placed his offering at the edge of the spilled powder.

Suddenly from without, a tremendous gust of wind rushed into the grotto. A cloud of green powder swirled into his face, gluing to his wet skin and hair, clotting in his eyes. He reared back, blinking. He sneezed.

Great pain overwhelmed his contorting body. He could not move. He could not breathe. As he slid sideways against the granite, he was absorbed into absolute darkness.

*

Allistair Rivers had once told James: there is really no such thing as absolute dark. As long as there are molecules moving about, they crash into each other, creating tiny flashes of light.

But James knew now he was in a place far, far from Allistair's experience. Yes, absolute dark. Uninterrupted by even microscopic light. Palpable, smothering, closer than his own skin, his own blood. Suffusing his cells.

But he was not alone. Unseen mouths darted out of the blackness to jaw and gnaw, bite and slaver. He could not escape. Tried to scream but silence broke in him, sharp teeth chewing from the inside. Unendurable agony, every bone crushed by angry molars.

They were his own teeth mutilating his flesh. He could not stop sinking into himself, thrilled by the warm wetness. Devouring and then excreting until there was no difference between flesh and feces.

Then a tiny pinpoint of light, immeasurably far away. But rapidly nearing. And within the light, a figure who smiled to palliate the terrible pain, but without kindness. It was Nonna. She was kneading dough into a round loaf, putting it into her stone oven, quietly humming a strange tune.

Nonna, he tried to ask, *Nonna what is happening to me?*

But he knew this was not Nonna after all. This was the Goddess creating *pa'at*, the loaf that connotes the beginning of time.

A sensation of being violently flung into the baking loaf. Tumbling into a vast desert. A sand-choked furnace abutting a sharp stone coombe. Within the coombe a dark cave. Within the cave, a bent wizened old man with a yellowed white beard that fell past his waist. Wearing nothing but a soiled, tattered knee-length linen kilt.

"What do you want!" the old man barked. Scratching at the cracked leathery moles covering his concave, drooping chest. "Ah, it's you." Sounding less than pleased to see him.

James ducked inside, relieved to be away from the burning red desert. The old man stooped at the back of the cave beside a tall Egyptian statue of blue granite. Noseless, one arm missing. The old man pointed with his stick at a tatterdemalion table containing dozens of books. "Choose one!" he ordered with curmudgeonly merriment.

The books were stacked in precarious columns. Large and small, worm-eaten, bindings torn, leather covers disintegrating. Each frayed spine contained only one or two words. Georgio Beato, said one. Kriegsmann said another. Newton. Kunrath. Fulcanelli. Others in Arabic, Hebrew. Still more in strange characters James could not identify.

James became aware that there weren't just dozens of books. There were thousands. Millions. Perhaps every book that had ever been written. He was lost in a forest of stacked volumes, sprinkling upon him the dust of their dissolution like pollen from desiccated flowers.

"Well?" the old man cried, rapping his staff across James's knee. "What are you waiting for?"

James chose Newton, only because it was one of the few names he recognized. He opened the cover, and it fell off.

"Read it aloud!" the old man snickered.

"'True it is, without falsehood, certain most true,'" James read hesitantly. "'That which is above is like to that which is below, and that which is below is like to that which is above, to accomplish the miracles of one thing. And as in all things whereby contemplation of one, so in all things arose from this one thing by a single act of adoption.

"'The father thereof is the Sun, the mother the Moon.

"'The wind carried it in its womb, the earth is the source thereof. It is the father of all works of wonder throughout the world.

"'The power thereof is perfect.

"'If it be cast on the earth, it will separate the element of earth from that of fire, the subtle from the gross.

"'With great sagacity it doth ascend gentle from earth to heaven. Again it doth descend to earth and uniteth in itself the force from things superior and things inferior.

"'Thus thou wilt possess the brightness of the world, and all obscurity will fly far from thee.

"'This thing is the strong fortitude of all strength, for it overcometh every subtle thing and doth penetrate every solid substance.

"'Thus was the world created.

"'Hence will there be marvelous adaptations achieved of which the manner is this.

"'For this reason I am called Hermes Trismagistus because I hold three parts of the wisdom of the whole world.

"'That which I had to say about the operation of the Sun is completed.'"

"My words on my tablet!" said the old man. In his lingering gaze, James recognized the alien being he had detected in Maggie. "For I am Hermes Trismagistus, the Thrice Great!"

His squeaky cackle brimmed with mockery, bubbled into a catarrhal cough. "The *Emerald Tablet* the Greeks called it – because they were fond of calling *any* green stone 'emerald'! Impetuous Alexander of Macedonia stole the Tablet from the arms of my mummy. Thought he was so clever, that he understood the riddle I'd written on it. Came to think of himself as the son of mighty Ra. Began referring to himself as 'the Great.'"

The old man snorted. "After *he expired*, those Greek idiots hid the Tablet so well they forgot where it was! But they'd done their worst, translating the Tablet's words, disseminating them. Grist for so many fools! Rogues! Thousands of them, century upon century, all seeking great secrets. Alchemists, ha! Quacks. Yes! They saw what you just read as the formula, the recipe for the Philosopher's Stone. The secret of immortality, of great fortune – as if fortune were the equivalent of wealth. Most of them driven mad by it. Like our mutual friend in the red cassock, the one who dares to call himself Hermes, his brain rotted away by mercury vapors and lead dust. That is why I love your language. For such a young tongue, English overflows with meaning. For instance, that *cupidity* rhymes with *stupidity*! How true, how true! All these idiots, searching for 'the secret' when all the time it stared them right in their stupid faces!"

"That the Emerald Tablet you made *is* the Philosopher's Stone," said James.

The little old man giggled and coughed again. "Just so! Sweat of the mighty Ra. More ancient than the earth itself. And now, it is yours! Ah yes, but that is the very equivalent of saying that *you* belong to *it*! You are but the Third Vessel. Just as the Templar Knight Gilles de Clermont was the Second. He rediscovered the Emerald Tablet in the midst of Jerusalem's rape, when the alleys ran ankle-deep in Saracen blood! While his compatriots burned infidel bodies to extract the golden besants the Saracens had swallowed in their final agonies, the Stone revealed its true form to his dull mind. He spirited it away to the Templar palace. For himself, all for himself. Or so he thought.

"His life was hideously prolonged by its power. And with the extension of his years came a bloating of his self-indulgence. He thought he had been granted the secret of immortality! But that is not the nature of things! All things must pass away. Change, inconstancy are the lifeblood of the universe. So when he realized death could no longer be cheated he was filled with great torment. As you will feel too, James Muir. You will pray for death. Of that you can be assured.

"Gilles's greedy pride dictated that no one else should ever possess such a wonder. No! Not ever! It happened that around the same time, word spread of heretofore unknown, vast empty lands across the ocean far to the west. He rejoiced. He ground my Emerald Tablet into dust. Keeping a small portion for himself, he sent men across the ocean and up the river that would come to be known as the St. Lawrence. Following ever-shrinking tributaries to their deaths in a remote, pitiless wilderness. Gilles presumed the Stone would never again be found." Hermes Trismagistus gave an evil, merry snort. "Well, *never* turned out to last exactly four hundred and eighty-four years. *Until you came.* He was only following the Stone's will, after all."

"You tried to hide it too, didn't you? In plain sight. The Emerald Tablet that you carved with this gibberish." James flung the dusty book onto the table.

"Not gibberish!" the old man boomed, and suddenly he seemed much taller, his voice vibrating the stone walls of his hovel. "It is a formula full of wisdom! Remember it and you will command great power!"

"What is it? What is this thing?"

The old man glowered. His face gray as the dusty residue of fire, splitting into a malevolent grin. "What is it that you want?" he drawled.

James did not hesitate. "I want to see my family."

All at once, the old man was a great scorpion-like beast with dozens of claws. It fell on James with a terrifying mewl, tearing him limb from limb.

*

Again, great darkness. The inevitable oceanic abyss that surrounds all things.

Then James saw them from afar. Divided from them by cloudy distance and great height, and yet able to see the smallest detail of mud pressed into the pores of Stacy's nose. The ugly scratch on Jenny's cheek. Sara's bruised hand that sought for warmth against Stacy's neck. Stacy was gripping both girls in her arms, her face set in a hard expression that robbed her of beauty. Eyes narrowed, fouled with distrust and fear. Only one face of dozens, crowded onto an acre of chilly mud dotted with tents.

Stacy! he screamed and she turned to him – yes! she'd heard his voice—

Abruptly he was torn away, just as he reached out for them, just as his fingers were feathered by Stacy's windblown hair.

No! he shrieked, but his voice was subsumed in the snicker of Hermes Trismagistus, wet and full, as if James was bathing in his phlegmy throat. *To see your family was your request, Third Vessel. That was all.*

And then, James was beside the steel shipping container. Ten years after. The female slave pen.

"So it's time travel you're hog-selling now, is it?" a female voice snarled from within.

James still so broken with grief at being robbed yet again of his family that he acted without thinking, rapping on the container door. Sheilagh was inside there. He must get her out. His knuckles drummed on the steel.

But it wasn't steel he was skinning his knuckles on. It was the bark of a tree. Gunshots, shouting voices all around. Amy fired her rifle. The Sicari horseman burst through the foliage upon them. Mike jumped out to defend her. The bravest and the stupidest act James had ever seen. James was filled with fury. He threw down the rifle and tackled Mike.

*

Five millennia ago, you find it. Far out in the desert, far from the nourishing waters of the Nile. Half dead of thirst, you come upon it. Alabaster is what it seems to be. In your language, *shiss*. Yet bizarrely green.

You are the first it seeks. Its First Vessel. You study its wiles. Bathe in its mysteries. You are very patient, ungreedy. Infinity you caress in your sure hands. *Shiss!*, the cobra's warning. It commands you to call it merely the Stone. It whispers to you the *logos* of the universe. Grants you hymns from a mind greater than the sum of all time.

Through this power you build a great city. Iunu, you call it. Place of pillars, for the huge temples you raise to the brilliant Ra, who bestowed the Stone upon you. Iunu, which the literal-minded Greeks will come to call Heliopolis. City of the Sun. Iunu, the seed of a civilization. Fantastic wealth comes to you, the ability to make and unmake, mask and unmask as you see fit. Kings of Kings pay homage at your temples and seek your counsel. Dynasty upon dynasty. Never it seems do you age or tire.

Your desire to become king is quashed by the Stone, which has other ends written for you.

Over several lifetimes you fuse your *ba* spirit, your character, forever into the Stone's eerie consciousness. You become its one true Voice. Wherefore you are called son of the divine scribe Thoth who is the father of all science and magic! Known to the barbarian Greeks as Hermes, messenger of the gods! Trismagistus, the Thrice Great. Thus you are honored by god kings as the crafter of deep magic by which they achieve *akh* and thus become stars in the heavens. They raise temples, obelisks, great pyramids at your behest.

Not satisfied with your wealth and fame, you also build the city of Khem, naming it so after the blackness of the Nile soil upon which Egypt was founded, as distinguished from the scorched red desert where creeps the demon Seth, cast out by Horus as vengeance for dismembering his father Osiris.

In such awe is your wisdom regarded that the Arabs will come to call your art *al-Khemia*, the study of blackness. From whence the savage inhabitants of a small, cold, rain-swept island derived *alchemy*. The Hermetic Art. This alabaster-skinned line who were draping themselves in animals skins when you were divining the whispered incantations of stars. These grubs who presumed understanding, who will themselves one day command the world.

All these things you see! Memories of the future troubling your four hundred and eighty-four years. Yours to behold because you possess secrets unknown to mere mortals.

They build a great statue to your name. Your features smashed into a slab of blue granite by the sweat of a hundred craftsmen. The story of your deeds to strike fear into the hearts of the very gods. Horus's eyes – that can gaze across time, that can behold endlessness – rolling, crazed with frightful awe at the accomplishments of Hermes the Thrice Great. A graven image to last forever, to match your immortal frame.

But you are deceived. You have taken credit for work that belonged to the Stone. You have beheld yourself as master when you are enslaved. Immortality is but a figment. You are dying. Suddenly desperate for time, you cast the Stone as a green tablet inscribed with your wisdom, to be woven into your mummy. No one will have the intellect to guess at its true nature. Your final act is your most brilliant: to impregnate the blue granite statue with your *ka* spirit, your life-force. Thereby cheating death. Within the statue you *will* live on into eternity.

Who else but you could divine such brilliance? Could know all that is signified by such words as life, magic, honor. To apprehend such depth requires different vision from that of the eyes.

But now your true nightmare begins. Entombment within the statue for millennia. Wars topple you, wrack you so cruelly, efface your incredible story, mark your wise face with cracks, smash away your noble nose so that you will spend eternity as a leprous freak.

Worse. The civilization you helped to found crumbles and dies. Trapped in your statue, a forgotten lump of stone, dumped by time into oven-hot desert sand. Sand that scours and whispers, ridiculing your name, skimming over your stone contours. Every particle an imp biting your lithic flesh. Millions upon millions in waves, in feathery tongues, in leaden impenetrable gales.

But your statue is of granite. The great grandfather of sands. As many grains of sand as there are stars in the universe could peck at you without effect.

Then in the fifth millennium of your hell you understand. Your conceit is finally broken. Finally! True understanding, total subjugation to all that terrifies you. It is the giant Betelgeuse! Magnificence to make even the prodigious Ra tremble, toady himself before his relentless might! Betelgeuse who smites the universe with such a mighty hammer as will ring against stars for a billion years.

And you hear Betelgeuse laughing at you. A low, contented laugh that lasts longer than you can imagine. You cannot imagine it because the length of time is so great it brims the breadth of your mind, spilling over and over.

Not millennia. *Millions* of millennia, until you are ground down and down by the sand, masticated into your most loathsome nemesis. Worn, bite by miniscule bite, into the sand that digests you. You are scattered, a million different directions, blasted by the hot wind of an empty, dead planet. And all the time, the wind despises your story, outlasting you until the world itself is gone.

And so you too have vanished. Utterly crushed. Swallowed by time. Your posterity not so long as you prayed for, but so much longer than you could bear.

*

The memory of sleepless eons crushed James. Only dimly aware of a low moaning. The stink of shit.

All over his body, his muscles felt hideous, wooden. As if he himself had become an ancient sarcophagus. He could hardly move. The back of his head very sore from resting against the rock. For a while he lay still, remembering only scrambled patches that were confused and intermingled. Something about a cave in the desert. Glimpsing Stacy and the girls.

Grimacing, he raised his head, propped himself on his elbows. Every movement a terrible effort. One of his shoes had been gnawed open, his naked toe exposed through a ragged hole. Jesus, he must have been comatose not to have noticed that. Perhaps for days. The thought chilled him more deeply than the wind howling across the mouth of the little cave.

Gnawed by a mouse—

just like the sand taking its tiny bites, sand sand sand millions upon millions of nibbles until he was reduced to sand sandsandsandsandsand—

He shook violently.

Just sitting up winded him, the smell of his own shit gulped into his panting lungs. Very gingerly he turned his head, cords in his neck creaking like the rigging of an old tall ship—

sandsandsandsandsandsand!

His body jerked violently. He cried out in pain. His calf muscles twitched and pulled. He knew he was badly dehydrated.

He managed to roll over onto his knees, wincing as the spasms leapfrogged up his legs. The sickly feeling of having something alive within him – *the Stone!*

The clay pots remained where he'd found them. Five plus the one that had cracked open, the green dust spilled like a child's play sand. But this was not play, no. He had just experienced an eon of dissolution, erosion, pecked and pecked and pecked away to nothing. Ultimate nothingness.

And above him the towering pine snickered. The way a cuckold would deride his former lover after she had been betrayed in turn.

The Stone. He expected a sign, some ceremony of its consummation with him. But there was nothing. He closed his eyes.

When he opened them again, he was suddenly outside the cave, eyes lanced by the daylight, dry tongue scraping his chapped lips. Somehow he'd crawled down from the pinnacle to the top of the slope on the southern side of the island. Overcome by vertigo, he rolled down the granite, elbows and knees clubbed by stone, one solid smack on the head and he splashed into the water.

And he felt as the granite did the slow, slow ache of erosion under the ruthless licking waves. Licking and licking, coldly erotic, always taking.

He panicked, terrified of rolling off the shelf into the deep black water. Reaching out, grasping for the edge of the rock shelf—

A man can drown in a bowl of chicken soup, sweets!

He hoisted himself on his elbows and maneuvered back onto dry rock. On his hands and knees he turned around, shakily bowing to the lake.

Gasping for breath, lips enfolding the water's skin, sucking, gulping and choking. Until his aching stomach could take no more.

He knelt, shivering, staring into the glacial blue October sky, bright enough to sting his eyes. Jumbled with grey-purple clouds, frosted brilliant white on top. Even these he saw as granite, reforming, blending, restive.

All the water vomited back out of him in groans. Milky bile slithered down the rock to haze the lake. Bile and something else. Black and gritty, a lump the size of a hazelnut. Old clotted blood, he thought at first – but no, it wasn't black at all, it was blue, very dark blue—

With shaking fingers he seized it. A lump of blue granite!

"What the fuck is going on?" he croaked.

Across one edge of the lump, he could see the mark of a chisel. A fragment of some hieroglyph.

Absentmindedly, he slipped the rock into his pocket. Then he crawled to the other side of the shelf and drank again, where the water wasn't polluted with his puke.

Using his hands, scooping water into his foul mouth.

Lord, the pounding in his skull!

"How the hell am I gonna get back?" he asked hoarsely.

Was this it? he thought, slouching on the granite. Chilled by the wind, already shivering. Soaked to the skin, October night coming in soon. A few flakes of snow drifted across his line of sight before being whipped away by the bullying wind.

Shit.

This was it? Had he the strength, he would have screamed it. *I came all this way – I brought all those people – I almost starved – for this!*

"I refuse to die of hypothermia," he croaked, gritting his teeth against the shivering. No, he must survive. If only for the possibility of seeing Stacy and the girls again. One day.

As quickly as he could, fighting his stiff muscles, he stripped off all his wet clothes – first his coat, then all the layers of his ruined underwear, soaked in piss and shit. There were a few broken branches on one of the younger pines that he used as pegs to hang his wet things. He hurried. He needed to stay warm, to get out of this damn wind.

Naked, he plunged into the shallow water on the rock shelf, doing his best to rinse away the feces caked on his skin. His plan was to crawl back into the cave, spend the night there. Perhaps bury himself in the pine needles as a makeshift blanket.

And then a voice from the water: "*Ecce homo!*"

The first thing to spring into his mind was vicious, animalistic greed: *Go away! It's mine!*

But it was Tribe! He and Graham were twenty yards offshore in a battered old aluminum canoe. Shivering violently, James wept with gratitude.

"Christ," said Graham from the canoe. "You look like cack!"

Tribe berated James. "Didn't I tell you to wait!"

They came ashore, gave him their spare clothes.

"How long?" James rasped.

"Four days, man." Graham shook his head, hardly able to believe it himself.

"Just as well we spied your pack sitting there, or we might never have found you."

Again, caustic jealousy sparkled in James's addled brain. *It's mine.* He snuck a peek at Graham, who was standing halfway up the slope. *Don't even think about climbing to the top!*

"What is it?" Graham asked, wide-eyed. "What's up there?"

"Leave it." Something between a warning and a plea.

Graham stared hard at him. Peered at the shit-smeared long johns twisting against the pine. Those apparently were enough of a warning. He crossed his arms and waited for James to finish dressing.

James kept flashing back to the eons of erosion he'd experienced. Day by aching day, lost in an ocean of sand. The wicked intensity of a fever dream that had lasted for billions of years. An immense onus he felt still, scalding lead where his marrow should be.

He eyed Tribe. *You think I went through that Hell just to hand it over to you? You're crazier than a bag of cats!* He smiled to himself. *And don't be thinking that goddamned sword is going to do much good. Not anymore!*

As if sensing James's withering look, Tribe turned to glare at him, the wind flapping his hair. James pretended to busy himself getting into Graham's pants. A couple of inches too short, but they'd have to do. *Leave it up to McMann to be a short little fuck—*

Jesus Christ, what is *wrong* with me?

—and I'm keeping my eye on you as well, you fucking mick—

"Enough!" James shouted aloud, pressing the heels of his palms to his temples.

Graham and Tribe looked alarmed.

"Sorry," James mumbled, focusing on tying his shoes. He was badly frightened. The Voice now fused with his own imagination.

374

Before they left, James got the Aspirin bottle out of his bag, went back up to the summit. He hesitated before squeezing back into the grotto, terrified of the Stone. Just as if it were a nest of king cobras waiting to inject poison into his blood.

But the poison was already there. As long as he remained alive. Even long after, decaying back to soil, the Stone would settle into the earth as his bones dissolved.

The Stone was silent. James understood. All sentient beings must sleep. What dreams haunted its imagination?

Very carefully, reverently, he scooped up some of the green powder and screwed the top back onto the plastic bottle. Only now did he notice that the little glass bell was no longer there.

James sat in the middle of the canoe, Tribe in the front, Graham sterning.

So short would this life be, just a faint blink. Not even the endurance of a meteor against the bold eternity that came before, that stretched ever on after. He recognized his own puniness within the world. He faded like a jellyfish, invisible against dim waters. Simply an abstract cloud of cells, he experienced the universe encompassed within his own mind. Vaster than the universe without.

It was as if his eyes had suddenly evolved the quality of telescopes and microscopes at once. The trees aglow, even in the shadow of rain soaked clouds. His lungs but part of winds flowing through him, bursting from every pore. Growth, decay, all teeming, wondrously fecund. Plants groping sunward, feeling their nourishment. Every leaf a green metropolis of capillaries and cells glorious with the light of a star ninety million miles away. One multifarious whole.

"Y'alright, mate?"

James blinked, his trance jogged but not snapped.

"It's all breathing," he said quietly. A voice filled with the wonder of a little boy.

"Mmm-hmmm..." Tribe jabbed a cranky glance at him over his shoulder.

The whole way across the lake, Graham complained about Tribe's paddling. "Ach, will you stop pulling us to the right, Captain Studly!"

Even these utterances, seemingly inane, came to James bursting with hidden meaning. The way of the canoe knifing through the waves. A heartbeat.

James had read once of a tribe in the Amazon basin who identified holy men very early in life and kept them strictly sequestered in dark caves all their lives. Until the age of eighteen, when they were suddenly released into the riotous rainforest, to see with stinging raw eyes that most intricate of living mazes. And so to touch the numinous.

He felt he now understood something of that dreadful exacting experience. Every atom in his body resonating, all of them born in the blazing heart of a star.

Tribe's paddle broke the surface. James saw the water ripple over the polished wood, the brief dentition of drops along the edge. More drops scattered across the scalloped surface of the lake, each kiss with the water's skin ringed by spreading ripples.

He sensed large-mouth bass lurking in jungles of lake weed, trout down in the dark with unblinking brass medal eyes. Diaphanous fins, plate armor silvery in the deep. On shore, even from hundreds of yards out, James saw insects burrowing in leaf litter, moths taking wing, bright green inchworms suspended from gossamer threads – all things that swam and crawled and flew. That hopped and dug and ran.

Had Betelgeuse been orbited by a watery planet long ago, before it bloated into a tumescent supergiant? James thought so. That planet's waves sprinkled with red points of fire instead of gold. Just as these waters honored the might of the star that ordained their movement. The chord of each wave capturing the sun in portraits, thousands, millions, winking across the lake's skin.

Abruptly, a powerful vision struck him. Remi's farm attacked by the Sicari. They must get back.

*

They ate on shore. James told them all that had happened. Struggled to explain what he was experiencing, but none of his feeble words matched the reality. Tribe remained skeptical, not of the quality of the vision itself, but of the fact that the Stone seemed to be an inebriant. A false god.

Graham was more blunt: "You just spent four fuckin' days on that island dropping acid, you wanker! Didn't you!"

James smiled faintly. "One thing I've realized, above and beyond anything else."

"What's that?" Tribe asked.

"Even you two are better than being alone." Tribe and Graham laughed, and James joined them. "Pass me the bottle, would you?" Tribe handed it over and James took a long pull.

When he put his head back to drink, he saw Graham eye him warily.

"What is it?"

Graham looked spooked, staring at one side of James's face, then the other. "Sweet Jesus!" he rasped. "Your ear's grown back!"

Tribe looked on in amazement. James touched the right ear, pleased by its warm pliancy. "False god, Tribe?" He laughed, ridiculing the look on Tribe's face.

James stopped chewing, hearing a distant crinkling sound. Very faint. And then it dawned on him that it was not distant at all. All around him, a patient tinking, crinkling. Hearing the sound of the trees growing. Building the last few microns of this year's ring before the snow started flying in earnest.

They hiked back in seven days, following the trail of broken saplings Graham had created, each one bent in the direction of their return. James, ever struck by the overwhelming span of time embedded in all things. Time as a gargantuan, crushing weight.

His pack started to feel very heavy. Too heavy, as if Graham or Tribe had slipped rocks into it. He even stopped and checked. When he pulled out the aspirin bottle, it rolled off his hand and thumped to the soil like something far bigger.

"Christ!" he said, "it must be thirty pounds!"

Graham tried lifting it. "Forty, maybe."

*

They by-passed Remi's valley on purpose, bushwhacking around the western end to meet the ATV trail they'd been following when Remi found them. Gradually, the scenario had gestated in James's mind until he knew what the Stone desired of him.

They concealed themselves on a mossy crag overlooking the trail. A column of Sicari appeared. Forty of them, ragged and dirty. Nguyen and Alvarro were not among them. James knew immediately that Nguyen had seen this coming and had been so spineless he'd sent his men on without him.

James actually found himself pitying the Sicari, but was compelled to act. If they made it into the valley, they would slaughter everyone. If only in revenge for the terrible privation of their mission. When they were directly beneath the crag, he opened the aspirin bottle. A blur of Sam's blood still visible on the label. Grunting under its weight, he held it aloft, needing Graham and Tribe to support his arms.

"*Didet pet kima'at ta'a innet hapi!*" His voice rang with such dreadful force that the Sicari cowered and cried out. *That which the sky gives, which the land creates, and which the inundation brings!*

The bottle's weight spiked, so heavy James felt his elbows would snap. The bottom tore wide open, releasing the Stone in a green cascade. The sudden release of weight flung James, Tribe and Graham backwards.

The Stone rumbled down upon the Sicari like thunder, trampling saplings as if every tiny mote of green powder were a huge rock. James felt the ground shake. Heard their screams.

"Holy shite!" Graham groaned, looking down on the scene of bloody bodies, torn uniforms and broken equipment. These were victims of a rockslide, but only sprinkled with a little green talc.

"That's what it is?" said Graham in a hushed voice.

James didn't respond. Overcome with grief, the sense of being possessed. Owned.

Tribe climbed down and finished off the few that still lived.

This was how that section of the trail became known to them for ever after as the Graveyard of the Sicari.

*

The valley beckoned in the cold wind, the chimney on the small fieldstone house trailing a wisp of blue smoke. Remi had just thrown a log into the airtight, James thought. At least it would be warm.

From a distance, they saw Gord and Amy in the sheep paddock with shovels over their shoulders. Lilac, Rohini and Sheilagh carrying bushel baskets down along the path that led up to the orchards. Behind them was Massimo with Clay. And another. A skinny figure. At first James refused to recognize him. Even now, he could not accept what it meant to see him. James's knees wobbled. He gestured for the ground, cushioning his slow fall.

Graham stopped in his tracks. "Christ, that can't be Mike!"

Tribe snorted. "Of course not!"

Everybody ran up to them. After many welcoming embraces, James, Graham and Tribe all gaped at Mike.

Mike crossed his eyes at them. "Stare much?"

Lilac laughed delightedly.

Sheilagh helped James to his feet, beaming. "Did you do this?" She hugged him again, kissing him on the mouth.

"It's like totally frigged," said Mike. "I mean, like Sheilagh keeps telling me I was shot, but all's I remember is coming here." He shrugged self consciously.

"I'm with Mike," said Lilac. "I don't remember anything about him being shot."

"None of us do," said Amy. "I'll be totally honest with ya, Sheilagh. I thought you were fulla shit." She turned to James, Graham and Tribe. "Till I saw the looks on your faces."

James touched Mike's shoulder. "But – but if he didn't die in the first place, then how – how can the four of us know he was saved?"

Sheilagh tried to put on a grave face, but her toothy smile burst through. "Ah, would you stop asking such stupid questions James!" Everybody laughed as they trooped towards the house.

"All I can think is, this means I'm doomed," said Mike. "The Oracle said one of us would die twice."

Tribe took him by the neck and gave him an affectionate shake. "We all must die, Mike. Nobody lives forever."

Epilogue

The Winery

Gradually the corrugated steel shipping container cooled in the evening. The pissy stink of the female slave pen abated. Still, the straw dust irritated Sheilagh's nose. She sneezed. Nobody said "Bless you." That was one tradition that seemed to have died with the old world.

"That's all I have to say for the moment," she rasped. The guards had gone off for their supper, but it was still best to keep one's voice down.

The severe woman with the barbed wire tattoos on her biceps shook her knobby head. "You can't expect us to swallow that crap. A quest for the holy grail, I mean, come on! And you really expect anybody to believe he brought somebody back from the dead!"

"I didn't ask you to believe. Only listen."

"I've heard tell of such things from others," said the girl. "Great works, so they say, are more plentiful now than in the time before."

"Mike wasn't brought back," Sheilagh added. "It isn't the story of Lazarus. He was prevented from dying in the first place."

"So it's time travel you're hog-selling now, is it?" she snarled.

They all jumped as somebody pounded on the door of the container.

www.ingramcontent.com/pod-product-compliance
Lightning Source LLC
Chambersburg PA
CBHW050906250626
47155CB00001B/122